Edward Lucas

The Life of Frederick Lucas, M.P.

Edward Lucas

The Life of Frederick Lucas, M.P.

ISBN/EAN: 9783337093570

Printed in Europe, USA, Canada, Australia, Japan

Cover: Foto ©Raphael Reischuk / pixelio.de

More available books at **www.hansebooks.com**

THE LIFE

OF

FREDERICK LUCAS, M.P.

BY HIS BROTHER

EDWARD LUCAS

IN TWO VOLUMES

VOL. II.

116307

BURNS AND OATES

LONDON
28 ORCHARD STREET, W.

NEW YORK
9 BARCLAY STREET

1886

CONTENTS OF VOL. II.

—⊷—

Book the Third.

Book the Fourth.

Book the Fifth.

Book the Sixth.

CHAPTER I.

CHAPTER II.

Book the Third.

LUCAS IN PARLIAMENT.

CHAPTER I.

THE Meath election being over, Lucas wrote a letter to Mr. Riethmüller, the following extracts from which will show with what feelings, and under what difficulties, in his own estimation, he was about to enter Parliament. He says :—

"I go into the House of Commons to stand, I fear, very nearly alone, a member of an unpopular minority, an unpopular member of that minority, and disliked even by the greater number of the small party with which I am to act, and having cast upon me in a prominent manner the defence of the two noblest causes in the world—that of a religion which requires great learning to defend properly, and that of the most ill-treated and (in all essential qualities of heart and character) the noblest population that ever existed on the face of the earth. I am very poorly and hurriedly describing to you what it is that weighs me down. But I think you will understand me. You talk of Burke and O'Connell; and indeed to do adequately what I ought to do would require a Burke or an O'Connell—that is, a man who, in an assembly of really able men, can stand *alone*, on his own resources and character, against every opposition from within and from without. I think my own course is the one I shall follow, and that you will disapprove. . . . It remains to be seen and tried whether I can hold as true to my convictions in Parliament as I have done in the press; and I am sure that, with my many weak-nesses of character, this will be utterly impossible without a special grace of Almighty God to save me from total political. extinction. . . .

"I have it in my mind that I shall fail in my endeavour; that my abilities are not equal to the task before me; that I shall be rudely thrust out of the saddle upon the ground; and that, before two years' time, I shall be digging gold in or near Port Philip."

The House met on the 11th of November, and Lucas was present at the opening. One of the first acquaintances whom he met in the lobby was his cousin, John Bright, who, with that *bonhommie* which distinguishes him, addressed him thus—"Well, Fred, and how goes on the old superstition?" "Why, John, a great deal better than the new hypocrisy," was the reply.

Referring to Ireland, the address from the throne spoke of restraining, if necessary, "that unhappy spirit of insubordination and turbulence, &c., in that portion of my dominions."

This evidently pointed to fresh penal and repressive laws, which the English press had been calling for, especially in order to justify the Titles Act. But the very next day the power of the Independent party made itself felt. Mr. Villiers had given notice of a motion regarding a threatened return to Protection, and Government wanted the Irish vote. The Attorney-General for Ireland and Lord Naas were asked to state clearly the import of the Queen's speech as touching Ireland; did it mean penal legislation? They both evaded the question, each in his own fashion. At length Mr. Serjeant Shee rose, and repeating the question in the name of the Irish party, rebuked Ministers for their evasiveness, and, with a significant reference to Mr. Villiers' motion, required an express answer whether the threats of penal legislation were or were not to be carried into effect. This way of putting the case altered the matter. Mr. Walpole was observed to be in conversation with Mr. Disraeli, and at once "Irish turbulence" was at an end, and in the most emphatic language all idea of penal legislation was disclaimed.

On the 22d November Mr. Napier brought in and explained in a long speech four Government Bills for the settlement of the land question; and on the 25th Mr. Serjeant Shee brought in the Tenant League Bill for the same purpose. All the Bills passed the first reading without opposition. It was agreed that the second readings should take place on the 7th December, Mr. Napier moving those of the Government measures, and Serjeant Shee explaining the League Bill. Mr. Napier had made a very remarkable admission on the first reading. He had conceded the principle that the property which the tenant has created is his own; that though the existing law gave it to the landlord, it was not the property of the landlord; that the Legislature might step in and do what neither Common Law nor Chancery would be able to do—that is, to take from the landlord a property in improve-

ments which the existing law gave him, but to
which in justice he had no sort of claim. " In
all these cases of past improvement," said Lucas,
" Mr. Napier concedes the principle and the right,
but I very much doubt whether the extension of
compensation which he gives in respect of the
right so acknowledged is worth much more than
the paper it is written on." But it was a great
thing to get the principle admitted, and that by a
Conservative Government.

On the 7th December Mr. Napier moved the
second reading without further remark. Mr.
Shee, after an exhaustive address on the whole
question, proposed to send all the Bills before
a Select Committee, and to this Government
agreed ; but on a motion of adjournment, Keogh
rose to attack the Attorney-General for Ireland.
This attack was in bad taste, seeing that the
Attorney had just been a party to the friendly
agreement. But it showed what was passing in
the minds of the " Brigade." The debate was
adjourned to the 15th, when Lucas made his first
set speech in the House. It covered nearly all
the ground with which the reader of the foregoing pages has been made familiar, and was a
signal success.

One thing he made very clear, namely, that
parity exists between English building leases and
Irish agricultural occupancies in the matter of
compensating periods. In the one case, the man
is a capitalist, who takes a piece of land at a low

ground-rent, builds upon it a house which is his own for a certain number of years, and for which he receives a rent sufficient to pay interest on the capital expended, and to repay that capital before the expiration of the lease. In the other case, you have a poor man, who, as soon as he has improved his holding, is forthwith rack-rented. So that it is the landlord who, for the ten, twenty, or thirty years the tenant remains on the land, benefits by the capital spent in improvements; "and then, when you come to the end of the period, when the man has been rack-rented and ground down like a serf, living like a pig perhaps, and sometimes with a pig, in a hut little better than a stye; a hard-working industrious man, not eating meat more than eight or ten times during the year, and who has been literally plundered of every farthing he could wring out of his farm year by year, during the whole time he possessed it; you turn round upon the man who has been robbed of everything, and you tell him that the privilege of having been thus robbed for seven, fourteen, or twenty-one years, is to be his sole compensation for his improvements."[1]

Strange as it may seem, Keogh gave Lucas the greatest encouragement, and was of material assistance to him in addressing an assembly so difficult

[1] Practical men assert that this theory of a compensating interest in the case of building leases is more often than not a complete fallacy. The builder, they say, does not recoup himself. At best, he makes a successful speculation; but more frequently a losing one.

for a stranger to please as the House of Commons.
This first effort was fully appreciated by the party
and by the House at large.   Duffy wrote that
Lucas had made one of the most powerful and
convincing speeches it had been his good fortune
to listen to ; that he had done two things at one
blow—advanced materially and computably the
position of the tenant question, and achieved a
parliamentary reputation for himself ; adding, that ·
the Tory party gave him perfect fairplay and bore
willing testimony to his success.

The *Liverpool Journal* said it would be wrong
to pass over the unexpected success of Mr. Lucas
as a Parliamentary speaker.   He made a really
splendid speech ; careful, moderate, and complete ;
and by the avoidance of contempt for Mr. Napier
and the Government he put himself right with
the House.

" Who ever thought the *Tablet* would talk its leaders in the
House of Commons without being yelled at ?   But there is
the fact ; and perhaps Sir Robert Inglis [a terrible Tory bigot]
would be the first to admit it, and with pleasure."

He was followed by Mr. Drummond (the same
whom he had characterised as a " filthy person "),
who agreed that he had made out a case, and
that Parliament ought to interfere on behalf of
the tenants.

Two days later the division on Disraeli's Budget
was taken.   It became a question how the Irish
party should vote.   Keogh, Sadleir, and others
of the " Brigade," at the private meetings of

the party, insisted upon the pledges given by members to oppose any Government which would not make Sharman Crawford's Bill a Cabinet measure. Napier's Bill, they said, was not Sharman Crawford's; it was a bad Bill; they were bound by their promises to vote against the Government. Lucas advised abstention at the least. They had not given the Derby Government a fair trial. Government had had no time to show what they would do under pressure. The Bill was capable of amendment; it admitted a principle till then denied; there would be no breach of promise in postponing an adverse vote for some time. On the other hand, the Whigs, Radicals, and Peelites had absented themselves on the land debate; the Irish would therefore be either great fools or great traitors to throw themselves away on such hollow and rotten friends. Keogh and Sadleir prevailed, the party voted against Government, and on 17th December Disraeli's Budget was thrown out by a majority of 19—286 to 305, of whom 52 belonged to the Irish party.

Lucas said: "The next step is to manifest the same impartiality towards their successors," and he asked, "Will the Irish members have the virtue to keep together and to act with tolerable unanimity for this great end? I hope, I trust, and what is more, *I believe* they will; and sure I am they have every public motive to do so."

It seemed impossible that such (and such recent) appeals to high principle could be treated as wasted breath. But Keogh had his private reasons; he was hopelessly in debt. His accommodation bills were being offered at a discount of 50 per cent. And when the list of the new Ministry under Lord Aberdeen and Lord John Russell was published, his name appeared as Solicitor-General for Ireland and that of Sadleir as Junior Lord of the Treasury. The defection of these men was bad enough, but so long as the rest of the party kept together, or any appreciable number of them, no great harm was done. Little did Lucas think that Dr. Cullen had already changed his tactics, and was playing into the hands of the English Government; yet such was the case.

A letter which Lucas wrote to Keogh on this occasion is an admirable specimen of his way of putting a dishonest opponent in the wrong, and of his absolute freedom from rancorous feelings. There is no reproach or vituperation; on the contrary, he congratulates Keogh on his elevation, and on personal grounds rejoices at it, never for a single moment having entertained any sentiment hostile to the gratification of his just and honourable ambition. But then he recalls the oath at Athlone, which had been repeated twice at Cork some four or five months later, and he expresses the hope that he and Sadleir have made terms with Ministers in accordance with those oaths. But if not, it would be the duty of every one in a public position to express his decided reprobation of such conduct.

Of what happened when Sadleir presented himself for re-election, all the reader will care to hear is related in the second chapter of the "Statement." The effects this defection produced on different minds were very diverse. The Northern Presbyterians looked on the treachery as a condonable offence. Dr. M'Knight, and the loud-mouthed Rev. Messrs. Bell and Rogers, and their co-religionists, wished for proof of Sadleir's dishonesty. The English press almost unanimously agreed, so the *Tablet* observed that "mere principle, mere honesty, mere integrity, mere honour should be treated as utterly unworthy of regard in this business." The Irish public in general thought differently. Sadleir was rejected for Carlow; a petition had been presented against Keogh, and till that was settled no new writ could be issued for Athlone.

CHAPTER II.

THE next time Lucas spoke in the House was on one of the annual Maynooth debates. Members were impatient for a division, and his remarks, which only occupied half an hour, were characterised by the parliamentary correspondent of the *Tablet* in eulogistic terms which were probably well founded, but which rather offended Lucas's sense of modesty. He wrote, therefore, to his Dublin manager requesting him in future not to insert anything which might seem like puffs of himself at second-hand. He had intended to speak at greater length, as will appear by the two following letters.

" *To the Right Honourable* S. H. WALPOLE, M.P.

"29 SURREY STREET, *Saturday*, 26*th February* 1853.
" SIR,—I believe that a few days after Parliament assembled in the autumn, Mr. Serjeant Shee was kind enough to convey to you, on my part, my very sincere regret for certain unhappy expressions used by me at a moment of great political excitement during the late election at a public meeting at Slane in the county of Meath.

"It was my intention in speaking last Wednesday on the Maynooth question to have repeated in public what I communicated to you through Mr. Shee, and what I now beg with great sincerity to communicate to you under my own hand—that is, my regret for having, in perfect ignorance of your character and person, and under a most mistaken impression, used the phrases to which I have referred. You may perhaps be aware that the anxiety of the House for a division interrupted my remarks, and this interruption prevented my doing what I had intended. I am informed there is a probability of the debate being partially renewed on Wednesday next; and if any opportunity should then arise, it is my intention to do then what I have just intimated. If I should be unable to use this occasion, I shall be both ready and anxious to take the next opportunity that may present itself for doing this public justice to you, and to my own feelings of regret for the pain I may have occasioned. It is proper to add, that in doing what I propose, the nature of my argument will probably oblige me to refer to the occurrences at Stockport and to the proclamation by which they were preceded.—I have the honour to be, sir, your obedient servant, F. LUCAS.

"I need hardly say that you are at liberty to make any use of this letter that you may judge proper."

To this Mr. Walpole replied :—

"EALING, *February* 27, 1853.

"SIR,—I beg to acknowledge, with many thanks, your frank and honourable assurances of regret (the more gratifying to me because they are spontaneous) on account of 'certain unhappy expressions used by you and applied to myself at a moment of great political excitement.' It is a misfortune common to all public men to be misunderstood and misinterpreted by those who are not acquainted with them; but it happens to few—I believe I might say to very few—to find an opponent who is generous and just enough voluntarily to make amends for his error as soon as he has discovered it.

" Pray do not think it at all necessary to recur to the subject either in the House of Commons or anywhere else. It has long passed out of my mind, and the only trace of it which will be likely to remain there is the pleasing recollection of the handsome manner in which you have expressed your regret at its occurrence.—I have the honour to be, sir, your obedient servant,   S. H. WALPOLE.

" F. LUCAS, Esq., M.P."

It would be interesting to know the grounds of the apology. But I cannot discover whether the regret arose from the violence of the language alone, or from my brother's having found out that Mr. Walpole believed his denial of the dormant condition of the law. Certain it is that the law had never been used, and that no apology was tendered to Lord Derby, whom in the same speech Lucas charged "with being utterly care-less whether even worse consequences than loss of life should be produced by the proclamation ;" declaring further that the "expectation of its promulgators was that it would create, develop, and inflame such infuriate Protestant mobs .in England as those which have lately worked their lawless will upon poor Irishmen."

This charge was as definite as that against Mr. Walpole, and, so far as I can find, was never retracted.

I will here leave the more direct history of the Independent Opposition party in the House, and come to Lucas's happiest effort in Parliament, I mean his speech on the Madiai question. It is altogether too long to give entire, and should, indeed, be read in Hansard. No abstract will convey an adequate notion of the speech, and it does not readily lend itself to extracts. The most striking points about it consist in two facts : first, that Lucas stood alone in a most hostile House, and with Serjeant Shee, who ought to have been one of his supporters, known to be upholding his opponents ; and, secondly, that, under these disadvantages, he exposed Lords Palmerston and John Russell so completely that the mover of the resolution had to withdraw it then and there.

The case was this. A certain Exeter Hall gentleman, furnished with sufficient cash to render pecuniary assistance to any persons whom he might induce to apostatise, had founded, some year or two previously, a sort of mission in Florence, where he had gained over a man named Madiai and his wife, and one Pasquale Casaccio. All these persons were put on their trial for "proselytising." The Madiai were condemned, whereas Casaccio, who had only tried his hand at domestic perversion, was acquitted. The papers were first filled with false reports of the case, and then with the necessary articles in condemnation of the Grand Duke of Tuscany, who was described as a "contemptible despot." Sir Culling Eardley wrote to Lucas a curious letter, to which he "required" a reply in Marseilles by a certain day. This reply was to be presented to the Grand Duke, and was to contain abuse and

condemnation of his government in this affair.
Lucas declined to pass sentence on a foreign
sovereign ; drew a distinction between Tuscany,
where the people were all of one faith, and a Protestant country where they were not, and never
could be ; and said that were he king of a Catholic
country, he would not permit the introduction of
heresy into his dominions.   But the case of a
Protestant country was different : in the first
instance, an apostate would be a criminal ; in
the second, not at all necessarily so.   This was
early in October 1852.   Towards the end of
the month a great meeting to advocate religious equality, especially in Ireland, was held in
Dublin, at which, among others, Serjeant Shee
proposed a resolution.   In the course of his
remarks he fell foul of the Grand Duke, and, by
implication, of my brother.   With a somewhat
peculiar logic, he began by speaking doubtfully
of the report as requiring confirmation, and ended
by taking the Protestant comments as unquestionable.   Lucas could not allow this to pass without protest.   Mr. Shee, he said, had been misinformed as to the facts ; and he added that he
would reply at length on a more fitting occasion.
When his answer came, it was very elaborate.
Shee had been praised in the Protestant press,
at the expense of, and by contrast with, Lucas
and the Catholic clergy in general, who had been
vituperated and traduced by the same authorities.
He informed Mr. Shee that his own knowledge of

the facts was derived from the Protestant papers, which reported the trial and the punishment fairly enough as for the crime of proselytising; whereas both Shee and the English press commented upon the case as if the punishment were for privately reading the Bible. Lucas said that if the facts were as stated by the Serjeant, he should agree with his condemnation, and he asked him either to correct him on the facts or withdraw his charge. He was grieved, he said, not at abuse of himself—that had been his daily bread for years, and continued so to be morning and evening; not for this did he lament, but that Mr. Shee, whom he respected and esteemed, and under whom he hoped to fight many a battle against the common foe, "should be mixed up even for a moment, and through a misapprehension, with such a crew, and should be exposed to the indignity of their heartfelt approbation." The Serjeant neither retracted his censure nor attempted to prove his facts, and there is no doubt that his authority greatly stimulated the Protestant bigots to bring the matter before Parliament.

On the 18th February 1853, then, Mr. Kinnaird moved an address to her Majesty, asking her to take steps, in concert with the Governments of Prussia and Holland, to remonstrate, not dictatorially or menacingly, but in the name of religion and humanity, with the Grand Duke. Lord Dudley Stuart, in seconding the motion, thanked the hon.

member for the opportunity which he had afforded of a fair discussion.

Lucas concurred with the noble Lord, and praised the manner in which the subject had been treated ; but he could not concur in the resolution, because a very different case had been submitted to the public from that stated in the papers just laid on the table of the House. The resolution declared that a persecution was "actively begun in Tuscany of those who secretly or openly professed principles in common with the majority" of Englishmen ; whereas, if the facts mentioned in the papers were true, the persecution was not for openly or secretly professing anything, but for engaging in a system of proselytising at the bidding and instigation of foreign emissaries. (No, no.) "That I say, is the case, and that I am prepared to prove. It is the entire case ; it is the form of proceeding before the Court." The defence of the accused was, that what they did was done privately, and the condemnation proceeded on the ground that they had not been able to establish that defence ; had not been able to overthrow the facts alleged in the accusation, namely, systematic proselytising, by the influence of foreign money paid from abroad. Mr. Kinnaird had attributed the persecution to religious reaction, Lord Dudley to political reaction. Lucas hoped they would settle that matter between themselves ; for his part, he believed the papers. From them it appeared that Mr. Scarlett had had an interview

with the Duke's Minister in August 1851, when
he had been told, and had informed Lord
Palmerston, that foreigners were perfectly free
to practise their religion in Tuscany, but not to
tamper with the religion of the natives. This was
especially reasonable at a time when pretended
conversions to Protestantism were being used as a
mask for carrying out political views, and designed
rather to sap the foundations of government in
Italy than to promote the cause of Christianity.
Such was the case for the Tuscan Government ;
and to interfere in the matter would be to transform
the House into a court of appeal against the
Court of Tuscany. He had thanked the mover
for bringing the case forward, because it opened
up a class of cases he wished particularly to submit
to the House, and without this motion he did not
know when an opportunity would have arisen.
The noble Lord had referred to the persecutions
which the nuns of Minsk had suffered at the
hands of the Czar. These atrocities had excited
a great deal of animadversion at the time. But
who ever heard of the Foreign Secretary remon-
strating with the Emperor, and telling him that it
was contrary to the enlightenment of the present
age to persecute and torture when mere Roman
Catholic nuns were concerned ? The atrocities in
this case were infinitely worse than any alleged
against the Grand Duke; but the Czar was an
awkward person to deal with, and the sufferers
were Catholics. Now how did this bear upon the

present case? Lord Palmerston had laid it down in a letter to Sir Henry Bulwer that it was a moral duty from which the Government could not shrink to employ their influence on behalf of Protestants. Whether the House would agree with that principle he did not know. But he made a particular appeal to Lord Palmerston, because, from some papers which proceeded from that noble Lord's able diplomatic pen, he thought, if the Grand Duke wanted an advocate of the highest authority, he might ask the noble Lord to undertake his case.

" The House would not have forgotten the events of 1847, when the Jesuits were expelled from Switzerland, in accordance with the advice of the noble Lord, for no crime—(Oh, oh !)—for no offence whatever. What were the words of the noble Lord? I find them in a despatch dated November 16, 1847—a despatch in which the noble Lord, in that calm, quiet, and easy manner which distinguishes all his productions, does not run violently on against the Jesuits, but, with characteristic skill, suggests all the reasons which would induce all the parties by whom the despatch would be seen to take the most hostile course against them. (Laughter.) The noble Lord wrote :—

" It appears to her Majesty's Government that the objection which the Diet makes to the continuance of the Jesuits in Switzerland is not destitute of good and reasonable foundation. The Society of Jesuits must be looked at both in a religious and in a political point of view." (" Hear, hear," from Protestant members.)

"When I got to that sentence, I think I put a construction on it which those gentlemen who cheer me now suggest; and I thought the noble Lord was going to exculpate the Jesuits as to religion, and take exception to them as to politics. But the gentlemen will find their cheers were premature." ("Hear, hear," from Catholic members.)

"In its religious character it is a Society avowedly established to make war upon the Protestant religion. What wonder, then, that in a small country like Switzerland, where two-thirds of the people are Protestants, the introduction of such a Society should give rise to dissension between Catholics and Protestants, and should be viewed with aversion by the majority of the nation?"

"Those were the grounds on which the Jesuits were to be expelled from Switzerland, not because they were bad politicians, not because they were advocates of a form of government which happened to displease those who opposed them, but because they were banded together to proselytise those among whom they lived—to disseminate the Catholic religion, and to make war as a religious body against Protestantism. That was the ground upon which the noble Lord, with the approbation of the whole Liberal and Protestant opinion of this country, recommended the Diet to exterminate the Jesuits out of Switzerland, and out of those Catholic cantons, too, where, in obedience to the invitation of the people, they wished to establish themselves in strict accordance with their laws and policy, and where the people

defended them at the hazard of their lives.   The
noble Lord recommended, in effect, that the Catholics of Lucerne should be shot ; that war should be
waged upon them because they maintained among
themselves a body of Catholic missionaries.

" The noble Lord proceeds, ' In its ecclesiastical character the Society is exclusive and en-
croaching,' and so on; and then he goes on to
speak of its political character.   ' In their political
character the Society are known to incline to
arbitrary power and to be averse to popular
rights.'   Well, the Duke of Tuscany uses language exactly analogous to this.   He objects to
those who, under foreign leaders, are propagating
Protestantism in Tuscany.   The Grand Duke,
exercising that right of private judgment which
I presume the noble Lord will not deny, takes
exception to revolutionary politics.   He says the
emissaries of Protestantism are really emissaries
of revolution.   And so, taking the same ground as
the noble Lord had taken on the religious and
political view of the question, he decides that those
persons ought to be banished from Tuscany, just
as the noble Lord advised that the Jesuits should
be exterminated from Switzerland.   But that is
not the whole of the case.   I have some other evidence with regard to the opinions of the noble
Lord, which I think fit him most admirably to be
the defender of the conduct of the Grand Duke
of Tuscany, and the consideration of which should
bring moderation into the fury against Catholicity

which this case has excited among the Dissenters of Great Britain. I refer to the case of Tahiti and Mr. Pritchard."

He then gave a short sketch of the doings of the Independent Missionaries in the South Seas from 1797 to 1835. The noble Lord had appointed Mr. Pritchard Consul there. Well, in 1835 a Catholic missionary, Father Murphy, went there to proselytise the natives. He was driven out of the country by Rev. Mr. Pritchard, and, when information of the facts was sent home to England, Lord Palmerston connived at the act. Next year other missionaries came. This time they were Frenchmen. They also were driven away. They appealed to a French captain sailing in those seas, and the matter thus assumed international importance. The noble Lord did not advise Mr. Pritchard to refuse the reception of French Catholic missionaries. He dealt with the question more astutely : he told the Consul that of course every Government had a right to make its own laws, and to refuse permission for any foreigners to reside within its dominions whose presence might be considered hurtful to the state. On this hint Mr. Pritchard procured the passing of a law forbidding under penalties the landing of such obnoxious persons. The terms of the prohibitions were conveyed to Lord Palmerston, who found nothing objectionable in them ; only, at that distance, it would be difficult for the British Government to contract with the Queen (Pomare)

to fulfil with proper punctuality defensive obligations.   At the same time, her Majesty felt the
greatest interest in Queen Pomare, &c.   Mr. Lucas
proceeded :—

"That law remained in force two or three
years, as I understand, and was put an end to—by
what and by whom?   By a French Admiral coming
from a Catholic country with the Popish religion
in his ships' bottoms.   He brought that sort of
freight with him ; he came with the Popish
religion and French cannon, and he established
for the first time in the history of Protestantism
in the South Seas the principle that 'every one
should be free in the exercise of his own form of
worship or religion.'   Mr. Pritchard was never
rebuked for conduct such as that for which you now
wish to rebuke the Grand Duke of Tuscany. . . .
Now, sir, if I believed that the resolution we are
considering expressed the facts with regard to
Tuscany, there is only one consideration that
would prevent me from adopting it and dividing
in its favour ; and that is, that I never can, and so
long as I have a seat in this House I never will,
recognise that the exercise of this power of
humanity and philanthropy is to be all on one
side. . . .

"I hold in my hand two volumes, laid on the
table of the House by the noble Lord the present
Foreign Secretary (Lord John Russell) as an in-
ducement to the House to enter upon a course of
persecution against the Catholic Church, when he

was animated by the same sentiments of friendliness towards the Roman Catholics which animate him now. The public legislation of Europe was the ground upon which the noble Lord professed to base his Ecclesiastical Titles Bill, and I will take some of those specimens of the public law of Europe."

He then enters in detail into the penal laws in force in Sweden, Denmark, and Mecklenberg, showing that quite recently people had been banished and their property had been confiscated, not for proselytising, but for privately adopting the Catholic religion; and he concludes thus :—
" I propose to begin by requesting the interference of the noble Lord with the Cabinet of Sweden; afterwards I propose to go through the Protestant states of Europe—to Mecklenberg next, and then perhaps to Saxony; and he would produce a wonderful change in the social condition of Europe. It cannot be allowed that it is the peculiar duty of the Foreign Office to teach the true principles of toleration to those Governments from which they differ in religion ; let them first apply their strength to those with which they agree—the Protestant Cabinets of Europe—and rebuke the evil spirit out of Protestantism. When they have accomplished that great work, performed that Herculean labour, cleansed that Augean stable, then let them begin with the Catholic states. Sir, I will conclude with repeating, that if this resolution did not contain

statements of facts which I believe not to be true, and to be at variance with the papers on the table, it should have my support. As it is, I cannot support it. But I am sure when I have made the motion of which I have given notice, I shall have it seconded by the hon. gentleman opposite."

The *Leader* newspaper shall describe the impression produced by the speech upon the editor of that journal :—

"The debate on Thursday, leaving the Madiai where they were, is not unimportant as having developed some individuality. In the first place, we may afford to admire the unequivocal success obtained by Mr. Lucas as a debater. . . . Cardinal Wiseman getting elected to the House of Commons, and attempting to secure a hearing, would not have had a more difficult game to play than Mr. Lucas has had; yet, against all the prejudices which met him on the part of the religious members for the violence of the advocacy of his creed, and on the part of the men of business for the political wrong-headedness of his general policy—against a general belief on all sides that he was a fanatic and a fool, who would merely talk fanaticism and folly, and must consequently be summarily put down—this very Catholic, and more Irish than an Irish gentleman, gained on Thursday night a great oratorical success, testified not merely by the chuckling cheers of the delighted 'Brigade' around him, but by the encouraging silence, the sign of close attention, of the House generally. . . .

"Mr. Lucas has spoken twice since his election—once on tenant-right, and the second time on this Madiai question, and the result is that he is safe of a hearing and of respectful treatment—of a House of Commons position, in fact, for the rest of his sitting life."

This the *Leader* attributed not only to his

mastery of the subject, but to his deferential and courteous manner.

Lord John defended Lord Palmerston. It was like Charles Kean offering the part of *Macduff* to Macready, said the *Leader*. As for Lord Palmerston, he replied in a speech as much as to say, " The idea of my caring one curse about Protestantism as opposed to Catholicism —the idea!" So far the *Leader*.

After some insignificant speeches, Mr. Kinnaird's resolution was withdrawn.

For this success Lucas took no credit to his own skill or power in debate; he attributed it solely and conclusively to the fact that the statement and argument were urged *in opposition*.

He had no idea of the advantage of dividing the Catholic party in any proportions between the other two parties in the House. It had not occurred to him that your bundle of sticks is strengthened by being untied. That application of physics to politics had not then been discovered.

The fame of this speech soon reached Sweden and Denmark, as I had reason to experience a year later both at Stockholm and at Copenhagen.

His father was present at its delivery and wrote to congratulate him on his success. He replied as follows :—

"SUNDAY, SURREY STREET.

"MY VERY DEAR FATHER,—I must be very busy indeed if I could not find time to acknowledge thy most affectionate letter, of which I am justly proud.   I am sure, my dear father, I am always very sensible of thy great care and anxiety for my welfare, though I have often feared that my return for thy kindness has been but small compared with what it ought to have been.   Since I have had a child of my own, I know by my own experience what the affectionate anxiety of a father is, and in judging of thy feelings by my own, I have often of late years blushed to think with what thoughtless indifference I have too often accepted as a mere matter of course those inestimable proofs of thy affection which have never been wanting when there was an opportunity.   However, I am sure, my dear father, that in this case it is only thoughtlessness, and not intentional ingratitude, with which I have to reproach myself.   Above all human things, I am, and ever have been, proud of thy approbation ; and if my conduct, public or private, has been marked by any degree of rectitude, this has been almost wholly owing to the influence of thy precepts and ex- ample, and to my unchangeable respect and reverence for thee.

" I was very proud to speak in thy presence the other day in the House, and to have thy commendation of what I said. Since I have been in Parliament, I have repeatedly called to mind thy prudent advice, and have endeavoured to regulate myself by it, and whatever success I have had has been mainly owing to my having done so.   I am more than satisfied with the success I have so far had—nor does the odd conduct of some of our associates at all discourage me.   I wish they would act better ; but in the House I believe I have a more honourable standing than most of them, and I feel certain that their notorious time-serving does me no injury.

" Thee will have seen that the petition against me is with- drawn, and that my seat is now secure.   This does not make much change, for I had not begun to be anxious about it ; but I fear the withdrawal of the petition will lead to my being speedily put on some Election Committee.

" My health, thank God, is very good, and I mean by a little more regularity to avoid all needless wear and tear. I shall get, I hope, some rest in the recess, but after Easter I imagine I shall be pretty hard worked in the House. However, I have no wish to be idle.

"And believe me, my dear father, as ever, thy most affectionate son,

"F. LUCAS."

While listening to the speech, a stranger who sat next my father in the gallery asked who the speaker was, remarking, "He's a very clever man; why, he has blown them clean out of the water;" as indeed he had.

At this time my brother's work was incessant. He kept the *Tablet* supplied from day to day with information of the progress of such affairs as could interest his readers, and his correspondence was very voluminous.

When the recess came, the desired rest consisted in managing the *Tablet* in Dublin, and attending numerous meetings, at which he made a succession of speeches.

CHAPTER III.

To return now to the state of the Independent Opposition party in the House. While others thought the defection of the Corruptionists had materially weakened the party, Lucas was of a different opinion. His view was, that everything depended upon securing a nucleus of men who would stand fast to their principles; that before, while the traitors remained, it was impossible to take effective counsel as to the details of the parliamentary campaign; that hitherto their movements had been impeded, but that for the future they would have no difficulty of that kind. But a weakness soon exhibited itself in the Irish ranks. Some were for dropping the title of "Opposition" and adhering only to that of "Independent." These people could then vote as they liked—against the Government when to do so would not inconvenience them, and for the Government in case of danger; and they always had their conscience—a sacred and secret recess, which could not, and must not, be scrutinised—to appeal to in justification. Such was the talk when the recess arrived. At this time a Tipperary elector wrote to the *Tablet* complaining that the priests of that county did not use their influence, as they were bound to do, to keep representatives to their pledges. At the same moment, Father Redmond of Arklow and Dr. M'Knight of Belfast fairly ratted. The latter, along with the Northern Presbyterians in general, Lucas had long ceased to trust. Indeed, it was only at his first acquaintance that he had any confidence in their fidelity. They were of a very peculiar type, and he soon saw through them. Elsewhere the cause looked prosperous.

During the recess, however, at an important meeting held in Dublin, Lucas showed what suspicions troubled him. He spoke of the coming election for Athlone, and thought it necessary to insist very strongly that, if Keogh were returned, it could only be through the neglect or active influence of the clergy. He declared that his return would be an immense disaster, and his whole tone showed the uneasiness he felt. He insisted strongly on the responsibility of the clergy for the conduct of their representatives. He did not, he said, believe that in all Catholic Ireland there was one constituency in which the people were not faithful. And he would say further, that wherever a bad representative had been returned to Parliament, a man treacherous to the people, the fault or defect lay with the Catholic clergy. Whether this arose from weakness, or from some other cause on which he was incompetent to pronounce, he could not tell. He evidently had in his mind what was afterwards proved beyond doubt, as the reader will see in the second chapter of the "Statement." He affirmed that such clergy violated their duty, and that at their door would be laid the deaths, the beggary, and the loss of every soul arising from neglect to fulfil their known obligations.

His suspicions were more than confirmed by the comments of the *Times* and *Herald*, who took up the cudgels on behalf of the Bishops and clergy. In speaking of the "constituencies," he had said that by this word he meant "on this question" the Bishops and clergy, "because the people were true and faithful, if they were truly and faithfully led." The *Times*, as a matter of course, misrepresented the statement, and, by leaving out the words "on this question," made Lucas say that on every question, and in every sense, the Bishops and clergy were the same thing with the constituencies. An obvious intention underlaid this suppression, an intention which was fairly realised in the end—for the false saying has been quoted numberless times since. But the mere fact of those journals undertaking the defence of the Bishops and clergy was in itself an indication of some secret, undisclosed information unfavourable to the cause of honour and honesty. Lucas was by no means led from his point. He said—

" The Catholic clergy in Ireland should know well, and I take the liberty most respectfully to remind them, that their political influence, based on popular confidence, is an inestimable jewel, which they have possessed, and which they have it in their power to throw away. Many of my clerical friends know this well, and feel it bitterly. They know very well that at this moment, in some places, in consequence of recent events, the influence of some of their brethren as political leaders trembles in the balance. They know the hopes which the clergy contributed to raise at the last election; the devoted courage of the people in facing hostile influences; the sacrifices that were made ; the risks that were run ; in too many instances, the ruin that was incurred, in reliance on the judgment, knowledge, and prudence of those clergymen whom the people supposed to be better advised than themselves as to the trustworthiness of the means and instruments employed.

" These things they know well and cannot forget. But when they witness the disappointment of the public hopes ; when they see how bitterly the Catholic electors resent the betrayal that has taken place ; when in their daily intercourse with the people they listen to the execrations poured upon those men who, for their own selfish interests, have made a mockery of the heroism and self-devotedness which sent them to the House

of Commons; and when they put before themselves the vision—not very distant—of another
election, of other contests with landlord power,
of fresh sacrifices to be made, new victims to be
offered up, new vouchers, new assurances, new
pledges, new promises to be given, new hopes
to be excited, new enthusiasm to be kindled, new
speeches to be made, old credit to be pledged
anew, and nothing better to be conjured up from
the past than that recent and ignominious bank-
ruptcy of public faith, upon which the dividend is
not even a miserable three farthings in the pound ;
a great many of my clerical friends know well that
unless this picture be very materially altered before
the next election, there are counties in which the
electors will not repeat their efforts ; will not follow
the old lead ; will not make enemies of the powers
of this world in order to be made fools of in return ; will abandon the struggle in despair as mad-
ness, and will make the election of 1854 a very
different thing from the election of 1852.

" Yes, hitherto the priests and the people have
been united ; and at the advice and with the encouragement of the priest the peasant has made
fearful sacrifices. Shall he do so any longer? Will
he do so any longer ? He knows himself to have
been betrayed by those he sent to Parliament. He
feels too humble—at all events he is too prudent—
personally to remonstrate with the men who have
betrayed him. He leaves that to the priest, who
vouched for the good character of the traitor, and

pledged his sacred word to the service that would
be achieved by electing him. At this moment,
and for this purpose, the priest is his spokesman.
If the priest remonstrates, makes known his indignation, and severs himself from the evil act—
all is well ; not so well as could be wished, because
public treachery always inflicts a grievous wound
upon public confidence, but a great deal will be
done to repair the mischief. But if the priest be
silent, if he does not remonstrate, his silence is
suspected, his power weakened, his influence
shaken to its foundations, and the next election
will show that the priest and the constituent are
not necessarily the same thing.

" It is not for me an agreeable thing to handle
these topics after this fashion ; but in matters of
real moment it is as well to be plain-spoken. For
myself (and many others), I can say that I did not
allow myself to be sent to Parliament as child's
play, and I am not disposed to treat what happens
in these matters as of little moment. They are
not of little moment to us or to the country.
Having the opportunity of forming a more accurate judgment of affairs than . many whom I
address, and having the means of making known
such judgment as I am able to form, it would be
criminal in me to hold my peace."

He thought there had never been a time when
silence on his part would be more criminal, because he believed that the very constitution of
society throughout the provinces of Ireland with

reference to politics and the future source of
political power was at stake.   The notion, he
said, that the people had been driven to the polls
by the priests against their will was, of course, a
base and baseless fabrication.   But if the priest
had lost the confidence of the people, they would
not be led by him again.   He thought the landlords would drive them.   He could not foresee
the rise of the Fenian Brotherhood ; but what
was very clear to him was the waning influence
of the clergy in certain quarters.

His worst fears were soon realised.   A petition had been presented against Keogh's return
in 1852, and had been pressed by his Tory opponent in a manner for which Lucas disclaimed
all sympathy.   And as he had taken, and considered it his duty still to take, a prominently
hostile part against Keogh on political grounds,
he thought himself bound to protest against the
course pursued by Mr. Lawes, the Tory candidate.
He had no personal enmity against Keogh, and,
even if he had, he would have been ashamed
to gratify it by a harassing and vexatious system
of personal annoyance such as the Athlone Committee had disclosed.

Mr. Lawes, the petitioner, having failed to
wrest the seat from Keogh, the latter had to
vacate his seat—a step which had been in abey-
ance since his taking office—and to undergo a
fresh election.   The nomination took place on
the 20th April.   Meantime people became very

uneasy as to the probable action of the Bishop
of Elphin, and somewhat openly expressed their
fears that he would be found supporting the perjured Solicitor-General. No Independent candidate presented himself, and Keogh was allowed
to say from the hustings that he had the support
of the Bishop and clergy.

CHAPTER IV.

*SESSION OF 1853 CONTINUED — SPEECH BY DUFFY —
EXCITEMENT IN THE HOUSE — CONVENTS INSPEC-
TION BILL — DEBATE ON GRANT FOR REPAIRS TO
MAYNOOTH COLLEGE — LUCAS ON CHAPLAINS TO
PRISONS—LORD PALMERSTON'S PROMISES.*

THE next occasion on which Lucas took a prominent part in Parliament was the debate on Mr.
Gladstone's Budget. At the time when Disraeli's
Budget was defeated, and when Irish votes were
wanted by the Whigs, negotiations had been set
on foot between the Whig leaders and certain of
the Irishmen. Among other terms, it was distinctly intimated on behalf of the Government,
that in any income-tax they might bring forward,
Ireland would not be included, as it had been in
the Derby Budget. Nevertheless, when the new
Chancellor of the Exchequer made his financial
statement, the bargain was found not to have
been kept, the tax was extended to Ireland, and
additional burdens were thrown upon that country
in the way of extra duties on spirits. In speaking
of the income-tax question, Mr. Duffy made use
of an expression which, however true, Lucas
thought was perhaps hardly prudent, and which

caused a great uproar. He said, " I don't think in the worst days of Walpole and the Pelhams more scandalous corruption existed than I have seen with my own eyes practised upon Irish members." Then followed what is called "a scene." Several members rose at a time, some called, " Order, order ; " some cried, " Name, name ; " some desired that the words should be taken down ; some said the words were not correctly heard ; some wished him to withdraw them. The chairman read the words, and Mr. Duffy said they were so nearly what he used that he did not quarrel with them. Lord John Russell called upon him to substantiate his charge by name. Lucas rose, as in duty bound, to defend his friend. The case was a difficult one, and for a moment he was puzzled how to act. Recovering himself, however, he pointed out that the words were not a charge against single members, but against Ministers, men occupying positions similar to those of Walpole and Pelham. Disraeli took the same side ; he found no imputation of corrupt motives ; what he found was a distinct charge of corrupt proceeding by high officials. To allege corrupt motives would be out of order, but a distinct accusation against a Ministry was perfectly in order, and might be a duty. A member acts, he said, upon his right in bringing such an accusation. After that it is his business to substantiate his charge. Lord Palmerston tried to coax Duffy into an admission that he meant nothing dishonourable to any member. Lucas reiterated his former interpretation of the words, and said further, that, if he might venture to give the member for New Ross any advice, it would be to stand upon his right and adhere to the true interpretation of the exact words used. Then Sir G. Grey said Lucas denied the accuracy of the words. Here Lucas interrupted. He had denied nothing of the kind ; all his observations were founded on the accuracy of the words. Duffy offered to prove his case if they would give him a Committee. Mr. Bright said the charge was that Government had taken measures analogous to those taken by former Governments to obtain the votes of Irish members. He felt sorry to have to defend the Government; but he advised the Committee to proceed no farther, because it was not alleged that the Irish members had succumbed to the temptation. The House laughed. Everybody knew what had taken place. Duffy was directed to withdraw from the House, and Ministers made a way for themselves out of the mess by pretending they thought he had meant to convey that money payments had been made to Irish members, whereas what he did mean was notorious.

In next week's *Tablet* Lucas congratulated Mr. Duffy on his signal and decisive triumph over Lord John Russell and the deserters, and gave his own account of the negotiations in the previous December. It was Mr. Hayter, the Whig Whip, who had made the proposals, through Mr.

Maurice O'Connell; with the result that the Derby Government was displaced to let in a Whig Administration, equally bad or worse.

Next Mr. Chambers came upon the parliamentary scene with a bill for the inspection of convents and for facilitating the recovery of the personal liberty of nuns in general. The *Tablet* described this gentleman as a man of considerable ability, of no deep-rooted bigotry, but one who, in fighting the borough of Hertford against the aristocratic influence of Lord Cowper, had found it necessary to discover some popular cry. The thing that took at Hertford was the nasty anti-Maynooth cry. " So," said Lucas, " Mr. Chambers takes out of the dirt the policy which the cry expresses; scrapes it and washes it in muddy water; tries to clean it a little and polish it; and having done his best to make it look decent, brings it into the House of Commons in the shape of a ' Bill to facilitate the recovery of liberty in certain cases.' " Lord John Russell opposed the Bill; and Lucas, as was his habit when persons and not principles were concerned, thanked " the noble Lord for the extremely generous and able speech which he had made, and which must have perfectly settled the question in the mind of every impartial and rational member of the House." He ridiculed stories of Mr. Drummond, of which he said there was a yearly crop; and, much as he respected English public opinion, he treated with contempt the pretence of protecting Catholics from Lynch law by any legislation of the kind proposed. Forty-seven Irish members being absent, the Bill passed the first reading by a majority of 23.

When the Bill was printed, it appeared that it had been prepared with the help of the Protestant Alliance, and that "a more atrocious production it was impossible to conceive." Going through it in detail, Lucas remarked, " Every man has his taste ; but for my part, if I caught the gentlemen (the inspectors) in my house under such circumstances (on a pretended search for imprisoned ladies), I should muster such help as I could find available, and, if strong enough, I should without a moment's delay fling them out of the window to end their researches with broken bones upon the pavement."

Nothing, as we know, ever came of these annual efforts in Exeter Hall.

Next followed a debate on the then usual grant of £45,000 to Maynooth, and on some other items for repairs there and at certain Protestant chapels under the Commissioners of Public Works in Ireland. Mr. Spooner moved to strike off £1235 for repairs at Maynooth. Lucas said he would vote for the reduction if similar items for other religious buildings were included. Mr. Williams, M.P. for Lambeth, moved such reduction accordingly. The Committee divided, and Lucas and Mr. Swift went into the lobby with Mr. Williams. There was so much confusion that the other Irish members voted against

Mr. Williams ; and Mr. Spooner, who would have done the same, was actually named teller to Mr. Williams's motion, which he disapproved. Mr. Williams was beaten, but the Maynooth amount was disallowed. Later in the evening Lucas indulged in a little obstruction, but in the most deferential manner. A vote for chaplains and general superintendence of prisons all over the United Kingdom was asked for. He said the question was a large one, and could not be properly debated so late at night. Lord John said it could not be postponed merely because Mr. Lucas was not prepared with his statement. The hon. member replied that he had not said that he was unprepared, but that that was not the time to discuss the question. He observed that while the amount demanded included payments to Catholic, Presbyterian, and Anglican chaplains in Ireland, no provision was made for Catholic chaplains in English prisons, and that, as matters then stood, the process of reforming Catholic prisoners was to make them begin with an act of hypocrisy. Lord John Russell had to give way, the subject was postponed, and only came on again for discussion on the 9th of August. Lucas had not been idle in the meantime. What success he had had is best told in the " Statement," chap. vi. sec. 8. But I must quote here two passages from Lord Palmerston's reply to Lucas's speech on the day named.

Lord Palmerston is thus reported : " He said

he was sure the hon. member who had just sat
down did not need to make an apology to the
House for having brought under their consideration a matter of great interest and deep importance.
Personally he had to thank the hon. gentleman
for the courtesy with which in private he had
communicated the views he meant afterwards to
state to the House."

This passage is of importance here in reference
to a charge made against him in Rome, and the
truth of which is denied in the "Statement," namely,
that his non-success arose from his unpopularity.
It is clear no unpopularity could be truly alleged
at that time, and the more so when we read Lord
Palmerston's concluding words.   He said—

"He was quite sure that in matters of this sort there
was no difference between Catholics and Protestants as to
what was the proper course to pursue, because it was quite
obvious that, as in a country like Ireland, where the great
proportion of the people were Catholics, provision ought to
be made for the instruction of such prisoners as were Protestant; so in England, where the great proportion of the
people were Protestant, provision ought also to be made for
the instruction of such prisoners as happened to be Catholics.
(Hear, hear.) We ought not to make our gaols arenas of
theological discussion or schools of proselytism.   They ought
rather to be made places of reformation and moral and
religious improvement, and for this purpose we ought to
manage them in such a manner as should most effectually
accomplish the object which we professed to have in view."

So far, then, Lucas's efforts on behalf of the
prisoners seemed in a very fair way of obtaining
a permanent removal of a crying grievance.   His

own estimate of the position he thus expressed on the next day. "In this matter of prisons, Lord Palmerston and the Government speaking through him have adopted, with the assent of the House of Commons, the principle of religious equality. Henceforward there are to be, what there never yet have been in Great Britain—Catholic chaplains for Catholic prisoners, duly remunerated for their labour, possessing exclusive spiritual jurisdiction over the Catholic prisoners; and the Catholic prisoners are to be secured from all interference on the part of Protestant and proselytising clergymen and laymen, chaplains or schoolmasters, who have heretofore enjoyed and exercised a nearly unlimited right of interference. Henceforward he is to find himself, when in prison, as comfortable in every respect when professing and practising the Catholic religion as he would be if he professed and practised the Protestant."

This, surely, was no small encouragement to continue to pursue the Independent line of policy which had been urged upon Catholic leaders at the aggregate meeting of 1851 by Dr. Cullen. How and by whom the advantages thus gained were so completely frustrated that to this day they have never been fully realised will appear in due course.

CHAPTER V.

LET us now go back to the month of June 1853, when Mr. George Henry Moore, the member for Mayo, brought on a motion "for a Select Committee to inquire into the ecclesiastical revenues of Ireland, with a view to ascertaining how far they were made applicable to the benefit of the Irish people." This motion was understood to be aimed at the Church Establishment in Ireland, and Sir John Young, the Chief Secretary, had complained that Catholics now were running back from their declarations made before Emancipation, when they gave assurances that they had no hostility to the Establishment. Now that the Establishment no longer exists, to follow the discussion in its details would be unprofitable and uninteresting to the reader. But two passages in Lucas's speech have a direct bearing upon subsequent events, and even upon the present condition of things. The reader will perceive their significance and applicability to arguments to which we have all become accustomed. In reply to the taunts of Sir John Young and others he says :—

" Honourable gentlemen had quoted a document dated 1792, which showed that the Catholics
of that time were content with, and almost grateful for, the ecclesiastical arrangements which then
prevailed and still continue in Ireland, sentiments
however which he (Mr. Lucas) neither approved
nor applauded.   An hon. gentleman had talked of
deception and fraud ; but did he forget that the
iron had entered into the souls of the Catholics in
those days ? or was it to be wondered at, if, long
oppressed as they had been by social debasement
and political degradation, in the first moment of
even their partial deliverance from the tyranny
under which they had groaned, their feelings of
thankfulness found vent in language which, if they
had lived in the present day, they themselves
would have been the first to condemn ?   Again,
when Catholic Emancipation was granted, was it
surprising that when the intolerable yoke was
removed from off the necks of the Catholics of
Ireland, they expressed their gratitude in rather
exaggerated terms ?   From observing the little
allowance that was made for the natural feelings
of men under the circumstances he had described,
and the use that was made of such expressions, he
confessed that he had been taught that the avowal
of political gratitude was a very dangerous thing ;
and it would perhaps be better if in future they
were rather sparing of that article, seeing that it
might be reasoned upon in the House twenty or

fifty years afterwards with all the dexterity of
hard-headed Nisi Prius lawyers."

The other passage runs thus :—

" He asked, what was meant by the constitution ?
He agreed with that great statesman, Edmund
Burke, that the constitution was not the mere
outward form of returning certain gentlemen,
whom they called representatives, to a body
which they called a Parliament, and investing
them with the powers of government. What did
they call the constitution in Ireland ? The constitution in England was a means to an end.
The means was representation, and the end was
making the permanent, settled, deep-rooted convictions of the people omnipotent in the management of affairs. Such was the constitution in
England. How different was it in Ireland!
They were told they had got a constitution in
Ireland ; and yet in the year of grace 1853 they
were discussing the vast and monster iniquity of
the Establishment. The constitution in Ireland
meant that the permanent, settled, fixed, and
irrevocable will of the people should be thwarted,
refused, and denied, trampled on and insulted
generation after generation. The constitution of
Ireland meant that the people should knock in
vain at the doors of Parliament for justice. It
meant an injustice under which no human beings
could be induced to live except by military violence and physical force. For years the people
of Ireland had endeavoured to get rid of this

injustice, but their demands had been rejected with contempt and insult, and they had been told that, because there were a hundred gentlemen re- turned to that House by a process that was called representation, they had the blessings of the British Constitution, which in England meant the accomplishment of the will of the people, but which in Ireland meant exactly the reverse."

With the debates on two Land Bills, the vain efforts of the Irish Independent members to make them into something more than waste paper, the arguments for and against various clauses, with discussions on the theory of compensating periods, and the rest, I will not load my pages; but will proceed to a subject of wider and of more lasting interest, Lucas's observations upon which may, perhaps, help to enable the reader to perceive more clearly the value of certain recent pro- nouncements on the same topic.

It was at this period that the Eastern question began to assume a very doubtful shape. Russia had occupied the Principalities, and the papers were talking of their evacuation : they had fixed the month, if not the day, of the withdrawal. In this state of affairs Lucas wrote :—

" Ever since I have been able to pay any attention to this portion of the field of politics, I have entertained no doubt, and every year has confirmed me in the opinion, that the great enemy of Western Europe—an enemy not able to injure if she be properly encountered, but to be dreaded

in the highest degree by all those who think that
by the Cabinets of Western Europe her systematic plans of aggrandisement are not properly
and effectually encountered—that the great and
really formidable enemy of everything civilised,
free, independent, and progressive in Europe is
Russia, whose designs, planned with skill and fore-
sight, and carried into execution by a far-reaching
and inflexible will, threaten danger to every state
and monarchy in Europe. When I hear and read
the talk that is current about the magnanimity of
Nicholas, the moderation of Russia during the
last few years, and the expressions of wonderment
which every now and then meet us that her proceedings during the last few months are so much
at variance with the moderation and equity of her
diplomatic language ; I confess I am very much at
a loss to understand how the people who use
this cant can look out upon the map of Europe,
look back upon the history of fifty years, and not
blush to utter such childish and insane fatuity. I
do not understand how any man gifted with the
use of reason can look out upon the world and not
see that, under all the phases of her policy, and
under all changes of political principle in the
states by which she is surrounded, Russia is
systematically aggressive ; that she unites with
the utmost coolness of perception and wariness
of practice a fanatical zeal in favour of the extension of her influence and her territory which never
flags. It is all very fine to talk about the magna-

nimity of Nicholas and the moderation of Russia, or even about the insanity of his Imperial Majesty driving the Russian Cabinet beyond the bounds of its accustomed prudence and disinterestedness. But really if any man uses this language believing it to be true—if any man really gives Russia credit for the absence of ambition; for a desire to remain quiet within the boundaries of her present acquisitions; for an unwillingness to trespass on the rights of her neighbours; and for a nervous anxiety, from her conservative principles, not to interfere with the *status quo* in Europe—such a man may, for aught I know, be fit for the function of a parish beadle, but he is not fit to enter the council chamber of any potentate, Christian or heathen, or even to hold a pen in the office of the humblest journal of this empire. Russia is the great standing, permanent, persevering enemy of Western Europe. She is a perpetual danger and an everlasting insecurity to us all, from the Dardanelles to the farthest shore that is washed by the billows of the Atlantic. If she refrains from seizing a present advantage, it is only when, by abstaining for the moment, she can double the force of the blow by delaying the hour to strike."

It is perhaps not necessary to pursue these remarks further. Of late years the ambition of Russia has not ceased to manifest itself in either an easterly or a westerly direction.

Parliament was prorogued on the 20th August. How the Irish party had been weakened up to that time; how the deserters looked in Lucas's eyes; what advantages they had gained for themselves; and how illusory the notion that place-taking was beneficial to the cause of the Church, the poor, and the Irish tenant-farmers, he told in a few words.

" Of the men who have sought and found office I will not say a harsh word, but I point to the row of them as they stand shoulder to shoulder together, linked in a delighted and congenial brotherhood — John Sadleir, William Monsell, William Keogh, Serjeant Murphy, Edmond O'Flaherty; others who are seeking office and have not yet found it I do not name. They are known by their works and by their fruits; but to these men I point, and of them I say that they have at least succeeded in part of their aspirations. They have got something for themselves. They have not yet pulled down the Church as by law established. They have not got the principle of perfect equality recognised. They have not got the sanction of Parliament to Sharman Crawford's Bill. Even for themselves they have not got power; but they have got place, emolument, money, and what they think honour. In return for these things they have surrendered liberty and they have surrendered power. There they stand, five of them, made rich and made impotent; utterly destitute of all political influence over measures and the remedy of grievances; powerful only in extending the circle of corruption, by bribing, as they have been bribed."

CHAPTER VI.

*VISIT TO BELGIUM—INDUSTRIAL FARMS—LORD PAL-
MERSTON'S RETIREMENT—DOWLING v. LAWLER.*

PARLIAMENT having risen, Lucas crossed over to
Belgium to gain information as to local industries
there, such as he fancied might be introduced
with advantage into Ireland.   For this purpose
he visited Meulebeche in West Flanders, a little
town with a population something under nine
thousand.   There he found that, what with the
potato blight and the introduction of machinery
into the larger towns, the condition of the inhabitants in 1846 had become so miserable that nearly
one-half of them were receiving, wholly or in
part, official or charitable relief.   This was in a
place that had been prosperous only three years
before.   The spinning and weaving of flax had
been displaced.   Even so late as 1847 the town
contained but one small and ill-arranged work-
shop.   But latterly no effort had been spared to
remedy this state of affairs, and by 1853 they
had in the arrondissement eighteen model workshops and schools of apprenticeship perfectly
organised.   Hospitals were established for young

and old, for men and women, which were conducted with a cheapness almost unintelligible to
Englishmen ; the inmates labouring according to
their capacity for their own support, the young
learning some useful trade, and the old doing
what they could in the fields, or spinning and
weaving within doors. Several of these establishments were to be found at Meulebeche, and
in almost every other town in the district. A
Government functionary explained the phenomenon. He said that the low daily cost of the
inmates—a penny to three-halfpence per day—
arose from the fact that these *fermes hospices* were,
as their name implied, small farms, which were
economically managed, the inmates employing
themselves in productive labour for the support
of the establishments.

The introduction of industrial reformatory
schools had been determined on in this country,
and as some of these *hospices* were of this
character, Lucas thought that a system which had
been so successful in Belgium might be advan-
tageously tried in the United Kingdom. The
plan was exactly in accordance with views which
he had expressed at length in the *Tablet* ten
years previously in some articles on the working of the poor-laws here and in Ireland.

On his return to Dublin, he made a report on
the subject to a Conference held in that city on
the Tenant-Right and other public questions. In
the course of his remarks he mentioned that the

farm of which he had seen most was an agricultural school. "It extends," he said, "over not less than three hundred acres of ground, and embraces in practice many varieties of farming, gardening, and stock-keeping. The soil is sandy and light, and requires peculiar care and labour to make it any way productive. The animals for the use of the farm, on 31st December 1852, included ten horses, twenty-nine cows, nine oxen, three bulls, thirteen heifers and bullocks, fifty pigs, sixteen sheep, besides animals of less importance. The crops of 1852–53 included rye (about ninety-four acres), potatoes (about forty-five acres), oats (nearly twenty-four acres), flax (nearly two and a half acres), carrots, trefoil, beetroot, Swedish and common turnips, buckwheat, beans and peas, Jerusalem artichokes, colza; with nearly fifteen acres set apart for a kitchen-garden and two and a half acres for an orchard. There is scope enough for agricultural industry and training of almost every kind. This is where the leading idea of the institution is to render the children whom the state takes under its protection useful members of society, a help to themselves and others, instead of being a burden to society."

The school was managed on a strictly religious basis, and its success so marked that Lucas exclaims, "Pray God that this success, unmarred by bigotry or malignity of any kind, may be repeated where it is so much needed, that is, on both sides of the Irish Channel." What was especially wanted in Ireland was a scheme of industrial as apart from reformatory schools; but the extraordinary conduct of the Northern Presbyterians and the action of the Archbishop of Dublin rendered abortive any attempt at unity, without which there could be no success. At the Tenant-Right Conference which was held early in October, Dr. MacKnight of the *Banner of Ulster* tried to discredit Lucas. He publicly charged him with having endeavoured to induce the Government, through the Chief Secretary, Sir John Young, to postpone legislation on Tenant-Right for that session. At first the charge was made against some nameless member, and the Doctor was only compelled by great pressure to name the supposed delinquent. When the name was mentioned, Lucas at once said the charge was an unmitigated lie, and called on Dr. Mac-Knight for the name of his informant. This Dr. MacKnight would not give, but he declared that Lucas had admitted as much to himself in the lobby of the House. Then said Lucas, "If you give no authority for your first statement, I have at any rate my own with regard to the second. If the second be a falsehooood, then the author cannot be believed as regards the first, and so I have two lies on one neck and behead them both with one stroke. The statement which Dr. MacKnight has now made is the most unmeasured falsehood I ever heard."

He apologised, however, for the vehemence of this language, not to Dr. MacKnight, but to the Conference, in the same edition of the *Tablet* that contained the report of the meeting. Dr. MacKnight was supported in his calumny by the Rev. Mr. Rogers, Presbyterian minister, and subsequently by Mr. Sharman Crawford.

But this was not the only fable invented against Lucas. It had been said, and the memory of the accusation was now revived, that he had congratulated Keogh on his appointment as Solicitor-General for Ireland, and had expressed approval of his action in the matter. This tale was fabricated out of the before-mentioned kind personal expression used to Keogh, an expression that only proved how little of personal rancour there was in his condemnation of even his most pronounced opponents. Such attacks as these did not augur well for the Tenant-Right or any other cause that required united action.

The end of the year saw two events which, directly or indirectly, had some bearing upon the short remainder of my brother's life. The first was the retirement of Lord Palmerston from the Home Office in connection with Russian affairs. The second was an action (Dowling *v.* Lawler) tried in connection with the Carlow election of 1852.

As regards the first event, a letter from Lucas to Lord Palmerston, dated three days after his resignation, but before the appointment of his successor, brought out the fact that investigations into the subject of chaplains to Government prisons, and of the registration of prisoners, had taken place in the autumn ; and that on the 14th December Lord Palmerston, in accordance with his engagement in Parliament, had expressed his official opinion to Colonel Jebb, chairman of the Directors of Convict Prisons, that arrangements should be made which were exactly what Lucas had asked for, and which would have been as perfect a safeguard for the religion of the prisoners as could be expected or as would be practicable. So that, said the *Tablet* on the 24th December, "though the matter has not been finally settled, it is ripe for settlement." And a letter from Mr. Waddington to Lucas, dated the 21st December, stated expressly that Lord Palmerston's "intention had undergone no change."

When the trial of Dowling *v.* Lawler came to a hearing, John Sadleir, the Junior Lord of the Treasury, who had failed to be re-elected for Carlow, as we have seen above, perjured himself so grossly that he was compelled to resign his post. Meantime a vacancy had occurred in the borough of Sligo, and John Sadleir had been chosen to fill the vacant seat. So ended the year 1853.

CHAPTER VII.

BEFORE Parliament opened in 1854 meetings were held in Louth, Kilkenny, Meath, and Tuam in support of the Independent Opposition policy, to confirm the members who had remained true to their election pledges, to express the sense of the constituencies on those who had forfeited them, and to determine the future course of the party both in the House and in the country. In all these meetings Lucas took part. They were all remarkable, and were preludes to consequences which have continued to be felt to the present day.

The Louth banquet was held on the 4th January. In speaking to the resolution of " Mr. Sharman Crawford's Bill whole and entire," Lucas brought forward fresh arguments in favour of the tenants. He mentioned that the Law Amendment Society of England, after studying the question for three years, had come to the conclusion that payment for every class of improve-

ments was not only just in principle, but possible
and practicable. He then spoke of the Code
Napoléon, which was in force throughout France,
Belgium, and the Rhenish Provinces. By this
Code the landlord is bound to provide a farm
with all requisites for enabling the tenant to carry
on the cultivation of his holding, and the tenant
who finds his farm not so furnished has an action
for damages against the landlord. And further,
in case of unforeseen calamity, such as famine,
inundations, or war, causing the destruction or
partial destruction of the crops, the landlord has to
bear his proportion of the loss, even to the extent
at times of getting no rent whatever. He said, too,
that he was informed that a similar law obtains in
Scotland, where during the potato famine a provision to the same effect was put in force against
the Scotch landlords. And again, that the Orange
Tory, Mr. Whiteside, had published a book advocating the application to Ireland of the Tuscan
system, which appears to be the same in principle,
whatever difference it may show in details. These
facts being so, he was sure the Louth men would
consent to no mutilation of the Bill agreed to by
the Tenant League.

The Kilkenny meeting was mainly organised
by the Callan curates, Fathers O'Shea and Keeffe.
The Meath Conference and banquet were especially
significant and impressive demonstrations, as well
by the numbers present as by the resolutions
passed, and the sober, solid, serious enthusiasm

of those who attended them. At the Conference Lucas again described the Belgian industrial school system, and urged its adoption, not as a Government measure, but as one to be undertaken and developed by the people themselves. As this plan has been given in abstract in the preceding chapter, it will be unnecessary to repeat it here. Mr. Tristram Kennedy, one of the members for Louth, reminded his hearers that though Lucas would do all in his power to further the proposed object, yet that real substantial success could only follow a patient, long-sustained effort on their part; success or failure rested more with themselves than with their member.

In his speech at the Conference at Tuam he replied to certain fallacies which are still rife; to arguments—if they can be called arguments— which have been adduced ever since. He remarked :—

" It is said the whole question is altered because of the diminution of the people caused by inhuman laws inhumanly administered, and that in consequence of that diminution, and the high prices of agricultural produce, and the large profits farmers are now able to make, the necessity for a Tenant-Right Bill no longer exists." He met that proposition by the declaration that that very prosperity and improved condition of the tenants constituted the strongest necessity for at once passing a Tenant-Right Bill; and for this reason, that the prosperity of the country, which was

about to make a new spring, should be ensured
and made eternal. Who, he asked, was to make
those improvements which the new condition of
agriculture invited? Who was to spend on the
soil the capital and labour which were to enrich
the land and perpetuate its prosperity? Why,
the tenant-farmers of Ireland, who wanted and
had a right to insist on this, that when they
began to expend their money they should be able
to build up a secure property, which should be as
much their own as the soil was the landlord's.
"The change of circumstances has not got rid
of the question, simply because it is a demand for
justice. Is there any change of circumstances
that can dispense with the necessity of protecting
the property of any man? And surely it is impossible that the largest class of the community
should constitute the class from which protection
shall be withheld."

The Tenant League was charged with wanton
confiscation. The charge was a ridiculous one.
"We struggle," said he, "against confiscation.
The present law is a law of confiscation, and we
struggle against the present law. The present
law and the present practice together impose on
the tenant the obligation of creating property,
but give him no protection for that property
when created."

What they demanded was to put the land laws
on something like the same footing on which
they stand in every country in Europe.

"Confiscation! there is nothing so extravagant as this charge of confiscation."

At a later period in the same speech he puts the matter very much more strongly. Speaking of the plea that the clergy ought not to be mixing themselves up with political agitation; that their place is in the sanctuary, beyond which they should not pass; and that they should not entangle themselves in worldly business, Lucas said :—

"Such is the wretched sophistry, the specious but unmeaning cant, which has always been in the mouths of designing knaves, who, under the plea of consulting for the dignity of religion, have in all ages proved the deadly enemies of the Church and society."

After proceeding to suggest—he was speaking in presence of the Archbishop—that the clergy not only lost no rights of citizenship by virtue of their sacred office, but that they were bound to employ every means not inconsistent with the laws of God in opposing new restrictions on the exercise of religion and of combating every assault upon their spiritual rights, he went on to say that they were, as a fact, engaged in advocating the cause of the poor, in demanding the redress of a crime crying to Heaven for vengeance —the crime by which the labouring poor had been deprived of the just wages of the sweat of their brow—the cry of which had been for ages beating against God's firmament, and which had reached Heaven itself. Nothing could exceed his

indignation at the robbery to which the poor
tenants were subjected. I do not believe there is
a single passage in all his writings which exo-
nerates the landlords from the charge of intolerable brutality and habitual injustice.

With regard to the other question here touched
upon, namely, the interference of the clergy in
obtaining redress of this and other grievances, he
asked, " Did they think that, if the clergy had been
silent when the ' hellish cry' was raised throughout the country in consequence of the establishment of the Hierarchy in England, the overthrow
of their enemies would have been so signal?"

In whatever form the cry of " No politics " presented itself, it was in Lucas's view sheer cant
which he could not stomach. We have seen how
he appreciated it in the case of the Catholic Institute ; we see how he regarded it in the instance
just chronicled ; and we shall see it more elabo-
rately and more forcibly exposed in the " Statement." Strongly as he condemned the cry in the
Institute discussion, his aversion now was very
far greater ; now he looked upon it with loathing,
as being employed directly in order to enable the
landlords to perpetuate their robbery of the poor.

But his was not, in the result, by any means the
most important speech at Tuam. An address delivered by a Mr. Christopher Kelly, and another
by Dr. Gray of the *Freeman*, bore earlier fruit.

Mr. Kelly made some damaging remarks upon
the Whig sytem of buying Irish votes. He said,

referring to Sadleir, Keogh, and Edmond O'Flaherty, that corruption could be practised otherwise
than by becoming a Junior Lord, or a Solicitor-
General, or an Income-tax Commissioner. He
knew of his own knowledge the case of a stipen-
diary magistracy which was negotiated in the
following fashion. An honourable member and
the would-be magistrate entered into a contract,
the former promising a place, the latter handing
over £500 in exchange for the promise, and
undertaking to pay £500 more when the place
was actually got. The Minister was hard up for
votes on a particular division; the place was promised for the vote, and the vote duly given, as
was the place; not so the second moiety of the
purchase-money. This the dispenser of justice
refused to part with as agreed, and Mr. Kelly
was appealed to in order to induce the man to
keep to his bargain. There was no concealment
in the matter. Mr. Kelly refused to use his
influence with the defaulter, and was prepared
to disclose the names to the proper persons.

Then came Dr. Gray, who related how, when a
certain number of Irish members had undertaken
to vote for Lord George Bentinck's proposal to
grant sixteen millions for railways in 1847, they
were sent for by Lord John Russell, and told that
if they supported Lord George, they would cease
to have any claim on Whig patronage; in other
words, that they must decide between the people
who were starving and their own personal in

E

terests. The bargain was accordingly struck on these terms: wherever there was an inactive clergy, and local leaders who sought places for themselves or their relatives, for such constituencies the members should vote with the Whigs and against the people; but where the constituencies would not brook a sale, the members should not vote at all. Such was the condition of a large portion of the Irish representation, and such was the mode by which the Irish vote was secured for the Whig Government. Dr. Gray vouched for the facts; and, as we shall see, these two speeches led to some particularly interesting passages in the House and in Committee, in both of which Lucas distinguished himself greatly.

It will be remembered that he had opposed Lord George Bentinck's proposal, considering that the country required productive works and not iron rails. It may be supposed, therefore, that the gentlemen who were bribed as above did no great violence to their consciences; but inasmuch as they had already pledged their votes to Lord George, it is clear that they gave up their convictions for Whig patronage. Moreover, it was no case of an alternative between rails and productive works; for the Whigs were free traders of such strict orthodoxy that they would not interfere with the principle of supply and demand by undertaking reproductive works. The reader will not overlook this statement of facts when reading that portion of the second chapter of the "Statement," entitled " The Great Scandal of all."

Before proceeding with the subject of corruption as it occupied the attention of Parliament, I may refer here, as in chronological order, to the Louth election of 1853. The verdict in a trial of Dowling *v.* Lawler practically branded Sadleir as a perjurer. He was compelled to resign his post of Junior Lord, and was replaced by one of the members for Louth, Mr. Chichester Fortescue, who, of course, had to seek re-election. The history of that lawsuit will be found in the third chapter of the "Statement ;" and will be found to throw light upon the general subject of Parliamentary venality.

To return, then, to proceedings at Westminster. Parliament opened on the 31st January 1854. On the 5th February an article appeared in the *Times* repeating Dr. Gray's tale, and calling upon some Irish member to move for a committee to inquire into the truth of the allegations. Next day Mr. Butt moved, first, to have the article read, and, when that was done, to appoint a Select Committee. There was no opposition to the motion. But Lucas having been appealed to as one who was present at the Tuam banquet, rose to reply. His speech was considered one of his cleverest efforts. The subject was calculated to bring all his ability into play, and he acquitted himself in a manner worthy of his reputation as a debater. He began by avowing his ignorance

of the specific charges, but, as he had been
appealed to, it was only becoming that he should
offer a few observations. He had frequently
brought similar charges himself in a general way,
which he had no doubt whatever were true. It
was impossible to mix in the management of
public affairs in Ireland without hearing evidence
which could not be disbelieved as to widespread
corruption. The difficulty in bringing these
matters forward was, that the conversations in
which they were detailed were confidential. Now
Mr. Butt had commented on the article in the
Times, and it might be supposed that the journal
in question had got its information from the
speeches at Tuam; whereas nothing could be
further from the fact. He had in his hand the
copy of an article from the *Times* of the previous
September, months before the banquet, which
contained far stronger statements than any which
were made at Tuam. Now they often heard
very exalted names mentioned in connection with
the leaders in the papers. He did not know—
probably nobody knew—but that the article was
written by a Secretary of State, or by the Secretary
of a Board. ("Hear, hear," and loud laughter.)
One of the proprietors of the *Times* was a member
of Parliament, and not the least efficient supporter
of the Government—a man perfectly cognisant
of all the talk of the Treasury bench; one who
would not insult his fellow-supporters by making
false accusations against them. He (Lucas) had

brought similar charges against Irish members who for a long course of years had been connected in a commerce of corruption with successive Whig Governments. (Loud cheers from the Opposition.) Of such transactions the editor of the *Times* was a very competent and fitting witness. He would read the article, or rather extracts from it. But before doing so, he would recall the scene which took place last session in connection with certain members charged, but not named, by Mr. Duffy. Could any one forget the phrenzy of indignation which that charge of corruption excited on the benches opposite? It was almost impossible to stand against the burst of fury. Even Mr. Disraeli was almost overborne. Less practised members were fairly overwhelmed by the torrent. For himself, such was the impression produced, that for a moment he believed the other side of the House to be pure. (Great laughter.) The House would recollect how the affair ended. As it was not alleged that any cash payments had been made by Mr. Hayter; as political corruption—prostitution of principle through the ordinary agencies of Government, was alone alleged; Lord John Russell, if Mr. Lucas understood what he said, declared that he thought there was no accusation to answer!

Then he read extracts from the article with humorous comments which kept the House in laughter and covered the corruptionists with ridicule all round; Irish members, Lord John, and the *Times* alike ; the *suaviter in modo* being combined with the *fortiter in re.*

All this is too long to be quoted here. But one point must not be omitted. The *Times* had said that after a vote has been tendered, used, and enjoyed on a promise of patronage, the promise must be kept—the Minister cannot refuse.

" The next sentence in the article will, I think, meet with general approbation :—The sentiment of the transaction is not high. But the writer doubts if Aristides the just would have refused to avail himself of a mercenary vote, or to give the voter a small place, if he thought the safety of the country depended on it. I have," said Mr. Lucas, " interpolated the word 'place,' because that is the obvious meaning of the writer." (Laughter.)

The *Times* said that the system of corruption was perfectly notorious, but that it might be denied. Mr. Lucas was prepared for any amount of denial, but no amount would destroy any sane man's belief in the fact that the Whig Government had been kept in office for a series of years by the means alleged. He had, of course, no objection to the appointment of the Committee, but he hoped its inquiries would not be confined to the two cases mentioned at Tuam. His attention to the subject had been first called by a speech delivered by Mr. G. H. Moore at Ballina, in which that gentleman said that the price of places was as well known as the price of stocks. Cases had been stated to himself which he had a difficulty in repeating, because he was not at liberty to mention the names of his informants. He said, " I believe I shall not be doing what is wrong if I mention those facts to the House—(Ministerial cries of " Hear, hear!")—not under any pressure, for I am perfectly free at this moment to mention them or not. If I mention them, I do so warning the House beforehand that I have them from authority which I am not at liberty to name. (A laugh.) Some gentlemen opposite laugh, and are, perhaps, very glad that the authority cannot be named. (" Hear, hear," and renewed laughter.) But the facts themselves are true, and I am merely cautious, before mentioning them, to guard myself from being called upon to name my authority, because I cannot in honour name it. (Oh! oh!) Honourable gentlemen opposite seem to think that this difficulty about naming throws a doubt upon the accuracy of the statement. (Ministerial cheers.) Then (addressing Irish members on the Ministerial benches) you don't wish to hear the statements made? (" No, no," and counter-cheering.) I am delighted with those frank admissions on your side. (Loud cheers.) I believe you do not want to have the statements made. I believe you do not want to have the facts known. I believe you agree with the writer in the *Times* that a system of corruption is necessary for the management of the affairs of this country, and you wish to have as decent a veil as possible thrown over the inevitable infamy. (No, no.)

Oh, then, you do wish to have the facts stated ?
(A laugh.)   Well, in order to please you, I will state
the facts."

And so he did.   Among others, he mentioned
a saying of the late Mr. Sheil to the effect that
a certain person connected with the Treasury
"held the Irish members in the hollow of his
hand."   This was in the interval between Lord
John Russell's Durham letter and the introduction
of the Ecclesiastical Titles Bill.   The explanation
of the phrase was that before a division, when
the Government wanted votes, the gentleman in
question (Mr. Hayter was Government whip in
at that time) went to the venal members and
promised places for votes, payment to be made
after a vote was given.

After mentioning the sale of a place in the
custom-house for the sum of £9, he read a telegram from Dr. Gray offering to come over and
prove his accusation before the Committee ; and
then, after apologising for the length of his remarks, resumed his seat.

The motion for the Committee was unanimously agreed to, and, in writing to the *Tablet*,
Lucas was able to say that he fully hoped the
debate would be a fatal blow to the existing
system of corruption through patronage.   The
subject of competitive examinations had been
alluded to in the Queen's speech, and a *Times*
leader declared that it was high time to put an
end to the barter of places for party support.

There were upwards of sixteen thousand salaried offices, and these it was proposed to throw open to free competition.

When the Committee was appointed, it consisted, among others, of Mr. Henley, the chairman, Mr. G. H. Moore, William Keogh, Mr. Bright, and Mr. Butt.

After some sittings, in which Mr. Kelly, Dr. Gray, and Dr. Power, Member for Cork county (who had taken a place), were examined, Mr. Lucas was called. It is quite impossible to do justice to these examinations. I can but give some specimens. The most striking, though not by any means the most dramatic feature, was the tactics by which he led and forced the Committee to let him give his evidence in his own way. Knowing what he wished to bring out; knowing that the disclosure would be extremely damaging to the English Government, as apart from mere party disgrace; and being quite aware that the Committee had a suspicion of what he intended, and that the majority would use every effort to thwart his design; with these considerations present to his mind, he played his opponents with admirable skill, while he elicited friendly questions from Mr. Bright and Mr. Moore, who were more or less in his secret and assisted him materially; as also did Mr. Butt.

A vain attempt was made to induce him to name his non-parliamentary informants as to cases of Government bribery; then he was asked by Mr. Moore if he knew any member of Parliament who could state cases.   He replied that he did ; but that he felt a difficulty in concealing some names and mentioning others ; however, as the chairman pressed him, he supposed he must take that as an intimation that if any member of the Committee had spoken to him on the subject, the confidence would be waived in his regard.   After long discussion, and after the room had been cleared several times, it was decided that he was not bound by any consideration of confidence. He at once replied that he thought Mr. Butt and Mr. Bright could both give information.   He had had a conversation with Mr. Butt in the lobby on the subject of the constitution of the Committee, and had objected to the Irish Solicitor-General, Mr. Keogh, being upon it, owing to his position, character, and previous conduct ; and owing to his being a principally accused party. This brought matters to an unpleasant point; and Mr. Vernon, a friend of Keogh's, tried his hand at an examination of the witness.   But he had to give it up, and Keogh took the questioning on himself.   After a few questions, he asked if Lucas charged him with corrupt motives in voting to turn out Lord Derby.   Lucas replied, " I have no means of saying what were your motives in giving the vote which got you your place."   The Committee laughed.   Then Keogh tried him on the statement made by Mr. Sheil, and asked whether his declining to mention the name of his informant was because his memory was at fault as to whether Mr. Tuffnell or Mr. Hayter was whipper-in at that time. He answered, "No; that Mr. Tuffnell's name never crossed his mind." This fixed the charge on Mr. Hayter. Then Mr. Bright put it to him whether he attributed corruption to Mr. Keogh because he took office in violation of solemn promises and oaths to the public.

Mr. Lucas.—"Yes."

This brought Keogh fairly to bay, and he fought desperately.

Keogh.—" It is now about fifteen months since I took office. Had not you and I very strong personal disagreements long before that period ; in fact, did not I describe you, in your presence, at a large public meeting in Athlone,[1] as one who would plunge a dagger in a man's back, but would never dare to do anything to his prejudice openly in his presence ?" The room applauded.

Mr. Lucas.—" I do not recollect that you used those expressions. You charged me with being a calumniator, using the strongest language that could easily proceed from human lips; and you did so because I had said that whenever a coalition was formed between Whigs and Peelites, Mr. Keogh would accept the post of Solicitor-General for Ireland." The tables were turned, and again the room applauded.

---

[1] This was a meeting before the general election, at which Lucas was present.

Keogh.—" Did you not solicit me, after using that language, to go to the office of Dr. Gray of the *Freeman* in Dublin and strike that identical passage out of the report ? "

Mr. Lucas.—" I will give you a distinct reply, Mr. Keogh. You called me to account after the speech was delivered as having charged you with conduct most dishonourable, base, and disgraceful, when I said that if a coalition were formed such as that which now exists you would take the office of Solicitor-General for Ireland. You insisted upon three Catholic Bishops, then present, disclaiming any participation in that charge,[1] because (you said) it was so disgraceful to you that if you remained under it without securing the Bishops' disclaimer, you could never enter a room where Catholic politics were being discussed without a scowl upon your countenance."

Mr. Moore.—" That is true. That is true." (Applause.)

Mr. Lucas.—" The result of the conversation that morning was what, I think, I may properly describe as a reconciliation, and before we left the town of Athlone, you and I shook hands. It was agreed that as the report of that meeting would contain strong expressions of mine against you, and as it was desirable, after you and I had shaken hands, that there should be no record of our differences, it was agreed, I say, that every-

[1] The charge was made in the article entitled " Log-Rolling," referred to in Book II. chap. iv.

thing on both sides that had an angry character should be struck out of the report, and that was accordingly done." (Loud applause.)

The *Freeman's* London correspondent thus describes the scene :—

"Amidst hushed expectation, a few preliminary passages of arms were exchanged between them, as if to try each other's strength, till at length, and after an effective pause and one of those triumphant and overwhelming looks with which Mr. Keogh knows so well how to add weight to his deliveries, he thundered before his antagonist a question so damaging, so well aimed, and so effectively delivered, that a buzz of admiration through the room expressed the anticipation of the old '*habet*' of the amphitheatre. But the '*habet*' was uttered in vain, for in an instant the deadly thrust was parried, and the sword of the assailed passed through the very sword-arm of the assailant. But the intellectual resources, the courage, and the skill of the accomplished though fallen Irishman were not yet exhausted, and, to do Mr. Keogh justice, he exhibited, even in the moment of conscious defeat, a self-possession and a capacity worthy of a better cause. Again collecting his energies for the encounter, he again directed against his antagonist an interrogatory so trenchant, so terrible in its bearing, that for a moment it looked as if he had restored the battle, and every man held his breath as he waited an answer. Deliberate and inevitable as death it came. Cold and pointed, it cleft the very heart of the vanquished gladiator, and a long, suppressed respiration from all around told that in this instance the '*habet*' was unmistakable. It was a sight which none that witnessed it will ever forget, the countenances of the two combatants at this juncture—rage and unconquered despair in the one face—derision, triumphant and ineffable, in that of the other."

The description in the Dublin *Daily Express*, the Tory organ, was even more vivid. Hating

Lucas, it declared that, though Keogh could not be pitied, yet his enemy awakened no feeling but aversion. The writer's account therefore would not favour Lucas. He says :—

" He played his part, I must acknowledge, with consummate ability, although it was over-refined. You must have been present to have appreciated his success. The air of determination or smile of indifference, the leisurely folding of the arms, and fall upon the back of the chair, the measured whisper of his voice and quiet look of attention, were all finished in their way, and after no inferior master. . . . To men who despised the instrument, there was something that seemed like retribution in the words he used to the Solicitor-General for Ireland. To lean forward amid the breathless silence of a hundred gentlemen, to point the finger at one figure, to italicise with shakes of the hand slowly uttered charges of awful perjury and deliberate corruption, is to do that which would make not a few spring to their feet in a paroxysm of honourable anger. But if Keogh was angry, he concealed his wrath."

I do not believe my brother had a thought of acting a part in those replies. As we know, *indignatio facit versum.* Good acting consists in a perfect counterfeit expression of a natural manner. In this case there was indignation enough, and no time to counterfeit or to think of posing. Question and answer were alike spontaneous ; both were equally unpremeditated. But this was not the end of the matter. The charge was made, but the proof still remained behind when the Committee adjourned.

It has been said that the visit to Athlone and the reconciliation were faults on my brother's part.

Perhaps so, but in that case they were happy
faults.

When next examined in continuation, he found
the chairman, Mr. Henley, apparently determined
to have the evidence in a form sufficiently con-
fused and mutilated to impair or destroy its effect.
Mr. Henley interrupted my brother so often and
with such an obvious animus, that Mr. Moore told
him unless he desisted he should move to clear
the room. This was presently done, and the
sitting for that day closed.

On the next occasion Lucas had a real fight
with the chairman, who wished to force him to
make his statement after a particular fashion.
This Lucas declined to do. The duel lasted,
according to my recollection, nearly an hour.
At length the chairman was beaten and had to
yield. Lucas stated his case in his own way.
He put in the article on " Log-Rolling," in
which he had charged Keogh with the intention of taking place notwithstanding his promises.
Then he read extracts from Keogh's speeches.
Keogh tried to trip him as to the authenticity of
the reports, but in vain ; Lucas was armed at
every point. Keogh had said at Cork :—

" Let the Minister of the day be who he may ;
let him be the Earl of Derby, let him be Sir
James Graham or Lord John Russell, it is all
the same to us ; and, SO HELP ME GOD, no matter
who the Minister may be, no matter who the
party in power may be, I never will support that

Minister or that party unless he comes into power prepared to carry the measures which the whole people of Ireland demands. . . . I have seconded the proposition of Mr. Sharman Crawford in the House of Commons, and, SO HELP ME GOD, upon that and every other question to which I have given my adhesion, I will be—and I know that every one of my friends is as determined as myself—an unflinching, undeviating, unalterable supporter of it."

The reason why such stress was laid upon the possible defection in case of a Whig and Peelite Coalition Ministry was, that Keogh had been a follower of Sir James Graham, and, as it turned out, money for his election was actually being subscribed by Mr. Sidney Herbert, who was another Peelite, at the time Keogh was taking these oaths. Having brought out all this, Lucas concluded by putting in advertisements from the *Times* of offers to buy Government situations. It was well known that the money was paid to members who got places, as before mentioned, in exchange for votes. It was the recognised system, and demanded exposure; and this Lucas was the first to effect in so public a manner.

Referring to the reports of the examinations before the Committee which appeared in the English papers, Lucas said:—

"The English newspapers, giving a hasty summary of what occurs every day, continue with considerable regularity to omit or misstate all the points." On Mr. Napier's examination, for example, they suppressed altogether a statement which confirmed the above remark about the advertisements ; and with regard to another charge, namely, that past Parliaments were no worse than the present, they made Mr. Napier say exactly the reverse. Lucas had no further dealings with the Committee, whose report was eminently unsatisfactory.

CHAPTER VIII.

*CONVENTS BILL—AGGREGATE MEETING IN DUBLIN—
VARIOUS MOTIONS IN THE HOUSE RENDERED ABOR-
TIVE BY DR. CULLEN.*

THE event which next claims our attention is a
motion on the 28th of February by Mr. Chambers
for a committee to inquire into the number and
rate of increase of convents, and to see if any
fresh legislation in regard to them was necessary.
On the former occasion Mr. Chambers had spoken
with such moderation, that Lucas looked upon
him as a not very bigoted man, but one bound
to make out a case for himself with his constituents. Now, however, he exhibited his true character. The Tories were mild and gentlemanly in
their tone, but the speech of Mr. Chambers was
insulting in its language and offensive in its imputations. It contained, moreover, several false
charges. By this time it had been discovered that
the Independent Opposition party were out of
favour with episcopal authority in Ireland. The
result was a large majority (67) in favour of the
motion.

This fresh move against the convents created
a great agitation among Catholics in this coun-

try and throughout Ireland. Numerous meetings were held and resolutions passed. The Irish papers were crowded with articles and letters all protesting against the proposed tyranny. An aggregate meeting to be held in Dublin was soon determined on, and it was thought necessary to have a declaration against the attack drawn up and signed as numerously as possible. Lucas went over to Dublin about the 20th of April, and the moment he saw the proposed declaration he objected to its terms.

It was indeed an absurd document, for it made the signatories " express our deep regret that we are compelled, as a separate class of the religious community, again to undertake the assertion of our religious rights." " *Again!* " as if there had been an interval, long or short, during which they had had no occasion to come forward as a separate class in defence of their religious rights ; whereas no single grievance of those detailed in 1851 had been redressed. On this ground Lucas protested against the terms of the " Declaration." And several of the Bishops, even while attaching their signatures, objected to it for the same reason that prevented Lucas from signing it at all. An article from his pen in terms that any unprejudiced person must consider moderate and respectful appeared in the next issue of the *Tablet.* The meeting was held a few days later. In the course of it, John Reynolds, in a vituperative speech, charged Lucas with having in that very

article stigmatised as "knaves or fools" the Bishops
who had signed the declaration. Lucas tried to
reply, but was prevented from doing so by the
Lord Mayor, who occupied the chair. He was only
able to say in two sentences that the charge was an
"untruth," and that if an opportunity were afforded
him he would prove it to be a "base, deliberate,
and malicious falsehood." He then withdrew,
and the report with this denial appeared in the
morning papers. Nevertheless, Dr. Cullen, having
not only the denial, but the article itself before
him, adopted and repeated the calumny.

Whether Lucas or his friends most keenly felt
the treatment to which he was subjected I do not
know. Publicly he made no complaint. Not so
his friends, who with one accord stepped forward
in his defence. With little delay they determined
to present him with a substantial testimonial. As
soon as the scheme got wind, Dr. Cullen wrote
to one of the English Bishops, a great friend of
Lucas's, to express surprise at the movement.
He could not, he said, understand how English
Catholics could select the very time when—so
the Archbishop was pleased to aver—Lucas had
been creating discord among his fellow-Catholics
in Ireland; how they could select such a time
for conferring upon him so public a mark of
honour. But it was a matter of notoriety that
Lucas was the party attacked, not the assailant;
that he had, without provocation on his part,
been maligned before a large audience, and had

been refused a hearing in reply. To complain, therefore, of his destroying any existing harmony was to repeat the fable of the wolf and the lamb.

Writing from London the following week Mr. Lucas says :—

" Last week I preferred saying nothing about the very curious meeting by which the supporters of the present Government did their utmost to protect the nuns. It seemed unadvisable in the first moment of excitement to write upon a subject with which all hearts, in Dublin at least, were set on flame ; and it was, of course, impossible for me to write with any serious indignation against the principal authors of that strange scene, who, in what they did, only followed the instincts of their nature, and showed themselves as they are. All anger apart, what remains for us to do is to reflect upon what has happened, to consider what is its meaning and to what it tends."

Unfortunately the meaning and tendency, viewed by the light of affairs in the House of Commons, were only too plainly revealed, as will be seen in the sixth chapter of the " Statement."

In the course of this session Mr. Lucas gave notices and brought forward motions on several matters concerning the welfare of the Irish people and Catholic grievances, not only in Ireland, but also in England, Scotland, and abroad. The day after Parliament opened he placed on the books a notice of motion for a Select Committee on the best means to promote Irish industry by training schools (on the Belgian model). On the 3d March he brought forward (on Supply) the wants of Catholic soldiers and sailors in time of peace. On the 30th of the same month he moved to postpone the further nomination of Mr. Chambers's Convents Committee. He was beaten, of course, but the nomination was obstructed, amid the usual cry of a "tyrant minority." The *Leader* remarked on this occasion, that, bored as the House was by Mr. Chambers at a moment when the thoughts of men were in the East (the Crimean war had just been declared), and unpopular as the Irish members in general were, yet the House listened to and admired Mr. Lucas. And further, that it was fortunate for Catholic Ireland that she had such a leader in the House, a man of genius and an accomplished orator, one who last year was a parliamentary success, but this session an accepted House of Commons personage, whose speeches were important and must be listened to, watched and comprehended. The O'Connells, Scullys, Fitzgeralds only whined; Mr. Lucas, on the contrary, said, "This Committee is part of a system. You want to crush and intimidate the Catholics; but you shall not; we mean to resist you and defy you." That, says the *Leader*, is intelligible, certainly dignified, and, by altering the tactics from the defensive to the offensive, keeps off and keeps down the sham fanatics and real sycophants of parliamentary Protestantism. In the end Mr. Chambers failed to carry his Bill.

On the 12th May Lucas complained of sailors in the navy being compelled to attend Protestant services on board ship. Sir James Graham and Mr. S. Herbert evaded the charge, declaring that the complaint originated not with the men on board, but with the Catholic priests ashore.

The 12th June brought a discussion on a sum of £550 for Catholic chaplains in gaols. This had been inserted in the estimates in accordance with Lord Palmerston's promise of the last session. Now it was rejected by a majority of 22; twenty-four Irish members being absent, and the Tories encouraged by the partial break up of the Independent Opposition party.

A resolution by Mr. Collier to modify the law of partnership, in the sense of limited liability, Lucas supported in a speech exhibiting considerable mastery of the subject, and designed to show that the principle was especially applicable to poor countries, and particularly to Ireland.

On the 5th July he spoke on the disestablishment of the Irish Church. This measure he strongly advocated, declaring that he wanted none of the money, and would be only too glad to give up the Maynooth grant in exchange for the boon of disestablishment. The measure was, in fact, postponed because it was said the Catholics were chargeable with accepting the principle of an Established Church by taking the Maynooth grant.

He spoke also on the question of throwing open the University of Oxford to the Dis-

senters. In advocating this step, he grounded
his argument on the speech of Mr. Gladstone,
who admitted the grievance under which the
Dissenters suffered, and which he said was, as
matters stood, a real grievance. But Lucas
wished it to be understood that he considered it
would be extremely injurious to Catholic interests
if, the door being open to them along with the
Dissenters, they were to take advantage of any
such right of admission to the University of
Oxford as by the resolution before the House it
was proposed to offer.

On July 7th Lucas spoke in a debate on a
certain Middlesex Industrial Schools Bill, the
real object of which was, he said, not so much to
have an industrial Bill as to have a proselytising Bill. This Bill was carried by a majority
of 27.

Three days later he placed on the books of
the House three amendments to a Reformatory
Schools (Scotland) Bill. This also was a scheme
for purposes of proselytism, and the amendments
were framed to counteract the intentions of its pro-
moters. The Committee reported progress, and
when, on the 19th July, the debate was resumed,
while Lucas strove for the insertion of a clause
to prevent the sending of Catholic children to
Protestant schools, Serjeant Shee, instead of
supporting the member for Meath, declared that
he thought "they were disputing about nothing."
The discussions were, however, in some degree

successful, and on the 21st it was agreed that, if certain amendments to which the Independent party agreed were thrown out in the Lords, the Bill should be abandoned. "Perhaps," said Lucas, "the justice of the case as regards Catholic children had not before been properly understood." The end of the session was now approaching. It was not till the 31st July that Lucas was able to bring forward the motion of which he had given notice at the opening of Parliament on the subject of industrial legislation. It was, of course, too late to take any effective steps then, even had the House been in possession of sufficient information to warrant it in granting the Committee for which the hon. member asked. But a somewhat elaborate exposition of his views was listened to with marked attention; was replied to by Lord John Russell in a not unfriendly speech; and created an amount of interest and approval in the country which augured well for the future. But the Tenant-Right question made no way. Bills were introduced into the House of Lords and passed by their Lordships. On coming down to the Commons, they were found to be worse than useless, and, in face of the opposition of the Independent party, they were withdrawn. How horrible a wrong was in this session inflicted upon the tenants by their professed champions, also how the action of Dr. Cullen and others rendered abortive Lucas's attempts to obtain redress of the grievances to which soldiers, sailors, and prisoners were subjected, will be seen from a perusal of the 7th and 8th sections of the sixth chapter of the "Statement," where the particulars are fully entered into. Suffice it to say, that it was not till 1868 that any material modification was introduced by which children of Catholic paupers were protected from proselytism; and even to this day there are comparatively few workhouses in which mass can be said or confessions heard with due convenience, and in which Catholic chaplains are paid for their services. The "Statement" shows that, in the writer's opinion, these reforms might have been extorted from our unwilling rulers thirty years ago, but for the break up of the Independent party. How many children have lost their faith in the meantime, and how far the ground which might have been occupied by Catholics was left open to the establishment of the Board School system of proselytism, will never be known.

Paid chaplains for the army in times of peace and security for the children of Catholic soldiers were not conceded for many years; and chaplains for the navy while the ships are at sea were first granted to Irish obstruction in 1879.

CHAPTER IX.

THIS proved to be the end of Lucas's parliamentary career, for though he attended two sittings of the House in the next session, he was too ill to speak. Before his return to Dublin two incidents occurred which must be mentioned here.

The first was his appearance as a witness in an action for libel brought by a certain Mr. Boyle against Cardinal Wiseman. The allegation was that his Eminence had published or caused to be published a libellous letter in the *Tablet*, and Mr. Lucas was called to prove the handwriting of the " copy " from which the letter was printed. His examiner was Mr. Edwin James, Q.C., a very clever man, but a great bully, and so overbearing that he had the sympathy of no one even at the Bar. He was engaged as the man most capable of making himself obnoxious to the Cardinal, whom he insisted upon bringing into court, though the judge had already decided that he could not

be sworn.   He was called, however, but retired
on the Chief Baron reiterating his decision.   Dr.
Grant and Father Spencer were then examined,
but did not assist the plaintiff's case.   Then came
Lucas's turn.   He said he knew nothing of the
letter and had never read it.   In obedience to the
duces tecum which he had received, he had written
to Dublin for the manuscript of the letter, and in
reply had received the roll of paper which he
now produced and handed to the learned counsel,
who asked if he were not the proprietor of the
Tablet, and if he did not look after its contents.
He said yes, but that he had not seen this.   Mr.
James did not believe him, or affected not to do
so.   How came it that he had omitted to see this
particular letter, a letter to which so great an
interest attached ?   Lucas replied that as the
matter was in the hands of the lawyers, of the
learned counsel especially, he thought the less he
knew about it the better. (Laughter.)   Then
followed a conversation, as nearly as my memory
serves me, in the following fashion.

Mr. James.—" Look at the manuscript.   Now,
sir, whose is the handwriting ? "

Mr. Lucas, looking at the paper.—" I would
rather not swear."

Mr. James.—" You must answer my question,
sir."

Mr. Lucas.—" I really would rather not."

Mr. James, angrily.—" Answer my question,
sir."

Mr. Lucas.—" My lord, am I bound to answer ? I don't like to swear to any man's handwriting."

The Judge.—" Yes, Mr. Lucas, you are bound to answer to the best of your judgment."

Mr. Lucas.—" Allow me to look again at the document." (Then looking very carefully at it and handing it back to Mr. James.) "I really would rather not swear."

By this time James was fairly out of temper, and the Cardinal's friends in a cold perspiration.

Mr. James.—" Answer my question, sir, and let there be no more hesitation."

Mr. Lucas.—" Let me look at it again, please." (Then scrutinising it with the utmost minuteness.) " If I must swear——"

Mr. James.—" Of course you must."

Mr. Lucas.—" Then I say, to the best of my belief, it was written by Mr. Ornsby, my sub-editor."

The court was convulsed. Mr. James, completely nonplussed, was not himself during the remainder of the trial ; and the Cardinal won the day.

The other incident was his visit to Birmingham, whither he went towards the end of August for the purpose of obtaining information relative to the industrial projects mentioned in the preceding chapter. On its being known that he was in the town, the Birmingham Catholic Association determined to present him with an address expressive of their regard for him. The ceremony took place in the house of the Bishop, Dr. Ullathorne, who still retains the See.

The chair was taken by the President of Oscott College, who was supported on the right by his Lordship, while Mr. Lucas sat on his left. The address told what was, acccording to other competent testimony, the bare truth when it said :—

"Let any one who is old enough to be able to make the comparison contrast the English Catholics of twenty years ago and the English Catholics of to-day. If he finds them in the year 1854 of a higher tone of mind and possessed of more elevated sentiments ; if he finds them better informed on what concerns the Church in her real character, of her relations with the world, and in the history of her transactions throughout the globe ; if they are less disposed to lead an amphibious life between two sets of maxims, the one kept like family secrets, to be used at home and in church, the other to be used in dealing with the broad world ; if a Catholic in this country is more a Catholic in all circumstances ; if he no longer shrinks from the logical, or devotional, or the social consequences of his faith ; if he has learned to view with a Catholic eye and to estimate with a Catholic judgment history, policy, economy, literature, society itself ; without at all undervaluing the influences or trenching on the merits of other distinguished men in either the ecclesiastical or the political sphere, it is impossible for him, if he be just, not to attribute a great share in these changes to the writings of Frederick Lucas."

And again :—

"It is because you are known to be a Catholic in the integral sense of the word, because, in a word, you are known to be a man of incorruptible Catholic conscience, that your words command the attention and respect of all parties in the House."

This reception could not but afford Lucas much encouragement, and when he reached Ireland he still had great hopes for the future of the Catholic cause.

The favour with which his industrial project was received in Ireland gave him great pleasure. His plan was to take the Libraries and Museums Acts (13 & 14 Vict., c. 65, and 16 & 17 Vict., c. 101) in their general character for his model, and to provide that under the Towns Amendment Act every town should have the power to tax itself for an institution to promote manufacturing industry, just as the larger towns have power to tax themselves for museums and libraries. Alas! he was not to live to carry out a scheme the realisation of which would have saved much misery. But given an earnest and able champion of the cause, and it may yet not be too late to hope for something of the kind.

Just at that time it was reported, on what seemed reliable authority, that Keogh was to be made a judge. This Lucas said was as it should be, "if precedents and analogies were to be followed. Mr. Keogh never was a Whig; his promotion, if it take place, will be due exclusively to the followers of Sir Robert Peel; not to the Whigs, but to the men of high moral sentiment and Puritan political integrity;" of whom Mr. Gladstone was one.

Shortly after Lucas's arrival in Dublin it was proposed to hold a Conference of the Tenant

League. To the objection that the work of the session entitled members of Parliament to some rest, and that they could not be got together, he replied that other members of the League could take counsel as to the position of the question. A meeting was accordingly held on 26th September, when it was determined to organise a series of meetings throughout the country. The first was to be held in Callan, and this was the more necessary because, in consequence of Serjeant Shee's defection, "a whole year had been deliberately thrown away." He had undertaken the conduct of the Tenant-Right Bill through the House. Yet "not the smallest effort was made to advance the question ; and we, to whose hands this business had *not* been trusted, but who were the followers of a leader named by two Conferences, had no alternative but to help one another in doing nothing." The fact was the Sergeant had gone over to the other traitors, and had been indulging in hostile letters to a Sadleirite paper, the *Telegraph*. The second chapter of the " Statement " contains an account of certain letters on this subject that passed between Father Keeffe and Serjeant Shee, dated 15th to 18th October, and which appeared in the *Kilkenny Journal*. Immediately after their publication rumours became rife about " reforms that were to be introduced into the connection of priests with politics," and about " scandals that were to be corrected." What these scandals consisted in was not divulged. But

Lucas remarked that "public opinion and the common reverence felt by every priest for the order to which he belonged tended potently to correct such as were open and notorious; and that the real danger lay in the concealed evil, in the mischief transacted in hidden corners and in the ante-chambers of the great." "God grant," he said, "that vengeance may not rage against acts of honest but indiscreet zeal, leaving the meaner, weightier, and less public transgressions to fester with an inward and more dangerous corruption."

He "had a kind of light what would ensue," or perhaps he knew what had already occurred. For before the Callan meeting was held, on the 25th October, two or three days after the above was penned, it was known that Father Keeffe had been ordered by the Bishop to abstain altogether from taking any part in it, or indeed publicly in politics at all. Father O'Shea was present, however, and spoke to a resolution which condemned Serjeant Shee's conduct in reference to the Tenant-Right Bill, and to his unauthorised publication of Father Keeffe's first letter to him, in severe yet temperate terms. When the immediate business of the meeting was ended, the whole of the clergy retired, and Lucas addressed the assembly. He told the people of the prohibition, silenced their cries of "Shame, shame," and begged them to express no feeling of anger or disapprobation. He said that the power of the Catholic members in the House, and their only means of accomplishing "the redress of

grievances and of protecting the interests of the
Church and religion, was through the intrepid
heroic action of the people—most of them very
poor—led and sustained by the exertions of the
Catholic parish priests and curates of Ireland."
He continued, "If we have not this support; if
the clergy are forbidden to take part in what some
call politics, but what I call religion; if the parish
priests are henceforward to be silenced, I will
always obey ecclesiastical authority. If that be
the final decision of the Church; if the final
decision of the rulers of the Church be to close
the mouths of honest priests who stand by the
people, and are ready to sacrifice their blood and
their lives for the liberties and salvation of the
people of this country; if it be the decision of the
rulers of the Church to close the mouths of these
honest men, and if free scope is given only to
hirelings, to the corrupt, the profligate, the place-
hunters, the pledge-breakers, the men who make
politics a selfish game of pecuniary profit; then
I speak in the name of some here present, but I
speak above all my own conviction, when I say
that I see no other course for honest and sane
men to take but to wash their hands of public
affairs altogether, and to abandon all hope of protecting the rights and interests of Catholic Ireland
in the Parliament of Great Britain."

At the same time he told them he had no intention of withdrawing from public affairs, because he
did not believe that the final decision of ecclesi-

astical authority would be to silence the mouths of honest men.

Authority had commanded Father Keeffe to abstain from politics, and Lucas was glad he had obeyed; but the ultimate authority in the Church is the Supreme Pontiff, who has the right to decide in all cases in the last resort. He went on to say that they intended as soon as possible to bring the question before the Holy See. What the Holy See might decide he would not anticipate, but whatever it might be, to that he would give "unreserved obedience."

"Before a month is over, some of us will cross the Channel, and will find ourselves, with the blessing of God, beneath the shadow of the Vatican." Giving credit then to the Bishop of Ossory for the best intentions, he said he believed he was mistaken, but that if the Church decided that the power of the Bishop was that of absolute and despotic authority, much as he would be surprised, he was resolved never to disobey—always to be obedient, loyal, and faithful; but in that case he would "leave without a sigh of regret the game of politics to the selfish, to the corrupt, to the men who thirsted after gold; to the men who sought to make the lives and hearts' blood of the people the mere raw material of coinage for their own pockets."

Within a week Father O'Shea was put on the same footing as Father Keeffe; and Lucas at once declared that these were no isolated instances, but part of "a systematic concerted plan to introduce an entirely new state of things into the relations between the priests and the people of Ireland ; " and that "on the success or failure of this plan, not the mere discipline of the Church alone, but the dearest rights and interests of the people of Ireland, of the Catholics of England and Scotland, of the Catholics throughout the Colonies, are concerned."

What the new rules were to be was not certain, but if they were as described, "every friend of the hostile Government, every oppressor of the people, every proselytiser, every souper, every tyrannical agent, every sworn Orangeman, would be a friend to this new order of things. Intended for a different purpose, it would answer most exquisitely the purposes of all these men."

It is necessary to note here, with a view to understanding many allusions to them in the "Statement," that the "new rules were not binding upon any man," being merely a new project, upon which the Holy See was asked to pronounce.

From this it is apparent that the mission to Rome was to prevent the promulgation of rules whose effect, in the estimation of Lucas, could not fail to be disastrous to Catholic interests in the British Empire.

The Corruptionists strained every muscle to prevent the appeal to Rome by blackening the practice of the Holy See, striving to make it appear that appeals by priests against their

superiors were always given in favour of the
Bishop. Referring to these efforts Lucas said,
"'The little dogs and all, Tray, Blanche, and
Sweetheart, see, they bark at me.' I shall not,
however, take any notice of the barking of these
little dogs. We have them in Limerick and we
have them in London. But as the cause is sent
to Rome, and as all the barking of all the little
dogs in the world cannot prevent the Holy See
from taking a just view of the matters before it,
we need the less heed the small hostile noises
that assail our ears." It is to be observed that the
little dogs were precisely the same people whom
Lucas had opposed on the godless colleges question, and who had rejected the Papal decisions
against them. Among other barkings, one was
to the effect that the speech at Callan was a
distinct threat; whereas all he had said was
that "if the new order of things were to prevail,
there would be no place for men of his views
and opinions" in the political world.

At this time a letter to the Archbishop of
Cashel, written in the year 1848, and supposed
to be by Cardinal Fransoni, but actually signed
by another distinguished Roman ecclesiastic, competent to speak the sentiments uttered by the
Supreme Pontiff, was republished in the *Tablet*.
It ran as follows :—

"ROME, 28*th February* 1848.

"MY LORD,—The Pope praised your Grace's letter very
much, and said you took a right Christian view of priestly inter-

ference in politics. If religion or necessity require that they should interfere, they have a right to do so ; if the religion or lives of the people be in danger, religion itself and charity call on them to interfere and speak out; but in mere political matters which are not connected with religion, priests should not take part. This is what the Pope said. He kept your Grace's letter, expressing great approbation of it, and said that he fully approved your views."

The journey to Rome having been determined on, Lucas delayed his departure a few days in order to be present at a great Tenant-Right demonstration at Thurles, in Tipperary, on 25th November. The meeting was an open-air one, and it was estimated to consist of not less than 25,000 persons. This was the last meeting Lucas attended, and here he made his last public speech. I do not know that this utterance calls for any special observation except this. It had been said that he dared not show his face in this stronghold of Sadleirism. There he was, however, and that huge gathering gave the lie, he said, to the assertion that the men of that quarter were satisfied with the conduct of their representatives. The meeting over, he returned to Dublin, of which he took what proved to be a last farewell.

On the following Thursday, the 30th November, he was in London, where he received a testimonial and address, the origin of which was as follows.

It was felt, immediately after the Dublin meeting in May, that my brother was so greatly discouraged and dispirited, that his friends could scarcely press for a continuance of his exertions against such odds and such opposition. But the letter already quoted, in which he spoke of the meeting as a "curious one," showed that he was disposed to take a more sanguine view of Catholic prospects than had seemed possible, and his friends felt cheered accordingly. But he needed all the sympathy he could get, and Canon Oakeley addressed a letter to him for publication in the *Tablet*, to uphold and encourage him. He divided the feeling which prevailed in his regard among (1.) those who hated him because he spoke the truth, which they hated; (2.) those who admired, respected, and had full confidence in him; and, (3.) those who admired him yet mistrusted his discretion. With the first he had nothing to do; among his out-and-out admirers, on both sides of the Channel, the Canon professed himself to be one. He did not believe him free from faults, like other men, but since experience proves that we must trust somebody, he considered the possibility of a mistake an infinitely better alternative than the habit of carping. As to the third class, they were tending more towards him; their confidence was increasing and their criticism more hesitating. The saying, " Lucas is our only man," was getting more and more general. Indeed, it was so often repeated that it sounded to him like a proverb.

Others only wanted the note to be sounded to

fall quickly into line ; and after a very little preliminary discussion the testimonial was determined
on, and within a fortnight a committee was formed,
of which the present Lord Arundel of Wardour
and Canon Oakeley acted as secretaries, to carry
out that purpose.   One of the early contributors
was Cardinal Wiseman, who wrote as follows :—

"In every religious question that has come before Parliament, whether it related to England, Ireland, the Colonies, or
the Continent, Mr. Lucas has always been at his post, and
ready to defend the Catholic cause, without reference to
political considerations, or to the party from which such questions emanated."

Dr. Briggs, too, of Beverley, the senior Bishop
of England, was not tardy in responding to the
call.   He said :—

" I have watched with particular interest and gratitude his
parliamentary conduct.   Since the Catholic body has lost the
never-to-be-sufficiently valued Mr. Langdale, I have been
delighted to see his place well occupied by Mr. Lucas, as to
the unprotected portion of our community.   Who among us
has not looked with grateful feelings on Mr. Lucas's dauntless
persevering efforts in the cause of Catholicity in his place in
Parliament ?   Who has not watched his assiduous labours in
behalf of the Catholic soldiers and sailors—in behalf of the
poor Catholic inmates of our workhouses and prisons?   What
Catholic Bishop or priest has not found Mr. Lucas always ready
to co-operate with him in behalf of the poor and unprotected
members of his flock ? "

The Bishop of Nottingham expressed his—

"Sense of the deep obligations we are under to Mr. Lucas,
for his noble and manly advocacy of everything that is
Catholic."

And Canon Oakeley wrote—

"The whole progress of our undertaking has been such as to fill us with satisfaction and gratitude. It began in a private meeting of three or four humble priests, who, whatever their own wishes, would never have ventured to proceed a step further but for the encouragement spontaneously offered them from unexpected quarters."

Adhesions came in from all sides—from the aristocracy, from the religious orders, among whom I may mention particularly the Society of Jesus, from English seminaries and colleges, from provosts, canons, prelates, chamberlains of the Papal Court itself, from the parochial clergy, from literary men and artists, and from the middle class.

" To this," said Canon Oakeley, " we must add what our noble-hearted Irish brethren have said and done in the cause ; and, on the other hand, no word of malevolence or detraction has broken the harmony of the act." [1]

A letter from the English College in Rome said :—" In our little world we are all great politicians, and we are *unanimous* on this point, that Lucas is worthy of the highest praise and commendation for his Christian conduct during his parliamentary career." Nor was it Europe alone that joined in doing Lucas honour. India and America were not behind-hand in subscribing.

---

[1] There was, as the reader will see in the Fifth Book, one opponent who felt rebuked by this movement, and who did his best to prevent its success.

It was, said the Hon. Mr. Arundell, the first testimonial ever presented by the English Catholic
body.   In view of Lucas's journey to Rome, the
subscription lists were closed, and the testimonial
prepared for presentation as he passed through
London on his way to the Eternal City.

The address, which was signed by the Rev.
Dr. Whitty, Provost of Westminster, after declaring that the list of names included those of men
"eminent beyond the limits of our own community," proceeds to say that, "distinguished as
it is," it "can give you but a faint idea of the
amount of sympathy, or rather of enthusiasm,
which the progress of its formation has been the
occasion of eliciting in your regard."

With such encouragement, then, was he cheered
upon his way to Rome.   He left London immediately after the presentation, and arrived in the
Eternal City on the evening of Wednesday, the
6th December, just in time to enable him to be
present at the definition of the Immaculate Con-
ception of her "whom he still had served," and
under whose patronage he fought to the last.

Book the Fourth.

LUCAS IN ROME.

Iᴛ was a fortunate concurrence of circumstances that took Lucas to Rome at that particular juncture, when so many Bishops were present in the Holy City. He lost no time or opportunity in seeing such of them as would be able to promote the object of his visit.

On the 15th December he wrote :—

"I have seen and had conversations with Dr. MacHale, Dr. Derry, Monsignor Barnabo, and Cardinal Wiseman. . . . Dr. MacHale did not—nor did any one else—understand the whole scope of the business at first; and he said he had written home . . . to dissuade me from coming to Rome, and to carry on the fight with vigour in Ireland. On giving him a further explanation, and showing him the extent of the move we were making, he completely came round to our view, and expressed great satisfaction at the deputation, and spoke re-peatedly with the greatest confidence of the result."

A memorial numerously signed by the clergy was to be prepared and forwarded from Ireland for presentation to the Pope. A draft was sent for approval before the text was finally agreed upon. Referring to this, Lucas in the same letter says that the Archbishop (of Tuam)—

" Had heard of it, and thought some of the clauses about appointments to benefices, &c., might do harm. I made his Grace understand that the memorial was not drawn by me, but by the clergy, and expressed the genuine sentiments of those who drew it."

Of an interview with Cardinal Wiseman he says :—

" He entered very fully into the subject of the danger to Catholic interests from the present English Government, a danger greater, he thought, and more definite, on the part especially of the old Whigs, than most people supposed. He said that their object was to suppress Catholic opinion in Ireland, and thus to have at their mercy the Catholics of the Empire. An expression dropped from him which I thought significant, that he did not wish to feel himself in direct opposition to Dr. Cullen. It seemed to imply that he felt himself in opposition as regarded opinion and policy, but that he wished still not to make it a complete break. He said he had already spoken to the Pope on the subject, . . . and should speak still more at length on the whole business. . . . It was clear to me from what the Cardinal said that . . . the Pope is favourable to us, and that it is against the influences which surround the Pope that we have to combat."

Dr. Cullen had lived in Rome many years, and his influence at the Irish College was supreme. Lucas therefore found the professors there dead against him. On the other hand, an effort Dr. Cullen made to secure, practically, the appointment of all the professors in the Irish College in Paris was a subject of discussion at this time, and, chiefly through the action of Dr. MacHale and Dr. Derry, his design was overruled. On the 16th of December Lucas wrote :—

"This result has put Dr. MacHale in great spirits. Barnabo assures him that Dr. Cullen, except as visitor of the religious orders, has no quality of apostolic delegate, nor any power in any diocese but his own. . . . Dr. MacHale treats the Irish College as the stronghold of corruption, and will have no terms with it. He holds his head high and uses strong language suitable to the time. He is above all things desirous to have the memorial, and to have it numerously signed. . . .

"I had a long talk to-day with Dr. Briggs, to whom I explained the whole case. He enters into it heart and soul, and undertakes with Dr. MacHale to see that the papers I send in supplementary to the memorials are suitable. . . . He is particularly of opinion that nothing should be published about what is taking place here till all is settled. A word in print might damage what is going on so well. . . . Dr. MacHale and Dr. Briggs are of opinion that other M.P.s coming over would strengthen the case. There can be no doubt about it."

The next day, 17th December, he saw Archbishop Hughes of New York, whom he knew in London. Referring to their conversation he wrote :—

"Archbishop Hughes, when I saw him yesterday, spoke at some length about the Pope, with whom he had lately had an audience. He said he never was so impressed with him as with a man fit by dignity and greatness of character to stand upon the summit of human affairs and to rule the world. His audience lasted for three-quarters of an hour, and for thirty-five or forty minutes of that time the Pope poured forth a discourse —it was no less—on the state of the world and of every kingdom in it. Dr. Hughes said he had rarely or never heard in so few sentences so much wisdom upon so many topics so well condensed. The United States he fairly admitted he did not understand. England he thought had reached the turn of her greatness. He spoke a good deal about Italy and the visionary hopes of those who sought to regenerate it, and addressed himself to all these and many other points, not as a priest merely, but as a man of the world and a statesman."

The reader will not have forgotten Dr. Cullen's opposition to the Lucas testimonial alluded to in the last chapter. In continuation of the above letter Lucas proceeds :—

"I forget whether I mentioned that Dr. Briggs made no difficulty of telling me all about the letter written by Dr. Cullen against my testimonial to Dr. ———, in which he charges me with having called the Bishops fools or knaves."

We shall see presently that Dr. Cullen denied having written the letter.

A few days later Lucas "rehearsed the whole story to Monsignore Talbot," who remarked, "The Holy See having so often pressed the Bishops to keep their priests out of politics, it will be difficult to persuade it now not to stand by their Bishop." Dr. Hughes also took a less sanguine view than some others of the position. On the 23d December Lucas writes to Mr. Duffy :—

" My Dear Duffy,— . . . All the time that I have been here has been a very bad time for business, and until I get the memorial, I can *do* nothing but talk. You say nothing about the M.P.s' memorial, nor have I yet the smallest indication of when I am to expect either of them, or who will bring them over. Father Keeffe indeed writes that he is coming, for which God be praised. I hope he will not change his mind. Dr. MacHale attaches the greatest importance to these documents being numerously signed and quickly sent, as also *to other M.P.s* coming here. As it is, it looks a great deal too much like *my* business, and I do most earnestly hope I may not be left alone. At least Moore and Devereux ought to come. Numbers and the appearance of a strong popular feeling will tell in Rome in a case which they feel they only half understand, and in which they must be guided by some one. Dr. Cullen is, or has been, in *possession*, and will remain so until his inability to manage affairs fortunately be demonstrated. But of course you know all this. Therefore make a great stir and send me helpers. . . . The statutes were agreed to before I arrived, but if we work well we are in time to stop their publication."

This last remark gives the clue to some portions of the "Statement" which are difficult to understand without such an explanation.

At the beginning of January he was eager for the coming of the deputation. On New Year's Day he wrote to Dr. Whitty :—

"Can you urge our men through Duffy to be prompt in sending men and memorial. . . . It is very injurious to the cause for me to be left alone, as if it were my case."

By the 3d of January affairs had progressed so satisfactorily that the "Bishops speak very confidently of "a certain proposal, which would naturally include the Callan cases, being accepted. . . . They speak so hopefully of an arrangement of this kind being palatable to the Holy See, that I am in hopes we shall yet very much shorten the business and get home long before Easter." In this he was doomed to disappointment. Four days later, 7th January, he writes to his wife :—

"I have now been in Rome a month, and am in the most delightful ignorance of what is going on in Ireland, and when any memorials or documents are to be sent to me. I have done *talking* with the people who are accessible ; and *doing* anything is out of the question. . . . . . Dr. MacHale was thinking of staying till something was done in our affairs ; but I am left in such ignorance of what time he will be required to stay, and when business will commence here, that he told me on Wednesday he thought he should go home.   I have written full accounts from here of all that has arisen, but I get no accounts from Ireland, and am left to amuse myself with antiquities, of which, under the circumstances, I am heartily sick.

"On Wednesday I met Monsignore Barnabo on the stairs, and he was delighted to see me. We had half or three-quarters of an hour's talk. . . . He seemed very much displeased with something Dr. MacHale had said, and repeated that such a course (whatever it was) made the Church a democracy and not a monarchy.   I told him I firmly believed the Church to be a monarchy, and was *therefore* in Rome at that moment. He wished very much that . . . . as Drs. Cullen and MacHale and myself were now in Rome, a union could be made.

" We spoke about Maynooth, I explained to him that Dr. Cullen had been violent in his opposition to me for wishing Maynooth to be disconnected with the Government.   I told him it was my firm conviction that Dr. Cullen had been the obstacle to the redress of grievances. . . . We talked of the answer given me last year, 'that others were satisfied though I was not,' and he said that Dr. Grant had been rebuked for what he had done on that occasion."

Notwithstanding Monsignore Barnabo's cordiality, Lucas's impression was that he was not very friendly to the cause. In recounting an interview with Cardinal Wiseman he says :—

" The Cardinal confirmed my impression of Barnabo's hostility, or semi-hostility.   He relies a good deal, the Cardinal said, upon Dr. Grant (of Southwark).   Dr. Grant is with him every day ; is always very sweet with the clerks and subordinates, and thus finds everything go smooth with him, at least in the details and execution of business. 'It is not,' said the Cardinal, 'in my nature to use that sort of means or take that kind of pains to gain a point.'"

It seems the enemy was anxious to prevent Lucas from having an audience with the Pope; but he was told, "I had only to send my name to the chamberlain on duty, and I should have an audience as a matter of course, and the Pope would probably speak to me about the state of affairs in Ireland."

Accordingly a day was fixed, and on the 9th January he had his first audience, which he thus describes :—

"To-day[1] has been an event in my life. I have had my first audience of the Pope. In a former letter I told you I had been advised to ask for an audience, not on business, but merely to ask his blessing, and to leave the Pope to introduce or not the subject of my visit. This accordingly was what I did. I cannot express to you the kindness and benignity of the Holy Father, not merely in his general character, but to me personally. The hour for the audience was eleven A.M., at which hour, in ordinary evening dress, I found myself, after passing through a considerable suite of rooms, in an outer antechamber, where I waited, while others were having their audiences, for a little more than two hours. Into an inner antechamber each person was called when it came to his turn, and there one waited till one's predecessor was dismissed. On entering, I confess I was for the moment too much flustered to notice whether my name was announced; but somehow or other the Pope knew who I was, repeated my name, and when I knelt to him, gave me, not his foot, but the ring on his hand

---

[1] Tuesday, 9th January 1855.

to kiss.   Mr. Kyne says this was a particular distinction, but I
have a vague notion that he is mistaken.   In giving me his
benediction, however, nothing could exceed the Holy Father's
kindness, which, both in countenance, in manner, and in words,
was most marked.   He sat at a little table, and motioned to me
to stand a little in front of the table, at the left hand.   My
interview lasted about twenty minutes, I imagine, and in every
part of it was most gracious.

" He began by asking me whether I would speak in French
or in Italian, and on my saying French, he asked me if I was
likely to stay some weeks at Rome—a question which he
afterwards repeated, as if he wished me to remain—and to
which I assented.   Without further preface except to say something kind about my efforts for religion, he at once plunged
into the business, and said that both on the business itself and
on persons he should speak to me 'with open heart'—if I
caught his French rightly, *à cœur ouvert.*   He told me he
was afflicted at the differences among the Bishops, and particularly between Dr. Cullen and Dr. MacHale ; and that his
great object was peace and union, by which only could anything be accomplished.   He said that Dr. MacHale was a little
strong ; that from the very commencement of his pontificate
complaints had been made of him, but they came from Englishmen—from persons whose motives he appreciated—and that he
gave no heed to them, but remained silent ; that during all this
period Dr. Cullen invariably defended Dr. MacHale, and that
everything continued well between them until the former
became Archbishop of Dublin, and then arose these misunder-
standings.   He said that in my position, in any intercourse I
had with either or both, it was my duty to sow the seeds of
peace and a good understanding between them.

" He then spoke about the Government and the proper
mode of treating it.   He did not profess to judge whether the
English Government was actuated by motives of political
interest or by hatred to the Catholic religion, but for some
reason or other he conceived them to be decidedly hostile to
us, and had no sort of confidence in their good-will.   There
were two ways of acting towards them ;—one, to show them
confidence, constantly to profess oneself obliged by what they

did, to make a great deal of little things, and to act as if dependent on them. This he decidedly disapproved. Another
course was to act towards them with rancorous hostility, denying them all merit, even where they made concessions or acted
well. This he also disapproved, and he referred to the sending
chaplains to the Crimea as an instance for which they should
get credit, though they barely did their duty, and perhaps did
it from a motive of self-interest.

"Here he interrupted himself playfully to remark on his
own bad French. He said he had only commenced speaking
French when he became Pope, and that was rather old to go to
school, but he hoped I understood him. I said perfectly.
Did I assent to what he had said? I answered that I did,
but I did not know what representations might have been made
to his Holiness about unreasonable opposition to the Government. I knew of no such opposition having been offered, and
I believed the most sincere disposition existed to give them
credit for whatever they did that was just; but that really their
concessions to justice were so small, that it was impossible to
make a large acknowledgment of them. With regard to the
chaplains, I said that no concession had been made which every
Government, even that of Lord Derby, would not have been
obliged to make, inasmuch as it referred exclusively to a time
of war; that, on the other hand, they had, in the most insulting
and resolute manner, refused on principle all justice to Catholic sailors, alleging the Established Church as an insuperable
obstacle. Having said as much on this point as seemed consistent with the ground-plan of the dialogue, I stopped, and the
Holy Father then went on to speak about priests interfering in
politics.

"Here also he said were two courses—taking no part and
going too far. He wished great moderation to be used; that
the priests should not act so as to raise a prejudice against
their sacred ministry, or give scandal, or give the Government
just ground of complaint by striking at the root of public order.
It was difficult to secure this moderation, but these were
difficulties which it was necessary to overcome. Here he
paused as if to give me an opportunity to say something.

"I said that unquestionably any such difficulties ought to

be overcome, but I thought they were of less magnitude than
had been represented. Whatever had been the case six or
seven years ago, when questions had been discussed affecting
the existence of the English Government in Ireland, at present
I knew of no politics in which the priests were engaged in
which the Catholic religion was not directly interested. (The
Pope here made an exclamation from which I gathered that
this statement pleased him.) The only question about which
any difference of opinion could arise was the Tenant question ;
but upon this at least there could be no difference between
Dr. MacHale and Dr. Cullen ; that Dr. Cullen had given his
formal assent to the interference of priests in this question out
of their own dioceses. Except this one question, all the other
points in which priests interfered were points of religious
grievance on the face of them—the Established Church, the
grievances of soldiers, inmates of workhouses, prisons, &c.
To all this the Holy Father listened with great attention, as I
am told it is his habit to apply his whole and undivided
attention and the whole force of his mind to whatever is the
business of the moment. Certainly it appeared so in this case.

"He then spoke about myself. He said I had two characters—that of an M.P., and a journalist, and that he took a
distinction between these two. In my character of M.P. I
had been 'a true apologist of religion,' and it was to mark his
very high appreciation of my conduct in that capacity that he
had that day given me his especial benediction ; that he regarded me as an independent man, who neither hoped on the
one hand nor feared on the other from any Ministry or party,
and who looked only to the interests of religion ; and 'on this
account, *mon cher*, I have given you my especial benediction,
that you may be encouraged and strengthened to proceed in
the same course ;' but, he said, 'I am afraid the editor of
the *Tablet* sometimes exceeds the bounds of patience and
escapes from the kingdom of moderation into that of impatience.'

"The Holy Father said this with the most perfect kindness,
smiling and half-joking. I took it in the same way, promised
that his words should have as much effect as I could give them,
and assured him that my object and wish were to conform

myself entirely to his will, to carry out the instructions of his Holiness, and to obey his commands. It is proper to add, that this little reproof about the *Tablet*, though evidently meant seriously, was lightly passed over, while the reference to the 'especial benediction' was enlarged upon and repeated two or three times, and in a manner so heartily kind and gracious that I was inexpressibly affected, and indeed for a time hardly able to maintain my small part in the conversation.

"The Pope then again asked me if I was likely to spend some weeks in Rome. I said yes; and he then added that he had already spoken to the two Archbishops on this subject, and should speak to them again, and that his great object was to bring about peace and union. He said also that if before I left Rome I wanted another audience, and would apply to Monsignore Talbot, he would have great pleasure in giving me one; and then intimating that the audience was ended, he again gave me his ring to kiss (saying *mon cher*), and giving me his benediction, and I left the room. When I came out, Monsignore Talbot told me I had had a very long audience."

The general result of the interview and of the representations Lucas had made to Propaganda and the Pope was conceived to set the cause on a secure footing. In another letter he says :—

"Everybody here speaks of the excellent position our case is assuming, and a leading Jesuit told me on Sunday that with perseverance we were sure to succeed."

At this moment the M.P.s' memorial reached Rome. It had only six signatures, those of G. H. Moore, Richard Swift, C. G. Duffy, John Francis Maguire, Patrick McMahon, and John Brady. Shortly after the interview with the Holy Father, Monsignore Barnabo proposed a meeting or conference with Dr. Cullen. This conference

was. brought about, it was believed, by the personal interposition of the Pope. The design was
that an understanding might be arrived at, which,
if it proved acceptable to his Holiness, might be
made a rule of action for the future. The conference then was arranged for; and in a letter to
his wife dated the 21st January, Lucas detailed
his mode of preparing the ground for the interview. By this time he had ceased to wish for the
deputations, and he wrote as follows :—

"I don't know how matters will end, but I know that unless
I play my cards very ill, the game, with God's help, will be very
much in our favour. You will have gathered this from my
previous letters, and that I am at this moment by no means
anxious for any deputation—so much have matters changed.
Perhaps another sweep of the wave may render a deputation
advisable, but not at this moment, except to help me with advice
and to diminish my personal responsibility; but the thing has
now got into such a train that I see a prospect of being able
next week to settle the whole matter to our entire satisfaction. A *prospect*—I should say a *possibility*—for it is only a possibility and may end only in disappointment. But it gives
grounds for a rational, though not for a very strong hope.

"In my last I told you of a conversation with Monsignore
Barnabo in which he had told me that Dr. Cullen agreed to
the conference with me, and that we were to settle time and
place with Talbot. On Friday I saw him and had a long talk
with him. I placed before him, as I had before Barnabo, all
the difficulties of the conference. I told Talbot that assurances
given to me privately by Dr. Cullen would not even advance
the pacification one step; that Dr. Cullen maintaining to me
his present identity with the Dr. Cullen of 1851 would be of
no value whatever if he were to go back and act as he had
been acting; that what alone would be of any service would
be a written statement of the course to be pursued in future,

such course to be communicated to the public and made known in the least offensive or displeasing way possible. I added that the Callan cases should also be amicably settled as part of a general pacification without going into their merits. I said I had no notion of Dr. Cullen, or any other Bishop who represented Rome, treating our party and the party opposed to us with impartiality as persons who were equally to be regarded; that, if we were pursuing politics for our own interest, it might be well for the Church to take her own course, and not be compromised with us ; but that we were pursuing politics for the sake of the Church and the poor, and for no other end ; that we were following a course laid down originally by the Bishops ; that whatever reason there was for us taking that course in our sphere, the same reason bound Dr. Cullen to use his influence in his sphere in the same direction; that if our help to the Church was thought useful and our course prudent, we were entitled to the help of the Church, and that if the Church did not think it prudent to give that help, I for one felt that I had no further vocation to meddle in the business.

"I put all these heads as strongly as I could, for this reason, among others—in order to make Talbot feel from the beginning the difficulties of the conference, and that in the event of an agreement being impossible, I might not be charged with raising difficulties in the course of it which had not been anticipated. . . . I declare to Heaven that now, with some prospect of success before me, I had rather, as far as I can discern the future, and for our personal interests, fail than succeed. Success will bring an intolerable burden of responsibility, and perhaps little cordial support after all. However, we must do our best and hope for the best. Talbot's part in this conversation was to mention the points Dr. Cullen would urge against me—my violence ; my late speech at Callan; my attacks on Bishops; my connection with Disraeli (!). To all these I gave suitable answers. . . .

Monday night.—This letter will be posted to-morrow. I have just come in from Monsignore Talbot, who is extremely friendly. Unless I hear to the contrary, it is fixed that I am to meet Dr. Cullen at the Irish College on Wednesday morning at eleven."

Among other charges against him was an habitual unchristian want of charity. For this, he said, "I shall certainly ask for proofs." Meantime, their positions being changed, he thought it prudent to call and leave a card on Dr. Cullen. In the same letter he says that a friend speaking a day or two previously with some students at Propaganda, found their tone quite changed.

"They said I had won good opinions in all directions. God be thanked if this is not flattery. For the last few days I have been incessantly seeing pictures and antiquities with John Mill. He feels rather better, and this day week goes to Naples. Perhaps, if my business be settled by that time, Mr. Kyne and I may go with him for a week. I think this letter will please you."

On the 26th of January he wrote :—

"Another sweep of the wave has come, and it has become more necessary than ever for our friends to be active. My last letter alludes to a conference with Dr. Cullen. It came off on Wednesday, and as my account of it may be of some importance, I did not like to write an account until I had seen Monsignori Talbot and Barnabo. The latter I have not seen. To the former I have stated pointedly my impression of the conference, as to which he is cautious enough neither to assent nor dissent, but he at least thinks it accurate enough to be communicated to Monsignore Barnabo. In a few words, then, to Monsignore Talbot I summed up the conference thus :— 'That in the course of it Dr. Cullen did not give one indication of a desire for any amicable settlement; that if any proof had before been wanting, his conversation of Wednesday furnished proof that he wished to get rid of me personally, to break up our party, to discourage opposition to the Government, and to put down public opinion in Ireland.' I added that Dr.

Cullen had in the course of that conversation said so many things that were untrue, that I should have the greatest possible objection to have any further personal communications with him of any kind."

Here follows his account of the conference. It will be found referred to again with further details in Chapter VI. of the "Statement." Lucas wrote to his friends :—

"The conference lasted two hours and a half, and of course I cannot give a shorthand report of it. A great deal turned on my speech at Callan, and on recent speeches and writings of others, also on Father O'Shea's conduct. On these things I said what may easily be imagined. Speaking about the League, he took credit to himself for allowing perfect freedom of opinion, and alleged that he had recently promoted a clergyman whose connection with the League he regretted, and whom he had advised not to have anything to do with it; but still, though he had continued a member of it, so unwilling was he to interfere with free opinion, that he had actually made him a Canon—Canon Redmond.[1] Upon my honour he said that!

" I interrupted him by saying that his Grace forgot that before he made Redmond a canon, Redmond had done his best to damage the League, to serve the Government, and to damage those who opposed the Government, namely, us. He said he did not see that there was any harm in supporting the Government; that if opposing the Government were a virtue, one ought in Italy to co-operate with Mazzini and in Hungary with Kossuth; that the first duty of every Catholic was to support the Government unless it attacked the Church. He then broke out into a violent tirade against Duffy, whom he described as a wicked man, to act with whom, after his conduct

---

[1] This was the Father Redmond whose abandonment of Independent Opposition has been recorded in Chapter III. of Book III.

in 1848, was impossible until he had fasted fifty years on bread and water. I defended Duffy, as you may imagine, referring to his conduct in the University question, to his conduct with regard to Mazzini and Kossuth, and also to the evidence on oath of Dr. Blake and Dr. Moriarty at his trial. At this time he became more violent. He said Duffy had been a party to getting the people massacred, ridiculed the idea of his being a pious man, declared he did not care what anybody had sworn, and turning upon me said it was a shame or discreditable for me to say a word on behalf of such a man or to act with him. . . . With regard to the services of any particular men in Parliament or elsewhere (which I did not press upon him, but somehow it got mentioned), he said Ireland would always produce plenty of excellent laymen, and that if one set of men passed away, another would be there to supply their places. The meaning of this was of course that we might go to the devil if we liked.

"On the part to be taken by priests in politics, he said the business of a priest was to confine himself to his spiritual duties, and in the intervals of these to devote himself to reading and meditation ; that if the Church was attacked in such a way that all Catholics must agree upon it, then they should come out ; but wherever two Catholics might differ, then they should take no part, lest by doing so they should get into collision with one part of their flock ; that with regard to elections, they ought to tell the people their duty, to avoid bribery and perjury, and to vote for a candidate favourable to the Church ; if a candidate avowedly hostile to the Church showed himself, they might warn the people against him, though with caution ; but if two candidates presented themselves, both not professing sentiments hostile to the Church, their business was not to interfere between them, but to stick to general principles.

"Monsignore Talbot turned to me and asked me if I concurred. I said that, on the contrary, I entirely dissented, and that the practical meaning of such a course was to hand over the constituencies in a very short time to the enemies of the Church and people.

"I can't, of course, tell half that was said, but I have told enough to show the animus of the dialogue. I had been requested by Propaganda (and I think by the Pope) to take my part in a conference tending to lead to an amicable arrangement. I was determined, therefore, to say nothing which could have the appearance of warmth or a hostile intention, and this kept me from saying many things which rose naturally to my lips. On Dr. Cullen's part, the conversation was carried on in a tone of shabby ——, ill concealing, and not intended to conceal, a resolute purpose of defiance ; and it rose into passion when he spoke of Duffy, whose recent articles seem not to have pleased him.

" But let all who read this understand that the passion and vehemence were the passion and vehemence of a man who was on the defensive, who has his back to the wall, who feels that his all is at stake, who, being personally compromised with the Government, *cannot* do what the Pope wishes, and who is therefore determined to fight it out against Pope and people with every appearance of submission to the Holy See and compliance with its spirit.

" Now, then, is the time to act in Ireland with firmness, spirit, and resolution, but avoiding every false step that might compromise the case here. I am sure Dr. Cullen's position is entirely changed for the future in Ireland as regards Rome, and I am satisfied we have on the cards, with temper, patience, and perseverance, the best possible game."

Lucas's next letter is to Mr. Duffy, and is dated the 27th of January. He wrote :—

" There is now every ground for hope, and I think a pretty tolerable certainty that we shall succeed—an absolute certainty that up to this time great good has been effected. Now then, if ever, we and our friends in Ireland ought to be alive and active. But pray don't let anybody abuse Barnabo. I believe your correspondent is quite mistaken in the particular case. I am sure it is our highest interest to keep him in good-humour, and certainly he puts on a most friendly appearance to me. He told me to-day, with reference to Dr. Cullen, that I was not to be discouraged by the hostile language of Dr. Cullen ;

that he had great hopes a friendly arrangement could be made, and that he would do his best to bring it about. When I complained of the paragraph in the *Evening Post*, and told him it represented him as having given me a rebuff or reprimand, he said, on the contrary, he told the Pope that I had been represented to him as a violent person, but that he found me complaisant and reasonable."

On the following Monday, 29th of January, he started for Naples with John Stuart Mill and Father Kyne. The road from Rome to Naples, the city itself, the bay and the objects of interest in the vicinity, have been so often described that little need here be said. Though the weather was not all that could be desired, the journey was very enjoyable. I have frequently heard Father Kyne, himself a man of considerable information, dilate upon the conversations, discussions, and casual remarks of the two men, which he said eclipsed all that he had ever heard in the way of conversation.

While he was absent in Naples, Dr. Cullen addressed a letter to Dr. Yore for publication in the papers. The animus with which it is written is very evident. The "one gentleman" who was "meritoriously employed in seeking spiritual advice" is truly delicious. The letter is as follows :—

"IRISH COLLEGE, ROME, 3*d February* 1855.

"Up to the present day no appeal has been lodged with the authorities here against the Bishop of Ossory, or any other Irish Bishop or Archbishop; neither has the famous memorial so much spoken of been presented. The lay and clerical deputation so often announced has not as yet appeared. There is indeed one gentleman here who took an active part in the meetings of Callan and Thurles, but he has not exhibited credentials from any party, and indeed I believe he is very meritoriously employed in seeking spiritual advice and instruction from the authorities of this city, who, being anxious to gain all to Christ and to bring those who are astray to the right path, receive all with truly paternal kindness and Christian charity. Should the members of the deputation arrive at any future day, they too will receive instructions and advice which may be very useful to them. From what I now state, after having made inquiries at the Propaganda and higher quarters, you may form an estimate of the value of the reports spread in Ireland that the appeal was going on successfully, and that the deputation was most active and zealous. The truth is, nothing whatever has been done as yet. There has been no display of zeal or activity. —Your devoted servant, PAUL CULLEN."

Four days later he wrote in these terms :—

"IRISH COLLEGE, ROME, *7th February* 1855.
"MY DEAR DR. YORE,—Nothing can be more reasonable than your anxiety to be made acquainted with the progress in Rome of the controversy on ecclesiastical jurisdiction, which was brought under the notice of the meeting held in Callan as far back as last October. From the vehemence and determination displayed by the orators on that and other occasions, and the promise made to carry without loss of time the controversy to the highest tribunal in the Church, some were led to expect that the most energetic measures would be forthwith adopted to have the order of the Bishop of Ossory to one of his clergy set aside—an order calculated, it was solemnly declared, to close the mouths of every honest ecclesiastic, leaving liberty to speak only to the evil-designing and corrupt. The business was at first taken up with haste ; it would brook no delay ; yet more than three months have now elapsed, and the first step, declared to be all-important, has not been taken.

This statement of the case will create surprise, as you must have heard from other quarters that great activity and talent were engaged in carrying on the Callan appeal; yet such is the fact —nothing, absolutely nothing has been done.

"First, no appeal has been lodged in any of the tribunals of Rome against the Bishop of Ossory; nay, more, no mention has been made by the appellants of the proceedings which took place at that meeting.

"Secondly, no appeal has been lodged against any other Bishop or Archbishop for any matters arising out of that meeting.

"Thirdly, no memorial has been presented to any of the tribunals of Rome. It is, indeed, reported that a memorial has been received here, but it is said that the person to whom it was sent, not thinking it fit to be presented, sent it back to have some alterations made in it. This, however, is only known by report, and it may be that the memorial, added to or taken from as the originators of it required, will after some time be forthcoming.

"Fourthly, no deputation that we have heard of has arrived in Rome to present the memorial; none certainly has as yet presented it to any of the tribunals.

"Fifthly, there is, indeed, one gentleman here connected with the Irish press, but he has presented no credentials from any party; he has given no formal statement of his business, and he has not undertaken to justify the proceedings at Callan against the Bishop of Ossory. Perhaps he does not intend to undertake and prosecute the business marked out for a deputation at Thurles and Callan. He seems to be more meritoriously employed in seeking counsel and advice, which are never refused by Rome to any of her children."

Lucas returned to Rome on the 10th of February, and next day he wrote that no papers had come to hand later than the 2d, but that a telegram said Lord Palmerston was Minister.

"What to make of all this for us I hardly know, and, to tell the truth, I hardly try to fathom or estimate it. I am tied here and can take no part in what is to be done. I hear nothing from Duffy ; his promised letter has not come. Your letters,, your pains and care, are my only resource, and a great resource they are. . . . Many kisses and much love to Angy. Tell him I have got, and keep, and wear his cross. God bless the darling child, and his most dear mother ! "

He had received letters mentioning that Dr. Walsh of Ossory had refused to allow Father Keeffe to go to Rome to prosecute his appeal. Referring to this in a letter dated 13th February he says :—

" To Monsignore Barnabo I spoke about the refusal of the Bishop of Ossory to permit Father Keeffe to come to Rome. They take these things very quietly at Rome."

Then he sets out the proper course for Father Keeffe to pursue. But an article had appeared in the *Nation* appealing to the public against the Bishop, and he said :—

" This article has, I think, ruined Father Keeffe's chance, and of course Father O'Shea's. The idea of arguing in public the details of the management of his case at Rome or in relation to Rome by Dr. Walsh ! . . . The last article, unless Father Keeffe has already, or immediately will, express in the strongest terms his regret at and disapproval of such an interference with his business, will ruin him. Great God ! Providence puts all possible chances in our way, and we make every possible effort to ruin them.

" I suppose it is best for us to be beaten, and therefore we should not repine at what is for our good. But certainly after what has happened—the delay with the memorial, which renders nearly hopeless everything that relates to the new statutes, and this escapade, which I think renders quite hope-

less the Callan cases—I hope I shall not be reproached if
our business ends in a total and ignominious failure. . . . It is
pleasant, when everything lies fairly well before me, to see all
chances cut off, one by one, by one's own friends ! However,
I neither do nor will despair."

By this time all the English and Irish Bishops
except Dr. Cullen had left Rome. Dr. MacHale
in particular, who had a contest with Dr. Cullen
on questions with which we have no concern
here—a contest that became critical—relieved himself from embarrassment by leaving somewhat
prematurely. It was a deep disappointment to
Lucas, who was entitled to count on his continued
counsel and assistance. It was thought at Propaganda that the circumstance might even prejudice
his case ; as the Archbishop had not obtained the
Pope's leave to retire. Lucas was advised to have
another interview with his Holiness, and discrimi-
nate between the case he represented and a proceeding for which he was not in any way responsible. There was the more need for this as the
Pope was about to issue a Brief on Irish affairs.
The interview took place towards the close of the
month.[1] Lucas began by reporting the failure of
his conference with Dr. Cullen. He continued as
follows :—

" I was proceeding in detail, when his Holiness interrupted
me, and said that he had not seen Dr. Cullen since the conference, and had only seen Dr. MacHale, who had left Rome a
little too quickly. He was about entering into the circum-

---

[1] 26th February.

stances of Dr. MacHale's leaving Rome, when he checked himself, and said he understood that with that business I was not
in any way mixed up; that I occupied *une troisième position*,
and that my case had to be judged on its own grounds. I
assented, and earnestly assured his Holiness that I did not
presume to meddle with those high ecclesiastical questions.
He then spoke about English affairs, and referred ;to the
probable dissolution of Parliament, and to Lord Palmerston's
Government, of which he expressed an unfavourable opinion.

"In this way he spoke with great freedom and kindness, but,
I thought, not wishing to come back to the subject of Dr.
Cullen, from which he had led the conversation. 'And now,
caro amico mio,' he said, 'I commend you to God,' &c., &c.

"Feeling myself at this point about to be done out of the
business part of the audience, I said that I had requested an
audience at the suggestion of Monsignore Barnabo, who had
shown me the Dublin resolutions, and had given me his own
personal impressions as to their meaning, and who had advised
me to lay before his Holiness the difficulties and objections I
had stated to him. . . . His Holiness then made some general
observations on the impropriety of priests entering into politics
when not necessary for the interests of religion. I ventured
to say that such necessity always existed in the present state
of things. He objected to meetings being held in chapels. I
said no such thing had happened within my knowledge. . . .

"Feeling that it was necessary to squeeze into this moment
of time as much as I possibly could, or lose an opportunity, I
urged these points with rather more earnestness than on any
former occasion I had ventured to assume. His Holiness had
no wish to commit himself by any expression of opinion, and
his answer was, therefore, in the most kind way, to inform me
that he intended to issue a Brief on this subject, that all might
understand the path they were to follow; that before he did
this he hoped to receive information from various quarters,
specifying Dr. MacHale, and, as I understood, referring to the
other Bishops; and that if before the Brief was prepared I
would put on paper the views I wished to lay before him, he
would give them his best attention. I might write it, he said,

in English, and give the document to Monsignore Talbot, who
would get it translated into Italian. (This was making it not
a document for Propaganda, but for himself personally.)"

Such, then, was the origin of the " Statement,"
and such the cause of the importance attached to it ;
both during its preparation and at all times since.
Dr. Cullen's letters, given above, came into
Lucas's hands after the last interview with his
Holiness. This was his reply to those letters :—

"ROME, 5th March 1855.

"The letters of the Archbishop of Dublin of the 3d and
7th February, which have just been published in the Irish
journals, oblige me to say a few words on the subject to which
they refer. Having taken the advice of persons best able to
speak with authority on such a point, I had come to the conclusion that it was unfitting to make any appeal to the people
on the progress of an affair referred to the Holy See and still
undecided. His Grace seems to be of a different opinion ;
but even his high example, and the provocation it affords,
shall not turn me aside from the course I had laid down for
myself, and of the propriety of which I am now, after making
fresh inquiry here, more firmly convinced than ever. But as
absolute silence on my part might seem to give a tacit assent
to the accuracy of the statements put forward by Dr. Cullen
and signed with his name, I feel bound to say that I protest
against it being supposed for a moment that in any essential particular those letters contain an accurate statement of
the facts. Beyond this decisive protest, it would, I think, be
unbecoming towards the Holy See to go. It is one of the
inconveniences of the Archbishop's appeal to the public that
my duty to the Holy See forbids me to enter into explanations
or to give any particulars, and compels me to limit myself to
this dry denial—by which, of course, I mean to convey no
imputation on my respected Archbishop, but simply to make
it known to all whom it may concern that about certain matters

of fact in which I am personally concerned, and of which I have personal knowledge, I am directly and decidedly at issue with his Grace.   F. LUCAS."

How little support he got from Ireland, either by way of memorial or deputation, will be seen from a letter under the same date as the last :—

" . . . Your letter and that of Father Dwyer of Doon filled me with such indignation that I tore the letter [one he had just written] up, intending at the moment to write nothing. Indeed, what is the use of writing at all, and of what use is Irish public opinion in a matter which primarily concerns the priests? Out of 27 dioceses and 3000 priests, not one can be found to give me an effective lift after having spent three months in Rome upon an affair in which it is my personal interest to be defeated. . . . I do not blame any individual, because I do not know who is personally to blame; but I feel that it is simply impossible to save or serve a people 3000 of whose picked men are capable of such inconceivable cowardice.

"Think of the —— Priests! God help us! I am, it seems, to make their meeting and resolutions stand in place of signatures to a memorial.   I neither can nor will do anything of the sort. Simply in conversation I make it serve for proof of the reign of terror that prevails in Ireland, and which bows every head down in the dust in hopeless servility.

"My first impression was to send in no representation of my own, but to content myself with a formal representation of the two memorials, and to return home content with having accomplished nothing. But calmer reflection has made me more inclined to the belief that, being here, it is a sort of duty to do what more I can do with little additional inconvenience —that is, to send in statements of my own on points about which I know that information is needed. Perhaps ultimately this may be my decision ; but after what has happened I have a right to say that I feel myself absolved from any obligation towards anybody else in this business; free to remain in Parliament if re-elected, or to quit Parliament, whatever turn the affair takes; and at liberty to break off from my labours here whenever I please.

"The failure of the memorial has given great encouragement to Dr. Cullen, and no doubt has betrayed him into the imprudence of writing those two letters. He thought, when he wrote them, that he was master of the ground, and it has made him less inclined to arrange the Callan cases amicably, which was our last chance. If the priests will not stand by themselves, I feel under no personal obligation to stand by them beyond my general duty to the Church and to the poor of Ireland. It is perhaps well that this total failure of cooperation leaves me at liberty to choose my own course, free from any ties whatever, except those which, as long as they trust me, bind me to my noble and glorious constituents. There are other priests to whom I have the same feeling, Fathers O'Shea and Keeffe, &c.; but on the whole, the last news from Ireland has put me in a state of the most ⸺ savageness."

He very soon set to work on the "Statement,' and was encouraged in a certain portion of it by a letter from London dated 15th March. The writer says :—

"The Cardinal [Wiseman] thinks you might well urge Dr. Brown's proposing Keogh in Athlone [1] last week, and that it will confirm in Roman minds all that you have said as to the real animus of the non-interference in politics. What is against Government is 'politics,' but never any conduct in favour of it. I am sure from the Cardinal's manner that you can make immense use of this fact in Rome."

On the other hand, Dr. Cullen was writing to Dr. Grant of Southwark to say that Lucas would

---

[1] *Vide* "Statement," chap. ii.

return as he went. "He has," says a letter dated 21st March, "evidently *reason* to think he has gained the day in Rome. . . . Barnabo has evidently been gained over by Dr. Cullen and Dr. Grant—his mind has been convinced."

This made it imperative on him to bring Dr. Grant's name into the "Statement," very much indeed against his inclination; for he had a great personal regard for the Bishop, however he disapproved of his political action.

The work of preparing the "Statement" was by no means easy. Writing to his wife on the 23d of March, he says of the document :—

"It will be a pamphlet, and the whole ground I have to go over is so difficult that it is slow work. I had written, as you know, a great deal, but I have had to go over it carefully again and rewrite a great deal. At length I think I have got it fairly under way, though I have still a great deal to add. Mr. Kyne has just left me, and we have settled to his satisfaction the first thirty odd pages, and he has taken away thirty more. . . . I have got it out of the form of a memorial, which was awkward. I now make it a 'Statement' in my own name; divide it into sections with formal headings like the chapters of a book. I do this of course to make it more readable."

At this time Fathers Keeffe and O'Shea were removed from their curacies, and their punishment is recorded in chap. iii. of the "Statement." In the above letter he exclaims :—

"I am heartily sorry for them, though not much surprised. God help them! We are all fools together, I think, if worldly prosperity is what we aim at. . . .

"Don't be disheartened, my dear wife. You are, I think and

am sure, the best and bravest woman in the world. I cannot
admire you enough for the quiet, brave, clever, sensible management you have displayed in the last four months.   My
heart aches sometimes to think what rising trouble you must
have had to keep down during that time.   God bless you, my
dearest, sweetest love !   What a blessing you are to me I can
never tell you, nor how much gratitude I owe you and feel
towards you. . . .

" Tell Mr. O'Byrne and Mr. Dwyer [his manager] most particularly from me that I thank them for their great care during
my absence."

Writing to Duffy on Good Friday, the 8th of
April, he remarks :—

"I think the point of the decision will be the expected
Brief of the Pope.   He told me it was to be a guidance for all
parties.   If that guidance is such as you and I can act with,
it seems to me we ought to remain in Parliament."

And in another letter he says, that if he does
remain in Parliament, he will " avoid scandal ; not
go beyond the line of a good Catholic ; and, in
fact, do against Dr. Cullen what with Dr. Cullen's
sanction and encouragement I did against Dr.
Murray."

For fully two months Lucas was engaged in
preparing the " Statement " for the Holy Father.
During this time he was subject to much depression of spirits.   Nor is this surprising ; for during
a whole month he was almost alone in Rome.
He had, indeed, the friendship and assistance of
Dr. Morris, Vice-President of the English College;
and Monsignore Talbot continued the kindness

he had exhibited throughout; but his health was giving way, and he had no cheering news from Ireland to sustain and encourage him. He never considered himself beaten however.

The want of support from Ireland which Lucas felt so bitterly is explained in the 5th section of the fourth chapter of the "Statement," and in further detail in Sir C. Gavan Duffy's "League of North and South;" where it will be seen how

While these pages are passing through the press, I find that I have omitted to give extracts from a letter which Lucas wrote to his wife, dated about 17th January. In it he says :—

"Tell Duffy I have read the *Nation* with real pleasure. I think he has done great service. When I wrote (if I wrote) querulously, it was because I sat in exterior darkness, knowing nothing and feeling shut out from the world."

Insert at page 137.

am sure, the best and bravest woman in the world.   I cannot admire you enough for the quiet, brave, clever, sensible management you have displayed in the last four months.   My heart aches sometimes to think what rising trouble you must have had to keep down during that time.   God bless you, my dearest, sweetest love !   What a blessing you are to me I can never tell you, nor how much gratitude I owe you and feel towards you. . . .

" Tell Mr. O'Byrne and Mr. Dwyer [his manager] most particularly from me that I thank them for their great care during my absence."

preparing the "Statement" for the Holy Father. During this time he was subject to much depression of spirits.   Nor is this surprising; for during a whole month he was almost alone in Rome. He had, indeed, the friendship and assistance of Dr. Morris, Vice-President of the English College; and Monsignore Talbot continued the kindness he had exhibited throughout; but his health was giving way, and he had no cheering news from Ireland to sustain and encourage him. He never considered himself beaten however.

The want of support from Ireland which Lucas felt so bitterly is explained in the 5th section of the fourth chapter of the "Statement," and in further detail in Sir C. Gavan Duffy's "League of North and South;" where it will be seen how the most strenuous efforts of himself and Mr. Moore utterly failed to infuse courage into the minds either of the clergy or of the Members of Parliament.

The following Book contains all the material portions of the "Statement."

Book the Fifth.

" It is God's truth, in God's cause, said to His Vicar ; and if it is for His service, He will make it good and secure for it belief."— *Letter to Duffy.*

IN presenting the "Statement" drawn up by desire of his Holiness, as expressed on the occasion of Lucas's second audience, I have thought it advisable for the reader's convenience to curtail some portions of the document. In doing so, I have been careful to give the substance of the original, epitomising some of the details, but in no instance softening or toning down any censure or any facts which involved a principle. Thus the first chapter is given entire. The second chapter enumerates cases of scandal at sundry elections, and reprehensible conduct on the part of certain ecclesiastics in connection with the same. The third chapter, entitled " Cases of Punishment," shows how some priests were punished for meritorious interference in politics. These two chapters are epitomised. They point out that the proposed new statutes do not touch the real scandals at all.

The fourth chapter consists of six sections. Of

these, the first and fifth are given entire. Of the other four, full abstracts will be found in the following pages. The fifth chapter is also divided into six sections, and is not curtailed by a single word. The sixth and last chapter is the longest, and contains eight sections. Of these, the introductory section is in the words of the original with some few excisions. The second, third, and fourth are nearly entire. The fifth is greatly epitomised, though much remains as it came from Lucas's pen. The sixth section is left out altogether for a reason which will be found in its place. The seventh section is perfect as far as it goes; the concluding pages are omitted, as explained at the end of the section. The eighth and last section is given almost entire.

CONTENTS OF STATEMENT.

CHAPTER I.

CHAPTER II.

RECENT CASES OF SCANDAL.

CHAPTER III.

CASES OF PUNISHMENT.

CHAPTER IV.

RELIGION AND POLITICS IN OSSORY.

CHAPTER V.

CHAPTER VI.

THE APOSTOLIC LEGATE.

CHAPTER I.

Section I.—*General Introduction.*

In common with a great number of laymen devoted to the interests of the Holy See, and also with the great majority of those priests in Ireland whose sentiments I have had an opportunity of learning, I have heard with dismay that a design has been conceived by some Irish Bishops, and specially by the Archbishop of Dublin, materially to diminish the liberty which Irish priests have hitherto used of co-operating with their flocks in those legal and constitutional efforts by which the rights of the Church and of the poor can alone be defended against the enemies of both.

The existence of this design was first made generally known by an extraordinary act of authority on the part of the Bishop of Ossory, who, in the course of the past year, commanded two of his priests to abstain altogether from interference in the public affairs of Ireland, under circumstances which have left a very general, and, I believe, a very well-founded impression, that the intention of the Bishop of Ossory was not to punish any breach of ecclesiastical discipline, or to prevent or remove scandal, but to introduce a new rule and a system of politics into the conduct of his diocese; and to do so by placing a mark of ignominy upon two priests who are generally believed to be second to none in the diocese for the discharge of their ecclesiastical duties.

This act of power is considered more significant and more alarming from three causes :—

First, it is known, by the statement of the Bishop of Ossory himself, that he was incited and encouraged to silence one of the priests in question by the Archbishop of Dublin. Secondly, this interference of the Archbishop of Dublin took place at a time when to silence that priest was to render a very material assistance to the late Government at the time of an election ; and thirdly, it is a notorious fact, and particularly known to me, that the Bishop of Ossory is a very strong politician, and that he does interfere in politics as far as the difference of opinion existing between his Lordship on the one hand and his clergy and flock on the other renders it possible for him to do so.

The inference drawn from these three circumstances, along with many others which it would be too long to relate, was and is that the act— silencing of the two priests in question—was not an isolated act of a single Bishop, well or ill advised, but that it was part of a general design entertained by the Archbishop of Dublin to fetter the liberty hitherto enjoyed by priests throughout Ireland ; and that the particular object is to discountenance and suppress certain opinions about religious politics which are in no respect at variance with the spirit of the Catholic Church or with the law and constitution. of England, but which are very much hated by the oppressors of the Catholic people and by the enemies of the Catholic Church.

From conversations which I have had on various occasions with the Archbishop of Dublin, and from many facts which have fallen under my own observation, I have no doubt whatever such are the deliberate intentions of his Grace; and that he labours diligently, in season and out of season, by all practicable methods, to accomplish this disastrous result.

To give greater weight to this project, it has been industriously circulated in Ireland that in so doing the Archbishop of Dublin and those who act with him are merely carrying out the wishes of the Holy See; that they are acting under instructions from the Supreme Pontiff; and that to differ with them, or to do otherwise than co-operate in their designs, is to oppose the wishes and commands of the successor of St. Peter. After making the best inquiries I have been able to make in Rome, I imagine that any instructions from the Holy See to the Irish Bishops have had reference to the preventing of scandals, if any such exist, among the clergy, and to the better maintenance of ecclesiastical discipline; but what is known in Ireland to be the fact is, that the pretended necessities of ecclesiastical discipline are made use of by some Bishops, whose natural leanings or timidity of character make them ordinarily the allies of the British Government, as a pretext for putting down, not all ecclesiastical politics, but all independent ecclesiastical politics ; and lending the whole weight of the influence of the Church to those who make Catholic politics a means of serving the British Government and promoting their own advancement, and an instrument for increasing corruption and venality among the Irish people.

Among these Bishops I am sorry to be obliged by a sense of duty to make special mention of the Archbishop of Dublin, whose eminent position, indefinite authority, and supposed omnipotence at Propaganda make him by far the most important of the Bishops referred to ; and give to their political designs that of which they would otherwise be altogether destitute—standing-ground and a possibility of success.

It is not rashly that I presume so to name the Archbishop of Dublin. In due course I shall state the grounds of these assertions ; but for the present it is sufficient to say, that having been now in Parliament for more than two sessions, labouring to procure a redress of Catholic grievances, the great difficulty I have had to encounter in seeking such redress has come from Bishops entertaining the views I have just described, and especially from the Archbishop of Dublin ; that

the known political friendship of his Grace to
the Government has diminished their motive
for making concessions to us; that his Grace
has himself co-operated with the Government in
creating some of the grievances of which I have
had publicly to complain; and that his Grace's
antipathy to the independent course pursued by
me in particular has been manifested in never-
ceasing efforts to reduce such influence as I was
exerting for the service of the Church by secret
whispers, private correspondence, and the most
unfounded imputations upon me and upon every
man who was acting with me in the same cause.
During the last two years Catholics have had
a great opportunity of procuring redress of their
religious grievances. That opportunity my friends
and myself have striven to turn to the best account,
in spite of the discouragement we have all received
from the Archbishop of Dublin; and I have no
hesitation in saying—what I know to be true—
that that opportunity has been almost wholly lost
in consequence of the obstruction placed in our
way by the Archbishop of Dublin and his policy.
Nay, to such a point have affairs now come, that
if Dr. Cullen succeeds in his political designs, redress of religious grievances must henceforward
be sought, not from the use of human means, but
from the miraculous intervention of Providence
alone

It seems to me the more necessary to state
these things plainly, because I have found, since

I came to Rome, that the decision of the ordinary details of Irish affairs rests with those who, to great merits of another kind, great zeal, vast diligence, and sincere anxiety to do good, add, unfortunately, a want of acquaintance with Irish affairs, an inability to read the language in which these affairs are ordinarily transacted; and an inability to make themselves familiar with the course of events and necessities of Ireland; and who therefore, on too many very important matters, are very liable to be deceived.

I would not say this if my own personal experience in Rome did not give me strong reason to be certain of its truth; and as I know that for a long series of years the Holy See has been studiously misinformed from all quarters about Irish affairs and Irish persons, I have the less hesitation in going pretty fully into detail.

SECTION II.—*Certain Misrepresentations Removed.*

It is easy to discover that the question of the interference of priests in politics has been distorted by grave misrepresentations, not merely of particular facts, but of the general aspect of the case, and of the intentions of those who take a side hostile to the English Government. Thus, for instance, I have heard stated as an abuse calling for immediate correction, the practice of priests holding political meetings in churches and chapels.

To this I answer, that I have been taking an
active part in Catholic politics in Ireland since
January 1850, and during these five years I have
attended and been a party to the holding, along
with priests, as many meetings probably as any
person in the country; yet I never was present
at a meeting held in a chapel (except one near
Dublin four years ago). I never heard during
all that time of meetings being so held. I am
sure there is no practice or habit of holding
political meetings in places of worship; and I am
satisfied that, whatever may (or may not) have
happened in half-a-dozen instances in as many
years, there is practically no abuse requiring the
enactment of any new law. The only objection
that I can conceive to the making of such a law
is that to make it would seem to take for granted
what is not the fact, viz., that a practice exists
in Ireland of holding political meetings in the
chapels.

Again, it is said that priests taking a part in
politics, even if they do so on proper occasions,
may give scandal by their imprudence or indiscretion. It is insinuated that we who are unfavourable to the English Government are indifferent to such scandals, that we wish to paralyse
the authority of the Bishops, and to make their
hands powerless for correcting disorders among
those subjected to their rule. Nothing can be
more unfounded than this accusation. We who
are so accused wish scandals to be prevented,

and, if need be, to be punished. But most un-questionably we do not wish that, under the pretence of maintaining ecclesiastical authority, any Bishop should use the powers intrusted to him by the Holy See to carry out political objects of his own, alike hostile to the wishes and interests of his flock and injurious to religion. We do wish scandals to be abated; but it is because we are firmly persuaded that the proposed legislá-tion will not put down scandals, but will increase them; that it is directly calculated to injure the character of the priesthood, to weaken the in-fluence of religion, and to destroy ecclesiastical authority, that we throw ourselves at the feet of the successor of St. Peter, entreating him to save us from this great calamity.

Again, it has been charged against us that we wish to take off the priests from their ecclesias-tical duties and involve them in politics, that is, in designs of mere worldly ambition or policy remote from their ecclesiastical duties. Here again I venture absolutely to deny the accusation; nay, I go further, and say that if such a charge can truly be made against any class of priests in Ireland, it can only be made against some who are favourable to the new policy of the Archbishop of Dublin and to the proposed new legislation. I shall have something to say hereafter about those priests who make use of politics and of their local influence with the electors as a means of enriching themselves or their families. These secret but not less scandalous practices exist in certain quarters ; and those who are guilty of them are guilty of meddling in secular business, convert politics into a commercial speculation, degrade the authority of the Church, and ought certainly to be discouraged.   But those are not the priests with whom the proposed legislation affects to deal.   Those venal clergymen will find their hands strengthened by the spirit of the proposed legislation, as it has been explained to me.   But as for the rest of the priests and their politics, I venture to say that there are no politics now current in Ireland amongst the clergy except those to which the duty of a priest towards the Church and towards the poor necessarily binds him.   To pass laws against sacerdotal politics, as if priests habitually transgressed their sacred calling to make themselves worldly or secular politicians, would be to act under the most extraordinary misinformation, and it would dismay one to think that such misrepresentation could have been made at Rome from quarters deemed worthy of belief.   The politics of the Irish priests are to protect the lives, the faith, and the dearest interests of the Catholic poor.   The new policy and the new legislation propose to discourage the clergy in the discharge of these duties.   None but venal priests who sell their sacred calling have any other politics but these ; yet the venal priests are not touched by the proposed legislation, and are positively encouraged by the new

policy. The politics of the Irish priests at this
moment are neither more nor less than those
prescribed, sanctioned, and commanded by his
present Holiness, as appears by a letter received
by the Archbishop of Cashel in February 1848
(Already quoted at p. 101 of this volume.)

SECTION III.—*Restrictions on the Action of the
Clergy viewed as a Concession to the Enemies
of the Church.*

Such being the only politics known to the Irish
clergy, or, at least, within the scope of the proposed legislation, the question arises, what will
be its operation upon the minds of those large
classes who are indirectly and very powerfully
affected by it, but upon whom it has no direct
operation ?   How will these new restrictions be
understood and appreciated by our enemies outside the Church, and by the laity within its fold?
Everybody in Ireland and out of Ireland who
has paid attention to this subject knows that for
a series of years the enemies of the Catholic
Church and of the Catholic poor have been
making representations, not only in Parliament
and in the public journals, but in Rome itself,
with a view of discrediting the interference of
priests in Irish politics, and persuading the Holy
See to bind them with some kind of restriction.

To accomplish this result I am credibly informed they have spared no pains and shrunk

from no misrepresentation. In particular, I am told that all the extravagant falsehoods printed in the anti-Catholic journals about the elections of 1852 have been translated into Italian and pressed upon the attention of the Holy See.

If this design should succeed, if—which God avert—they should at length have persuaded the Holy See to comply with their demands; there is no doubt that in England and in Ireland to the enemies of the Church such a decision will give the greatest possible satisfaction. They will hail it as the triumph of their past exertions, and as an encouragement to assail us for the future. They will say—and justly—that our Church condemns us; that those efforts for the poor and for religion which have been so offensive to them because they are the enemies of our religion, are also offensive to the rulers of our Church and the guardian of our religion. They will rejoice that they have at length accomplished through the Holy See what they have long desired to accomplish through penal laws. They will boast that they have persuaded the successor of St. Peter to do the work which the successor of Elizabeth had in vain striven to accomplish in her own name.

On the other hand, the effect of such a decision upon the bulk of the Catholic people and clergy of Ireland would be not dissimilar—only that they would lament at what to their enemies would be a source of rejoicing. They would draw the same conclusions, but would regard them with a

very different mind. They would feel that the
hand of their father had smitten his faithful children, calling to him for help against their common
enemies. They would regard such a compliance
with the wishes of our foes as a proof that the
hereditary influence of England in Rome, which
has been so powerful for six centuries, still flour-
ishes in its pristine vigour.

I but repeat what I have often heard. Not I,
therefore, but the Catholic people of Ireland,
would say that the fatal predilection for England
through which Adrian IV., deceived by false
representations, gave Ireland to the murderer of
St. Thomas of Canterbury; through which Alexander III. was persuaded to confirm what Adrian
had done; through which John XXII. was induced to reward with excommunication the heroic
struggles of unconquered Irish chieftains for the
maintenance of their rights ; and which, to come to
later times and to this century, has given to the
capital of the land a succession of Archbishops,
eminent indeed for their piety and zeal, but pre-
eminent alike for their influence in Rome and for
their unhappy subserviency to the enemies of our
Church and people—that that same fatal predilection still exists which made Adrian and Alexander
the remote instruments in the hand of an inscrutable
Providence for inflicting centuries of persecution
upon this faithful portion of the Church of God.

If, which I cannot believe, the new policy
should be indeed sanctioned by the Holy See, I

am sure that, whether this language be well or ill
founded, it will be very generally used, and that
feelings most injurious to the Holy See will
penetrate deeply and rankle long.

SECTION IV.—*Omissions of the New Proposed Legislation.*

Monsignore Barnabo has had the kindness to
show me the Dublin statutes recently approved
by Propaganda, and also a letter addressed by
his Eminence the Cardinal Prefect to the Archbishop of Tuam in explanation of the general
views of the Sacred Congregation on this subject.
Not having these documents before me, I cannot,
of course, undertake to refer very accurately to
particular words or phrases, and can speak only
of their general purport.

What first struck me in these documents was
what they did *not* contain—what seemed to me
their omissions. What precise degree of relative
importance the Holy See attaches to the redress
of the religious grievances by which poor Catholics are afflicted and thousands of souls are
annually lost, is not for me to say; but having
regard to the fact that these grievances are inflicted by law, and that their removal can only be
brought about by a change in the law (that is, a
change in the spirit of the Legislature), it has
always seemed to me, and to those whom I have
consulted, that the defect in the Irish clergy with

reference to politics and elections is the very opposite of that taken for granted by the proposed statutes. They take it for granted that the priests are too zealous, too forward, too careful about elections, occupy too much of their time with public affairs, and assume altogether too prominent a position in these respects. As one of those laymen upon whom falls the duty of trying to extort a redress of these grievances from a reluctant Legislature, and also as having some experience in Irish elections, I feel no doubt that the very opposite of this is the case. If grievances are to be redressed, not by the use of human means, but by prayer and fasting and miraculous interposition, then it is easy to understand the spirit of the proposed statutes. But if it is our duty to use the human means at our command—and it is only on this supposition that laymen need trouble themselves about the business—then I am sure that the reason why the redress of grievances is so long delayed, and why year after year so many souls are lost by the operation of unjust laws, is precisely because the clergy in many parts of Ireland are not zealous enough; do not use all the strength they possess; are not sufficiently systematic and persevering in their political exertions; are too often apathetic, timid, lukewarm, and indifferent; do not sufficiently appreciate the greatness of the trust committed to them; have too little thought of the good they might accomplish by increased exertions, and of the evil they perpetuate by their want of diligence; and sometimes, as we shall see hereafter, make even a selfish and corrupt use of the powers which God has bestowed upon them for higher and nobler purposes.

If I know anything of Ireland or of the spirit of the Irish priesthood, these are the evils that require a remedy and that demand the intervention of the Holy See. We laymen, who have devoted ourselves to this service of the Church, cannot but be both *im*pressed and *de*pressed by the fact that at the moment we are labouring with the utmost zeal and at greatest inconvenience, the Church proposes to inflict upon us the greatest discouragement, by depriving us of three-fourths of our support. Fainting as we are under the burden of the day; compelled, if we continue our labours, to stand as few amongst many; exposed to obloquy and discredit of all kinds; supported solely by the intrepidity of the poor electors and by the public spirit of the more courageous of the priests; crippled by the apathy of the less zealous and by the open hostility of the venal; we find, to our amazement, that the authority of the Church itself is invoked to complete our destruction. The Holy See is asked to speak, and for what end? Not to breathe into the hearts of the clergy and of people alike a fuller measure of that zeal by which the Holy Father is inflamed; not to inspire them with a higher magnanimity; not to implant in them a more self-devoted spirit, a more undaunted perseverance, or a greater disinterestedness; but exactly the reverse of all this. The documents I have seen, and the language I have heard, strike exactly in the opposite direction. It is for us to serve the Church, if we think fit; to give up our days and nights to this service; to sacrifice our health, to abandon every hope of worldly advancement; to expose ourselves to obloquy, derision, and hatred in a cause in which, without clerical co-operation, we are absolutely powerless; and while we are engaged in this thankless labour we are suddenly told that to give us the help which is indispensable to our work is not the business of the clergy; that if any clergyman co-operates with us, he does so at his peril; that those who stand aloof or help the enemy are most sure of favour; that those who show themselves most diligent to help us are most sure of chastisement and displeasure; that the business we are engaged in is not a religious but a secular business; and that if we choose to trouble ourselves about it, it is our own concern only, in which the Church takes no interest.

That this is the true meaning of the proposed statutes, and of the language used to me with regard to them, I shall presently show.

In the meantime, I am, and I profess myself, an obedient son of the Church. I have engaged in politics from a religious motive and as a religious work. I have done so under the notion that in this business the Church and the clergy were the principal agents, and that I was their very humble assistant.   I always believed that the work upon which we were engaged was primarily the work of the Church, and that from the necessity of the case laymen took a part in it, but only a secondary part, in order to secure the rights of the Church and to help her to fulfil her duties.   I held this opinion in the most perfect good faith, and if it is a wrong opinion I am prepared to change my course.   In Parliament and in politics I have no secular objects to pursue ; and if the Church should really proclaim that Irish Catholic politics are merely or mainly a secular business, a pursuit of secular ambition, with which the Church has no concern, and in which the clergy have no right to meddle, I, and every man who shares my opinions, will of course feel that our function has come to an end, and that our desire to serve the Church makes us intruders in a field which is sacred to the designs of selfish and ambitious men.

But this is not all.   We who have foolishly thought to serve the Church in Parliament are not the only laymen concerned.   In all the Irish elections within the present generation, it has been the teaching of the Church to the Catholic electors —that is, to the poor farmers dependent on their Protestant landlords—that the election of a member of Parliament was a sacred and religious duty ; that they were bound to vote for representatives properly qualified to defend the interests of the

Church; and that in the performance of this duty they were bound to disregard the threats of their landlords and considerations of private interest.

Never was this doctrine of religious duty more solemnly inculcated than by the present Archbishop of Dublin in immediate anticipation of the very last election. He solemnly proclaimed to the people that it was a " strict religious duty to select as representatives of the people those men who are best fitted from integrity, ability, and zeal to support our religious rights and to remove the many grievances under which we laboured." He took the lead in forming an Association of which Bishops and priests were to be the leading directors, and of whose operations his Grace was to be the mainspring; and one of the principal functions of that Association, so guided by Bishops and priests, or rather its " imperative duty "—for so Dr. Cullen formally proclaimed—was to interfere in every election in Ireland ; or, to use Dr. Cullen's own words, " to organise and marshal the elective power of each constituent body so as to ensure a right direction being given to every available vote." Nor was this a mere theory. The Association under his Grace's direction was very inefficiently managed, and lost the confidence of the country, and was very soon dissolved ; but while it lasted it assumed the power of interfering in every election in which it could get a hearing, and priests and laymen indiscriminately took a part in the electioneering work. In every county in Ireland priests acted on this theory at the election of 1852; and in the county of Dublin itself Dr. Cullen's priests took as active a part in the election as they knew how; though, from their want of practical knowledge and experience in the political guidance of their people, they were ignominiously beaten, and enemies of the Church were sent to Parliament as their representatives.

The high lessons of religion in connection with elections then taught to the people by the Archbishop of Dublin and the other Bishops, impressed the public mind in Ireland the more deeply because from his Grace's position he was supposed to bear with him the blessing of the Holy See upon the course he then recommended, and was supposed to act in accordance with the views of the Supreme Pontiff. The people of Ireland took what fell from his lips as if it had fallen from the lips of the Holy Father, whose mouthpiece they believed him to be; and nobly and faithfully did they do their part under the active guidance of the Bishops and the clergy, to whom they and their fathers before them have been in the habit of looking for direction and advice. Nobly did they do their part, braving the tyranny of landlords and the threats of the powerful, in order to fulfil the duty towards the Church which the Church had taught them, and which at that very moment the Church was sounding in their ears through the lips of the Apostolic Delegate.

The result was that, by the sacrifices of the people, a large number of members were returned to Parliament pledged in the most solemn manner to pursue a particular course in Parliament, which the priests told the people was indispensable for the service of the Church. Seduced by offers of place and Government patronage, a great many of those representatives have broken their pledges in the most disreputable manner. A great many priests and some Bishops have leagued themselves with these betrayers of the people, have given sanction to this scandalous breach of faith, and are now before the public as men utterly indifferent to public morality, men who by their acts teach the people that even Catholic politics are a selfish game, to be pursued for selfish ends, and by the use of the most abominable means.

Under this state of things instructions are to be given to the people of Ireland as to the duties of their priests in regard to politics; and, so far as I have seen, it is proposed that not one word shall be said about the duty of priests, when they engage in politics, to do so disinterestedly; about the scandal of making Catholic politics a means of promoting mere private interests; about the infinite disgrace of priests preaching duty and sacrifice to the people, and then turning the sufferings of the people to their own pecuniary account; not one word to encourage the clergy to take a lofty view of their own mission and to stimulate them to a more zealous and complete fulfilment of their duties towards the people whom they guide ; but, on the contrary, regulations and language every word of which tends to discourage zeal, to make cowardice the safe course, to give the whole clergy of Ireland to understand that in leaving the helpless people to their fate, they are best securing their own interests with the Holy See ; and that henceforward, in regard to public duties, nothing will be more dangerous for a priest than Catholic magnanimity, intrepid courage, and a never-failing perseverance in behalf of the poor of Christ.

I cannot but think that for the Holy See to take notice only of the occasional indiscretions of which, for aught I know, honest priests may now and then be guilty before the world ; to treat these as the only evils ; to interfere so as to make an honest advocacy of the people's rights dangerous, and at the same time to say not one word against the apathy and selfishness which are the real scandals of the time and the real enemies of the Church and of the poor, and not one word of encouragement to those clergymen and laymen who are labouring disinterestedly to serve the Church—such a course would, in my judgment, place the Holy See in a very false position ; would make it seem to take part with the Government against the people, and would be a course both very disastrous in Ireland, and very dangerous to its own honour and authority.   Above all, I do most

earnestly implore, if the Holy See shall decide
that Irish politics are a secular business with
which clergymen have no concern, that the same
doctrine may be taught plainly and loudly to the
poor electors; that on this important subject,
which to the elector is a matter of life and death,
we may not have a double teaching to suit the
caprice of the moment; and that the fathers of
families may no longer be led astray, to the
ruin of their wives and children, by such solemn
exhortations as those of the Archbishop of Dublin in 1851, that the duty of an elector to choose
"the best" representative for the interests of
the Church is "a strict and religious duty."

SECTION V.—*Monsignore Barnabo's Interpretation
of the New Statutes.*

The general intention of the new statutes
unquestionably is not to encourage the priests
to stand by the Church and the people in those
matters that depend upon the power of the
Legislature, but most directly to discourage them.
Upon this I think there can be little difference
of opinion. They convey the notion that hitherto
the priests in Ireland have been too busy in
these matters, and that they need to be checked
and discountenanced.

To those indeed who have paid attention to
recent affairs in the kingdom of Sardinia, they

suggest the idea that the wish of their authors
is to confine the Irish priests within the limits
in which the Piedmontese clergy kept themselves
at the last and former elections; to discourage
the exercise of all public influence beyond that
of which the utter inefficiency has in this very
year brought the kingdom of Sardinia to the
verge of an interdict. With that instance in
our hands, I am justified in saying that priests
may interfere too little as well as too much ; and
that in a constitutional Government the Church
may be grievously damaged, and the very foundations of the faith shaken, simply from this
one cause—that in the details of election politics the well-meaning Catholic electors are not
sufficiently habituated to act with their clergy
and to follow their direction and advice. To
the position of Piedmont the British Government
(which has been the first to insist upon this new
course of policy for Ireland), would be delighted
to assimilate the condition of Ireland as regards
the political action of the clergy; and, that I
have not exaggerated the possible meaning of
the Dublin statutes in this respect, will appear
from what follows.

In one of the conversations with which Monsignore Barnabo has, favoured me, our conversation turned upon the Dublin statutes, and
he told me that they forbade the attendance
of priests at meetings. Having read the
statutes hastily before, I expressed a doubt of

this, when Monsignore Barnabo produced a printed copy of them and referred me to the text. On reading it over, no such prohibition was to be found in express words; but Monsignore Barnabo told me that that was the spirit of the new regulations; that under those regulations it would be the most difficult thing in the world for a priest to attend what is called a political meeting; that whatever was the meaning of the Irish Bishops, this was the meaning of the Roman authorities in confirming them, and that these regulations, where not quite explicit, were the seed (*la semence*) from which the Holy See intended gradually to develop a complete prohibition of all clerical interference in politics. I am sure Monsignore Barnabo must mean well to Ireland, and can have no feeling towards that country other than one of good. But unfortunately his explanation of these new rules would give the greatest possible satisfaction to the enemies of Ireland and the Church. If Lord John Russell or Lord Derby had been explaining to me the letter and the spirit of some new law intended to crush the Catholic religion in Ireland and to give the state complete control over its concerns, I think in their most unguarded moments they would hardly go further than the secretary of Propaganda on that occasion. The meaning of the Dublin statutes is not very clear. As I read them, any Bishop may put upon them almost whatever interpretation he pleases. But what I have a right to infer, and what I do infer from the words of Monsignore Barnabo, is that if any Bishop chooses to forbid the priests of his diocese to attend public meetings or to take part in elections, Propaganda is at present disposed so to construe the new statutes as to uphold him in such a course. If this be so, it would surely be far better at once to tell the people of Ireland to abandon all further struggle for their religious rights, and to lay themselves and the Church of their fathers in the dust before the enemies of their faith.

SECTION VI.—*Practical Effect of this Interpretation—Irreligious Politics—Young Ireland.*

This command to the clergy to abstain from public meetings will either be obeyed or not. My own belief is, that, being altogether impracticable and unsuited to the circumstances of Ireland, it will hardly be possible to obey it ; that the first persons to disobey it will be those who now clamour for it ; that the next general election will see it broken and set at naught; that it will be taken merely as a party triumph achieved in Rome by the friends and clients of the English Government ; that it will be used as an instrument for persecuting good priests when their honesty becomes too troublesome, but that nobody who

knows the state of Ireland dreams for a moment
of enforcing any such rule.

But suppose that by some strange accident it
should happen to be obeyed, what would be the
result ?   The first result would be to weaken, still
further than the Archbishop of Dublin has already
weakened, the strength of the Catholics in Parliament, to increase enormously the numbers of our
enemies in the House of Commons, and by publish-
ing our weakness to stimulate against us their zeal
along with their power.   The second effect would
be this, that though priests might not attend meetings, meetings would still be held. They would
be attended prominently in many instances by men
smarting under the belief that the Church has
abandoned the people, and from this circumstance
prone to new and dangerous projects.   Hitherto
the presence of priests at public meetings in Ireland has been a powerful guarantee for the Church
in all popular movements.   It has checked the
rashness of well-intentioned men ; it has kept in
awe those who in secret may have meditated evil
things against the Church ; it has infused a spirit
of religion, wanting in too many other countries,
into the popular politics of the time.   But once
exclude priests from all participation in public
movements ; once tell the people that these things
are so strictly secular that it is unfit for a priest to
appear in them ; depend upon it the people in the
long-run will take those who tell them so at their
word ; popular politics will *become* so secular that

in very truth no priest *ought* to be connected with
them. The rule will become a prophecy and will
ensure its own fulfilment; and the guidance of
popular movements, instead of being, as now, under
ecclesiastical control, will fall into lay hands little
careful about the Church, less and less imbued
with the spirit of their faith, and more and more
disposed to treat the Church as an impediment, if
not as an enemy.

The Archbishop of Dublin is known to speak
as being much afraid of the party called " *Young
Ireland*," and of course those who think that
" *Young Ireland*" and " *Young Italy*" are the same
thing may be deceived by his representations.
The fact is, that at the present moment the party of
" *Young Ireland*," considered as a party hostile to
the Church, is as dead as the Archbishop of Dublin
will allow it to be. Some of its members are
actually dead; some have abandoned politics altogether; some are no longer in Ireland; some have
renounced the party, have given their services
openly to the English Government, and are allies
of the Archbishop in the disputes now raging in
Ireland; while others, imbued with a more Catholic
spirit, have made a public recantation of their
errors, and have shown on certain occasions a
much greater alacrity in publicly obeying the
Holy See than has been shown by some even of
the Bishops. But if a new "Young Ireland"
party is indeed to be dreaded, the very best way
to create the danger will be to take the course now

recommended; to withdraw priests from politics, to place public affairs uncontrolled in the hands of laymen, and to leave to the clergy as their only weapon against the open enemy on the one hand, and false friends on the other, the power of preaching certain abstract truths separated from everything which in common minds can give them strength and efficacy.

If I wished to create in Ireland an anti-Catholic (and more especially an anti-Roman) popular party among Catholic politicians, I solemnly declare that I know no better way of ensuring this pernicious end than the course explained to me by Monsignore Barnabo. At the present moment the popular politics of Ireland—would to God the same could be said of Piedmont and some other countries—being in the hands of the clergy, are essentially and intensely Catholic.

The clergy, indeed, are not impeccable; but I will venture to say that on this very point they have rendered immense services to religion by keeping and using that political influence which, being devoted to the interests of religion and the poor, increases the love of the people for the priest, and makes more indissoluble the bond which unites them to religion. This leadership might, perhaps, sometimes receive a better direction. In particular instances its use might sometimes be animated by higher motives and purified by a loftier spirit. But woe to the Church in

Ireland when from the priests of the living God
it passes into other hands!

Section VII.—*Interpretation put on the New
Statutes by his Eminence the Cardinal Prefect of Propaganda.*

The second interpretation I have seen given
of the practical meaning and intended operation
of the new statutes is contained in so much of
the letter (27th January 1855) of his Eminence
the Cardinal Prefect of Propaganda to the Archbishop of Tuam as was read to me by Monsignore
Barnabo. This letter, as far as I can pretend to
recollect it, while leaning most decidedly in the
same direction as Monsignore Barnabo's verbal
statements, contained some special matter on
which I wish to say a few words.

The Cardinal Prefect, if I rightly understood
his letter, does not contemplate the entire aboli-
tion of the political influence of the clergy. To
a certain extent, I think, he even recognises its
necessity. His Eminence is of opinion that in
some way it should continue to be exercised, but
without scandal, without noise or public notoriety;
without the hard rough work of actual business,
and all by the silent and unseen operation of a
good priest's life leading his flock to follow his
whispered counsels. This would be an extremely
admirable theory if it had any relation to the
actual facts of the case. The Holy See of course

will do what it sees fit, and I shall not resist its commands directly or indirectly; but if it takes the course of enforcing such a system as this, and if it succeeds in enforcing it—which I am persuaded is hardly possible—it will have succeeded in extinguishing in almost every county in Ireland the influence of the Church in elections and in those public affairs in which the Church and the poor are interested. If it be any comfort to reflect that the political influence of the Church will have died by the hand of the Church itself rather than by a penal law enacted by its enemies, this is a consolation which will be relished equally by the enemies and by the friends of the Catholic religion. We shall at least have saved our enemies the obloquy and the danger of inflicting the death-blow upon us.

First, then, I wish the Holy See to consider the position of the priest in Ireland towards his flock, especially in those districts remote from great towns (such as Dublin), which constitute more than three-fourths of Catholic Ireland. The flock consists mostly of farmers of a humble class, who hold their farms very much at the good pleasure of landlords, for the most part Protestants of a very bigoted and malignant stamp. In any ordinary state of society, the advisers, guides, and counsellors of these poor Catholic farmers in all secular affairs would be either their landlords or some well-educated and benevolent neighbour belonging to the class of landlords or richer persons. But in Ireland between these poor and these rich there is a great and insuperable gulf. The rich, as a class, with many individual exceptions, are Protestants, who hate the Catholic religion with a very deadly hatred; who have a mania for proselytising; who have become oppressors of their dependents from religious hatred as much as from personal cupidity; and who lose no opportunity of undermining and destroying the religious influence of the Catholic priest with his flock. On the other hand, the poor, loving their religion, naturally distrust and dislike the landlord, whose hand is heavy upon them. Both in secular and religious matters it is obvious there can be no social confidence. In the thousand affairs of daily secular life in which dependent and uneducated men require counsel and advice, the Catholic farmers cannot receive it from the class of educated laymen by whom they are surrounded.

With this complete separation of feeling, interest, and religion between the rich and the poor in Ireland, the priests have a peculiar function to perform. They occupy towards the Catholic people the place of a gentry or local aristocracy. Between them and the people religion is not a gulf of separation, but a bond of the tenderest union. They belong to the same race as the people, and feel for all their sufferings, temporal as well as spiritual. At the same time, the sacerdotal character, the higher views of life, the

greater experience of the world, the more culti-
vated intellect, raise them above the rank in
which they were born ; and as they form the *only*
educated class which truly sympathises with the
people, they necessarily form the only class to
whom, in those temporal matters in which the
poor Catholic farmer requires an adviser better
educated than himself, he can have recourse, and
from whom he can receive guidance. It is not
merely in the politics of the people that the priest
takes a part, but in all their temporal affairs in
which they need counsel and advice ; politics are
not an exception to other temporal business, but
stand on precisely the same line with all the rest.
The priest leads, guides, chides, interferes, and
advises his people in temporal affairs of all de-
scriptions. To say the contrary and to forbid
this habitual interference would be to revolutionise
the country even worse than it has been revolu-
tionised by the English Government. Unless,
therefore, politics are to be made an exception
from all other secular business, the ordinary course
for a priest to take—the course which the people
expect and wish him to take, from the known
social relations between them ; and which they
believe it to be for their interest and for the interest of the country for him to take, is to interfere pretty actively in politics in a proper manner
and on all fitting occasions.

But how is the priest to interfere in politics ?
of course every kind of work has its own rules

and necessities.   To interfere in the secular business which constitutes a man's private affairs is to interfere privately and as a private friend. But elections are very different from a man's private affairs; they are essentially public, involve the co-operation of multitudes, and, as a general rule, in Ireland cannot be dealt with effectually except in public.   To say that a priest shall not interfere in politics is intelligible, though I think pernicious.   But to say that a priest may interfere—that it shall be his duty in certain cases to interfere—but that his interference must be private, is equivalent to saying that he must speak without a tongue, walk without legs, see without eyes, and hear without ears.   It is enjoining upon each of three thousand priests to work an annual or triennial miracle.

To understand how this really is, let us consider what Irish elections would be without the active intervention of the priests.   We are able to answer this question pretty exactly, because the intervention of priests in elections is of very recent date, and within the memory of numbers of men now alive.   Up to 1826–28 the line taken by the clergy was pretty much that which is now so strongly recommended.   The farmers—that is, the Catholic electors—were under the dominion of their Protestant landlords, and voted as their landlords—that is, as the enemies of their faith—bade them.   If a Catholic elector came to the priest and asked his advice, the priest gave it him.

In many instances no doubt he volunteered his advice to an elector when it was not asked. But on the whole, he did what it is now wished he should do again—he kept out of that secular business called elections, or, if he played any part in them, it was a subordinate one. His business was religion, not politics, and the secular business of elections he left to the laity. In other words, he left elections to the rich and powerful—that is, in Ireland, to the enemies of our faith and of the poor. In the business of elections the flock of the Catholic priest were sheep without a shepherd. Their natural shepherd was the priest, but he had not yet learned the art of putting himself at their head. Their only other guide was the wolf, that is, the landlord; and as the pastoral staff and its guidance were used with unskilful hands, the snap of the wolf's teeth was the guidance which the flock followed. Under this *régime* the elections of Ireland were all in the hands of our enemies, and thousands of Catholic electors were compelled to send up to represent them in Parliament their worst and most malignant enemies. A very few years before Emancipation, this state of things generally prevailed. Emancipation was carried, because, under O'Connell's guidance, the priests began to act in a manner which it is now sought to stigmatise and forbid. They began to take the management of elections into their own hands; they came prominently before the public; they co-operated on a wide scale. Priest combined with priest and parish with parish; they attended public meetings; they organised committees of management; they took the lead, threw themselves into the struggle with their whole souls, and laboured with a firm determination to succeed; and as they took the right means, it naturally followed that success crowned their efforts.

Between 1826–30, county after county, long bowed down in subjection to the Protestant landlords, shook off this influence, and succeeded in returning members who represented a little more accurately their feelings and their wants. At length came the great Clare election, in which even O'Connell would have been powerless but for the combined, public, active, vehement, and gigantic efforts of the priests, and by this signal triumph Emancipation was gained. It is now proposed to renounce the experience of the past, and to throw us back to the year 1825, and to make us as if the battle of Emancipation had not been fought.

But to bring this matter a little more closely home. Let me suppose a county in which the Catholic electors are far more numerous than the Protestant, but in which the Protestant landlords, powerful, united, and unscrupulous, have hitherto contrived to keep the representation in their hands by compelling the farmers to vote against their real wishes and opinions. It is thought desirable to change this state of things, and to send to Parliament a sound Catholic representative. How is

this to be done ?   Politics are a secular business ;
leave it to the laity ; leave it to the poor farmers,
every one of whom, taken singly, trembles under,
the frown of his landlord and the lash of the
agent.   Leaving it to the laity as a secular business, means leaving it to men who are morally
incompetent to do anything in the matter, because
they are too dependent to come prominently forward individually ; because no man amongst them
would be willing to take the lead in resisting the
landlord's will ; because if such a man, or a few
such men, came forward, the people would not
have sufficient confidence in them to follow their
guidance in so perilous an undertaking.   To say
" Leave it to the laity," means " Don't do it at all,"
but leave the representation in the hands of the
enemies of the Church.   No sane man who says
" Leave it to the laity" says so with any other
intention than to prevent the work being done
at all.   In no county in Ireland have the farmers
ever combined to resist the will of their landlords
and to choose a Catholic representative except
under the guidance of their priests.   They have
never done so, and, unless the state of society
becomes fundamentally changed, they will never
do so while the world lasts.

Take the county of Dublin, for instance.   It is
a model county in this respect, and forms part of
a model diocese.   For two or three generations
it has been governed by Bishops who have
discouraged the interference of their priests in

politics. There is a large majority of Catholic voters, but the influence of the landlords and the forced neglect of duty on the part of the priests enables the landlords to return whom they please. In the House of Commons the member who is called the "whipper in" of the enemies of our faith is returned by Dr. Cullen's own county of Dublin, in spite of the preponderance of Catholic voters there. At the last election (1852) an attempt was made to return two Catholic members—made under Dr. Cullen's auspices and by his management, through the Defence Association. It was a time of peculiar enthusiasm, but the attempt failed. The priests, indeed, at the last moment took an active part in the election, but they did not understand their business ; they had been studiously kept out of politics ; they had no practice in the management of elections ; their flocks had not been used to co-operate with them in elections, nor they with their flocks. The whole business was ludicrously mismanaged, and Dr. Cullen's policy thus returns for the metropolitan county two hostile members of the House of Commons, one of whom is most practically active against Catholic interests. Under the same policy, Dublin city, which, if priests and laity were united under the Bishop, could easily return Catholic representatives, returns two preeminently active anti-Catholic members. Dublin University being a Protestant University of course returns anti-Catholics, nor can Dr. Cullen

be held responsible for that. The county of
Wicklow, which is also in the diocese of Dublin,
returns to Parliament one—I think two—anti-
Catholic members. It is impossible to imagine
anything more humiliating to religion than the
representation of the Catholic people in this part
of Ireland. As regards poor-law guardians and
municipal offices, it is getting worse under Dr.
Cullen's management ; nor can anything happen
more disastrous than the introduction into other
dioceses of the suicidal policy pursued by Dr.
Cullen and his predecessors.

But to come back to our supposed case of a
county coerced by Protestant landlords to return anti-Catholic representatives. To procure
the return of Catholic representatives for that
county, it is, I suppose, admitted that the priest
must interfere. But how ? Not in public—not
at meetings—not by open active intervention—
not by incurring the risk of indiscretion or scandal
—but by the quiet unobtrusive influence of a good
life and a persuasive example on his own flock.

Let us try it in detail. Such a county as we
have supposed consists of thirty or forty parishes,
with thirty or forty parish priests and sixty or
seventy curates. The property is held by a small
body of landlords, who are united in their determination to keep the representation in their own
hands, and to punish by eviction any refractory
tenant who dares to disobey them. The parish
priests differ too much in zeal, ability, influence,

and disposition to take a part in this disagreeable and difficult business. The people themselves differ in zeal or readiness to act, partly according to their character, partly according to their pecuniary relations with their landlord.

The landlords, agreeing in the main in their wish, differ in character, influence, and power. One is an absentee; another has a Catholic agent, or an agent who desires to stand well with the priest, who is his next neighbour; another is a humane person, adverse to strong acts of arbitrary power. Where the landlord is the most arbitrary and powerful, and the farmers and electors most dependent, it may happen that the priest is the most zealous and the most capable of taking the lead in such a business. Around him are half-a-dozen parishes where the priests are less zealous and capable, and where the farmers are unwilling of themselves, and, unless impelled to do it, to risk a collision with their landlords. The priests in these half-dozen parishes are not adverse to the proposed movement, but are unwilling to be too prominent in it, and have not the necessary energy. The one priest in the one parish has both the energy and the capacity, and if he were at liberty to attend public meetings of the surrounding parishes—meetings perhaps in his own parish to which the surrounding parishioners might be invited—he could make up for the deficiency of the neighbouring priests, infuse a resolute spirit into the electors of the whole district, and set an example

that might tell upon the county at large and
ensure the success of the election in a Catholic
sense.

. But under the new *régime* this power is to be
taken from him. He is not to be at liberty to
attend public meetings. He is to be rigidly tied
down hand and foot, as the landlords would wish
him to be tied down. He may influence his own
flock in a quiet underhand way, but he is not to
give scandal by coming noisily before the world.
Of course, if such an order is issued, I hope—it is
my duty to hope—that he will obey it to the very
letter ; that he will hold no public meeting, and
neither in the chapel nor out of the chapel
address words of exhortation and explanation to
his assembled people ; that he will do nothing to
dispel the apathy of the surrounding parishes and
the political inability of the neighbouring priests ;
that he will not think of encouraging the people
to stand firmly together by so profane an instrument as eloquence ; that he will calmly see them
beaten down by the excitement of terror, and will
make no effort to raise them up by the counter-
excitement of enthusiasm ; that he will not follow
the example of Peter the Hermit with the first
Crusade, or St. Bernard with the second ; that he
and all his fellow-priests will studiously avoid
giving their people any assurance or visible mark
of that general co-operation which is essential to
their success in the election in the first place, and
to their protection from the landlords' vengeance

afterwards ; that he will leave them single, isolated, unconnected, disheartened, weak, impotent, contemptible. In such an event it will be my duty to hope all this, knowing at the same time that from all this there will follow disaster and discomfiture to the Church. But I very much doubt whether anything of this kind will happen ; because I am persuaded that the first persons to break the proposed rule, in their zeal to serve the English Government, will be the Bishops at instance they have been passed.

The truth about Irish elections lies in a direction exactly opposite to this new policy. If the people have a duty to perform to the Church on those occasions, they must be trained and taught to perform that duty. The more thoroughly they are taught and the more universally they are taught, the more chance there is of a quiet election, and the less danger that the landlords will provoke against them a contested election. But who is to teach them their political lesson ? The landlords are the enemies of the Church whom they are to combat ; newspapers are not habitually read by one out of six of the rural electors ; and thus either the people must be left untaught, or they must learn their duty by chance, or in the intervals of elections they must somehow or other be instructed by the priests. To the priests ultimately we must come, not merely as the teachers of religion in Ireland, but as the teachers of politics, because God has so made

society in Ireland, and we cannot unmake the
world. In actual practice, the difficulty is that
too many priests are not systematically active;
that they do not keep their people sufficiently
informed about public affairs ; and thus when the
time for action comes, everything has to be done
at once, hurriedly and convulsively, because sufficient preparation has not been made. Sure I am
that if the people have a duty towards the Church'
in this matter, the Church has a duty towards
the people—the duty, namely, of teaching and
instructing them ; and it is my humble judgment
that, instead of rendering impossible the discharge
of their duties, the priests should be made to
understand that the Holy See regards the systematic training of those electors who depend upon
them for this kind of knowledge as a most indispensable obligation, a duty upon the general and
regular discharge of which depends, humanly
speaking, the protection of the Catholic Church
and poor against the assaults of their most malignant enemies. For these, amongst other reasons,
I regard the theory propounded by his Eminence
the Cardinal Prefect in his letter to the Archbishop of Tuam as utterly untenable, unless the
defence of Catholic rights by human means is to
be abandoned altogether. If this alternative is
to be adopted, let us all, clergy and laity, adopt it
together. Let us renounce human weapons, and
plainly avow that we place our sole reliance on
supernatural means. But if we are not prepared

to go this length, then I respectfully submit that the doctrine of his Eminence's letter supposes an entire misapprehension of the social and political state of Ireland.

SECTION VIII.—*The Archbishop of Dublin's Interpretation of the Proposed Statutes.*

The third exposition of the proposed legislation I had the honour of hearing from the lips of the Archbishop of Dublin in Rome, at the conference between his Grace and myself which took place in January at the request (to me) of the Secretary of Propaganda. The theory of his Grace, as I understood it, was partly borrowed from the Cardinal Prefect, but adapted to his own political views. He relaxed something of the severe rule contemplated by Propaganda, and would sometimes allow a priest to come publicly before the world in order to express his approbation or his disapprobation of particular candidates.

" If a candidate was proposed avowedly hostile to the Church," said the Archbishop, " I would allow the priest to tell the people not to vote for such a candidate ; that it was their duty to vote against such a candidate. But if two candidates came before them, both promising pretty fairly to the Catholic Church, and not expressing any decided hostility, then I think the priests should not be allowed to interfere, but the choice should be left to the unbiassed judgment of the electors."

To make this opinion (which I have given nearly verbatim) quite intelligible, it should be stated that in Irish elections we have to do with three kinds of candidates. First, " Tories," members or partisans of Lord Derby's late Administration ; these candidates are what the Archbishop of Dublin would call open and avowed enemies of the Church. Secondly, "Whigs " or " Peelites," members or partisans of Lord Aberdeen's, Lord J. Russell's, or Lord Palmerston's Government. Such candidates are in the habit in Ireland of using a great deal of smooth language about the Church, and labour to injure it as much by treachery as by open violence. If they wish to make Maynooth Gallican, they try to corrupt it by large grants of money. If they wish to de-Catholicise the people and to loosen the bond which connects them with Rome, they spend large sums in establishing what are called liberal systems of education and godless colleges. Sometimes, as in the case of the Ecclesiastical Titles Act, they display their true nature by an open per- secution. Amongst the candidates of this class of politicians are many Catholics. Some of these, if they are honest, are weak ; but the great majority of such candidates are needy or am- bitious men, utterly indifferent about Catholic principle or practice, and for the most part very ignorant of both, who engage in politics solely to serve their own interests, and to whom the

smooth speeches of Whigs and Peelites afford
a very convenient pretext for combining the
pursuit of pecuniary emolument with pretended
service but real injury to the Church.   In 1851
Dr. Cullen openly and deliberately proclaimed
his opinion that such mock friendship and real
teachery was more disastrous to the Church
than the open enmity of the Tories.   The third
class of candidates consists of those who engage
in politics to serve the Church and the poor;
who have bound themselves to renounce all
personal advantages from politics until the
wrongs of the poor and of the Church be redressed; who have kept these promises hitherto,
and have shown a determination to keep them
hereafter.

Now with regard to these three classes of candidates, Dr. Cullen's rule would have at once a
curious and characteristic application.

His Grace's present political party is Whig or
Peelite, and accordingly he lays down a rule
favourable to Whigs and Peelites.   He will allow
the priests personally and publicly to oppose the
Tories—they are his enemies, and the enemies of
the Church.   But his present friends, those whom
in 1851 he denounced as worse enemies to the
Church than its open enemies, candidates of this
party, he will not allow the priests openly and personally to oppose.   The Whig or Peelite may be
in character most disreputable, in intentions most
corrupt, in religion either hostile to our faith or a

public scandal to the Church; his promises may
be known to be valueless and his oaths habitually
broken, and his disposition may lead him to make
himself at any time a convenient instrument to
our enemies; yet the rule laid down by Dr. Cullen
would forbid priests taking part against such a
man, and trying to secure the return of an upright,
sincere, devout, and incorruptible Catholic.

In plain English, the rule recommended by the
Archbishop of Dublin is a mere rule of party
politics. The priests may give open opposition
to the Tories; they may give open support to
the Whigs or Peelites, but under no circumstances
may they try to replace treacherous Whigs or
Peelites by independent Catholics, so long as the
former find it to their interest to use smooth language, and do us all the injury in their power
without actually professing open enmity. Such
a rule is too glaring in its partisan intentions to
be carried into practice. It admits the principle
of open and active interference. It limits the
application of the principle by party views which
are merely arbitrary, and which the people of
Ireland do not share. The first general election
would shatter it to pieces as simply and merely
impracticable.

CHAPTER II.

RECENT CASES OF SCANDAL.

THE second chapter opens with the remark that the general scope of the proposed statutes is to deal with a supposed public scandal, and that though, as a layman, the author may not be competent to pronounce as to the sort of legislation applicable to such cases; yet that, as they have fallen under his own observation, he may not be incompetent to form an opinion as to whether the statutes in question would have any application whatever to the known instances of abuse.

In the abstract the law may be good or bad, but in the concrete its effect would be to encourage and increase the scandals very decidedly. The writer says :—

" I begin with selecting two cases that seem to tell most against my view and most in favour of the new rules."

These cases were the Clare and New Ross elections in 1852. In the first case, loss of life, by what Lucas regarded as "an accident foreseen by no one," had taken place at Six-Mile Bridge.

It is true that priests were present, and were possibly a little imprudent; but they were supporting, not Independent Catholics, but Whig Protestants devoted to Lord Aberdeen's party; they were not active members of any particular association; they were without experience in political movements, and were, in fact, acting in strict accordance with Dr. Cullen's rule to oppose the return of an avowed enemy of the Church. It follows that the proposed statutes, as explained by Dr. Cullen, could not, and would not, have prevented the unhappy occurrence.

In the second case, other circumstances, which one of the new rules professes to remedy—the scandal, namely, of one priest openly quarrelling with another about politics and elections—did not occur. At this election there was no quarrel. The curate, Rev. Thomas Doyle, took one side, and the parish priest the other. The former supported Mr. Gavan Duffy, a man "hateful to all to whom the will of the English Government is the supreme law;" a man "whose excellence as a Catholic two Bishops have sworn to in a court of justice, and whose character as an honourable man is unimpeachable." The parish priest, on the other hand, advocated the return of "Sir Thomas Redington, a Catholic gentleman, who remained a member of, and had continued to support, Lord John Russell's Government while it was enacting the Ecclesiastical Titles Act." The people and clergy were, of course, highly indignant at this conduct, and were very strongly in favour of Mr. Duffy, who was actually elected. But as between the Rev. Mr. Doyle and his parish priest there was no quarrel whatever, therefore the new rule, which does not forbid "differences of opinion," but only personal quarrels, would not touch this case, in point of fact.

Pursuing this subject, the "Statement" goes fully into the Athlone election of 1854, the Carlow elections of 1852 and 1853, the Sligo town election of 1853, and the Cavan election of 1855. The Sligo (county) election of 1852 is also mentioned, but this case had already been laid before the Holy See. What is entitled the "greatest scandal of all" consisted in a "regular system of corruption, organised and methodised, by which Whig statesmen have contrived, year after year, to augment the number of Catholic clergy, whom, by the basest and most naked methods, they use as the instruments of their perfidious hostility against the Catholic Church and the Catholic poor. . . . This is the great scandal and danger of the present times, because it pollutes and debases the sanctity of the ecclesiastical character, and accustoms the ministers of the altar to lower their habitual thoughts and aspirations to the level of usurers and money-jobbers."

The system consisted in offering to influential priests, whose near relatives were known to be in want of situations, places for their friends in exchange for co-operation at elections —

a co-operation which was not unfrequently accepted.[1]

The last case, that of the Athlone election of 1855, had happened while Lucas was in Rome, and it occupies a place in the " Statement " before those of the earlier elections.   It was an instance in which "more scandal was given than could have been given by a hundred noisy and riotous elections. . . . There was no riot, no violence, no abusive language, no contest even. . . . The only candidate was a high official, a follower of Lord Aberdeen and Mr. Gladstone ; his proposer was a Bishop who everywhere proclaims himself a partisan of Dr. Cullen, and who makes no secret of it that the Apostolic Delegate upholds him . . . against the Archbishop of Tuam (Dr. Mac-Hale) ; a Bishop, moreover, who had followed the Archbishop of Dublin in his recent changes in politics.

" This scandal is pre-eminent both in kind and in degree. . . . The case may be stated in a few words.   A few weeks ago, Mr. Keogh, Solicitor-General for Ireland under Lord Aberdeen, accepted the office of Attorney-General, and had to go back to Athlone for re-election.   His most influential constituent was Dr. Brown, the Bishop of Elphin, who came forward on the hustings to propose him for re-election.

---

[1] This, and the history of the Cavan election at p. 197, explain Lord Palmerston's remark in the debate on the Ecclesiastical Titles Act, when he said that he did not expect much opposition from the Irish Bishops, vol. i. p. 439.

"Mr. Keogh himself is a man who, for the sake of office, had deliberately broken public engagements deliberately contracted, often renewed through a period of eighteen months, and confirmed by three public oaths. The same Bishop was, both in public and in private, a most active party to making those sworn engagements; nevertheless he had been, both in public and in private, a most active party to the violation of those engagements and to the breach of those oaths. Mr. Keogh was, therefore, before the world as a most notorious perjurer, and the Bishop had made himself his public apologist and defender. Is it possible to exaggerate the scandal of such a case as this? Yet it is not an isolated case. . . . Other priests and Bishops do the same thing on behalf of the Government which Dr. Cullen is supporting. It is indeed understood by everybody that the proposed statutes are brought forward to strengthen the hands of those by whom this public immorality is taught and practised, and to weaken those by whom it is opposed." For these statutes pass over venality, perjury, and gross public immorality, while all their vengeance is levelled at men who in honest zeal outstep the bounds of discretion. And what makes the case worse is, that Mr. Keogh is a man in himself of "no political importance whatever, being without property, family influence, character or consideration, . . . a man without power for good or evil," except what he derives from his supporters among the Bishops and clergy; a man, therefore, "whom it was quite unnecessary to conciliate."

And further, although Dr. Cullen "has not had the indescribable rashness to appear upon the hustings and vouch for Keogh's integrity and trustworthiness," yet it is known that he fully confirms Dr. Brown's conduct, and "would regard Mr. Keogh's defeat as a calamity and his triumph as an advantage; . . . that he is considered in Ireland to be a partaker of this scandal;" and that he has said nothing to correct such an opinion, if it were not well founded.

The other elections mentioned above had each its own peculiar scandal. The town of Carlow was "particularly prominent." This was remarkable, because here dwelt the Rev. James Maher, uncle to Dr. Cullen. He was a known politician; but then his connection with the Archbishop should have prevented scandals where he lived. He "discouraged politics," unless on the Whig side. According to him, the duty of the clergy was to "attend closely to their spiritual duties, to think only of the pulpit, the altar, the confessional. This was the story for Rome. But at Westminster or Dublin Castle he is known as an active politician who can always be relied on by the Whig Minister of the day."

So also was " Dr. Healy, Bishop of Kildare, but residing in Carlow." He was one of those "who never interfere in politics. . . . So strict is his rule, that when his clergy go on vacation, they are recommended not to discuss politics even in private." In accordance with this very strict discipline, a certain priest, going to Meath for a holiday, declined all such conversation; nevertheless when, after his return, an election took place the same summer, this priest was so extremely active as to get a voter sent to prison, where he lay for some months, on a debt not yet due, in order to prevent his voting against John Sadleir.

John Sadleir had, like Keogh, broken the pledges which secured his return, and having, as the price of his dishonesty, obtained the place of Junior Lord of the Treasury, he had again to present himself for election. " Promise-breaking of this public and solemn kind, where priests and Bishops were parties to the promise, and had it in their power to punish or reward the breach of faith, was then comparatively new, and people generally through Ireland were greatly scandalised at Mr. Sadleir's audacious perfidy. But this was in the beginning of 1853. Two years have since elapsed, and the example set by Bishops and priests in that interval has very much hardened the conscience and blunted the public sense of morality and rectitude. Mr. Sadleir's was the first case, and the Bishops and priests in Carlow did very much surprise people in Ireland by the unqualified way in which they gave him their cordial support. The clergy generally supported him. The Rev. James Maher, having first con-

sulted his nephew the Archbishop of Dublin,
supported him ; and the Bishop (though no politician) supported him and canvassed for him with
unwearied diligence."

In neither of these cases do the proposed statutes
touch the evil ; and if sent to Ireland in their
present state, it will be fully understood there,
however little in Rome, that they are intended to
whiten the sepulchre externally, not to cleanse it
within.   This election was followed by that of the
town of Sligo in the same year.

"John Sadleir was not elected for Carlow in
1853, and for some time he remained out of
Parliament.   In the meanwhile his character became more and more damaged before the public.
The illegal arrest of the Carlow elector was the
subject of a trial in a court of law, and Mr.
Sadleir was not only proved to have grossly
perjured himself as a witness in that cause, but
the jury before whom it was tried found a verdict
in direct contradiction to his oath.   A more
scandalous transaction was hardly ever made
public ; and in consequence of his part in it, Mr.
Sadleir was compelled to resign his office in the
Treasury, and to become again a private citizen.
When the notoriety of his bad character and the
scandal of his proceedings were at their height, a
vacancy occurred for the town of Sligo, and the
priests of Sligo, with the Bishop of Elphin's
sanction, thought, whatever Mr. Sadleir's character,
it was good enough for the town of Sligo, and

they returned him to Parliament accordingly. A scandal like this is not touched by the proposed statutes. The Bishop of Elphin, supported by two bad Catholics and known perjurers in the House of Commons, boasts everywhere that, in the strange course he has recently pursued, he has the support of Dr. Cullen."

At the County Cavan election of 1855 a scandal of another kind shocked simple and gentle, and confirmed Lucas's prophecy that the first to break the new statutes would be those in whose behalf they were to be enacted. "The new statutes distinctly forbid priests to speak about elections within the church. On these matters they may address the people, but it must be *extra ecclesias*, and no distinction is drawn between priests and Bishops. Nevertheless the Bishop of Kilmore, another Dr. Brown (not he of Elphin), took occasion to break through the regulation. He was a non-political prelate, that is, when he did interfere in politics, it was always on the side of the Whigs. It was under his direction that Sir John Young, late Secretary for Ireland, . . . was elected in 1852 ;" and when, in 1855, Sir John Young vacated the seat on promotion, this Bishop and his clergy selected a Mr. Hughes as their candidate. He was a Catholic, who, on the hustings, "avowed with pride" that, though a Catholic, he had his children brought up as Protestants, and declared that "he had the sanction of the Bishop and clergy for addressing

the electors." He had been Solicitor-General in
1851, and had stuck to his place all through the
passing of the Ecclesiastical Titles Act. He was
taunted publicly by one of the multitude with this
treachery towards the Church. His reply was
this : " The Rev. Bishop of this diocese and his
clergy know all the facts connected with that
measure, and, knowing those facts, they approve
my conduct." But this was not all : in the same
speech, referring to the National system of godless education—a system, as we have seen, condemned by the Synod of Thurles, at which the
Bishop was present, and by the Holy See—referring to this system he said, " I do believe the
happiness of this country is greatly dependent
upon bringing the youths of all creeds together,
and imparting to them a sound and useful education, and *teaching them to sink all differences for
the promotion of their own welfare.*" Here was
the candidate, as painted by himself. But while
on these grounds Mr. Hughes claimed the support of the Bishop, the Bishop himself came boldly
before the public and pledged himself for Mr.
Hughes's " integrity," " sincerity," and " high character ; " and he assured the people they might
"repose confidence in Mr. Hughes."

But more : after the morning service on April
8th, the Bishop, having unvested, came forward and
addressed the people from the altar in a speech
"entirely devoted to the question of Tenant-
Right," for which he professed a wonderful zeal.

Now the Government hated the very name of Tenant-Right, *but the farmers were strong advocates of it.* Mr. Hughes wanted a "place under Government," and the Bishop wanted to return a Government candidate, one who would break his pledges on the first fitting occasion. This was "the explanation of the comical mixture." For these noble objects it was necessary "to make fervent professions in favour of Tenant-Right."

Accordingly the Bishop broke the statutes since they interfered with his liberty of action. But the statutes did not touch in any way the selection of such a candidate as Mr. Hughes. That scandal they left unchecked ; and Lucas contends that the whole transaction justifies him in the belief he has always entertained, that the Whig Bishops never had the least intention of being bound by the statutes which they had been at the pains to get framed.

The above, though an epitome, is as far as possible in the very words of the "Statement."

CHAPTER III.

CASES OF PUNISHMENT.

" HAVING gone through the chief cases of scandal which had been spoken of during late years," the " Statement" proceeds to show that " punishment had been actually inflicted upon innocent priests for their meritorious interference in public affairs, and that the punishment has been the scandal." Three cases are brought forward ; those of Dr. O'Connor in Sligo, and the Revs. Thomas O'Shea and Matthew Keeffe in Callan. It will be observed that it was the same Bishops who were implicated in the scandals who inflicted the unjust punishments.

Dr. O'Connor had taken some pains to inform the Holy See of the scandals connected with the countenance given by the Bishop of Elphin to the two perjured Catholics, as already related. " The only person," says the " Statement," " who has been really punished for the late transactions in the diocese of Elphin is the priest who has taken the greatest pains to put the Holy See in possession of these shocking scandals, . . . the Rev. Dr. O'Connor, P.P. of Lough Glynn. For the crime of communicating with the Holy See Dr. O'Connor has been subjected to daily and public insult, to threats of personal violence, to a painful and degrading espionage, and to a life of habitual mental torture." This is the first circumstance in connection with these punishments.

" The second is the more important, because in Ireland every effort has been made by Dr. Cullen's partisans to represent appeals to Rome as hopeless, and to denounce them as criminal; and because Dr. O'Connor's case is appealed to as a warning to all priests how they dare to communicate with the Holy See in cases in which Dr. Cullen takes an interest. To myself in private this language was uniformly held by Dr. Cullen's friends before I came to Rome. I was told in so many words that Dr. Cullen was omnipotent in Rome; that the Holy See had practically made over to Dr. Cullen its functions of superintendence and control; that in the Eternal City his will was recognised as the measure of justice, and that the mildest fate of those who dared to displease him was to die of a broken heart. The very phrase in which all this novel and scandalous doctrine was summed up repeatedly to myself by Dr. Cullen's personal friends and partisans was, that 'to appeal from Dr. Cullen to the Holy See was to appeal from the Pope to the Pope.'

" The case of poor Dr. O'Connor of Lough Glynn up to the present moment lends indirectly

a certain countenance to this disloyal representation. He has carried information to Rome and
proved guilt against some of his brother priests.
The result has been that they have been rewarded
with parishes and he with persecution; and all
that the world understands or supposes beyond
these patent facts is, that this distribution of
a cross to the innocent and a diadem to the
guilty proceeds from Dr. Cullen's influence. ·I
earnestly hope this may not be true; but when
his friends inform us that he is omnipotent, we
naturally look to him as one great cause of whatever happens."

The next priest mentioned is the Rev. Thomas
O'Shea, C.C. of Callan. His case arose in this
way. Mr. Chichester Fortescue (now Lord Car-
lingford), the member for Louth, having accepted
office in 1854, was compelled to seek re-election.
He was a gentleman who, during the debates on
the Ecclesiastical Titles Act, had made a speech
insulting and hostile to the Church, and in favour
of a new law to limit the influence of priests
at the bedside of the dying . . . . . ; he "re-
pudiated the foolish and arrogant pretensions
put forward by the See of Rome" (in establishing
the Hierarchy), and expressed the opinion that
"a real aggression had been made on the Church
of England." "A candidate who expressed such
sentiments," says the "Statement," "might be
very acceptable to the Piedmontese Government,
but could not be acceptable to an honest Irish

Catholic constituency." He had been elected in 1852 through his family influence, in spite of those words. But in 1854 the Catholic Defence Association of Louth, which was under the patronage of Dr. Cullen himself, determined to oppose Mr. Fortescue's election, and chose as his opponent a Mr. Cantwell, a member of the management committee of the Association

Some charges were afterwards made against Mr. Cantwell, but as he was a visitor at the house of Dr. Cullen in Dublin, there was no reason to doubt his eligibility in all respects, and he "was selected on public grounds to defend the interests of the Catholic Church and to secure the acknowledged rights of the Catholic people."

Mr. Fortescue's family interest in the county being great, a well-known custom was resorted to by Mr. Cantwell's committee. They looked round for influential speakers to press his claims upon his constituents and to engage their sympathies in his behalf. Amongst others, they invited Rev. Thomas O'Shea, of Callan in Ossory. He was very much disinclined to go, but having obtained the leave of his parish priest, he went to Drogheda, where he called on the Archbishop, Dr. Dixon, to explain the object of his visit, to which Dr. Dixon made no objection whatever.

Mr. O'Shea soon found that some of the priests were devotedly attached to Mr. Fortescue, while the bulk of them took the Catholic side. The common feeling of the people was that Mr. Fortescue's clerical supporters were induced to aid him, not by any regard to public principle or the interests of religion, but by pecuniary considerations of the lowest kind. In this county the scandal of taking bribes from wealthy and influential persons (as alleged in the last chapter) was of old standing. " This belief produced a most painful state of feeling in the minds of the people towards the priests in question, and was no doubt injurious to religion ; just as it would be injurious on a much larger scale to have it supposed that the higher authorities of the Church, from any motives whatever, take part with the enemies and oppressors of the people."

The painful belief existed in Louth before Mr. O'Shea arrived, and he said no word to encourage the belief. This statement of facts is vouched for in a document forwarded to Mr. Lucas in Rome, and signed by six priests, personal witnesses of what occurred.

There was great excitement among the people, who, in one parish, had, before Mr. O'Shea's arrival, threatened to nail up the doors of a chapel of one of Mr. Fortescue's supporters. With this great scandal, therefore, Mr. O'Shea had nothing to do. But his speeches to the people produced a very great effect on them, and were likely to do much injury to Mr. Fortescue's interest. It was deemed necessary, therefore, by his supporters to do two things. First, to convince the people that Mr. Fortescue never made the speech in Parliament; and, secondly, to procure, through the Bishop, the removal of Mr. O'Shea.

For the first object the clerical friends of Mr. Fortescue took the short and direct course of denying flatly that Mr. Fortescue had ever made the speech. A document to this effect was signed by about a dozen of them, and fixed up for the people to read. The denial was quite unfounded; the signatories had no personal knowledge of the matter; whereas the speech was reported in the London morning papers at the time, and was not denied by Mr. Fortescue himself. This document thus publicly displayed made the people express some very strong sentiments about the means by which the supporters of the enemies of the Church sought to accomplish their purpose.

These persons next took to calumniating Mr. O'Shea; and at the request of the Archbishop of Dublin, to whom the calumnies were communicated, the Bishop of Ossory peremptorily recalled him to his parish under the pain of suspension. This was done without inquiring into the charges, and without even telling him in what they consisted. Mr. O'Shea obeyed to the letter, returning by the first train, and calling on the Bishop, as he was ordered to do, on his way to Callan.

Dr. Cullen's animus was shown in this, that, in absence of any proof of misconduct, he desired the Bishop of Ossory to " ascertain from his parish priest whether he (Mr. O'Shea) has leave of absence, and, if not, to put him on his trial and suspend him." Fortunately for Mr. O'Shea, he had leave, and had not been guilty of any of the unpriestly conduct necessary to justify the arbitrary proceedings of the two prelates. " Dr. Cullen," says the " Statement," " knew and felt, and therefore practically admitted, that Father O'Shea had done nothing in Louth to justify suspension ; and therefore he urged the Bishop to look out for some technical and pretended reason, which, though not the real reason, would be sufficient in strict law to warrant the chastisement he had determined to inflict."

In the entire absence of any delinquency, Father O'Shea was ordered as a punishment to abstain even from such political action as was allowed to other priests. He had broken no ecclesiastical rule, he had committed no crime, he had not set priest against priest, as was proved by Dr. Cullen trying to get him punished for something not connected with Louth. His real offence was that he was the ablest man on the side of the opponents of the Government, and he must be got out of the way. They had not long to wait. The following autumn Father O'Shea attended, without speaking, and in strict accordance with the understanding between himself and the Bishop, a meeting in Callan ; and for this invented offence he was removed from one of the best parishes in the diocese to a miserable locality, where there was absolutely no society for a man of his mental capacity. So far as regards Father O'Shea. The

"Statement" indeed urges the facts at greater length and emphasises the proofs and arguments ; but I think that, with these exceptions, nothing is omitted which would make either the history itself or the manner of placing it before the general reader more attractive.

The next case was that of Rev. Matthew Keeffe. It was determined to hold a meeting at Callan to express the opinion of the county in favour of the Irish Independent Parliamentary party. Mr. Keeffe undertook some of the preliminary private correspondence, and among other letters wrote to Serjeant Shee, one of the members for the county. In this letter, written in a perfectly friendly spirit, he told the Serjeant that a good deal of dissatisfaction had been expressed at certain actions of his, including especially his desertion of Tenant-Right, his defence of the Madiai (in the debate already mentioned), and his advocacy of mixed education, and even of sending Catholic youths to Protestant universities. The letter was a private one. Father Keeffe was in no way before the world, and his only act was this friendly letter to the Serjeant. The Serjeant, however, was determined to drag him before the public, and accordingly wrote him a long and insulting reply which he sent, not to Father Keeffe, but direct to the press along with the private letter referred to. In this he "charged him with want of sincerity, assailed his motives, and in a covert but perfectly intelligible manner imputed to him conduct unsuited to the duties and character of a priest." Father Keeffe replied to these charges in a letter to the same journal—a letter which contained no word unbecoming a priest. Two days later, Serjeant Shee being then a guest in the Bishop's house, Father Keeffe received a letter couched in most arbitrary phrase commanding him to refrain henceforth from all "agitation," and to attend only to his spiritual duties. This command was strictly obeyed, and, as a reward for the obedience, the Bishop of Ossory published the details of a clerical memorial on this case prepared in private for presentation to the Holy See. Further he descanted in the public journals on the memorial in question, indulging in an offensive personal attack upon the two silenced priests. Among other things, he compared them to men "addicted to habits of intemperance in food and drink." Dr. Cullen's uncle also assailed them in the Government journals, and the Bishop refused permission to Father Keeffe to go to Rome in order to conduct his appeal. Propaganda also "has equally refused permission ; and to crown all, Father Keeffe, punished, calumniated, assailed, denied all justice, and refused permission to act in his own right by the advice of skilled advocates in Rome, is removed from all communication with his friends in Callan, and, like Father O'Shea, is exiled to another parish. God and man know that he is innocent and that he is guiltless of offence. His

Bishop . . . knows that he is innocent; but because he loves the poor, because he is zealous
for religion, because he will not sell his independence to corrupt and wicked men, all the powers
of man's injustice are let loose upon him, and even
the gates of this, the very Temple of Justice itself,
are for a time closed in his face."

The conduct of the Bishop was the more
striking because "at an ecclesiastical conference
in 1852, the same Bishop earnestly invited his
assembled clergy to exert themselves to the utmost, by the ordinary means of political agitation,
to secure the return of Serjeant Shee. In compliance with the Bishop's injunction, the Rev. Mr.
Keeffe did take an active part at the last election,
recommended Serjeant Shee most actively to the
electors, . . . and in some measure made himself
responsible to the people . . . that he would
honourably fulfil his promises."

The reason for this conduct on the part of the
Bishop in 1854 was plain enough. Father Keeffe
had committed no offence ; but the Bishop was
a Government Bishop; the Serjeant was the
Bishop's friend, and the Serjeant was meditating
(what he had already accomplished before this
Statement was written) the desertion of the party
and principles on which he was elected, and the
transfer of them to the British Government. The
Bishop wished him to do this, and at the same
time to retain his seat. Father Keeffe was too
formidable an opponent to be left free to speak

even in private, and must be struck down acccordingly.

The memorial then contrasts this treatment of Father Keeffe with that awarded to Father James Maher. One seldom wrote in the press, the other was an indefatigable letter-writer on politics; one had been dragged by no action of his own into publicity, the other had voluntarily and constantly obtruded himself; one had used no unpriestly or abusive language, the other, as we shall see, was most intemperate; yet the one was put to silence while the other passed without a rebuke; but then he was Dr. Cullen's uncle.

These personal disputes might be forgotten at this distance of time, did they not serve to illustrate the lengths to which the Government Bishops went in their determination to crush the popular party, and the tremendous difficulties which stood in the way of obtaining justice either for the poor or for the Church.

To make it clear that there is no exaggeration in these charges, the memorialist quotes a book published by Dr. Crolly, one of the Professors of Maynooth, and the nephew of the late Archbishop of Armagh, in which he remarks on the "indelicacy and ferocity of an attack made by Father Maher on the memory of the deceased Archbishop, as well as on his talent for creating mischievous dissensions among the clergy; but above all, on the peculiar delight which he took in attacking archbishops;" for it was not the deceased

Archbishop alone whom he attacked, but, at con-
siderably greater length, Dr. MacHale, Archbishop of Tuam.   Nor did Lucas fail to come in
for his share of abuse from the Bishop's friends,
particularly from one Canon Redmond,[1] who
had been created Canon by Dr. Cullen; who
had, as we have seen, cited the promotion to
Lucas in Rome, taking credit for it as a proof
that he allowed his priests great latitude of
action.   Father Redmond, up to the time of his
promotion, was a great letter-writer, but always
on the side of the Government, and pre-eminent
for his attacks upon Lucas and his friends.   But
then, as the "Statement" says :—

"*We* of course are lawful game.   Every priest
may indulge to the utmost in public vituperation
against *us*.   It is not politics to come before the
world as *our* assailants.   We are the offscouring
of the earth, and if a priest holds *us* up to the
general indignation, he is performing the true
work of a priest; he is doing God's service; he
is earning a Dublin canonry.   But let him be-
ware how he ventures to defend even his own
character and honour against the public assaults
of one of those sacred animals who (like Serjeant
Shee) is engaged in the holy work of earning
for himself a judgeship by political prostitution.
For such a priest there is no mercy under the
present rule of Dr. Cullen."

Again, in commenting upon the unjust arrest

---

[1] *Vide ante*, Book iv.

of the Carlow election, above mentioned, the
editor of the *Tablet*, after remarking upon the
unfairness of the judge in throwing the chief
blame on the priest, whereas it properly belonged
to John Sadleir, had taken occasion to warn
priests of the danger they ran, whenever, for
Government purposes, they involved themselves
in the questionable acts of ambitious and greedy
politicians ; and that they always ran the risk of
being deserted by those whom they had laboured
to serve, whenever real danger presented itself.
Referring to this article, the "Statement" says:—

"The priest in question was very angry at
these comments, and his clerical friends in Carlow still more so. A number of them got together,
and in Carlow, the Bishop's own town, jointly
concocted a letter of reply. To this they put
the name of the Bishop's curate, one of the persons who had a principal share in preparing that
reply, and who was one of the Bishop's professors
in the Seminary.

"Here then were two cases which on the surface
ran very well together. Serjeant Shee, member
for Kilkenny, attacked Mr. Keeffe for an affair
which the Serjeant was the first to bring before
the world. I censured a priest for an act scanda-
lously patent to all the world, and for which an
eminent Catholic judge had already publicly censured him much more strongly than the *Tablet*.

"Father Keeffe defended himself in language
which could not be considered indecorous or im-

proper. A confederation of priests, representing
the Bishop's palace and seminary, defended the
said priest. And in what terms did they defend
him? With decorum? With propriety? Like
bishops? Like priests? Like gentlemen?"

The following words, applied to Lucas, and
which he was called upon to publish, as he
did, are rehearsed in the "Statement":—He
was accused of "infamous slanders," of "base
iniquity," of "excessive depravity;" he was described as "unconscientious," "unscrupulous,"
"unprincipled;" he was charged with "malignity of heart;" he was called "a spy" and "a
hypocrite;" he was likened to "the lowest ruffian
in the land," and was called a "characterless
reviler;" "ruffianly hardihood" was imputed to
him, and "artful iniquity;" he was told that he
had a "corrupt heart;" that his journal was a
"besotted page;" that his words were "infamous
lies," and "false and lying as well;" and that his
manner of censuring Father —— was "the most
diabolical mode that Hell itself could invent."

This letter appeared in the *Tablet* on 7th
January 1854, but no censure was ever passed
upon it by bishop or archbishop. "Against Mr.
Keeffe, therefore, Serjeant Shee had the fullest
and meanest and most public satisfaction; [but
in my case] no such vengeance was inflicted, I
rejoice to say." These are striking contrasts;
scandals which the new rules in no way touched
nor were intended to remedy.

CHAPTER IV.

SECTION I.—*The Parish of Callan and the late Parish Priest.*

THE Archbishop of Dublin, by the letter in which he urges the Bishop of Ossory to put Father O'Shea upon his trial, has shown me that, according to the practice of that part of Ireland, a priest who has given offence may be put on his trial for one thing and punished for another; that the real motive of his condemnation may have very little connection with the ostensible, and that at the end of the trial the supposed conduct for which he is really chastised may never once have been investigated or even mentioned. In Ireland we have a number of strange stories satirising the way in which angry jurymen carry this sort of law into the jury-box; and a case is cited of a prisoner being found guilty of the murder of a man still alive and produced in court, because the foreman of the jury was under the impression that a few years before the prisoner had stolen his mare. This method of jurisprudence I certainly did not expect to find borrowed from

rustic judgment-seats by episcopal tribunals; and
as the ostensible accusation under this Dublin
practice affords no clue whatever to the real
grounds of the proceeding, this alone would furnish very good ground for the suspicion that,
after all, Father O'Shea may not really have been
punished for his conduct in Louth, nor Father
Keeffe for any impropriety in his reply to Serjeant
Shee.   Some other cause totally unconnected with
the alleged pretext may be the real cause of the
Bishop of Ossory's "harsh proceeding."   Of course
it is impossible for me to prove a negative.   It
is impossible to demonstrate that no secret or
hidden occasion may have been given by the two
curates to justify severity towards them.   But
as some loose general accusation of misconduct
may be alleged by the Bishop, or on his part, to
excuse what he has done; it becomes necessary
for me beforehand, by such evidence as I have
in my possession, to show that the two curates,
being innocent altogether of the specific fact
alleged against them, their general conduct has
been also unexceptionable; and that the relations
between them and the diocese on the one hand
and the Bishop on the other have been such as
to negative the presumption that the Bishop has
acted, even in mistake, on any fair ecclesiastical
ground; and to establish that his general objects
and purposes are not such as can meet with the
approbation of the Holy See.   In making this
inquiry I shall not in the least wander from the

question before us; and if I mistake not, I shall be able not merely to vindicate the two curates, but go far towards confirming the suspicion that the Bishops who have been most prominent in setting on foot this crusade against the liberty of the clergy have done so not so much from a zeal for ecclesiastical discipline as from political motives of their own, and from a desire to force the unwilling clergy to become their instruments in fastening upon the necks of the Catholic people a yoke which they and their fathers before them have always steadfastly abhorred.

Let us then spend a few moments in inquiring into the condition of Callan itself in late years; the conduct of the two curates during their residence there; the conduct of the Bishop of the diocese towards them and others, both in politics and in religion.

In the diocese of Ossory and the county of Kilkenny, Callan, after the town of Kilkenny, in which the Bishop resides, is, I believe, the second in importance. Before the famine it contained a population of ten thousand (10,000) souls, which number by famine, fever, and emigration has been reduced to seven thousand (7000). It is the head-quarters of a union of parishes for the relief of the poor, and contains a workhouse in which during the famine there were not less than 2000 paupers. The inhabitants are either agriculturists, or practise such small trades as are immediately dependent on agriculture. One of the principal landlords of this and the neighbouring parishes is the Earl of Desart, a member of Lord Derby's Government, a nobleman very remarkable for his bigotry, for his great hostility to the Catholic religion, and for the inhuman cruelty with which himself and his agents have driven from the face of his estates the industrious and deserving Catholic tenants.

As one of the complaints against Father Keeffe and Father O'Shea is their connection with the agitation for the protection of the tenants, it is right to make it clearly understood that their activity on this question had its origin in no abstract notions of political or social justice, but in the personal experience they had in Callan itself of the frightful sufferings of the Catholic poor, and of the shocking injustice which these miserable tenants were compelled to endure at the hands of their landlords.

Lord Desart's property extended into the adjoining districts of Callan, Ballycallan, Castletobin, in the parish of Callan, and Ballingarry—this last parish being in the county of Tipperary and in the diocese of Cashel. In Callan Lord Desart had twenty-six tenants previous to the famine. Of these, as early as 1850, twelve (12), or nearly one-half, had been ejected, and I believe that others have since been driven from the estate to find refuge in America or the workhouse.

In Ballycallan Lord Desart had forty-three (43) tenants on his property before the famine.

Of these, in May 1850 thirty-four families (34), numbering 184 individuals, amongst whom are a due proportion of widows and orphans (and of every one of which families the names and particulars now lie before me), had been driven from the estate.

In Castletobin Lord Desart had on his estate before the famine ten (10) tenants, whose names and the number of each family are now before me. Every one of these, numbering fifty-seven individuals, all Catholics, were expelled, and their place was supplied by a certain Doctor ——, a medical practitioner resident in Callan, to whom the occupation of that entire district was made over. Doctor —— is a bitter and rancorous Protestant fanatic, and a steady enemy of the religious rights of the Catholics in his neighbourhood ; and his son, who lives with him, is an open and notorious debauchee, a systematic corrupter of female innocence. Ten virtuous Catholic families have been driven to ruin by Lord Desart in this one spot in order to make way for a family whose perverted religion and depraved morality make them a pestilence to the neighbourhood.

In Ballingarry Lord Desart had sixty-three (63) tenants before the famine. Of these, twenty-six (26), whose names are now before me, making about 141 individuals, had been driven away in June 1850, and the houses in which they lived have been destroyed. A statement published at that time, and not contradicted, adds that in parts of this parish "the ordinary fences along the road and through the fields consisted too often of bedsteads and fragments of broken furniture" from the houses of the ejected tenants.

It thus appears that from the estate of one landlord alone in and around Callan eighty-two (82) families, numbering at least 442 persons, were ejected, their houses for the most part destroyed, and the unfortunate inmates left to shift for themselves, at a time when the famine raged in all its intensity; when fever added its ravages to famine; and when the general misery of the county rendered the misery of any particular district utterly hopeless and irremediable.

The sufferings of those times it is impossible to describe, and Callan, I believe, suffered more severely than any other part of that county or diocese. Upon the priests of Callan, of course, fell a great part of the active duty of attending to this enormous mass of misery. At one time there were not fewer than 2000 persons in the Callan workhouse; four hundred (400) wretches whom famine had starved into fever were lying at the point of death in the rude, temporary hospitals of the town; and throughout the parish and neighbourhood the houses of the poor everywhere contained their dying victims. What an increase in the spiritual duty of the parish this awful state of things brought with it, and with what danger to life that duty was discharged, and how faithfully it was discharged, I need not say. Two curates in

Callan—the only priests in the diocese who sunk under this labour—caught the fever in 1847–48, and died ; and those who survived, besides their spiritual duties, had to act on relief committees, and as far as they could to supply the temporal necessities of their unhappy people.   Personally witnessing these miseries, and—while these were raging—seeing hundreds of good and pious Catholic families driven by anti-Catholic landlords from their homes without mercy, while law gave no protection to the tenants—these were the circumstances which gave rise to the first local association in Callan for amending the law of landlord and tenant.

During all this time, and for a period I imagine of not less than twenty or five-and-twenty years, the Rev. John Mullins was parish priest of Callan, and continued to be so till his death, which happened about six or eight months ago.   Before this time the spiritual condition of the parish was far from edifying, and for the best part of a century events had been occurring which showed the evils to which the peculiar character of the people exposed them.   There had been disputes constantly recurring between the parish priests and their curates, and between the secular clergy and a convent of Augustinian monks.   These disputes among the priests had produced their natural effect in dissensions of a rather fierce kind amongst the laity who took one or the other side. The people also, of warm and impetuous dispositions, became involved in disputes among themselves, so that, I am told, for above half a century the parish of Callan had been the scene of the most heartrending disorders, in which religion lost too much of its practical influence. These disputes went so far that the Bishop of that time had on one occasion to direct the people to take from the altar a contumacious priest.

The late parish priest, Father Mullins, by his prudence, wisdom, and discretion, dried up the sources of all these scandals. He lived in perfect amity with the Augustinians; he loved his curates; the whole people revered and loved him; and the flourishing state of religion in Callan at his death proved at once his piety, the goodness of his heart, and the excellence of his judgment. He was a warm advocate of Tenant-Right as a necessary remedy for the wrongs and sufferings of the people. The late Bishop of Ossory (Dr. Kinsella), though opposed to him on many public grounds, acted towards him, wrote and spoke of him, with the warmest terms of affection and respect; and so venerated was he by the clergy of Ossory and the surrounding dioceses, that his funeral and month's mind were both attended by the very unusual number of sixty priests. In a word, I believe he was loved, honoured, revered, respected, and treated with respect by every human being but one; and that one was the present Bishop. How this happened we shall have occasion presently to see.

SECTION II.—*The Two Curates who have been Punished.*

Father Keeffe received priest's orders in 1836. After serving for two years as curate and then for six years as Professor at the Diocesan Seminary, he was sent (about 1843) to Callan, where he has been curate for upwards of eleven years to the Rev. Mr. Mullins. After he had been there about three years, Father Mullins had an attack of paralysis, which, though it left his faculties unimpaired to the last, rendered him very infirm in body; and thus for eight years Father Keeffe, though only curate, had in fact the administration of the parish, for which he was practically responsible. During the dreadful years of famine and fever this duty fell upon him with particular severity, and was discharged with exemplary self-devotion. In 1847 one of his fellow-curates fell a victim to the fever; and in 1848 Father Keeffe was summoned hastily home from the fever hospital to the bedside of another fellow-curate, whom on his return he found dead of this fatal pestilence. During these years of danger and suffering, which fell upon him perhaps more severely than upon any other priest in the diocese, Father Keeffe remained faithful to the scene of his duties, from which he never asked so much as an hour's absence.

When the second curate died, Father O'Shea (ordained in 1840) was sent to fill his place; and for the last six or seven years these two curates have discharged together the duties of this mission; with what result we shall presently see.

In 1849, when the augmented extermination of the people, the decrease of their numbers, and their frightful sufferings, filled every heart with pity, indignation, and alarm, the two curates, with the entire approbation and concurrence of their parish priest, and with the active assistance of the best and most prudent among the laity, founded a society called "The Callan Tenant Protection Society," the object of which was to check by public exposure the frightful acts of tyranny which were being perpetrated in Callan and its neighbourhood; and further to obtain by legal means for the tenants some small share of that protection for person and property which both in theory and in practice has always been denied to the Irish tenant.

From Callan, under the direction of the local clergy, similar societies spread into other parishes and districts and counties where the same local necessities prevailed; and in order to strengthen the action of these local societies and to give them a common direction, they were all united together in the year 1850 in Dublin into a National Society called "The Irish Tenant League." This was not done until, in 1847 and

1848, the Bishops of Ireland had twice unanimously made earnest application to the Government for "an equitable arrangement of the relations between landlords and tenants, founded on commutative justice," as "necessary" for the "protection of the poor" and the "peace and prosperity of the country." And the very year in which the Tenant League was founded (1850), the present Apostolic Delegate and all the Bishops of Ireland told the people, in their Synodical Address, that they were "the victims of the most ruthless oppression that ever disgraced the annals of humanity;" and that they were "treated with a cruelty which would cause the heart to ache if inflicted on the beasts of the field, and for which it would be difficult to find a parallel, save in the atrocities of savage life."

Is this teaching of the Apostolic Delegate true or is it false? If it was all a mistake, the Apostolic Delegate must be a very unsafe and uncertain guide. But if it is true, as the Callan curates believed, their duty, and the duty of every priest in Ireland, was and is, by every lawful means in their power, to try to find a remedy for these terrible calamities. This remedy could only be found in a change of the law; this change of the law under our constitution could only be the result of a general and combined effort made by an association like the Tenant-League; and in this combined effort the selfishness of the upper classes of Catholics, their indifference and the indifference of the people of the larger towns, to the rights and sufferings of the agricultural poor, rendered it necessary that the country priests—that any priest who loved God and the poor of Christ, and had a heart of flesh in his bosom—should take a prominent part.

For six years and more the great ability and zeal of Father O'Shea have enabled him to fulfil this function. Most usefully to the people and most honourably to himself he has been a leader on this question. Wherever a struggle was to be made his voice was to be heard; and his honest and manly understanding secured him the confidence of the people. Father Keeffe co-operated with him in this good work, and gave him every encouragement to persevere; but from many circumstances he was much less prominently before the public.

Two objections I have heard taken to this conduct of the Callan curates by their ill-wishers, and by enemies to the cause of charity which they advocate. It is said, first, that they have done wrong in going out of their own parish and addressing the people in other dioceses and provinces; secondly, that they have done wrong in giving up too much time to these public questions, to the neglect of the spiritual requirements of their own parish. To these objections I trust to give a conclusive answer.

To the first I say, that if the Callan curates have done wrong in going out of their own parish and diocese to carry on the movement for Tenant-Right, Dr. Cullen, the Apostolic Delegate, is the author and encourager of that wrong.

In October 1851, more than a year after the Tenant League was founded, and when it was in full operation, Dr. Cullen being then Archbishop of Armagh and residing in Drogheda, a deputation was appointed by the council of the Tenant League sitting in Dublin to collect in Drogheda funds for its exhausted treasury. Of that deputation I was, as secretary to the Tenant League, a member. Beside me there was no other layman, but there were three priests—Rev. James Dowling, P.P., Rev. Patrick Kelly, P.P., and Rev. Robert Mullen, C.C. Not one of these three priests lived in Drogheda, nor in the county of Louth, nor in the diocese of Armagh. All of them were priests of the diocese of Meath, and two of them had to travel about forty miles to reach Drogheda. The deputation waited first of all upon the Archbishop (Dr. Cullen), just as, at the recent election, in the very same town and at the very same house, Father O'Shea and his deputation waited upon the present Archbishop (Dr. Dixon). Nothing could exceed the kindness with which Dr. Cullen received us ; and he went very far indeed beyond Dr. Dixon in the encouragement which he gave these priests agitating out of their own diocese. His Grace not merely did not object, not merely encouraged, not merely gave us his authority, but gave us authority in writing under his own hand, and encouragement out of his own purse. Dr. Cullen was kind enough to give us one pound sterling as his personal contribution, and an authority to collect from priest and layman in his town of Drogheda. And to whom was this written authority given? Not to me, the only layman of the deputation, but to the Rev. James Dowling, P.P., the priest who, to reach Drogheda, had to go farthest from his own parish and diocese. The following is the letter which Dr. Cullen gave to Father Dowling :—

"DROGHEDA, 27*th October* 1851.

"DEAR SIR,—I cheerfully add my mite to the collection now commenced, which has for its object to aid in obtaining legal relief for the suffering agricultural population of Ireland. Their case is sad indeed; every man endowed with Christian charity must feel a deep interest in it. It is most desirable to have the matter brought in a full and satisfactory manner before Parliament, with the view to get some measure adopted by which the rights and interests of both proprietors and occupiers of the soil may be regulated and protected. It is clear that the present state of things has been most detrimental to landlord and tenant; and it is undoubted that the country will be irretrievably ruined unless the Legislature will adopt some wise and just measure to save it.

"Wishing you and your colleagues every success in your charitable endeavours to assist the poor and oppressed, I have the honour to be your obedient servant,

"✠ PAUL CULLEN.

"Rev. Mr. Dowling, P.P., Clonmellon."

With this letter in hand we went from door to door to the principal Catholic inhabitants of Drogheda. The chief spokesman of the deputation was, of course, the priest whom the Archbishop

had selected as in his judgment its fittest representative.

The "Statement" goes on to relate that in the
interview which Lucas had in Rome with Dr.
Cullen in accordance with the wish of his Holiness, Dr. Cullen gave a very strange account of
the visit to Drogheda.   He felt that he had committed himself in writing, says Lucas, and had to
find some excuse.   This he did by alleging that
he was induced to give the above letter because
Lucas had said that the League was in his debt
£80, and that he had told Dr. Cullen he intended
to retire as soon as he got back his money.

According to this version, which Lucas felt
bound to contradict in every particular, Dr. Cullen
not only contributed himself, but wrote a letter
soliciting money from his own subjects upon false
pretences; thus making not only Lucas and the
deputation, but himself also, co-operators in a
fraudulent design.

"I indignantly defend him," exclaims Lucas,
"against such an imputation, even though it proceeds from himself."

The letter itself shows that its real object was
to enable the deputation to collect money for "*the
suffering population of Ireland.*"

But to whose hands was the money to be intrusted.   To the League, "three-fourths of whom
were [as the Archbishop knew], priests of another
diocese.   [So that if] Father O'Shea erred in

leaving his own diocese to support the view of the Tenant League, he was led astray by the counsel, encouragement, advice, and example of Dr. Cullen himself."

But, says the memorial, if the Callan curates did no wrong in going now and then out of their parish, county, or diocese, perhaps they were absent too long or too frequently.

As to Father Keeffe, he preached every Sunday morning, catechised the children every Sunday afternoon, was never complained of for neglecting a sick call. He hardly ever went out of his district to advocate Tenant Right or any other subject. His most frequent absences were in 1852, when, at the Bishop's request, he made himself as active as possible on behalf of the Bishop's friend Serjeant Shee, to protect whom in his desertion to the Government Father Keeffe was now silenced.

Father O'Shea had been out of the parish upon League business more than Father Keeffe. He had, indeed, during the previous four or five years rendered inestimable service to the cause of the "poor and oppressed." In fact, his co-operation had been, and continued to be, indispensable to the remotest prospect of success. He had been to the cause almost what O'Connell was to the cause of Emancipation; to strike him down was seriously to cripple those engaged in the same charitable undertaking, and it was to accomplish this result for the British Government that, without a fault, he had been so grievously chastised.

His service to the " poor and oppressed," long and good as it had been, was not at the cost of neglecting his parish, but at great self-sacrifice. Every priest has two or three weeks' vacation each year. But from the beginning of the famine in 1845, never but once till 1854 did Father O'Shea allow himself that indulgence. While others were taking their lawful recreation, he remained at home. He was absent, not weeks, but two or three days at a time, taking a toilsome journey to some distant county, labouring hard there, and returning without delay, stinting himself of the necessary sleep and refreshment. Then he was slandered by those who hate the service of the " poor and oppressed," who said, " See how he neglects the duties of his parish." But neither the poor, nor Dr. Cullen, nor Dr. Walsh thought so ; but the enemies of the poor were pleased to *say* so, in order to slander the good work they hated.

What then was the state of the parish ? " By their fruits you shall know them."

On the 26th March 1855, a public meeting was held in Callan, attended by " nearly all the respectable merchants, farmers, and traders of the town," to adopt an address of sorrow and condolence with the curates on their removal and degradation. This address, signed by 150 inhabitants, refers to the incessant preaching of the gospel while the curates were in Callan ; it speaks of their extraordinary labours during the famine and fever ; it speaks of their exertions in the founding of schools, the number of which had been doubled by them ; it speaks of their successful efforts to resist the proselytisers, who in the famine year established a soup-brigade there, in order to allure the starving children from their faith ; they had money without limit, soup, meal, Bible-readers, tract-distributers, and preachers, but they were beaten by these two curates. But more ; the Bishop, said the address, never failed during all this period to praise them for their care of the parish, declaring that the people were highly instructed, the children well educated, that they were filled with accurate know-ledge, and that there were in the parish no scandals and no abuses.

The Bishop could not deny the fact ; but there was other testimony besides his own. The Provincial of the Augustinians, a prudent man, one in no way mixed up with these disputes, the Rev. Dr. Furlong, who had lived long in Callan and knew it well, had drawn up a carefully-prepared paper on the state of religion in that town. This paper, from which the memorialist copies two or three pages of extracts, declares that in the schools, which were got up and brought to their then state of efficiency by Father Mullins and Father Keeffe, education was so flourishing that there was constant application for boys who had been there educated to act as teachers ; that the opportunities given for going to confession surpassed almost any other parish in Ireland ; and that Father O'Shea's catechetical instructions were so interesting that people came from ten miles round to hear him. He said further, that these two curates had put an end to the practice of keeping the shops open on Sundays; and that in so doing, intoxication, quarrels, and faction fights had been stopped. He said, moreover, that the Bishop, at his last visitation, had admitted that there were scarcely any absentees from their Easter duty, and again and more fully, that the morality of the people was up to a very high standard. So far Dr. Furlong. This was the condition of affairs according both to the Doctor and to the Bishop himself on the 22d of July. Exactly three months later this garden of roses had become a desert. What had happened in that very short interval? Nothing in the religion of the place, but something in its politics. His Lordship had found out that Father Keeffe kept a sharp watch on his Lordship's very particular friend Mr. Serjeant Shee. If this vigilance were not checked, the servant of the Government might lose his seat at the next election. The Serjeant sent Father Keeffe's private letter to the *Kilkenny Journal;* the Bishop read it, and the whole face of religion in Callan became instantaneously changed. The people, from being marvellously well instructed and filled with "accurate knowledge," became miraculously ignorant. "Callan presented no longer a society in which every member blossomed and flourished, but a 'large uncultivated field.'

The priests were no longer models of spiritual zeal, but shepherds who ran after their own idle fancies and left the sheep to wander into the desert and poison themselves with noxious food. All this was brought about because it was found that unless episcopal authority did its best in Serjeant Shee's behalf," he would lose his seat, and the Government a supporter.

The priests had not been guilty of employing their time in secular business condemned by the Church ; they had not unduly absented themselves from their parish ; they had not followed such charitable and religious politics as had occupied them against the wish of the people. On the contrary, it was the misery and want of their own people which had driven them into public affairs at all. They had not, for the sake even of these works at once of corporal and spiritual mercy, so acted as to neglect the more obvious duties of their office.

But alas ! one great crime outweighed all their innocence and all their merit. Dr. Cullen had changed his politics, and they had not followed his example. Dr. Walsh patronised a dishonest politician who had broken his promise, and they had manifested an obstinate and perverse attachment to the poor, to honesty, and to truth.

SECTION III.—*The Curate who has been Rewarded.*

The priest who was chosen to take the place of Father Keeffe was, of course, "not a politician," that is, he was a supporter of Serjeant Shee ; for it was quite understood by all parties that to support the Government was not politics. Of 105 clergymen in the diocese of Ossory, he was the only one who did not belong to the Tenant League. This remark is important, as showing to how few the charges made throughout this statement applied. The great, the overwhelming bulk of both Bishops and priests were honest men. It was a comparatively small number who were themselves corruptionists or who sided with them. This curate was the only one in Ossory who stood by Lord Desart and who opposed the Tenant League. In 1850, it will be remembered, Dr. Cullen and all the Irish Bishops publicly denounced the landlords for inflicting upon "virtuous and industrious families" "the most ruthless oppression that ever disgraced humanity," by the cruelty with which they "exterminated" the poor, "levelled cottages," and "unroofed the abodes" of the poor.

When all Callan and Ballycallan (Rev. Mr. ——'s parish) were ringing with the groans of the three hundred wretched creatures whom Lord Desart had driven from their "levelled cottages" and "roofless abodes," and treated with all the atrocious inhumanity of "savage life," as described above, this reverend gentleman alone took his side, thanking him, though not in these express words, for his oppressions, and for bringing in, to replace Catholic innocence and virtue, the abominations of Protestant lust.

He came out boldly as an agitating priest; from the altar he attacked the Tenant League, and applauded Lord Desart. Nor did he confine himself to his own parish, his own county, or his own diocese. No; he made a foray into the parish of Ballingarry, in the county of Tipperary, in the diocese of Cashel, to denounce a Tenant-Right meeting in that parish. Neither did he stop short at mere denunciation. While the above horrors were being perpetrated, he came publicly forward with Lord Desart's agent to coerce or cajole the tenantry who remained on the estate into presenting an address of thanks and congratulation, declaring that hitherto mutual goodwill had existed between him and his tenants. And in a second address to the same effect, and to which he affixed his own signature, he did so, as he said, with the sincerest pleasure. The tenants' address went on to assert that an "amicable concurrence between landlord and tenant" "was happily at work on the estate;" and, further, that they, the tenants, were "pressed by no peculiar difficulties, had no complaint for the present or fear for the future;" and, to conclude, that the agent, a Mr. Lane, had "invariably enjoyed the attachment, the confidence, and the respect of the tenantry."

In reply to this, a meeting of the Callan Tenant Protection Society, Father Mullins in the chair, passed a resolution that "the sentiments which this address embodies are such as no Christian having a regard to truth and a knowledge of the estate would subscribe to."

This was the non-politician whom the Bishop appointed to preach the gospel in the town of Callan. "Politics," in the dialect of the appointment, meant to love the people and serve them. Those only were politicians who stood between the people and their oppressors. Alone, the new parish priest could not do much ; an agitation cannot be carried on single-handed. But he could do something, and he was not idle. A certain poor woman, Mary Kearney, had died of starvation. She had applied for relief to the Union ; but, after a consultation between Lord Desart and another of the guardians, relief was refused, and in two days the poor woman was dead. At an investigation on oath, Dr. Cronyn, a Protestant bigot, swore that she died for want of food. In other words, this poor wretch had been deliberately killed by the inhumanity of Lord Desart and the Board of Guardians ; and the coroner's jury found in accordance with these facts, charging the guardians with failure of duty. Two other similar cases occurred within two months, one being the case of a poor pregnant woman within a month of her delivery.   The verdict was "died of starvation."

Lucas was in some doubt as to whether it was politics to endeavour to remedy this state of things.   At any rate, the clergy prepared lists of Catholic candidates to replace at the next poor-law election the inhuman guardians by men having the bowels of compassion.   The curate of Bally-callan, where he was graduating for a Parish when the fulness of time should come, exerted himself to the utmost to defeat the Catholic can-didate, and to support the Protestant, put forward by the Board.

"See," says the "Statement," "how the Bishop's words and acts hang together."

In his letter of 22d October 1854 he affects to believe that the spiritual interests of Callan have been neglected by reason of the attention of the priests to politics, and to remedy such an evil, so arising, his Lordship makes choice of a parish priest who is remarkable for his disposition to active politics; whose politics have been against the people and in favour of the oppressors; who has openly taken part with those bigoted Protes-tants whose remorseless cruelties have been prac-tised upon the Catholics whose pastor he is to be; a man whom they might (if such a thing could be) justly hate, since they cannot but feel that his cassock is steeped in the blood of their brethren; a man not neutral, but chosen for his known enmity to the late parish priest; one about whom

the late parish priest and the most respectable
men in Callan had publicly pronounced the judgment that he was either "no Christian" or had
"no regard for truth." This was the man who
was to till the "uncultivated field" of Callan.

By way of commencement, he within a month
began a public attack on his own curates from the
altar, giving the people, on one occasion, to understand that, in his opinion, Father O'Shea ought
never to have been ordained.

Other scandals too disgusting to repeat here
are contained in the "Statement," and then the
memorialist thus sums up the case :—

"The Bishop affects to believe that the salvation of souls in Callan requires a more zealous
ministry. To bring this about he removes from
Callan two of the ablest priests in the diocese,
second to none in their zeal for missionary duty,
for attending the sick, for education, for catechis-
ing, for preaching, and for confession—two priests
adored by the people, and endeared to them by
the memory of countless services rendered at the
hazard of their lives. He sends there a priest said
to be deficient in understanding, ridiculous in his
manners, hated for his past conduct, regarded by
many inhabitants of his new parish (connections
of Lord Desart's victims) as a personal enemy, a
bad preacher, indifferent about Catholic education,
despised by all who do not hate him.

"One merit he has, and one demerit Father
O'Shea and Father Keeffe, which accounts for

this strange phenomenon. He openly professes and actively practises the politics which the Bishop wishes to thrust upon the people; the others stand as the great obstruction between the Bishop and the gratification of his political will.

" The real question at issue in these appointments and removals is, not to render spiritually fertile the 'large uncultivated field' of Callan, but to re-elect for the county of Kilkenny, in spite of his breach of promises to the people, the Bishop's personal friend and the servant of Lord Palmerston—Mr. Serjeant Shee."

SECTION IV.—*The Bishop of Ossory as a Politician.*

It was said that the Bishop of Ossory himself took no part in politics. Nevertheless it was the fact that, previous to the election of 1852, he had at various conference dinners of his clergy told them "that he expected they would exert themselves in favour of Serjeant Shee." The priests of Ossory throughout the county did so exert themselves, travelling from one end of the country to the other; and none was so active as Father O'Shea. It was indeed entirely attributable to the exertions of the clergy that the Serjeant was elected; and it was Father Keeffe and Father O'Shea who persuaded him, in the midst of great discouragement, to persevere with his canvass. To all this the Bishop made no objection, the "uncultivated field" of Callan was not supposed to be neglected at that time.

Thus it would appear that it was religion to support Serjeant Shee, and irreligion to oppose him.

It was true, indeed, that the Bishop did not in 1854–55 attend public meetings or make public speeches on behalf of the Whigs. To do so would be a dangerous experiment in the then state of popular feeling. But his Lordship did, at dinner tables and in private conversations, make known his opinions and wishes; and thus gathered round him all those Whig Catholic gentry who looked upon politics as a means of personal advancement, and who cared nothing for the poor. His priests he influenced by means of ecclesiastical patronage. Other Whig Bishops employed the same means; and, with these two instruments in hand, it was not necessary to make public speeches or to write letters in the public journals in order to be very active and very mischievous politicians.

Dr. Walsh had always been a Whig, and had always opposed O'Connell; and to such a pitch did his hostility to that family run, that in 1848, at a time when the Repeal Association, of which John O'Connell was the leader, was supposed to be a sort of barrier to the warlike designs of the Young Irelanders, who had seceded from it, he (Dr. Walsh) compelled Father Lynch, who was acting as treasurer to a fund collected for the Association, to return the money to the clerical contributors.   Yet when John O'Connell (who had retired from public life in 1851) again came forward in 1853 as an opponent of the Independent party, his Lordship contributed £3 to a fund raised for the same John O'Connell for his support to the Whigs.   This countenance of the Bishop was given in the most public manner possible.   " Such," says the " Statement," "are the evidences which his Lordship has given of his aversion to intermeddling in politics. Unhappily they have only served to convince the world that he is a vehement and intolerant partisan, and that his Lordship's protestations against clerical politics are made, first, to serve as a pretext for punishing politicians from whom he differs, and, secondly, as a convenient form of words by which to mislead the Congregation of Propaganda and the Supreme Pontiff."

Section V.—*The Reign of Terror.*

As I approach the ecclesiastical part of this question, and find myself obliged to speak more freely upon the practice of ecclesiastical discipline, I feel it necessary to explain why I, a layman, venture to treat of such subjects.   My answer to such an objection is very simple.   Even if these matters were not in point of fact intimately connected with politics and secular affairs, I conceive it would not be beyond the province of any layman to lay before the Holy See whatever he prudently conceives important to be known, and not likely to reach the Supreme Pontiff by any other means. In the present instance, everything I have to say about ecclesiastical discipline, besides being, as I conceive, important in itself, has unhappily a direct bearing upon secular affairs, and upon the relations of the laity to the Church. Moreover, I am sorry to say that, though a vast number of clergymen concur in my views ; though almost all the facts I have to state are derived from clergymen of the highest respectability, and in many instances are confirmed by irrefutable documentary evidence ; yet the difficulty to a clergyman of approaching the Holy See ; owing partly to positive obstructions interposed by certain Bishops, partly to the reign of terror which Dr. Cullen has introduced into Ireland, is so great that, practically speaking, it is not possible for these things to be conveyed to the Holy See except through the agency of a layman.

Yes, I am sorry to say, under Dr. Cullen's rule a reign of terror prevails in Ireland. Not a reign of authority, respect, willing obedience, cheerful submission, founded on a sense of justice and of right ; but obedience with discontent ; submission with a bitter, rankling sentiment of injustice ; authority reverenced for the function and the office, but not for the uses to which it is applied, or the person by whom it is wielded. I know the sentiment prevails in certain quarters that this reign of terror will answer all practical purposes, will overbear all obstacles, and will enable those who exercise it to carry out their designs to a successful issue.   For my part, I think this is a very mistaken calculation.   I take for granted that what the Holy See wishes at all times, but what is especially necessary at the present time, when great works like the founding of a university have to be accomplished by the general co-operation of the clergy and the people, is not an unwilling but a willing obedience; an obedience willing to sacrifice much, to make extraordinary efforts, to go a good way beyond the dull track of a common routine.   If at this time it is thought that no extraordinary effort is needed; perhaps the rule of a rod-of-iron obedience produced anyhow; war made upon the noblest; and direct preference given to the basest and most corrupt; for aught I know this method of government, though never very wholesome, may answer all the ends in view.   On such an hypothesis it is idle for any of us to trouble ourselves about the public service, and the sooner we are made to understand this the better.   But if great deeds are to be done and great ends nobly struggled for, then I venture to say that the present unquestionable reign of terror is to the last degree mischievous in itself and dangerous to the authority of the Holy See.

The prime agent in this reign of terror is, I am sorry to say, the Archbishop of Dublin.   The nature of it is very simple ; it arises *from the belief* that he is omnipotent in Rome; that in all things, from the highest to the lowest, his will is law; that what he wishes with regard to the appointment of new Bishops, the enacting of new statutes, the administration of the details of discipline, the rendering of justice or injustice between priest and Bishop, the punishment and the promotion of every ecclesiastic—that everything of this kind, in every province, and almost in every diocese in Ireland, depends upon his single will.   Sooner or later, directly or indirectly, in one way or another, he is supposed to have every priest in Ireland (or almost every priest) at his mercy.   Woe, not to those who fail in rendering canonical obedience to their lawful superior, but to those who in any way presume to obstruct his will.   Nor is his will supposed to be regulated by justice or guided in all things by truth.   The notion is that with this "will," a corrupt, selfish, subservient, untruthful spirit has a better chance than uprightness, heroism, and high-minded magnanimity; and I must say that the experience which I have been in a condition to acquire rather confirms than overthrows this gloomy view of our position.

The cases of Father O'Shea and Father Keeffe in part illustrate this system and the reign of terror which flows from it.   Here are two priests, whom everybody knows to have committed none but a political offence, most severely chastised at Dr. Cullen's instigation ; and as to one of them, an attempt made by Dr. Cullen himself, at variance with every notion of justice, to get inflicted upon him a yet more terrible punishment. Dr. Cullen has not yet succeeded, but no doubt the very first opportunity will be taken to suspend Father O'Shea or excommunicate him, or whatever worse can be inflicted upon him by an ecclesiastical tribunal. So people think, and to common minds the attempt already made to have him suspended without cause fully justifies this gloomy anticipation of Father O'Shea's future treatment.

This blow has struck, as it was intended to strike, terror far and wide. Not the wholesome fear of breaking the law, for no law has been broken, but the slavish dread of offending the arbitrary will of one man believed to be unjust. But the blow does not stop here. It is believed that the Callan curates were punished not in reliance upon right, but upon Dr. Cullen's omnipotence in Rome.

Father Keeffe applies for leave to come to Rome, where alone he can effectually prosecute his appeal. The Bishop flatly refuses him permission. It is believed that the Bishop puts this obstruction in the way of justice in full reliance upon Dr. Cullen's omnipotence at Rome.

And is this belief without plausibility? Dr. Cullen's letters from Rome to Ireland during the pendency of this affair have been expressly calculated to create and confirm this belief. True or false, I am sure Dr. Cullen wishes to have it so understood. To two of his Grace's letters, intended to convey this idea, and published—one of them by his vicar-general—I have been obliged to give the flattest contradiction that was consistent with the respect due to so high an ecclesiastic. In those letters about an affair yet pending before the Holy See, in which I had followed with scrupulous exactness the exhortations of his Holiness to seek peace and concord, and had carried out most exactly the advice of Propaganda—in those letters Dr. Cullen informed the people of Ireland through the newspapers that I was treated here as an erring and unfaithful son of the Church, ridiculed me for my supposed practices of devotion, and held me up to the contempt of the Irish people for the docility with which I followed the counsel of the highest ecclesiastical authority. Personally I am quite willing to endure much more ignominy than Dr. Cullen has cast or can cast upon me; but it is of the impression made or intended to be made upon the public mind in Ireland with regard to the general state of this question that I have a right to complain. The impression intended to be conveyed was that, right or wrong, Dr. Cullen could carry anything at Rome, that he could trample upon any opponent however just his cause, and make merry over him when he had achieved his unjust victory.

But these *published* letters were not all. Now and then we get indications of unpublished letters which are privately producing the same effect and with the same regard to truth.   There lies before me a pretty full minute of a very curious conversation which on the 6th of February last Father O'Shea had with the Bishop of Ossory at his Lordship's request.   At that time, though the Callan case had been a good deal spoken about, it will be remembered that no formal application about it had yet been made at Rome in any shape, and therefore that no decision could have been taken.   At this very moment no decision has been taken, nor can have been taken, because the case has not yet been formally laid before Propaganda.   Yet on the 6th February, two months ago, the Bishop of Ossory had received (or said he had received) from Rome the statement which he used in the following conversation :—

"I called," says Father O'Shea, "at one o'clock, and saw his Lordship, when a conversation of nearly an hour followed. No one was present but ourselves.   His Lordship began by saying that as he had received a document from Rome, in which, as far as he was concerned, he was told that he was out of this business, he wished to speak to me on some matters, &c. &c.   I asked him did he mean the Callan case, in which I and Father Keeffe were concerned, was decided in his favour. He said he did.   I asked his Lordship to show me the document.   He said he would not.   I told him my reason for wishing to see the document arose from the fact that I was in possession of information of an entirely opposite character. The Bishop, however, persevered in saying that he had the document referred to, and in refusing to show it.   After a long conversation on other matters his Lordship again told me that the Callan case was settled in his favour.   I again expressed surprise, as I had information to the contrary.   He said his object in sending for me was to tell me this, and that what he had said to me was also meant for Father Keeffe ; and that now, as the matter was decided in his favour, he wished to tell me, &c. &c."

Any letter from Rome on this matter on which the Bishop of Ossory could rely must, I suppose, have been directly or indirectly from Dr. Cullen. I the more readily believe it came from Dr. Cullen because long before the 6th February I had the honour to receive through a Bishop a message from Dr. Cullen to tell me that my business was settled, and that I had better leave Rome, as it was only a waste of time to remain there. At that time I had not laid my business before the Holy See, nor could a decision have been taken ; but the purpose of the message was to convince me that my business was decided before it was proposed, and that any business proposed against Dr. Cullen was decided before it was heard.

But whether the "document" referred to was sent by Dr. Cullen or invented by the Bishop of Ossory, the main fact is the same. Last February the Bishop most interested on Dr. Cullen's side did not scruple officially and authoritatively to promulgate a decision of the Holy See in his favour about a case which had not yet been brought under the cognisance of the Holy See. In this announcement there was not, and there could not be, the smallest shred of truth. But the object of such an announcement, whoever was responsible for it, is very clear.

At that time, and for several weeks previous, efforts had been made by certain priests in Ireland to procure signatures to a memorial to be presented, on the part of the clergymen signing it, to the Holy Father, laying before his Holiness statements of considerable importance respecting the condition of affairs in Ireland. On the other hand, every effort was made to deter by terror clergymen who wished to sign the memorial from doing so. One powerful means of influencing the ignorant by terror was falsely to persuade them that Dr. Cullen's omnipotence had procured for the Bishop of Ossory from the Holy See a final decision in his favour even before the complaint had been made known. To show how this and things like this have operated by terror to prevent priests saying to the Holy See what they believe to be true in matters of importance, I will transcribe part of a letter which I have received from the priest who acted as secretary to the committee for preparing the memorial :—

"Many are the reasons given in reply to my application for not signing the memorial. One parish priest writes to say that he could not prudently sign it, as he dreads the vengeance of his Bishop if he came to know it, and adds '*ex uno disce omnes.*' Another writes that very many of the priests of his diocese would sign it, but are in dread of their Bishop. Another writes that he must not sign it because he never would have any business to go near his uncle (the Bishop of a neighbouring diocese) if he did so; others could not ascertain the feelings of their

Bishop on the subject, and would not sign it on that account. Two priests from two dioceses very remote from Dublin write to say that Dr. Cullen through his agents was doing all he could to prevent the memorial being signed, and that many who aspire to a high position in the Church are deterred from giving their signatures in order to curry favour with the Apostolic Delegate, and thereby gain the object of their aspirations. And so on. I have a large heap of letters which show that the best wishes of the great majority of the priests of Ireland are for the memorial, and that fear of the displeasure of their spiritual superiors is the prevailing cause of their refusal to put their signatures to it.

"I may here add that the Wexford priests wish that their requisition and resolutions, in which seventy (70) of them co-operated, should take the place of the memorial and be represented in that way at Rome. The same may perhaps be said of the Mayo priests, and again of the clergy of Clare."

Other communications from other quarters employ similar language with a more general application. "The priests of this diocese," says one, "are afraid to give expression to their sentiments; they are afraid even of each other—such is the reign of terror." I have myself heard priests express similar sentiments, particularly in the diocese of Dublin. Several priests in that diocese were anxious that some representation of the present calamitous state of things should be made to the Holy See, but they dare take no part in it. One of them said to me very emphatically, "I will sign such a memorial if it is necessary, but I know that I shall be victimised." Another, who equally dare not sign the memorial, said, "If our Archbishop succeeds in Rome in his designs, I fear it will create a schism."

What very many priests in Ireland believe to be true—believe it to be of the last importance to have said in Rome, but dare not say through the reign of terror which, under the present rule, stifles the honest expression of what is thought and known by hundreds if not thousands of priests loyal and devoted to the Holy See—that I venture to say as their representative, knowing the sentiments which they dare not utter, relying on the facts and documents which most respectable members of their body have told me or written to me or put into my hands, and in all material points as far as I am able, copying their very words.

Section VI.—*The Bishop of Ossory as Bishop.*

In entering upon this part of the case, my object is to show that the Bishop of Ossory's unjust treatment of the Callan curates not only proceeds from his strong political feelings and antipathies, but is part of a system of management regularly pursued since his Lordship was made Bishop to enforce, not canonical obedience, but abject and absolute submission on the part of his clergy to his own will, however extravagant that will may be; to reward all priests, however theologically incompetent, who are the fit tools of his will, and to punish all, however meritorious and venerable, who have sufficient manhood to guard their

canonical and legitimate independence. How
this has been done it now becomes my duty to
explain ; and I enter upon the subject in behalf of
those whom a reign of terror silences, because I
have always understood that the principle of
ecclesiastical discipline is not arbitrary will and
personal favour, but rule and law ; that the Church
from her subordinate ministers exacts obedience
indeed, but obedience according to the canon ; and
that she trusts none of her subordinate rulers with
absolute power, does not permit those in authority
to tyrannise over their subjects, but requires
everything to be brought to the test of rule as
regards conduct, and of merit as regards personal
treatment.

How the present Bishop of Ossory has acted
since his consecration is in part explained in the
following extract of a letter written last year by
one of the most experienced priests of his diocese,
not addressed to me, nor written with any notion
of its being quoted for any purpose whatever, but
simply the private letter of an Ossory priest, very
friendly to the Bishop, which has accidentally
come into my hands :—

"The Bishop began his reign by rewarding those who voted
for him, which you will see by a little reflection. There was
not one of them who did not receive some mark or other of his
gratitude. That was the first process of corruption, and it has
gone on ever since."

Of course, even if in all cases promotion had
actually gone by personal favour, I could not

prove, nor could anybody prove, that the promotion was of an absolutely unworthy person. Many priests who gave their votes for the present Bishop were worthy and excellent men, and · I have specified this in order to put on record and illustrate the belief which on this subject is very widely spread. But the true test for favour, as I am informed, in this diocese is not so much past service as subserviency to the Bishop's present will, even should that will be in opposition to the Holy See. This is a grave charge. Let us see how it is borne out.

Here Lucas narrates in considerable detail how the proposal of a simultaneous collection throughout Ireland for the Catholic University on St. Patrick's Day, 1851, originated with the Callan curates. Their parish priest, Father Mullins, communicated it to the University Committee, who recommended it to all the parishes in Ireland.

On that occasion, neither the Bishop nor either of his Vicars, nor his Vicar-General contributed; nor was any collection made in any of the city parishes, nor any appeal to the faithful of the diocese to carry out the personal wishes of the Holy Father. It was understood, on the contrary, that whoever complied with the injunction of the Apostolic See incurred the reprobation of the See of Ossory. Only thirteen out of thirty-nine parishes contributed. The contri-

butions were from earnest friends of the Independent party; the arch-supporter of the Holy
See being Father Mullins of Callan.

, He was, with little delay, made to feel the
displeasure of the Bishop, who kept up a fire of
insulting letters addressed to himself, importing
gross and calumnious imputations against him as
a priest. This the Bishop did without inquiring
into the truth of the charges, but taking Father
Mullins's guilt for granted on the word of persons of disreputable character. How the Callan
curates were treated has already appeared.

Another priest, the Rev. William Lynch, who
contributed £5 to the University collection, was
removed from one of the Bishop's parishes in
Kilkenny to a remote rural curacy, being told
by the Bishop at the same time that he had no
fault to find with him. And again, of four
benefices disposed of since March 1851, three
were given to clergymen who had not subscribed
to the University.

On another question also, on which the Holy
See had pronounced an opinion, the Bishop
sided against the Holy See. Pope Gregory XVI.
had, in a decree already quoted, exhibited the
most marked suspicion of the National School
system, and had recommended strongly, as the
reader will remember, that where schools for
Catholics were established under the National
Board, the buildings themselves should remain
the property of the Bishop or parish priest.

Now, the Bishop of Ossory agreed with the late Dr. Murray of Dublin in liking the National Board and the Queen's (godless) Colleges, and in liking the politicians who founded them. So strong was this liking, that he did his utmost to persuade the Archdeacon of the diocese to invest the school-house of his parish (Ballyhale) in the hands of the Board of Commissioners. The Archdeacon, having the directions of the Holy See before his eyes, and desiring to please God rather than man, resisted the pressure put upon him by the Bishop. The effect upon himself is declared in a letter addressed to his Lordship, long before the present disputes began, in which the writer complains that, ever since his refusal, he has felt the absence of his Lordship's usual courtesy, and which concludes with these words :—

"Come weal, come woe, I hope, with the blessing of God, ever to be found standing unflinchingly by, not only the decisions, but also the admonitions, which emanate from the Chair of Peter."

As part of the same policy of Ossory against Rome in the matter of education, the Bishop co-operated in the erection in Kilkenny of a National Model School, which is only a sort of godless college under another name. It was said that the Bishop not only gave his countenance, but that he subscribed his money to this school. It was opened in November 1854, and the Protes-

tant and Government party in general triumphed
in what the Bishop had done.   In this school,
even at the very outset, the mistress who had to
teach the Catholic infants was a Protestant, and
to this arrangement the Bishop tacitly assented.

There was nothing whatever to prevent the very
danger which the editor of the *Tablet* had foreseen with regard to the godless colleges being
actually carried into effect in the Kilkenny Model
School ; a danger on which the vehement articles
referred to before were written.

To return to the government of the diocese.
Besides censures conveyed in speeches at conferences and in letters, there were other ways of
"influencing" the clergy.   The chief of these was
the patronage engine.   This was worked by practising on the hopes and fears of the curates, who
were seduced into an obsequious conformity with
the will of the Bishop on matters which the canons
of the Church leave free.   Thus, when a parish
of the first degree of excellence became vacant,
a skilful "promoter" created other vacancies by
appointing to the first, not the most deserving
curate, but the occupant of some parish of the
second grade ; and so on throughout the number
of parishes whose incumbents it was desired to
influence by hope.   Other curates were worked
upon by the fear of removal to remote places, as
had been Fathers Keeffe and O'Shea.

The "Statement" then gives in tabulated

form the names of both priests and parishes where such removals have taken place; and mentions, in addition, that offers of promotion had been made to, and rejected by, others whose names are not contained in the list.

CHAPTER V.

SECTION I.—*The Case Statea.*

THE questions discussed in the former chapters, looking at them from their political side, are for the most part questions of the means to be taken to attain a particular end. The end in view is the formation of such an Irish party in the House of Commons as may secure the rights of the poor, the interests of the country, the redress of Catholic grievances, and the protection of the Church. The means to that end are the election of members of Parliament, and specially the interference and action of the priests. Hitherto we have been speaking about *the means*, and we have seen that on this subject there are two very opposite opinions. But when we come to consider *the end*, that is, the organisation of a party in Parliament for the redress of grievances, we find a difference of opinion exactly analogous to that which prevails about elections and the conduct of the priests. For the most part, those who think and say that the intervention of priests at elections ought to be public, general, energetic ;

that it should be inspired by high motives, free from all taint of personal interest or profit, uncontaminated with corruption, and devoted solely to the Church and the poor, think likewise, and say, that the parliamentary party to produce which such an agency is to be directed should also be devoted solely to the Church and to the poor; should also be inspired by high motives; led by a disinterested sense of public duty; seeking favours from no Government until public grievances be redressed; opposing every Government that refuses to redress these grievances; employing all their strength and influence to procure this redress, and wasting neither in the pursuit of mere personal advantages.

Those, on the other hand, who say that priests should not interfere in politics (though they do the exact opposite of what they say and are most energetic politicians), say also, and encourage other men to think and say, that the members to be returned to Parliament—at the risk and suffering of the people—should straightway connect themselves with what is called a Liberal Government, if such a one exists, or with some section of the Protestant Liberal party, if the Liberals are out of office; should apply their minds to secure offices and promotion for themselves, and smaller places for their friends and supporters by a diligent service of their Protestant patrons; that if the diligence and ability of this service entitles them to some return from the Minister, they should be encouraged to take as much of that return as they can, in profit and emolument to themselves and their friends ; and that only the refuse of their time, their thought, their labour, and their influence—so much of all these as they can conveniently spare from the pursuit of their own personal ambition and interest—should be given to the service of the Church and of the poor.

These two sets of opinions almost always go together. Those who wish the priests to be active in elections, and are loud in insisting upon their disinterestedness, also wish and strive to maintain in the House of Commons an Independent party whose primary object shall be the Church and the poor. Those who profess to dislike the public interference of priests in politics, and really patronise amongst them venality and the pursuit of self-interest, strive to maintain in the House of Commons a servile body of Catholic members, devoted to the Protestant Liberals, active only in the pursuit of place and emoluments, and whose well-understood principle it is never to go so far in advocating Catholic rights as to endanger in the smallest degree the pursuit of their own interests.

Of course I cannot and do not expect that the Holy See will pronounce a formal opinion upon a question of policy which depends upon an intimate knowledge of the mechanism of our constitution and government. But yet it must be borne in mind that this is not a question foreign to the interests of the Holy See, nor is it one with regard to which the Holy See can well refrain from acting in one way or another.   Indeed, it is too true that, if the Holy See has not already pronounced an opinion on this subject, it has, I believe, without intending to do so, engaged and committed itself in public opinion on one side in this dispute. As matters now go, it is not neutral between the two parties.   It has already taken a side, and the side which it has taken is the side of those who make politics a selfish game and give the refuse of their labours to the Church and the poor; while in the name of the Holy See everything is being done by the highest authority to crush every unselfish and generous effort for the service of the Church and of the poor, and to discourage, discountenance, and defame everybody who shows by his actions that he is determined to prefer the public cause to the pursuit of his private interest.

I speak now not of the act of any simple Bishop, but of the acts of Dr. Cullen, the Apostolic Delegate, the especial representative of the Holy See, who has abandoned the former and more honourable policy in order to adopt the latter and less honourable, and of whom it is carefully spread abroad in every direction that he has changed his political course in order the more fully to carry out the views of the Holy See, which wishes the Catholics of the British Empire to continue in a degrading slavery to the author of the " Durham Letter " and the founders of the Queen's Colleges, and the most resolute upholders of the Established Church.

Whatever, then, may be the real wishes of the Supreme Pontiff, this much at least is certain, as I shall hereafter prove, namely, that by the conduct of Dr. Cullen the Holy See has been made a party to this dispute ; has been deeply immersed in the party politics of England ; has been made to take the side of its worst enemies and most treacherous friends ; has had its honour deeply involved in the course pursued ; and at this very moment, by the choice that has been made for it, strange to say, is a party to the designs against itself.   It is, therefore, no longer a question as to whether the Holy See shall or shall not interest itself in the internal politics of England.   If Dr. Cullen does indeed represent the Holy See, we who stand by the policy to which, in 1851, his Grace invited us to adhere, now find ourselves subjected to the vigorous opposition of the Holy See, which, in the person of him, its Delegate, is our most resolute antagonist.

At the same time I cannot but remember with great thankfulness and satisfaction that however opposed by the Apostolic Delegate, it was my peculiar fortune to receive here in Rome from the lips of the Supreme Pontiff a very high and flattering encomium on the course I have pursued in Parliament ; than which approbation I desire no higher honour upon earth.   If in any respect my course in Parliament or out of Parliament has been mistaken, I am anxious to amend it; but in the meantime so many false rumours have been so industriously circulated, and so much misconception prevails about the reasons for pursuing one course rather than another in Parliament, that I think it well to offer here a few words of explanation derived from my own practical experience.

SECTION II.—*The Policy of Independent Opposition.*

Every man who wishes to make politics a game of personal ambition or personal profit, and everybody who, for whatever reason, desires to serve the English Government, employs himself, as a matter of course, in decrying and misrepresenting this policy, which was that of Dr. Cullen in 1851; was by him recommended to us at that time; has been by us faithfully pursued to the best of our ability; but by his Grace most unaccountably deserted. In the conference which, at the suggestion of the Secretary of Propaganda, I had recently the honour of having with Dr. Cullen, his Grace went even so far as to compare our legal opposition in Parliament with the revolutionary projects and designs of Mazzini; from which and from some other circumstances I am not, I think, very rash in inferring that Dr. Cullen has been trying here to represent us as the advocates of a revolutionary policy. These flagrant misrepresentations make it necessary for me to explain exactly what is the " Policy of Independent Opposition " which in 1851 we adopted with Dr. Cullen's instigation, and to which we have since steadily adhered.

To any one who is practically acquainted with the English constitution this policy needs no explanation. It springs from the admitted practice of our form of government, and is the course which every other body of politicians, circumstanced as we are and whose efforts are exclusively directed to public objects, would and must necessarily pursue.

Our government, as it exists in Parliament, consists of two parts, the Ministry and the Opposition. Both these are essential parts of the machine of government, the Opposition quite as indispensable as the Ministry. It would be a great mistake to consider the parliamentary opposition to a Cabinet of Ministers as anything hostile to the Government, as an anomaly, as a thing to be deplored or got rid of, if it were possible. These may be Continental notions, but they are not the views entertained by any wise Englishman conversant with the working of our institutions. Far from being a thing to be deplored, an Opposition in Parliament, a vigorous and active Opposition, is a thing habitually to be desired ; a thing which no intelligent supporter of a Ministry deserving to exist would object to ; a thing which every Minister of any sense or capacity would desire to see meeting him face to face.

On the Continent, wherever parliamentary government has been attempted, opposition in the Chamber has ordinarily been little more than a cloak for revolutionary purposes; and the leaders of Opposition have been little more than agents to revolutionary clubs. There have been brilliant exceptions to this even on the Continent; but in England very different notions and a very different habit prevail. With us, a good Opposition is necessary to the perfect organisation of a good Ministry. The one is the necessary complement of the other, and where the Opposition becomes feeble and contemptible, the organisation of the majority which supports the Government loses its strength — the force of cohesion is weakened or disappears—discipline becomes loosened—and the Minister himself very often regrets that, in place of an open hostility from without, which would have kept his partisans true to their allegiance and firm in support of him, he has had to encounter mutiny within his ranks, and a discontent which turns the whole system of parliamentary government into confusion. In England, then, parliamentary opposition is never objected to, never connected with revolution, but always considered, whichever side is in Opposition, as an essentially conservative part of our representative government. It is not revolutionary, but, according to our habits and experience, is a positive safeguard against revolution and preservative of our laws. In accordance with this view, a phrase is in use amongst us which speaks of "her Majesty's Opposition;" the opposition being not directed against the Crown or form of government, but being, within the limits of the law, the most convenient expression of that moderate and reasonable divergence of opinion which must exist in all human affairs.

This being premised, it will be more easily understood that, with us, the immediate purpose of a parliamentary Opposition is not always or necessarily to turn out the existing Government. Sometimes for years together an Opposition, though powerful by the talents and character of its members, is too weak in numbers to have any such object immediately in view. Yet, night after night, it maintains its opposition with a hopeless minority, strong only in its conviction of being right. Though weak in numbers, it may be powerful in reason and eloquence ; and even Ministers of State are often preserved from blunders and deterred from acts of injustice by the dread of public exposure and rebuke before the eyes of the whole country on so exalted a theatre, though inflicted by the leaders of an insignificant minority.

The immediate purpose, then, of several very brilliant Oppositions in our late history has been not at all to turn out the Ministry, but to modify public opinion in Parliament and out of it; to control the Ministry by discussion and argument ; to render them more cautious by fear of exposure;

and to save the opinions entertained by the Opposition from sinking into that contempt which naturally awaits opinions that have no public defender or exponent.

This function is one which, as a general rule, every reasonable supporter of a Ministry desires to see well and vigorously performed by an Opposition. Those who most warmly and honestly support the Ministry know very well that, however good it may be, like all human things it has its imperfections; and they desire to see those imperfections corrected. If it acts amiss, or if in any respect it adopts a less prudent course, it is not the function of a supporter of the Ministry to lay bare its errors, or to make the most of its shortcomings. Any supporter of the Ministry, however, whose patriotism was stronger than his party zeal, would desire, in the interest of the whole community, to have those errors laid bare and those shortcomings exposed. He would not do this work himself in any particular instance, because he would not feel it to be his function or consistent with his general and ordinary position. But he would wish in the interest of the whole community to see it done by some one, and he would look naturally to the leaders of the Opposition to do it as effectually as they could; nay in his own heart, perhaps privately with his own lips, would thank them for doing it well. In England we all know that every political combination and question has two sides; that in politics the

truth never lies wholly on one side; that the
interest of the public consists in hearing all sides
of every political question thoroughly discussed,
and all possible light thrown upon it from every
point of the compass, and even from the feeblest
and most flickering taper.   I do not say that this
mode of carrying on affairs is suited to every state
of society or to the habits of every country; but,
as a matter of fact, I say that it is suitable to our
state of society, and to our habits and traditions;
that with us to maintain this within reasonable
limits is conservative, and to oppose it is revolutionary.

Again, the business of an Opposition, according
to our notions, is not to oppose everything which
the Government brings forward.   In our notions,
in our practice, and in our language, we distinguish
between a factious and a constitutional Opposition; one which uses its place and the means at its
disposal to ensure fair discussion, and a reasonable
exposition of every side of all important questions,
and an Opposition which without reason simply
makes use of the forms of the constitution to obstruct and interrupt, which opposes without really
objecting, which says *No* to everything, and which
never allows its zeal for the public good to over-
ride its hostility to the Ministers.   With us, the
strongest, the ablest, the most eloquent, the most
unscrupulous Opposition dare not oppose indiscriminately.   If it attempted such a course, it
would injure its own character, and damage itself

more than the Ministry. If the Ministry brings forward a measure generally acknowledged to be good, the recognised duty of the Opposition is to give it its support, to improve it if practicable, but to give the Minister credit for whatever excellence it may contain. To oppose everything without regard to the public service would be simply to ruin the Opposition. In short, the business of an Opposition, as practised with us, is to give the fullest and ablest expression to those differences of opinion which in every assembly and in every community must prevail, and to help both Parliament and the public to understand more fully the projects and the policy of the Ministry by saying without reserve whatever can honestly or plausibly be said against them.

The business of an Opposition, therefore, is not to object to everything, but to support what it thinks right and to oppose what it thinks objectionable. Its business is not necessarily to turn out the Ministry, but to do everything which can be done by public discussion to expose its misconduct and correct its mistakes. Its business is not to promote revolution or a violent overthrow of the Government, but to render revolution at once needless and impossible by giving effect to all just complaints, and by providing a remedy for all grievances within the constitution itself.

With us, those who should discredit constitutional opposition would be considered the great friends of revolution. Nor with reference to our

habits or our state of society can there be more
dangerous revolutionists, propagators of more mischievous and insurrectionary doctrines, than those
who confound our legal method of taking a cus-
tomary part in parliamentary warfare with the
practices of Mazzini.. Those who know our form
of government, know well that, as regards the
dominions of Queen Victoria, a more revolutionary
sentiment than that which, as I have said, Dr.
Cullen uttered on the occasion referred to was
rarely uttered by man. Of course it is not Dr.
Cullen's intention to teach revolution, but his
Grace has little experience in our form of government, and however able a theologian, I fear that,
with his opinions, he has little turn for safe or
prudent guidance upon these subjects. He is a
revolutionist *maigré lui*, and his Grace's doctrines,
if carried out, would be the most infallible receipt
for uprooting the foundations of society amongst
us and plunging us into all the horrors of anarchy
and civil war.

Suppose a man sent to Parliament without party
connections, without pledges or promises of any
kind, with a constituency disposed to leave him
at full liberty to follow his own opinions and be
guided by his own judgment. Let us suppose
that he finds a Government in power from which
he differs on the questions which to him are the
most important; that he sees grievances to be
redressed which they are not disposed to remedy,
principles by them maintained to which he is

strongly opposed, and interests which to him are overwhelming that have to be pressed forward against the Government, and that require the fullest, the amplest, and the most unrestrained discussion.   The natural place for a man entering Parliament with such views is Opposition.   He may or may not join the main body of members who constitute the Opposition ; but his function, even if he stands alone, if he wishes to accomplish any such object as I have described, is essentially a function of Opposition.   If he has any such work to do, and if he does it, he does the work of Opposition.   His business is to press on the attention of the House the principles and interests of which he is the advocate, regardless of the interests of the Minister or the wishes of that party.   He is to seize every reasonable opportunity to get from them a public discussion.   If the Ministers act at variance with those principles or trample on those interests, he is to visit them with an unsparing exposure.   If they deserve reproof, he is to reprove them, and if possible to make them ashamed and repentant.   He is not indeed to oppose them when he believes them right, but until they do justice to the cause he advocates he is not to go out of his way to give them on party questions which do not particularly interest him a support which, as far as he is concerned, they have done nothing to earn.

This course of conduct, whatever name you give it, is really Independent Opposition.   Such

a member may not have the most distant notion
of turning out the actual Cabinet. They may
appear too strong to render any such attempt
feasible. It may be a matter of indifference to
him whether they remain in office or are replaced by another set of Ministers who perhaps
will be just as bad. His sole object may be discussion, the propagation of truth, the advocacy of
justice, the alteration of opinion, the making use
of the great tribunal of Parliament to direct public
attention to abuses and acts of injustice which he
believes cannot bear the light, and which, when they
have been thoroughly discussed and exposed, must
ultimately be redressed, from whatever party the
Prime Minister may happen to be taken. But
even so his function in the House of Commons is
Opposition. He is labouring to do a great work;
in behalf of that work he holds himself free from
party trammels; he opposes the Ministry whenever they deserve it, and, as a matter of course,
he is not numbered amongst their supporters.

Now this is exactly the case of those who went
into the House of Commons in 1852 to maintain
the rights of the Irish poor and of the Catholic
Church. If anybody has gone into Parliament
to promote greater interests than these, I honour
and respect him; but at the present moment I
know no interests more pressing, as none can
be of more vital importance. Those members
with whom I act have not gone into Parliament
to forward their own interests, to advance their

fortunes, to get promotion for their relatives, or in any way to serve themselves. They have set before their eyes great public interests to advance, which is the end and scope of all their endeavours. No wonder, therefore, that they differ in their calculations of policy from men who, even if personally honest—and many of those from whom they differ are notoriously the reverse—seek first their own advancement, and regulate their actions and their policy by this end.

Coming into Parliament to promote these objects, we see a Government either resolutely opposed to us, and openly proclaiming their opposition, or seeking more effectually to neutralise our efforts by astute contrivance and pretended friendship. We see this Government doing its utmost to render us powerless by practising, towards men who have sworn to take the very course which we have taken, a corruption so open and shameless that in any part of the United Kingdom but Ireland it would not be tolerated for a moment. We see them trying every artifice and practising every seduction to corrupt the priests of God, and to thrust political prostitution within the gates of the sanctuary. We see them partially successful. We see the hopes we once entertained of speedy redress of grievances vanishing under these arts. We see that as our strength diminishes through this corruption, so the insolence of the Government—not against us personally, but against the rights of the Church and of the poor—increases also. We find ourselves, in every effort we make for the Church and the poor, opposed by the Ministers; and by this their resistance to our just demands, we are, as a necessary consequence, placed in opposition to them. It is a literal fact that no man with his eyes open and with the ordinary use of his senses, unless he has some other object in view than that of serving the Church and the poor, can be otherwise than opposed to the Ministers. He is opposed to them because they are insolently opposed to the Church and the poor.

Nor is it true that we have pushed this opposition to extremes. In itself, Opposition is, as we have seen, the mode ordinarily taken to force difficult questions upon a reluctant Ministry. It is the conservative method of changing the views of an Administration provided by our system of laws. But in handling that weapon we have not misused it. We have not practised any factious or uncandid opposition. We have attacked that which was grossly censurable, and have made good our attacks by argument and proof. But in laying before the House our demands for redress, we have invariably avoided an angry hostility; have given the Ministers credit for good intentions even when we were hardly justified in doing so; and have afforded them every opportunity to concede our demands with a good grace and without wounding their self-love.

I believe this has been the case with all those

with whom I have been acting. I can speak, of course, with a clearer recollection of what has happened to myself, and therefore I will merely say, that when I laid before the House the claims of Catholic prisoners, I was publicly thanked by Lord Palmerston for the courtesy with which I had pressed that subject upon his attention ; and in pressing upon Sir James Graham and Mr. Sidney Herbert the claims of the Catholic soldiers and sailors, I distinctly said that " I did not make that statement from any feeling of hostility to the Government; that I believed they would not refuse my demand; that I believed the right honourable gentlemen sincerely desired to do what was right in the matter ; " &c., &c. I am not aware that I have treated these questions differently from any other member of our party. Wherever it was possible to give the Ministers credit for what they had done, for what they intended, for what they had promised, we have studiously done so ; and if we have erred at all, we have erred in sometimes going even a little beyond the truth in their favour, and using words of compliment and acknowledgment which they have done very little indeed to earn.

It is strange to find oneself obliged to vindi-cate to the Holy See the attempt to render to religion this difficult and thankless service; to have to apologise for not being selfish, venal, and ambitious ; and to be put on one's defence in Rome for sacrificing one's own worldly interests in an endeavour to vindicate the Church. But so it is, and so let it be. For my part, I shall never regret any sacrifice or any labour that may accompany my very humble and imperfect endeavours to pay back—if such a thing were possible—a part of the infinite debt which every Catholic owes to the Church of his redemption.

The practical working of this policy of parliamentary opposition is in great part explained by what I have already said. A member of the House of Commons of great experience once said to me that, "with a good cause and ability to speak, two members were a party." That is, that two members having justice on their side; insisting only on what was right, however unpopular it might be; free from all suspicion of dishonesty, insincerity, or corruption; capable of enforcing with a moderate amount of eloquence the cause they had in hand, and able (by there being two of them) to defend one another when attacked—that two such men might produce an impression upon the House, upon the country, and upon the Minister, and labour usefully to whatever question they applied themselves. A parliamentary party of two is unquestionably a small party; but my experience in the House of Commons tells me that in substance this saying is quite true. A small party able to take a creditable part in the discussions and business of the House, known to represent a considerable opinion out of doors, devoted to the public object which they have in view, demanding only what is just, and seeking that justice with integrity—a very small party under these conditions, perfectly independent, properly supported by the country, and shrinking from no labour and responsibility in the House, is really able with the blessing of God to accomplish a great deal. Two men can do something, but twenty men acting with united strength are a very powerful force.

And how are they powerful? In part by their influence in critical debates and divisions. Twenty men acting together are always formidable. They make a difference of forty according as they take one side or the other in a division, and how many Administrations are there whose fate has been sealed by less than forty votes? No Minister, however strong, can despise a compact body of twenty members. The strong Minister of to-day is in a minority to-morrow, and the next day he finds himself in opposition. A dissension has arisen in his Cabinet, a colleague has seceded, supporters fail him, and friends become lukewarm; a critical division approaches, and then the leader of the Government and the leader of the Opposition both look with a wistful eye upon that compact force of twenty votes. All leaders of politics are accustomed to expect such incidents as these; and when a party of twenty seems likely to remain compact and to grow in strength, it is always treated with a good deal of respect by both sides of the House of Commons. If it is not wanted now,

both sides know that before very long its votes
may be, if not necessary, exceedingly convenient
and profitable; and though an honest politician
will not abandon his own principles to purchase
twenty, or indeed any number of votes, yet it is in
human nature that every party leader and every
party will avoid giving needless offence to a body
of members of Parliament whose votes by the
strange caprice of fortune may at some not very
distant day stand him in good stead.

But though this tacit and never-forgotten calculation is a not despicable element of strength,
I place far before it, and far before any acci-
dental political management, the power of directly
influencing opinion through discussions in the
House.   A party like that I have described may
sometimes find an opportunity to outvote and
overturn a Cabinet.   They may keep a Minister
in a wholesome fear of such a disaster.   But in
my judgment a much greater check upon every
Minister, especially in dealing with such grievances as those under which the poorer classes of
Catholics labour, is the fear of having to defend
himself, not once nor twice, but often, and night
after night, against repeated exposures and attacks
for failing to do justice to the poor.   Such attacks
can only be made by, and are only dreaded from,
those members who are in what we call "*Independent Opposition;*" upon whom the Minister has
no *claim* because they have received no favours,
and upon whom he has no *hold* because they

neither hope nor expect, nor would accept, anything. It always requires considerable boldness
to speak out the whole truth on behalf of the
poor and of the Church ; and the member who
has other objects in view, who has ambition to
gratify, who looks for office, or whose social
predilections make him particularly anxious to
stand well with the enemies of our faith and with
those who trample on the poor, such a man cannot, does not, never did, and never will speak out
the whole truth on these subjects ; and for the
most part, such a man dare not even think the
whole truth in the solitude of his own heart,
where none can penetrate. But even these truths,
however unpopular, being true, will make their
way and ultimately produce conviction, if boldly
stated and skilfully enforced by argument. For
this a small party of forty, thirty, aye, even
twenty members, personally competent to the
task, is fairly adequate. A party of forty, or
more than forty, pledged to these principles we
had in November 1852. Not all were honest—
many were known to be corrupt; but we thought
the Apostolic Delegate was with us ; that we had
the benediction of the Holy See upon this
glorious crusade ; and that the influence of the
Church would restore in due time whatever
strength we might lose at the beginning from the
temptations and corruptions of power. But, alas!
the event has turned out otherwise. Wicked
and perjured men have gone from us as we

expected, and our ranks are thinned by an anticipated desertion.   But along with these deserters
has gone from us the Apostolic Delegate.   His
influence, instead of being with us to repair the
losses in our ranks, has been against us to
weaken, to infuse distrust, to dishearten, to
encourage fresh deserters, to put new life and
spirit into the men who, after having scandalised
the world by their shameless effrontery, find
themselves, to their infinite amazement and
amusement, the favourites and darlings of the
Church ; while we, because we have remained
true to what were once the principles of the
Apostolic Delegate, because we have not forfeited our honour and have not betrayed the
Holy See, find ourselves treated as outcasts alike
of Church and State, and obliged to defend ourselves here in the Holy City from the imputation of being little better than the disciples of
Mazzini.

SECTION III.—*The Policy of Place-Taking and
Place-Begging.*

The only other mode of parliamentary conduct
for a Catholic party which has been placed in
competition with the policy just described, and
to which some persons give the preference, is
the "policy of place-taking and place-begging."
These words express very tolerably the policy
to which they refer.   The notion is that the

Catholic members of Parliament should connect themselves with the Liberal party, especially when in office; that such of them as are suited for the minor places under the Crown should try to get such places for themselves; that all of them should try to get yet smaller places such as are obtainable for themselves and political supporters; that they' should thus bind themselves to the Ministry by personal obligations and the pursuit of personal advantages; and that for the Church and the poor they should exert themselves just so much as is not displeasing to the Ministers by whom they are patronised, and as will not in the smallest degree interfere with the promotion of their own personal interest and that of their friends.   To make this statement complete, it should be added that many understand this policy to mean that, in the event of any direct and new assault being made upon the Church, the Catholic members should renounce their allegiance to the Ministers, separate from them, and, in a very extreme case, actually go into Opposition.   I put this qualification in order to act with perfect fairness.   But it is notorious that the Episcopal supporters of the place-begging policy are not agreed in setting even this moderate limit to the subserviency which they advocate.   We have already seen this in the case of the Bishop of Kilmore, who from his own altar has strongly urged the poor peasants of Cavan to expose themselves to the vengeance of their landlords

on behalf of Mr. Hughes, who was Solicitor-
General under Lord John Russell, and whom even
the Ecclesiastical Titles Bill could not induce to
sever his connection with office.   This man the
Bishop of Kilmore holds up to the people as
a man whom they may absolutely trust.   It is
not impossible that other Bishops are of the same
opinion, more especially when we remember that
several Catholics who held office at the time of
the Ecclesiastical Titles Bill, and who were ready
to resign office if they had been urged to do so,
were, on the contrary, urged to retain office, and
did actually retain office, by strong Episcopal
advice to that effect.   It is known also that
Catholic members who were in the habit of
supporting the Ministers at that time believed
it to be their duty to continue to support the
Ministers, and did actually continue to support
them, in spite of that penal measure.

With many, therefore, Bishops and laymen, the
doctrine is that we ought to connect ourselves
with the Ministers called Liberal ; to get out of
them, in the first instance, all the places we can
for ourselves and our friends, and then whatever
redress of grievances they may be willing to
concede ; and to stick to them, right or wrong,
even when they turn against us and begin to
persecute the Church and insult the Holy See.
Which of these two versions of the theory is
adopted by Dr. Cullen I cannot feel certain.
His Grace has so thoroughly changed his course

that on such a point it would be hazardous to express a confident opinion. My own notion is that those who presume most in favour of the Government will in reference to his Grace be the nearest to the truth.

A third modification of this policy has been suggested to myself. If, indeed, I have rightly understood some of Dr. Cullen's conversation, his Grace has more than once advised me to separate myself from all my present friends in Parliament and to stand alone; to raise no objection against any Catholic member who may wish to sell himself to the Ministers; to allow all Catholic members to take part with the Ministers; to separate myself from everybody; to take upon myself alone the duty of defending Catholic truths and Catholic interests in their integrity, and to try to increase my force in the House of Commons by diminishing the number of my coadjutors as much as possible. This suggestion has an aspect complimentary towards me personally; but the least inspection shows it to be too whimsical to be meant for a practical adoption.

At all events, and without arguing the point, I will merely say, as it is addressed to me personally, that I did not and do not choose to put myself in any such isolated position. I do not find myself made of different materials from my fellow-men, neither do I understand why one rule should be laid down for everybody else and an opposite rule for me. If, in the present state of our affairs, place-begging and dependence on the Ministers is good for everybody else, it is good for me also. If any other member is to be encouraged to get a good office for himself and to make that the primary object of his parliamentary career, the same liberty and encouragement should be given to me. Nay, a greater liberty and encouragement should be given to me than to many other members, because in a pecuniary point of view place would be a greater convenience to me than to them. Some of them are rich—I am poor. I have never, therefore, been able to understand why I am advised to continue the Independent course, and to devote myself at every sacrifice to the service of the Church singly, while others, whose duty to the Church is as binding as mine, are advised to take the opposite course, to get the best places they can for themselves, and to cultivate in the first instance, and with all their might, their own ambition, interest, profit, vanity, and advancement. Declining, therefore, the special honour which this view of things offers to me, I come to consider the place-begging theory in its more ordinary and favourable aspect.

Indeed, I think that to those who know anything of our political system I have already said enough to condemn this theory by merely stating it. No one who understands the working of our constitution could look for the redress of grievances from any such mode of acting; nor have any grievances affecting the lower class of the community, and which the ruling classes were unwilling of themselves to remedy, ever been remedied by the use of such means.

In the first place, the theory supposes (and the existing practice realises the theory in that respect) that no Catholic party, as such, is to have any existence. Those who adopt this theory are no longer a Catholic party in any rational sense of the term. They form a section of the Ministerial party, and nothing else. Some of them are in subordinate offices which give them very little influence over the decisions of the Government, but bind them to co-operate with the Government and to serve it on all occasions consistently with the spirit of the original contract into which they have entered. Beyond this neither the Prime Minister nor the Catholic subordinate can be made to go, so long as the contract lasts. The Prime Minister, of course, could not compel, and could not think of compelling, any honourable Catholic who had taken office under him to vote for a penal law against his religion. He might indeed expect, and in 1851 three Catholic gentlemen justified the expectation, that even a penal law should not break the connection between the Catholic and his Ministerial patron, and that while voting against the law itself he should continue to support and to receive the wages of the Minister by whom the penal law is introduced. Such complaisance is naturally expected sometimes from a Catholic lay official, because it is known to have,

up to this very hour, the approval of Bishops of
our Church; and what Bishops approve in his
favour the Prime Minister will take as a matter
of course and of duty from the laxer and harder
conscience of a lay politician.

On the other hand, whatever may be the
precise line of duty with regard to new penal
laws, the case with regard to the redress of old
grievances is perfectly clear. The Catholic has
taken office with no contract, express or implied,
as to the redress of grievances. The Ministers
are known to have uttered certain sentiments
more or less favourable, but they have committed
themselves to nothing. They have promised
nothing. They do not approve all the demands
we make for the Church and for the poor, and
indeed the greater part of our demands they
utterly and expressly repudiate. Even that of
which they approve they do not promise to
concede. They will do what they can. Many
obstacles are in the way. They dare not violate
the prejudices of the people of England. They
will examine the matter carefully, and whatever
is perfectly consistent with their own official
convenience that they are willing to do. Beyond
this the Catholic subordinate official, speaking
even in private to the Minister, dare not and
cannot seriously go. In all questions between the
subordinate and his chief, the safety and prosperity of their common partnership—the Ministry
—is and must be on both sides the main con-

sideration. In his heart the Catholic official may sometimes wish to go farther, but he cannot seriously ask the Minister to damage the Administration by conceding demands which involve risk and danger. Each of them in his place, as higher and lower members of the same Administration, must equally look to the interests of Administration in the first place, and to the redress of grievances as a quite subordinate consideration. From the nature of things this is the case even in private, where men speak more openly to each other what they mean. If Mr. Monsell, for instance, were to press upon Lord Palmerston the redress of any particular grievance, and Lord Palmerston were to answer that the redress of that grievance would injure the Government and could not be attempted, Mr. Monsell's mouth is shut by that rejoinder. If he wishes to carry the matter farther, he must resign his place and speak to the Minister as an Independent member.

But in public how does the matter stand? In public the mouth of the Catholic member is shut upon all Catholic grievances the moment he accepts office. As to speaking in the House, the subordinate official is absolutely under the control of his Ministerial chief. This rule is as stringent as military discipline. The Clerk of the Ordnance, or the Irish Attorney-General, cannot speak on any subject without permission, and must speak when they are ordered. There is

nothing humiliating in this ; every man who takes
service must obey the laws of the service, and the
official must conform to the rules of the Ministerial camp.   The moment a Catholic becomes
an official his public advocacy is lost to us.
He cannot publicly state our grievances in the
House, nor out of it, for fear of compromising
the Government to which he belongs.   On the
interests of the Church and of the poor the
tenure of his office compels him to be silent.
If Catholic principles are attacked he cannot
defend them.   Nay, even if liberal laws are proposed, and the Government Ministers think fit
to resist the proposition, the voice of the Catholic
official is never raised in vindication of his faith.
On the contrary, here too he is obliged to be
silent for fear of compromising the Administration.   I say this from the experience of the last
two years.   During that period we have had
plenty of Catholic debates ; many efforts have
been made to enforce in the House of Commons
the justice of our demands for redress of grievances ; attacks have been made on our convents ;
the principles of education have been discussed ;
Protestant proselytism in Catholic Continental
states has been brought under consideration ; but
to the best of my recollection in no single instance
has a Catholic official condescended or dared to
say a word in our favour.

Now, without going into questions of recrimina-
tion, observe how this system works necessarily

and ordinarily. Of all those Catholics who are willing to take office, the Ministry try to select those who can be most serviceable to them. They pick out the best speakers, the ablest men of business, the most influential, and sometimes those whose character gives them most weight. One part of our weakness consists in this, that we are sadly wanting in men qualified for public affairs. Of the few whom we have and who desire office, the Government takes the best, and gives them a subordinate place on condition that for the future they shall not open their mouths in public on Catholic affairs ; office buys them to be dumb ; and thus, if the system were carried out, and we were all, as Dr. Cullen wishes, to take the line of place-seeking, no one would be left for the public advocacy of Catholic interests and the defence of Catholic principles and rights but the incompetent and incapable. Every competent and every capable man would get a place for himself, and would take it on the condition of being dumb in public, and in private of pushing his advocacy of Catholic interests so far as may suit the interests of the Government, and not an inch farther.

But in the ordinary course of things, before a Catholic gets a place he has a novitiate to pass through. He spends months, perhaps years, as an expectant. During all that time he has to earn the office which he expects to hold ; he must show a certain amount of industry, capacity, and

influence; he must prove that he is both able and
willing to serve the Government; that he is discreet; not too zealous in seeking redress of Catholic grievances; not too Catholic in his sentiments
or his language; careful in avoiding the utterance
of any unpopular Catholic principle; and, better
still, if possible, ready to deny, renounce, and vitu-
perate any such principle if advanced by others.
In a word, the expectant must show in embryo
the virtues which as an official he is expected to
display in full maturity.   His main object, as that
of the official, must be to serve and please the
Government of which he expects to be a member.
This must be his leading purpose, and every act
and every word must be regulated so as to serve
that end most effectually.   A little more latitude
in speech is allowed to him than to the official,
but not much; and exactly the same virtue of discretion, the same want of zeal for Catholic interests, the same readiness to abjure or ignore
Catholic principles, the same silence on unpopular doctrines, or, what is better and more
frequent still, the same readiness to renounce and
condemn unpopular doctrines; to advocate false
views on education, on the powers and duties of
the Church, on proselytism, on the Papal authority;
on every mixed subject that comes under discussion—these same virtues must in their degree,
and very often in a high degree, be manifested in
the Catholic expectant quite as much as in the
Catholic official.

But when you have picked out these two classes from the body of Catholic members who are content to serve the Government, you have in effect taken every man of ability, and a great many of very little ability; every man whose vanity makes him ambitious, even if he has no talent to justify that ambition; and you have placed all these in a position in which all the most powerful motives of self-interest are brought to bear upon their minds, to render them weak, sluggish, ineffective, and unfaithful advocates. If all the Catholic members pursue this course of serving the Government and seeking for place, all the men of any ability and fitness for place, that is, all the men of any ability and fitness to serve the Church and the poor, are so placed that their first great, overwhelming, preponderating motive necessarily impels them to serve the Church and the poor as little as possible; to avoid these subjects whenever they can be avoided; when they cannot be avoided to treat them so as just to avoid heresy, even if they do that; and, in one word, to betray the truth rather than to advocate it.

Who then remain of those Catholic members who desire to serve in the Administration ? Every man of talent, every man who thinks he has talent, has already been disposed of. There remain none but the rank and file; men whose value consists in their numbers and their votes, and whose connection with the Government consists in getting a smaller class of places for their friends or near relations, and in paying for these places by votes for the Ministry in the House of Commons. What benefit can accrue to the Church or to the poor towards getting redress of grievances from this class of members it would be difficult even to pretend.   They are, for the most part, men of no parliamentary ability ; they have not the faculty of persuading, either in public or in private.   They do not follow leaders who are zealous for the redress of our grievances, for their leaders are the Protestant members of the Administration. They are valuable to the Minister for their votes on party divisions.   Their votes, too, are available even for the Church when new aggressions are attempted ; and the presence in the House of Commons of a certain number of Catholic votes, apart altogether of the use made of them, does in itself tend somewhat to deter our enemies from aggressions.   But in the way of procuring a redress of grievances, forcing upon a reluctant Administration changes of the law in our behalf, I defy any one to show, during the long course of years in which we have been blessed with a pretty numerous brigade of this class of Catholic sena- tors, that we ever benefited by them to the value of one half-farthing.

Nor can it be justly said that in the picture I am now drawing I have at all been guilty of exaggeration. On the contrary, up to this moment, by treating the matter in the abstract, I have very much understated the case. I have described the inevitable consequences of a particular line of policy by speaking of the relations of men and parties, without much reference to the individuals themselves. But if from these general considerations I could come down to the individuals; if I could paint in their true colours the Catholic members who now aspire to serve the Ministry; if I could render visible to the Holy See the want of intellect in some, the want of character in others; if I could show how the natural influence of great abilities has been neutralised by a shameless prostitution which discredits the Church instead of supporting it; if I could make it understood what depths of public and acknowledged baseness the greater part of these men have had to go through in order to become servants of the Government—how very few there are who, in reaching this position, have been able to keep even a shred of decent worldly reputation; and how, of the whole body of Ministerial Catholics, there are hardly two that can be trusted to speak on a Catholic subject without grossly belying Catholic principle and Catholic truth—it would be admitted that my delineation has been a very faint copy of the original.

SECTION IV.—*Experience—O'Connell and his Successors.*

The things of which I have spoken in this chapter are not questions of mere speculation and theory. We have already had upon them during a long course of years as full and decisive an experience as it is possible to have on any matter of politics ; and all this experience points in one direction. We have tried both systems of policy, under various circumstances and in different generations of men. We have tried both of them more than once ; and the experience is uniform and undeniable, that the policy of subservience to the Administration of the day is productive of nothing but disappointment, humiliation, and disgrace, while the Independent policy has procured for us all the concessions of which up to this day we are able to boast.

In far darker and more desperate times than these, both for Ireland and the Church, what was the policy of O'Connell ? He had precisely the same difficulties to contend against that we have now, only of an infinitely greater kind. The same objections were urged against the course pursued by him more than forty years ago, only with infinitely greater plausibility. His enemies were the ancestors of the very men by whom we are now opposed. The same phrases, the same cowardice, the same selfish ambition, the same calculations of a mistaken prudence, the same misplaced reliance upon Protestant patronage, the same attachment to English Liberals, were thrust as obstacles into his path.   For many years there were more Bishops in Ireland opposed to him than are opposed to us, and he had to struggle against an Archbishop of Dublin whose zeal for religion, intellectual capacity, wisdom, and knowledge of affairs were quite on a level with the great qualities of any Archbishop who has succeeded him to the present day.   Dr. Troy had indeed this excuse, that in his time the experiment had not been tried, and the policy recommended by O'Connell had not been, and could not have been, tested by experience.   Forty years have since elapsed; the experiences of those years have been manifold and multiform; they all tell one story and point in one direction; and we are coolly asked to throw them all aside, to take for granted that it was a mistake; to renounce in our own day the teaching and the policy which gained Emancipation; and to take Dr. Troy, or his representative in spirit as in jurisdiction, for our guide along a path which we know in Dr. Troy's own day could have led to nothing but disaster.

When O'Connell began his struggles for Emancipation, he had against him the very same classes that obstructed us by their opposition.   The respectable Catholic nobility and gentry hated him with a cordiality to which nothing in the present age affords a parallel.   They said that he was rash; that he was violent in speech and writing; that he advised extravagant and dangerous courses; that his policy was turbulent, un-Catholic, and democratic. They blamed him for separating from the English Whigs and Liberals; they reproached him for adopting Utopian schemes, to the neglect of projects of redress which, though smaller and less brilliant, were more certain and nearer at hand; they objected to him the unpopularity he had acquired by a bold advocacy of Catholic truth, and an equally bold exhibition of political courage.

They said that he had damaged himself by the outrageous course he had pursued, and that no concessions would be ever made to one who had raised up against himself so many enemies. They said, almost in the very words of to-day, "We must not ask for too much; we must temporise; we must conciliate; we must make friends with every English statesman who will condescend to cajole us; we must take their advice; we must put our business of Emancipation into their hands and follow their guidance; we must have nothing to do with any man whose language is not perfectly smooth and complimentary; we must have no connection with anybody who is so shockingly ill-bred as to use strong phrases in denouncing crimes and frauds; and above all, we must aim at doing only a little bit at a time, and that little bit we must get somebody else to do for us; and we must seek to carry it by private solicitation, by arrangements made in whispers, and by confidential compacts transacted in dark corners and behind half-opened doors." All the nonsense, all the cowardice, all the selfishness, all the blindness of forty years since are revived and brought out into full daylight, as if they had never been considered, condemned, executed, buried, and covered over a generation or two ago.

Everybody knows that Emancipation was carried because O'Connell deliberately rejected the policy now urged by Dr. Cullen; and that by Dr. Cullen's policy, Emancipation could never have been carried till the day of judgment.

It would be too long a history to relate here, but the notorious truth is, that we are not only following the great O'Connell's example in the means which he took—that is, combining and organising the priests in public and energetic activity to influence elections and to keep alive the public spirit at all necessary times—but we are following his example in the policy by which, to carry Emancipation, he wielded the power which the combined action of the priests and people put into his hands.

For many years the question of Emancipation had made no progress. It was supported by the public sentiment in Ireland, not only of the Catholics, but of the Protestant Whigs and Liberals. With equal zeal and sincerity—I am sure with very considerable sincerity and very great zeal after their kind—it was supported in

England by all the leaders of the Liberal party
and Whigs, and by all their organs of public
opinion. These excellent persons out of our own
ranks did for Emancipation a thousand times
more, and a thousand times more earnestly, than
ever did Lord Aberdeen, or Mr. Gladstone, or
Lord John Russell, or Lord Palmerston for the
redress of our existing grievances. They filled
the press with our complaints ; they wrote long
articles in the leading reviews ; they published
pamphlets full of wit, and argument, and humour,
which were then circulated by hundreds of
thousands, which the booksellers still reprint,
and which have become classic writings in our
tongue for their admirable combination of thought
and expression. In Parliament all the greatest
names of the first quarter of this century laboured
for us incessantly after their fashion. In 1800,
Pitt, because he could not carry into effect an
arrangement for Emancipation which he had
made with the Irish Bishops and with the
Catholic gentry of that day (an arrangement, to
be sure, by which these Bishops and gentry had
contracted to sell the liberty of the Church),
actually resigned his power, ceased to be
Minister, and went for a time into Opposition.
In 1808 or 1809, the Whigs, being then in office,
also resigned their power because they were not
allowed to carry for us a very small instalment
of Emancipation.

It was part of our grievance and part of our

weakness that we were then excluded from Parliament, and that we had no Catholic members to advocate our case. Year after year, distinguished Protestants and distinguished Whigs, the greatest orators in the House, men to whom the Catholics of Ireland are still grateful, and whose names are still held in reverence, took this task upon themselves and made yearly motions and speeches in our behalf. Grattan and Plunkett had the management of our cause, and some of the very ablest speeches that ever were delivered in the House of Commons were delivered by them to serve and support us. The help we received from the Whigs and Liberals of that day, the sacrifices they made, the ink they shed, the pains they took, the eloquence they uttered, not once or twice, but for a great many years in succession, are incomparably greater than anything their successors, the present Whigs and Peelites, have ever done or shown the least inclination to do. As far as regards service or help, or claim to gratitude or confidence—even leaving out of account the Queen's Colleges and the Ecclesiastical Titles Bill, for which we are indebted respectively to the Peelites and the Whigs—it would be a sheer mockery to draw any comparison between the Liberals of those times and the Liberals of the present day.

Yet what was O'Connell's course? He found that by these means, and by leaving other people, however distinguished, to do our work, we made much noise but no progress. He found that our claims and our rights were not properly stated to the House of Commons ; that our whole case was not fully proclaimed there, and that our demands were not urged with sufficient earnestness. He found that in Ireland public spirit was not sufficiently aroused, because the Irish Catholics were depending upon others to do for them the work which they had it in their power to do for themselves. He broke away, therefore, from the old, timid, worthless, barren, routine method. He persuaded the Catholic people of Ireland to take the management of their case into their own hands. He made them wrest violently, from the venerated hands of Grattan and of Plunkett, the trust in our behalf, which for a long series of years had been reposed in them. He resolved that we should state our own case in our own way, make our demands upon the British Parliament in full, and support them by our own reasons. Feeling his power with the constituencies, he began to make war upon Irish representatives who were either open enemies or false friends, or who, if honest in their friendship, were too timid, and too prudent, and too conciliating, and too little zealous for the occasion.

All the world of Catholic Whiggery and gentility, aye, and many Bishops to boot, cried out at various times against the rashness of this course, and did their best to discountenance and discourage him. The Holy See was not, for a long time, very strongly in his favour, and whatever encouragement it gave, it gave to the other side. Great numbers of respectable people cried out against O'Connell's ingratitude for treating so harshly tried friends who had served us so zealously and so long.   They repeated by anticipation, and with much greater reason, words like those which I have heard fall from the lips of Dr. Cullen and Mr. Keogh, about the gratitude due to the Gladstones and Aberdeens of thirty or forty years ago.   But O'Connell flung aside all this small obstruction and puny clamour with the indifference it merited.   He declared war against politicians, however civil their language or friendly their professions, who would not go all lengths with us, and would not postpone all other political objects to the concession of our demands.

The Clare election of 1828, which was the greatest field on which, up to that time, the priests had displayed their politics actively, was memorable on another account.   It was the election in which O'Connell set himself up as a candidate against a member of the existing Government; not hostile to us; not treacherous, but friendly and honourable in his views; a Minister who had no other fault than this, that the Administration with which he was connected would not make the redress of our grievances what is called a "Cabinet measure," would not stake its existence as a Cabinet upon Emancipation, and would not exert themselves to the utmost to procure for us the repeal of the laws which forbade us the exercise of our rights. For this sole crime—a crime in which at this day Messrs. Monsell and Keogh the Catholics are the accomplices of Lord Palmerston and Lord John Russell, and Dr. Cullen their supporter — for this sole crime O'Connell declared war against Mr. Vesey Fitzgerald (the Minister who stood candidate for the county of Clare, and who always voted and spoke for Emáncipation), and offered himself as a candidate to replace him. Great was the outcry against this act of ingratitude raised by the Whigs and time-servers, the Monsells and Keoghs of that day. But O'Connell disregarded their remonstrances. He gathered together the whole Catholic strength of Ireland for one gigantic effort ; he mustered priest and layman on the same peaceful battle field ; he drew out the highest energies of all and each ; he defeated Mr. Vesey Fitzgerald, the professed friend of Emancipation, on the Clare hustings, and by the beating of such a friend of Emancipation, Emancipation was carried.

Messrs. Monsell and Keogh occupy towards the Catholic grievances of this day exactly the position which Mr. Vesey Fitzgerald occupied towards the Catholic grievances of 1828. One of them, at least, is an honest friend of Catholic rights, and is sincerely anxious to obtain redress, just as was Mr. Vesey Fitzgerald. Mr. Vesey Fitzgerald would not make the redress of those grievances the first and principal object of his politics. Neither will they. He supported and made part of an Administration which left the redress of our grievances an open question, but of which the more prominent members opposed this redress, and openly refused the concession of our rights. So do they. Emancipation was carried when the Catholics of Ireland took and acted upon the bold resolution of treating all such half friends and cowardly partisans as enemies. The emancipation of our day will be carried on no other terms.

After O'Connell and the Irish Catholic members got into Parliament, his practice varied from time to time according to circumstances. He enjoyed such immense authority and led so great a force, who placed in him such absolute reliance, and were willing from time to time to change their policy at his bidding, that he was able to make experiments in policy, take advantage of opportunities, and adapt himself to the occasion in a way peculiar to himself. After Emancipation, too, he had other objects in view than to procure the redress of grievances depending on a mere vote of the Legislature. The administration of justice was at that time in a most frightful state ; the judgment-seat was filled with enemies of the Catholics. The custom, handed down from many previous generations, was to treat the Catholics of Ireland with the grossest and most revolting injustice. All offices in every town and in every county, from the highest to the lowest, were in

the hands of our enemies ; and it was very important at that time, before devoting himself wholly
to procure the redress of the remaining Catholic
grievances, to postpone these for a time in order
to work out in the administration of the law the
fruits of Catholic Emancipation.

Yet even with so strong a motive as this to
actuate him, O'Connell commenced his parliamentary career by opposing all Administrations alike,
as all equally the enemies of Ireland and of the
Catholics. He first opposed the Tories or Conservatives under Sir Robert Peel. When they
were driven from office he opposed the Whigs or
Liberals under Lord Grey and Lord John Russell.
But at a later period he changed his course. He
made an alliance with the Whigs, hoping to get
from them certain concessions which were never
made, and to gain advantages which the Catholic
people of Ireland never received. The first of
such alliances was supposed to have been made
at a meeting of members of Parliament held at
Lichfield House, and was popularly called " The
Lichfield House Compact." The result of that
alliance I cannot describe better than in the words
deliberately used last year by Serjeant Shee, on
whose behalf Father Keeffe and Father O'Shea
are now silenced, and who has this year deserted
the Independent party and joined the Government. These are not my own words, but the
words of the friend of the Bishop of Ossory, and
who boasted everywhere that in his treachery to

the Independent party he has Dr. Cullen for his approver. I quote his words as corrected by himself :—

"From the time O'Connell entered into the contract at Lichfield House, by which he sacrificed the parliamentary independence of his country to the convenience and exigencies of an English party, what single memorial did he place upon the statute book of the wisdom of that policy? Innumerable suggestions of the utmost value did the great O'Connell make to every Liberal Ministry which he supported, but where are the results? If his monument were to be raised to-morrow, nothing more can be inscribed upon it than that which certainly is sufficient for immortality—the one great word, 'Emancipation.'"

Perhaps these words overstate the case a little. It was impossible for twenty years to pass in such hands without some advantages being secured. Of these, the most prominent was the improved administration of justice, by the appointment of impartial magistrates and judges. But certain it is that no man of his great ability ever wielded so enormous and absolute an authority as he enjoyed, for nearly twenty years after the Lichfield House Compact, with such insignificant results. And it is also certain that, whatever he gained after Emancipation, he gained by showing a resolute front against all parties, by throwing off the bonds with which he had shackled himself, and by making Whigs and Tories alike afraid of him.

But this alliance with the Whigs, maintained, as it was, by Catholic constituencies returning to

Parliament a number of representatives, most of
whom were utterly worthless except so far as
they were compelled to be his instruments and
the elements of his power, produced a state of
representation very disgraceful even in his time,
and utterly unendurable when he had passed
away.   These are not my sentiments merely, but
the sentiments, and almost the words, of Serjeant
Shee, when, by my side, in my presence, and, with
the help of Father Keeffe and Father O'Shea, he
was defending our policy of Independent Opposition.   These are his words : " Language is too
poor to describe the state into which the Irish
representation had fallen, with very few exceptions, shortly after O'Connell's death."

My language certainly cannot describe it.   It
was everything that can be imagined of corrupt,
immoral, and scandalous.   It was to the last degree a disgrace to the Church of God, of which it
pretended to be a part and an emanation.   If the
tree is to be judged by its fruits, the Church which
sent forth such representatives of itself could for
them certainly not be praised.   It is enough to
repeat here, that the Catholic representation of
Ireland had sunk so low, that Lord John Russell
actually calculated on the support of the Irish
representatives in his attack on the Church by
the Ecclesiastical Titles Bill.   This was the
account of Lord John Russell's calculations given
in Dublin to his friends, in December 1851 or
January 1852, by the late Mr. Shiel, a Catholic

member of Lord John Russell's Government ; and my authority for that statement is an Irish Bishop, who has never taken a part in politics, who told me the fact within a few days after Mr. Sheil had given this explanation, and who has confirmed it to me with great emphasis very recently. But the fact is indisputable. The Catholic representation had fallen so low in 1851, had become, under the system of place-taking, so abject in their slavery to, and such devoted instruments in the hands of the Whigs, that Lord John Russell counted on them as his supporters even when he commenced a new war of penal laws against their own Church. Public indignation in Ireland was too strong even for the corruption of the majority of those Irish Catholic members. But Lord John Russell's estimate was not without foundation. Three Catholic members of Parliament, acting, as it was then said, by the advice of the late Archbishop of Dublin, and, as we have lately seen, with the approval of the present Bishop of Kilmore, did actually continue in office under Lord John Russell, and received his wages, after he had begun to persecute the Church ; and several other Catholic members not in office, but staunch partisans of the Whigs, continued to give them a general support, remained their partisans, and refused to have any hand in the attempt afterwards made to inflict political chastisement upon them by turning them out of office.

And what was the result of this state of things upon the interests of religion ? In all discussions in the House of Commons, Catholic principles were ridiculed and ignored; the rights of the Church were sacrificed and despised; there was no one to defend publicly the requirements of the Holy See ; Ministry after Ministry, Peel, Graham, and Gladstone one year, Lord John Russell the next, used all the powers of the Government to sap and undermine the Church without encountering resistance, until Dr. Cullen himself welcomed and declared his preference for open persecution rather than the subtle and treacherous semblance of kindness by which Catholic principles were then combated. I quote Dr. Cullen's words to this effect—words delivered on a great occasion, after infinite preparation and forethought, from the chair of a great assembly in Dublin, on the 19th August 1851, in the presence of many Bishops (and I may say of the assembled Church of God in the United Kingdom), and which I saw his Grace—not hastily deliver—but carefully read from a roll of papers which he held in his hand, and which he transmitted to the public press :—

"Should we not, however, be thankful to God for having given such a turn to late events ? If we are threatened with the persecution of violence and force, an end is put to a more dangerous sort of persecution—the persecution of false friends, whose smiles and trifling favours were scattered for the purpose of enslaving us, and gradually depriving us of our religion or our religious rights, who, under the pretence of being perfectly liberal, would put truth and error, light and darkness, on the same footing; and who, to propagate their principles more effectually, would take into their own hands the whole education of the rising Catholic generation of the country. It was in this way, not by violence or the sword, that Julian the Apostate persecuted his Christian subjects. It was in this way that the Arian Emperor Constantius persecuted the Catholics of his time. St. Hilary describes his last persecution, and declares that it was worse than that of Nero or Diocletian. I will read a few of his words:—*Pugnamus contra persecutorem fallentem, contra hostem blandientem, qui non dorsa cædit sed ventrem palpat, non proscribit ad vitam, sed ditat in mortem, non laetra vexat sed cor occupat,—non caput gladio desecat, sed animam auro occidit—non contendit ne vincatur sed adulatur ut dominetur—ecclesiæ tecta struit, ut fidem destruat.* Such was the way in which we too were treated by false friends; but they have been unmasked, and we may thank God that the course of events has taught us to put no trust in them, but to rely on Heaven and ourselves."

Such were Dr. Cullen's sentiments in 1851, when he was as yet only Archbishop of Armagh; such the nature of the call which his Grace made upon us laymen to come forward in our political capacity and to oppose, as the worst enemies of the Church, not its open enemies and avowed persecutors, but its "false friends;" those who bestow "trifling favours" and gratify us with "smiles;" those who, like the late, the present, and every possible Administration for some time to come, have tried, try, and will try, to "take into their own hands the whole education of the rising Catholic generation of the country." We have answered this call; we have adopted these sentiments; we have acted upon these instructions to resist those false friends; we have made it our policy "to put no trust in them, but to rely on Heaven and ourselves;" and it is precisely because we have responded to this call of the Archbishop, and have faithfully carried out his solicitations, that we have the misfortune of being now exposed to his Grace's bitterest hostility.

I am told that now in Rome Dr. Cullen professes that, though he has not changed his principles, further experience of Ireland (and I suppose of the English Ministers) has changed his opinion as to the best mode of ensuring their success.

It is hard upon us poor laymen that this increase of experience on the part of his Grace should place us under the sad necessity of either changing our politics and incurring public disgrace and dishonour, or else of offering the best and most uncompromising opposition we can to the new course upon which he has entered. For most certain it is that his Grace now persecutes the good which he once encouraged, and now encourages the evil which he once persecuted.

SECTION V.—*Relation of the Church to the Two Policies.*

Between these two courses of policy, either of which might be taken by Catholic members in the House of Commons, what line should be taken by the Church, by the Holy See, by the Bishops and clergy, so far as their course is determined by the wishes or the influence of the Holy See?

In the first place, it is, one would say, impossible for the Church to be neutral in such a matter. Her own interests, the spiritual welfare of her own children, the salvation of souls, such questions as that of education for all classes, rich as well as poor, the property of the Church, the rights and independence of the Church—all these things, in various ways and forms, are more or less at stake in the issue that is now raised. One may say almost without exaggeration that nothing else is at stake but these things and things like these— matters in which the Church is bound, as a matter of positive duty, to interest herself, and about which she cannot in point of fact be indifferent.

But if the Church is interested in the end to be attained, she cannot but be interested in the means. She cannot but look with much interest and anxiety at the weapons with which her children defend her; cannot but examine narrowly whether the best means are chosen for that purpose; cannot but feel most desirous to have corrected any imperfections or defects, and to have removed any impediments to the success of endeavours which she has so much at heart.

Apart, however, from these general considerations as to what must be, we know very well, as a matter of fact, that the Church does actually interest herself very much in all these questions; that she does not stand neutral or indifferent;

that not merely do the clergy of the lower grades busy themselves about these points of Irish politics; not merely do the Bishops show themselves active; but the influence, the authority, the active intervention of the Holy See is most discernible in all the political contests in Ireland. Whether the Holy See wishes to interfere and take part on one side or the other, I cannot say; but that through its representative it does interfere; that it does take a side; that it does not merely pronounce on abstract questions of right and wrong, but help one candidate at an election and obstruct another—help one party in English politics and obstruct another—help one side in a hundred divisions every session in the House of Commons and obstruct another—that it is felt, and known, and appreciated as a definite and tangible power in all our political contests in Parliament and at the hustings, is a proposition, which cannot be denied.

The Holy See may not wish to interfere at all; or may wish to interfere very cautiously, very moderately, and very little; but in point of fact it does and must interfere somehow; and the sole question is as to what extent it shall interfere and on what principles.

The question now to be considered is what course it ought to take between the two policies I have now described. Neutral or indifferent between them it cannot be; and in point of fact it is not. In the short space of three years and less, its practical influence has been exerted first for one policy and then for the other; its encouragement has been used to tempt men to the adoption of a particular course of public conduct, and when they have yielded to the solicitation and committed themselves beyond recall, its encouragement has been transferred to the other side, and they have found themselves discountenanced and rebuked for the crime of continuing honourably to obey its first behests. Thus the Holy See, or those acting in its name and supposed to wield its authority, have not merely interfered, but have interfered too much; that is, they have interfered on two sides, in two opposite directions, in favour of two inconsistent courses of action. Whichever policy be right, this change of policy has been grievously wrong. It is a blunder which has thrown everything into a confusion beyond calculation, destroyed all confidence, paralysed every effort for the public service, afflicted with unspeakable weakness the devoted servants of the Church, and instead of being a terror to the evil-doer, has made us the scorn and derision of our enemies. Whatever may be right, it is certain that what has been done on the part of the Holy See is wrong.

Another proposition seems equally indisputable. In Ireland, an Independent party such as I have described is either fitted to render service to the Church and to the poor, or it is not. If it is not fitted to render service, it has no business to exist at all. If it is fitted to render service, it ought to be supported by the whole strength and influence of the Church, so far as that can prudently be brought into play.

The difference between an Independent Catholic party and a Dependent and Place-taking party, as regards the Church, is simply this. The former exists only for the sake of the Church, and in order to serve the Church; if it does not do this, it does not accomplish the end of its being, and had better not exist at all. But the Dependent and Place-taking party exists first of all to serve itself, to serve the interests and private purposes of its members. Every member of it enters Parliament for some purpose of his own; not necessarily a dishonest or unworthy purpose, but still for some purpose distinct from, though not opposed to, the interests of the Church and the poor; and his main purpose may very fully be answered in Parliament even if no service whatever is rendered to the Church. He goes to the House of Commons because he is interested in its secular business; because he desires scope for his abilities in public life; because he has strong opinions about the general interests of the country; or simply to gratify his vanity or promote his worldly interests. Such a party as this has no particular claim upon the support of the Church. As Catholics, they have a duty to the Church and to the poor which they are bound to fulfil; and if they enter public life

primarily to serve their own purposes and interests, it is their duty, being there, whenever
the opportunity presents itself, to serve the
Church and the poor. Such a party does not
go out of its way to serve the Church, does not
devote itself to any such service. The very
principle upon which it is constructed is that the
Church requires no such exclusive and self-
sacrificing devotion; that the best course, even
in the Church's interest, which can be taken by
any Catholic politician is to serve his own interests first, to pursue his own views of politics,
to carve out his own fortune, and, while promoting
these main ends, to act like any good Catholic
engaged in commerce; that is, take every reasonable opportunity of serving the Church in his
leisure moments. To a party acting upon these
principles the Church has nothing to say, except
that its members are bound to do their duty.
The Church may desire to have in the House of
Commons as many such members as it can get,
and to have them as able and virtuous as they
can be procured; but beyond this it has nothing
to do with them except to keep them to their
duty.

Very different is the case with regard to an
Independent party. Such a party is formed to
serve the Church and the poor as the primary
object of its existence. In entering Parliament
each of its members takes upon him this solemn
engagement. He contracts with his constituents

and with the Church to make the service of the
Church and the poor his principal end and aim.
As a means to that end, he engages not to seek
his own interest or to gratify his own ambition
until that service be thoroughly fulfilled.   It was
altogether optional with him to have made such a
contract.   There was no obligation on him to do
so, unless a policy of this kind is obviously the
best means of rendering a necessary service to
the great interests in question.   Indeed, to enter
into such an engagement and to bind oneself to
such a policy is clearly an exceptional course.   It
lies out of the beaten track of politics.   If some
great necessity or some very great advantage does
not demand it, it is, like all exceptional courses,
unwise and foolish.   Such a policy of exclusive
devotion to the interests of the Church and of the
poor cannot be justified to common reason, unless
it may reasonably be hoped that these interests
will be very much promoted by it.   If such a
hope be reasonable, the party and the policy have
a right to expect the support and countenance of
the Church.   If such a hope be unreasonable, the
party and the policy will have no right to exist at
all, and the sooner they are got rid of the better.

This, then, as it seems to me, is the simple
question to be decided.   Does the Church want or
does it not want—will it be served or will it be injured by—the labours and efforts of twenty, thirty,
or forty Catholic members devoting themselves
exclusively or primarily to its service?   Are the

affairs of the Church in the United Kingdom in
such a position that it needs or does not need
this kind of service? It is a very troublesome
service to render. It cannot be rendered without
incurring much odium and ridicule, nor without
making many sacrifices. Nobody wishes to render
it if it be not needed. We hitherto, partly guided
by our own knowledge and observation, and partly
following the lead of the Apostolic Delegate in
1851, have judged that such service was extremely
needed; that all that could be done was too little;
that the thousands of souls who yearly perish and
are perverted through the operation of bad laws
badly administered require far more vigorous
exertions in their favour than any existing party,
however zealous or able, can render them. But
perhaps we have been in error; and I for one,
if the responsibility of the decision be removed
from my shoulders, if the highest authority in the
Church inform me, in direct terms or by implication,
that I have been mistaken; if I am assured by an
authority which has a much higher guidance and
inspiration than I can pretend to, that no special
service of the Church is required; that self-
sacrifice in such a case is wholly needless; that
everything is going as well as can be expected,
and that the Church will be best served or sufficiently served by every Catholic member following his own interest and convenience; whenever
this decision is authoritatively communicated to
me, so as to relieve me from the responsibility of a

conclusion which I now believe to be a fatal error, I promise not only to pay to that decision the most implicit obedience, but to make it as widely known as I can, and to procure for it the implicit obedience of every man whom I can influence. In that event, I take it for granted that it will be my duty to preach the same easy doctrine to the poor electors, which will have been decided to be applicable to the wealthier and more ambitious representatives. From a member no sacrifice is to be expected if he can best serve the Church by pursuing his own interest. If Catholic interests are so well protected and secured that on the part of the representative no special service is required and no sacrifice of self, of course the poor electors will get the benefit of this new doctrine, and will no longer be urged by Government Bishops from the altar to incur the displeasure of their land-lords and to risk the ruin of their families. If the doctrine be true, it applies to all ; let all have the benefit of it. Let all of us, rich and poor, thoroughly understand that the Church needs no public service except what we can render at our perfect convenience, and with the most devoted attention to the worldly advancement of every one of us. It will save a great deal of trouble if this doctrine, which is now practically enforced, as far as the rich are concerned, by the authority of the Apostolic Delegate and too many of the Bishops, be taught plainly and in terms, so that all may have the benefit of it, and simple people

may be saved from the unprofitable delusion that
the Church just now requires any other service
than the spirit of self-interest.

If, on the contrary, the Holy See judges that
special service, great devotion to the interests of
the Church, and a peculiar spirit of self-sacrifice
to do its work in relation to the state, are useful
and necessary in all classes and conditions of men ;
if it should decide that an Independent Catholic
party in the House of Commons, primarily devoted
to the interests of the Church and the poor, is
very much required—then I humbly submit that
it is better for such a party to be strong than to
be feeble, to be numerous than to be few in
numbers.

At present, the entire influence of the Holy See
in the hands of the Apostolic Delegate is applied
to decrease our numbers, weaken our union, and
diminish our strength—a very proper course if an
Independent Catholic party is an evil to be combated and a danger to be put down. If that is
the position which we hold towards the Holy See,
if it is we who are the public enemy, and if it is
indeed intended to direct uniformly and steadily
against us the authority of the Holy See until
our extinction is secured—let us be told this
plainly at once, that we may know how to regulate
our conduct. But if the Holy See thinks otherwise, then I humbly submit that the power placed
in the hands of the Apostolic Delegate as representative of the Successor of St. Peter has not

been legitimately used; has been employed—as I think it has been employed—to the detriment of the Church. If an Independent Catholic party be needed in the House of Commons, the influence of the Apostolic Delegate ought most certainly to have been used to strengthen and increase and improve its efficiency. Instead of doing so, our great obstruction in labouring for the Church and trying to procure redress of grievances affecting the souls of thousands has been not so much the Government or Exeter Hall as the Apostolic Delegate, and those Bishops who have co-operated in his designs. I shall show this more in detail in the next chapter, but for the present I say—what I presume Dr. Cullen will not deny—that his influence has been steadily used to discredit the Independent party; and that while we have received from him many discouragements, and while the servants of the Government flourished in the smiles of his countenance, we have enjoyed his Grace's frowns and symptoms of his perpetual displeasure.

In saying that an Independent Catholic party, if needed, ought to receive the support of the Church, I hope not to be misunderstood. No person and no party can deserve support, especially the support of the Church, merely by giving themselves a plausible name and professing to uphold certain useful principles. It may be that they are not able to do justice to the principles which they advocate; that they are incapable, or insincere, or dishonest; or, however right in the abstract, their personal disqualifications may render them unable to accomplish any good. All this may be very true.

It may be true that we are personally less competent to render service to the Church than the mass of perjurers and promise-breakers who, with a very small sprinkling of honester men, have taken the Government side. If this be true, or if it be thought true, let it be said frankly, and let us understand our position; we shall then know what course to take.

Again, in saying that the Independent party deserve the support of the Church, I do not mean to say that the Apostolic Delegate ought to be drawn into such a position of embittered personal hostility to the Government of the day as may render it difficult or impossible for him to transact his ordinary business with them. Such a course is not necessary, would be of no sort of utility even to us, and would be in the highest degree injudicious. It would not, for instance, be necessary for the Archbishop of Dublin to take nearly so prominent a position in public affairs as has been taken usefully for so many years by the Archbishop of New York. Nor does anybody wish the Archbishop of Dublin to appear upon the hustings, to attend public meetings, to appear before the world by his public writings on the Catholic interests of the day, as many great and renowned Bishops of the Church have appeared

before him in every age and in every country.   If
his Grace feels that these public demonstrations
would be unsuitable to him, or injurious to the work
he has in hand, we have never wished to interfere
with his perfect freedom in that respect.   What
we venture to complain of in his Grace perfectly
illustrates what we think we have a right to ask,
not of the Archbishop of Dublin, but of the
Apostolic Delegate.   Our complaint is not of acts
before the world so much as of private acts and
secret conduct which are continually but accidentally coming to light.   Dr. Cullen does not
openly commit himself to the world by publicly
opposing us and supporting the Government, but
in private he so acts that every man who supports
the Government feels him to be a friend ; every
man who opposes the Government feels him to
be an enemy.   It is not a public epistle that
reveals this, but a private letter ; not a speech
upon the hustings, but a whisper carried through
the lobby of the House of Commons ; not a public
denunciation, but sometimes (I grieve to say what
hereafter I shall prove) a private calumny ; not
an open profession of principles, but conduct
which favours one party and disfavours the other.
Without further avowals of any kind, Dr. Cullen
is able to serve the Government very effectually.
By the choice of less exceptionable means, but
by the same private communication of his views,
Dr. Cullen, without public demonstrations of any

kind, might serve the party which he now studiously injures.

Nor would a calm, measured, moderate behaviour of the kind I have described, in any way injure him with the Administration of the day. He would not be personally responsible for any particular acts of opposition which we might judge advisable. They would be our acts, undertaken upon our sole responsibility, and in obedience to the dictates of our judgment. The Apostolic Delegate would not be mixed up, or supposed to be mixed up, with our special parliamentary tactics. He would be known only as giving a general approbation to our zealous efforts in defence of the Church, which everybody would take to be his natural course ; which could give no offence, and could not implicate him in the details of our parliamentary conduct, any further than it directly touched upon the Church. For that we should indeed be responsible to his Grace, as we are to every Bishop in Ireland. We should be bound to account to him and to all for the demands we made upon the Government, and for the principles on Church questions which we might advocate. But for the prudence of the means we might take to give effect to those principles, his Grace would never be held accountable, unless he himself chose to claim a share in the parliamentary management. No man could or would blame the Apostolic Delegate if, allying himself with no party in the state, he gave his countenance to a body of Catholic

representatives who treated all parties with perfect impartiality, and knew neither friendship nor
enmity except on behalf of the Church and of the
poor.

And surely such a course would at least have
nothing ignoble about it. My belief, of course, is
that it would ensure, at no very distant period, the
complete redress of all those minor religious grievances which press upon thousands of the poor and
produce so much spiritual evil. I am satisfied
that the redress of these grievances is within our
reach if we chose to take the proper means. I
venture to say that an Independent parliamentary
party of twenty members, enjoying the support and
countenance of the Apostolic Delegate, and countenanced by him wherever his influence extends
throughout Ireland ; of which it was believed that
its strength was on the increase—and its strength
would increase if, through Dr. Cullen's management, the Holy See were not supposed to be our
enemy—becoming more numerous and therefore
more entitled to consideration, more feared by its
enemies and more respected by its friends ;—such
a party which he might incalculably strengthen,
and which he has done his best to destroy, might,
and by the blessing of God would, in five years
obtain the redress of every religious grievance
that presses directly upon the Catholic poor.
This truth is as clear and certain to me as the
sun at noonday. I am sure that redress is
speedily attainable.

God may of course give us His benefits in any way that best pleases Him, and by the use of the most unlikely means. But speaking of human means and human calculations, and taking into account the ordinary chances of political life, I am not rash in asserting that if the Apostolic Delegate and those Bishops who act with him would take as much pains to build up and improve as they have taken to pull down and to destroy an Independent party, they would in a very short time carry out in these respects what I am satisfied they can hope to carry out by no other means—the dearest wishes of the Holy See. We, at all events, shall have done our part.

With proper aid the strength of such a party may be indefinitely augmented and its power to serve the Church increased threefold. If the Church opposes us, we are powerless; and for my part I wish to be powerless against such an opposition. We have offered our services; we have shown at least a good deal of zeal, and—in the opinion of many—some capacity to render service; and we wish for nothing better than an opportunity to spend and be spent in behalf of the Church and of the poor. If our humble endeavours—mistaken though they be, but at all events well meant—be rejected; if we are told by the highest authority that our efforts injure the cause of the Church instead of serving it, we shall then at least be absolved from blame, and not upon us will rest the responsibility if at the end of the century, as at the beginning, the rights of the Church are still stubbornly withheld.

Section VI.—*English Political Parties.*

As the Church holds a neutral position among various forms of government, so I take the liberty of thinking that in a popular government like ours, it is, or ought to be, the policy of the Church to hold a neutral position among contending parties. The character of parties changes from generation to generation; I had almost said from year to year. In regard to the Church itself, the disposition and character of parties change, sometimes very suddenly, from seeming friendship to deadly hostility, and as readily from hostility to friendship. The recent history of England abundantly proves this proposition. For years the Catholics of Ireland had been in close alliance with the Whigs. Repeatedly, even within my short experience, the votes of Catholic members of Parliament have saved the Whigs from expulsion from office, and have replaced them when expelled. Yet in 1851 the Whigs found it for their interest to commence against us a new course of persecuting law. We quarrelled with them, and the quarrel seemed likely to be lasting. Dr. Cullen publicly thanked God that from the condition of false friends they had passed into the category of open enemies, and expressed his satisfaction that a new code of persecution had taught us to trust them no longer. Three or four years have passed away and the scene is again changed ; our sworn enemies are once more changed into our dearest friends. Dr. Cullen, in the person of Mr. Monsell, has enlisted the Catholic members under the flag of Lord Palmerston, and no man, not even a priest, finds favour with the Apostolic Delegate unless he is prepared to unsay the words which his Grace deliberately uttered in 1851.

But this is only the most recent experience. A little more than a century ago the Whigs were our special and most inveterate enemies, and the Tories pretended to be our allies. In those days the cast of parties was exactly the reverse of what it is now. The Whigs were then the authors and defenders of the penal code, which they afterwards helped partially to repeal, and which in our day they have laboured partially to reimpose. The Tories pretended to defend us from the Whigs, as the Whigs now pretend to defend us from the Tories. To that party in the state our forefathers attached themselves with devoted but mistaken fidelity, and on the battlefield and on the scaffold poured out their blood like water in support of a political alliance from which they never could have reaped advantage. To-day the fashion is to repeat this sacrifice of our public interests in favour of the Whigs; but our modern politicians differ from our ancestors in this, that when by a foolish policy they really did injury to their faith, they at all events, with a chivalry which cannot be too highly praised, staked and threw away every worldly possession; inheritance, family, fortune, name, and life itself, their last shilling, their last acre: and the head upon the block, a ruined house, and a family in exile, attested the heroism with which they played the desperate but impolitic game. We have fallen upon a more commercial era. We attach ourselves to a party that hates and despises' us, whose friendship, as Dr. Cullen told us in 1851, is more fatal than their enmity, and we damage the Church of God by the cowardice and selfishness which forbids us—I use Dr. Cullen's words—"to rely on Heaven and ourselves." But, unlike our forefathers, we have no thought of risking anything upon the cast. If the Church of God is injured, let us be thankful that Mr. Sheil's and Mr. Monsell's dignity and income are increased.

From this retrospect, however, amongst other things, I am led to the conclusion that for the Church to identify itself with any particular party, to make that party its friend and ally, and all other parties its enemies, as a general rule, is very bad policy, and very inconsistent with its own dignity. Outside the Church the Church has no sincere friends. At bottom, not all individuals, but all parties dislike the Church pretty equally. Political convenience and other circumstances modify the action of this animosity; and convenience may modify it in one party just as much as in another. An alliance between

the Church and one of the great parties in our
English commonwealth is an alliance offensive
and defensive. It is, if you will, a treaty for
mutual defence and protection; but it is also a
treaty in which each of the contracting parties
takes upon it the enmities of the other. It is a
communion of friendships, but it is also a communion of political hatreds. The Church makes
a treaty with the Whigs to receive Whig help,
and, when the time comes, Whig treachery; but
the same treaty binds her to political enmity
against the Tories, and, what is worse, it binds
the Tories to political enmity against us. If it
gains for us allies of whom we know that any
momentary convenience may change them into
active assailants, it ensures us the lasting hostility
of adversaries whose enmity is much more persevering and tenacious than the friendship of
those whom we call our friends.

When we have struck up an offensive alliance
with the Whigs against the Tories, we have by
that very act given the Tories a special political
motive to assail us. If we stand alone; adopting
an attitude of impartiality; treating each political
faction as it deserves at our hands; and declaring
war against none except so far as they declare
war against us; we may be exposed to attacks;
but in an ordinary way it will only be the attacks
of those whom genuine religious bigotry inspires
with an active and revengeful fury. But when,
as Dr. Cullen now wishes, we shall have enrolled

ourselves in the Whig party, the immediate
interest of the Tories who are out of office is to
attack the Whigs who are in office, in their weak
point, which in the present temper of the English
public mind is their alliance with us.   The mere
politicians of the Tory party care very little about
the Catholics, have comparatively little hostility
to us, like us perhaps rather better than .they like
the Protestant Dissenters, because of the principle
of authority in the Church, the antiquity and
venerableness of our faith.   But it is their political trade when out of office to find out points of
attack against the Whigs; and if the Catholics
will enlist in the Whig army, it is a matter almost
of necessity for the Tories to assail the Catholics if
they present the most vulnerable point of attack.
It thus becomes the interest even of those Tories
whom no religious bigotry inflames to inflame
the religious bigotry of the country against us,
because the Catholics are the most vulnerable
portion of the Whig line.   It becomes their interest through our act.   We make it their interest.
We invite them to adopt a course of religious
bigotry against us by making it profitable in the
sense of their political calculations.   They might,
I have little doubt they would, let us alone if so
many of us, and Dr. Cullen amongst the number,
were not Whigs.   But if we will be Whigs, if we
will take Whig pay and put on Whig uniforms,
we must expect to be specially honoured by
thrusts from Tory bayonets.   The Tories have

no political enmity to us as Catholics. Their political enmity commences when we join their enemies the Whigs. When we do so, it is we by our own folly who turn religious bigotry into a political weapon and direct that weapon against our own breasts.

If we would stand alone the Tories would let us alone; and why? A body of twenty, thirty, or forty members acting together (we might have as many if Dr. Cullen would allow us), able to help sometimes one side and sometimes another, are never lightly offended by the discreet leaders of either of the great parties. Remaining neutral, our votes may go to either side according to circumstances. We vote with one party to-day, but we may vote with the other side to-morrow. Each party hopes something from us, and fears something from us also. The interest of both parties is to stand well with us; and, except at moments when popular frenzy raises against us an overwhelming burst of religious bigotry and fanaticism, both parties will pay their court to us and give us as little offence as possible. As I state this broadly, it may perhaps be called a mere theory, but I shall presently show that it is fact and practice.

There might be a reason for uniting ourselves with one political party if the mode of treating the Catholic Church formed the ground of difference between that party and its political opponents. But the truth is, that both parties profess in regard

to the Church exactly the same principles.   The
heads of both parties are equally unwilling to
engage in an open contest with the Church unless
some very pressing motive urges them; in the
mass of both parties there is about an equal
amount of genuine religious fanaticism, and the
greater hostility shown towards us by the Tories
than by the Whigs has arisen, especially in late
years, far more from the connection we have
habitually maintained with the Whigs, and from
the hostile front we have always shown against
the Tories.

I am not blaming those who managed our
affairs in past times.   Every epoch has its own
special circumstances and its own policy; but
looking at the present circumstances of the times,
nothing is clearer to me than that, if it ever was
politic to maintain exclusive alliance with the
Whigs, it is so no longer, and what may have
been wisdom ten years ago is the height of imprudence now.

For indeed we have reached a new order of
things in English political opinion as regards the
interests of the Church.   Since Lord John
Russell's movement of 1851, the worst and
bitterest assaults upon us have proceeded from
what is usually called the Liberal side of the
House.   The attacks upon our convents have
been initiated by Mr. Chambers, a Whig lawyer,
returned by a Whig constituency, having for his
colleague Lord Palmerston's stepson; an ambitious

and rising barrister, who looks to Lord Palmerston for promotion. He is a man to whom I do no wrong when I say that everybody believes Mr. Chambers to be vastly indifferent to this question on religious grounds, and to have set himself to assail our convents solely from calculations of worldly ambition and advancement. He is a man of considerable shrewdness and ability. He is a lawyer looking—as most lawyers look—for place. His opinion as an English Liberal, looking for promotion to English Liberal Ministers, is that his furious assaults on the Catholic Church will not impede, but will very much assist his own legal and official elevation. Mr. Chambers is a man of humble origin, has no family connections to support him, and depends for the success of his career solely upon his own personal ability and on his adapting himself to the temper and spirit of the times. Such then is his estimate, as an English Liberal, of the general tendency of things around him.

Nor is this a single case. The recent traditions of the Whigs and Liberals in England as regards political principle are in favour, not merely of toleration, but of the widest and most comprehensive impartiality in dealing with all religions. Yet, from personal observation, I am· sure there is on the Liberal side of the House quite as much anti-Catholic bigotry as among the Tories. Indeed the case is that quite of late years the Tories have begun to lose something of their old bigotry and to receive an infusion of a better spirit. The Liberals, on the contrary, have begun to lose a great deal of their old pretensions to candour and justice, and have received a large infusion of fanaticism ; nor, indeed, is this to be wondered at. Everywhere on the Continent the sympathies of the English Liberals are against the Church and in favour of its worst enemies. At the same time the disposition of the English Tories with regard to Continental affairs is rather to look with a more friendly eye upon the Church, as an authority opposed to revolution, and to consider the acts of the Continental Liberals as foreshadowing the downfall of the English Protestant Church.

When an attempt was made last year to establish Industrial Schools for the poor on such a basis as literally to give the police power to steal Catholic children in the streets and thrust them into proselytising schools, the members whom we had to encounter and resist were quite as often on the Liberal as on the Tory side. Indeed, the author and promoter of one of the worst of these Bills is himself a distinguished Liberal. I believe that the bitterest enemies of religious orders, of the integrity of Church property, and of the purity of Catholic education, are unquestionably the Liberals. The Irish system of National education (which was once thought very dangerous, but perhaps that opinion along with others has been abandoned) is an invention of the Whigs or Liberals.   The Queen's Colleges had for their authors Dr. Cullen's dearest friends, the followers of the late Sir Robert Peel, and Sir Robert Peel himself; and these Peelites (now Liberals), up to the time of their leaving office in this year, were still their warmest and most vigorous upholders against us.   The motion with which we are now threatened against Maynooth proceeds, it is true, from the Tory side of the House.   But I see in the newspapers that, by a special arrangement, it is to be moved from one side of the House and seconded from the other ; and that the Bill when brought into the House is to have printed on the back of it names taken impartially from the Liberal and Conservative parties, in order to establish the fact that henceforward these questions of anti-Catholic malice are to be restricted to no special faction or party in the Legislature.

Depend upon it, the lesson contained in Lord John Russell's movement of 1851 has not yet produced all its fruits in the Liberal ranks.   The leaders of the Whigs, as they have proved, would, at any moment plunge a dagger into our hearts if their political interests required it.   At the same time, the worst assaults upon us in the public journals proceed from the Liberals, and they are becoming every year worse and worse. Of course there are some brilliant exceptions to what I am now saying ; there are, indeed, exceptions on all sides to any general statement that can be made ; but I am persuaded that I have now described pretty accurately the tendency of things with regard to anti-Catholic bigotry in England, and that this is the state of opinion with regard to which we have to take our course.

How stands the case then ? A spirit of fanatical opposition to the Church is developing itself in England, and making itself visible in various directions, new as well as old. It has eaten deep into the ranks of the Liberal party, and it is but four years ago since the leaders of this new-born anti-Catholic fanaticism were the men who then were, and still are, the leaders of the Whigs. This disease has eaten into all classes and ranks of men, and in many quarters has been potent and virulent enough to displace many old traditions of political opinions.

In former periods of our history, when religious bigotry has waxed strong and furious, we have suffered most when political calculation has blown the coals of religious animosity. It has done so at all times from the Reformation down to the year 1851. It was so in the reign of Charles II., when the profligate Lord Shaftesbury put himself at the head of the religious frenzy of the time and used it as an instrument for overturning his political opponents. It was so after the Revolution, when the two parties of Whig and Tory—the Tories in the House of Commons and the Whigs in the House of Lords—employed themselves, as Burke has well described, in the evil emulation of adding clause after clause to the worst portion of

the old penal code, not from any religious bigotry
or feeling whatever, but from the coldest calculation of political expediency, and to further the
interest of their respective parties. A repetition
of this very game between Whigs and Tories was
witnessed in the discussions on the Ecclesiastical
Titles Bill, in which the same political rivalry
produced precisely the same results, to our dis-
advantage.

If these facts from history are of any value as
lessons, the inference I draw from them is that
we ought to be very careful not to make political
engagements with one of the great parties which
shall oblige us to permanent political hostility
towards its opponent; not to create political animosities in addition to the religious animosities
by which we are sure to be assailed; not so to act
towards any political party as to give it to understand that our enmity towards it is permanent and
unchangeable; not to deprive any political party
of those motives of repentance which the prospect
of thirty or forty votes always gives to a prudent
assemblage of parliamentary politicians; not to
act so that one of the great political parties shall
feel that, whether they attack us or whether they
let us alone, we are equally their enemies, and are
bound by a political alliance to show them enmity
on all occasions.

My notion of wisdom for the Church and of
safety for the Church at this moment is that these
are to be found in an attitude of prudent neutrality.

We have much to fear from every party, and we have something to hope from all parties in their turn, if we act so as to command their respect, and not so as to create and perpetuate their enmity. We ought, in my opinion, to keep ourselves in such a position that we can treat all parties from time to time exactly as they deserve at our hands. I think there is no party on the continuance of whose friendship we can rely, or on whose enmity· we may not equally calculate on a change of government. To procure the cessation of that enmity, to make all parties respect us and fear to lay their hands upon us in the way of persecution, depends upon ourselves alone.

It is said indeed, that, as matters now stand, the Whigs or Liberals are as a whole more favourable to us, and the Tories or Conservatives as a whole more hostile ; that no man can calculate the changes which time may produce ; but that, as matters now stand, it is more for our interest to have in office a party which is to some extent friendly, even though its friendship should be treacherous, than a party that is openly hostile.

I know not why this principle should be conceded. Sure I am that it is at variance with the deliberate, written, and recorded opinion of Dr. Cullen in 1851. His Grace then thanked God that instead—not of any other false friends—not of false friends in the abstract—but of these very identical false friends—the same men holding the same opinions, and nourishing the same designs

—Lord John Russell and Lord Palmerston, with Catholic colleagues to keep them straight—that instead of false friends like these, with a tranquil and seemingly favourable state of public opinion, we had got a Government of open enemies, threatening and performing acts of violence, and directing the tempest of a furious popular bigotry. His Grace publicly thanked God that we had open enemies in office, and a frenzy of bigoted fanaticism rather than a tranquil state of public opinion, with these very treacherous friends in power. I know not, therefore, why I should be compelled to differ with the Dr. Cullen of 1851, or why I may not assert in 1855 what he asserted four years ago.

If the Tories were now in office, I should oppose them as zealously as I oppose the Whigs, unless they granted justice to the Church of God and justice to the poor of Christ. To me the men are nothing; but whoever refuses justice to the Church and to the poor, to him I cannot but be opposed. When Lord Derby was in office in 1852, I opposed him, and with my vote helped to turn him out. But if I am asked my opinion, I should say that the Tories are much less dangerous to us in office than out of office; and that the Whigs, on the contrary, are, and have always proved, much better friends to us out of office than in office.

When in office, the Tories have the responsibility of governing; the peace of the country is in their hands ; they wish, naturally, to make affairs run smoothly and easily ; without renouncing their principles, they wish, at all events, not to make enemies ; and to make friends they would be glad so to act that Catholic gentlemen could take office with them, or at least show towards them a friendly feeling ; and if they saw a willingness to treat them not with a mere undistinguishing party hostility, but strictly according to their merits, I am persuaded they would do nothing to stir up popular bigotry against us, but would do whatever they could to allay the anti-Catholic frenzy of their followers, and allay rather than increase the bigotry of the public mind.

Lord Derby's Government of 1852 commenced by a violent opposition to the Catholics, of which the Stockport riots were an unhappy symptom and result. At that time the excitement arising from the Ecclesiastical Titles Bill had not yet subsided, and the Tories calculated, as the Whigs had done before them, upon getting a certain amount of popularity out of that public frenzy. Besides, they knew many of the Catholic members who had been in Parliament before the general election of 1852, and they judged (very truly) that most of those members had made their arrangements with the Whigs or Liberals ; that they had nothing to hope from them ; that neither kindness nor justice could change their course ; and that, as a matter of calculation, it being out of the question to conciliate or soften the party hostility of the Catholics, they could lose nothing and might gain much by bidding high for the support of anti-Catholic fanaticism. Upon this calculation they acted in the beginning of their short tenure of office; but when the elections were over in the summer of 1852, they found that a good many new Catholic members were returned to Parliament, and they at once applied themselves more diligently than ever to find means of earning favour and disarming the opposition of the Irish Catholic constituencies. When Parliament met in the autumn of the same year, Lord Derby's Administration laid on the table of the House of Commons the very best Bill for doing justice to the Irish tenants that up to that time had ever been proposed by an English Government; and even at the risk of offending the Irish landlords, who formed some of their strongest adherents, they fully recognised the justice of the Irish tenants' claim. The measure that we proposed on that subject they were not prepared to adopt : but the very instant we announced in the House of Commons that we were not going to act as partisans, but to treat the Government strictly according to its merits ; to receive acts of justice from it with precisely the same candour and gratitude as if they came from the Liberals ; and, in a word, to treat all parties with the utmost impartiality ; the Government without a moment's hesitation made us a concession which had never been made before. They agreed to give our Tenant Bill a

second reading, to put it on a level with their own
Bills on the same subject, and to refer all the
Bills (ours included) to a Select Committee, in
which we were to be amply represented.

I don't say that Lord Derby approved of our
Bill ; he strongly disapproved of it.   He approved
of it no more than Lord Palmerston, or Lord John
Russell, or the Peelites.

They all bitterly disliked it ; and it is because
Lord Derby disliked our Bill, because his Protestant supporters disliked it so much, that I insist
upon the lengths he went in giving it countenance,
as a proof of the efforts a Tory Government may
be ready to make even for us, and on matters of
the first importance to them, in the hope not
exactly of purchasing our support, but of mitigating
our opposition.   The concession made by Lord
Derby on that occasion was the greatest help the
Irish tenants had ever received from any official
personage towards obtaining a just settlement of
their claims.

Lord Derby's Administration was overthrown
soon after this incident, and nothing passed with
reference to Catholic questions from which a
deduction could be drawn as to his purpose upon
these.   But when his party were driven into
opposition, and throughout the whole session of
1853, there was exhibited by the members of that
party—I say what I witnessed—a marked disposition to avoid everything hostile or offensive
to us.   Offensive things were said and done now

and then by partisans of Lord Derby ; but rather
fewer and less offensive, I think, than were said
and done by partisans of Lord Aberdeen and
Lord John Russell, and indeed by Lord John
Russell himself.

But to any one who witnessed what took place,
it was clear that the Tory leaders, seeing a considerable section of Catholic members on the Opposition benches, unconnected with the Whigs,
and not bound by any party ties to their enemies,
did what they could to restrain the bigotry of some
of their own followers, and to avoid as far as they
could whatever might displease us. And this
endeavour continued as long as we appeared to
have the preponderating strength in Ireland, to
have the support of the leading Bishops, and above
all, to be sustained by the good wishes of the
Apostolic Delegate. But when it began to be whispered that the Apostolic Delegate was our enemy,
and in proportion as it became more confidently
asserted and more generally believed that all his
influence was given actively though privately to
support Lord Aberdeen and uphold the Whigs,
this forbearance of the Tory leaders became less
and less visible, and the whole party began once
more to use the anti-Catholic fanaticism of the
multitude for their own factious purposes. And
so it will continue as long as human nature remains the same. If we persist in making ourselves the tools and servants of the Whigs, we
shall always have the Tories prompt and active

to stir up whatever bigotry they may find in the country ready to their hand and useful for damaging their opponents. Nor, if we consider the thing as a matter of political calculation, can we blame them for doing so. It may be dishonest, but selfish dishonesty is the vice of political partiès ; and if we make it the interest of half the politicians in England to be our enemies, and declare war against them, we cannot reasonably complaiń if they take us at our word and inflict upon us all the mischief in their power. For these reasons I am of opinion that the Tories, as we generally manage matters, are more dangerous to us when in opposition than when in office ; and that if office gives them increased power to do us mischief, it generally diminishes the motive and the inclination.

As to the Whigs or Liberals, on the other hand, I have no occasion to go into any lengthened reasoning to show that out of office they have always exerted themselves much more in our behalf than when they have been Ministers of the Crown. It is a known fact that they always have done so. Out of office it is easy to make professions, which entail very little responsibility, and it is the cue of the Whigs when out of office to make great professions of religious liberality and great promises of service to be rendered. Out of office they are indignant at our wrongs; they smart at every injustice inflicted on us ; they make our cause theirs, and take a pleasure in exposing any unfair treatment of which we may have been the victims. But once seated on the Ministerial benches the case is wonderfully altered. In Opposition words are breath; they cost little, and very often mean less; but with the Minister of the Crown words are things, and what he promises in his capacity of Minister he must endeavour at least to appear to fulfil. When the Whigs are in office, therefore, they do us little or no service in act, and we lose even the service of their tongues. They cease to be our impassioned advocates; they shrink from too great an appearance of complicity with our demands; they inflict upon us rude repulses; and happy is it for us if they do not find it convenient to demonstrate the strictness of their Protestantism by aiming at us a treacherous stab, or meeting us with scornful and insolent hostility.

For these, amongst many reasons, I agree cordially with the Dr. Cullen of 1851, that the presence in office of the treacherous Whigs is not better, but much worse, than to have our open enemies in power; and for these reasons also I retain the opinion which Dr. Cullen then held, that the true province of the Church in Ireland is not to be the purchased instrument of a party, but to hold herself aloof from all parties; and to use her influence to send men to Parliament who will simply do her work, and defend her rights and the rights of the poor; to treat all

men and all parties according to their deserts;
to make herself needlessly the enemy of none;
but with indefatigable and unremitting vigour to
oppose and resist all, whether in or out of office,
who dare to lay a hostile hand upon her, or to
refuse justice to those unprotected poor of whom
she is bound to be the protector.

I am sorry to know that Dr. Cullen entertains
a different opinion. I wish I could agree with
his Grace; but if I were to do so, I should have
to disagree with prelates who know Ireland much
better and have much greater experience in its
affairs. But even were it otherwise, I cannot but
feel that the course which I advocate is at all
events the safest and least dangerous. What has
happened before may happen again. The Whig
persecutors of 1851 may become the persecutors
of some other year not very distant or remote.
Dr. Cullen is now reconciled to them, and in
their behalf is trying to disband the parliamentary
army which was enlisted against them and for
the protection of the Church; wishes us to desert
our standard and become recruits under those
who have made it penal for him to claim the
See of Dublin or to receive a Papal Bull; and
labours to subdue the spirit of the country and
render it tame, and to make it tremble beneath
the hand of its Whig taskmasters. The policy
of 1851 is no longer to his Grace's taste, and
he wishes us to go back to Pharaoh again to do

his work and eat of his flesh-pots. We thought him Moses and gladly followed him. He (not we) repents of the manna in the wilderness, and he would carry us back to the rich feasts and unspeakable degradation of the land of Egypt.

CHAPTER VI.

SECTION I.—*Introductory.*

THE name of Dr. Cullen has often been mentioned in the course of this "Statement," incidentally, and as the necessity from time to time arose.

I must devote some few pages to a more systematic explanation of what I have to say respecting his Grace and the course he has recently been pursuing. I am sorry that this should be necessary. It has been throughout at once my wish and my interest to believe that Dr. Cullen had not changed his politics since 1851 ; that he was still pursuing a line in which I could humbly co-operate with him ; that he was still willing to give his aid to the principles and to the policy to which, in the fullest reliance on his support and sympathy, I and others had in a very particular manner publicly and irrevocably committed ourselves.

. . . . . .

Nothing could be more hostile to my interests than to have it supposed that Dr. Cullen had seen reason to change his policy, and that, instead of the support which he formerly vouchsafed to give me, I was henceforward to struggle with his hostility. . . .

I therefore shut my eyes to the truth as long as possible, and longer I think than was perhaps prudent. All around me were long since convinced, . . . but it was not, I may say, till his Grace's uncle, the Rev. James Maher—supposed to be his most trusted counsellor—had conveyed to me personally the impression that his nephew's policy had undergone a radical change . . . that I practically admitted into my mind this (to me) sad and unprofitable truth. . . .

Nor in Rome have I been less unwilling to treat the points at issue in a hostile spirit; and I say with perfect truth, that I have done everything in my power to carry out what I understood to be, and what I am sure was, the wish of his Holiness, that the points of difference should be as much as possible smoothed down. I put myself for this purpose unreservedly into the hands of the Secretary of Propaganda, and begged of him to dictate to me the manner in which these views of the Holy Father should be carried out. . . . He advised that we should speak out very plainly. . . .

The details of the conference it is not necessary to give here. I need only say that I adhered as strictly as I could to my purpose of avoiding all topics of mere complaint and irritation; that not

less than three times I recalled to Dr. Cullen's
recollection that the purpose of our conference
was peace, and I hoped it would not end without
something being said or done to promote peace;
while, on the contrary, from Dr. Cullen's lips not
one word dropped having the remotest tendency
towards peace; his Grace did nothing to meet my
advances; his tone was hostile throughout. . . .
His Grace distinctly intimated his wish that I
should retire from public life; his desire to destroy
an Independent Catholic party; his strong preference for a Government connection; and his
resolution to have, with every man entertaining
the sentiments of his Grace in 1851, no peace, but
war. . . . After that conference it is not a matter
of deduction, but of certainty, that Dr. Cullen
nourishes views of public affairs . . . which are
fatal to any hope of the redress of Catholic grievances, . . . and which if they could be fully
carried out, would lay the nation prostrate at the
feet of the English Minister.

Nor was this all. The conference had hardly
ended when Dr. Cullen sat down to write letters
to Ireland about my proceedings. Those letters,
evidently written for publication, and published
in the Government journals by his Grace's Vicar-
General, held me up to ridicule before the people
of Ireland for the very efforts I made to seek
peace, . . . endeavoured to lower me in public
estimation . . . by representing me as an erring
son of the Church, and the paternal condescen-

sion of his Holiness—how far beyond my merits —as the benevolent artifices of a benign father labouring to reclaim the guilty by kindness rather than by severity.

Section II.—*Past and Present.*

It is not easy to know to what extent I should go in establishing the point that Dr. Cullen has completely changed his politics within the last three years. In Ireland, as I have already said, the thing is notorious, and to set about proving it would be like attempting to prove that black is not white. . . .

But in Rome I don't know what is understood about this business. . . . Sometimes I hear it said that his Grace denies that he has changed; at other times, that he admits a change, and justifies it by alleging some trifling change of circumstances. . . . In a conversation I had with his Grace's uncle . . . that gentleman in words denied any change, but admitted that his nephew . . . now acts politically with Mr. Monsell—that is, with a member of Lord Palmerston's Government—who never joined the Defence Association in 1851, but was on principle opposed to it.

In the conference with Dr. Cullen in Rome his Grace seemed also in words to deny any change, but used expressions which showed an entire and radical alteration. Amongst other things, his Grace was good enough to institute a comparison between those who, acting in Parliament according to the ordinary forms of our law and constitution, oppose peaceably a particular Minister because they disapprove his principles —and the revolutionary followers of Mazzini. I could not at the moment refrain from thanking his Grace for this compliment.

.   .   .   .   .   .

To me this (question of change) is a matter of no little personal importance on public grounds. Once I enjoyed Dr. Cullen's favour. I am now the object of his bitterest enmity. . . . He has found out that I deserve great reprobation and has gone the length—I blush to say it—of inventing articles that I never wrote, and phrases that I never used, to help the good work of my personal ruin. . . . I am told that Dr. Cullen is highly indignant at me for writing in the *Tablet* about clergymen in such a way as to excite towards them the disrespectful feelings of my readers. . . . But it is a singular fact . . . that the first time I had the honour of seeing Dr. Cullen and making his acquaintance . . . was when he introduced himself to me in London to instigate me to make an attack upon a priest . . . who had misconducted himself very grievously in Philadelphia, but had atoned for his errors, had made his peace with the Holy See, and was then living in Dublin under the protection of the late Archbishop, Dr. Murray, . . . who, with many other Bishops, took the Government side on the question of University education. Dr. Cullen took the other side, and judged it important to have that priest's character ruined. . . . He did not tell me that the priest had made his peace with the Holy See. . . . In the most perfect good faith, and with no other view than that of rendering a public service, I complied with Dr. Cullen's wish. . . . Looking back at my past life, . . . I am sure that, if ever I did an unjustifiable act with regard to the character of a priest, it was this act to which I was directly stimulated by Dr. Cullen.

.   .   .   .   .   .

I begin with this case because it is the earliest indication I ever had of Dr. Cullen's views and wishes; and if I have since erred in the freedom with which I have spoken of priests, who, I thought, were injuring the Church by their public conduct, I say, before Heaven, it is to the encouragement I have received from Dr. Cullen that I must in part attribute my mistake. For not merely in 1846, nor with regard to a single priest, but with regard to the last Archbishop of Dublin, and since Dr. Cullen became Archbishop, he has been my instigator and accomplice in the commission of this kind of offence. For nearly a year in 1850–51 (as I remember the dates), I was engaged in strong public opposition to the late Archbishop, Dr. Murray, on the question of the University and the degree of support and trust to be placed in the present Ministers, who were the Ministers of that day. In doing so, it was my fortune to incur great unpopularity with large classes of men, who loved the late Archbishop, and thought my opposition to him was too severe and unsparing. Whether it was or not, I repeat again that at that time I was an humble instrument in Dr. Cullen's hands, whom I believed to be the organ of the Holy See; that I obeyed his commands to the best of my ability; that I laboured at all risks to carry out his wishes; ·and that for my public opposition to the late Archbishop of Dublin I received the countenance, support, and distinct approbation of the present Apostolic Delegate.

.   .   .   .   .   .

This, then, is one of the proofs which I adduce of Dr. Cullen's altered sentiments. Before 1852, in the way of attacking the Government—other people doing the work and incurring the unpopularity, while he supplied the secret direction, incurred no risk, and received the benefit—nothing was too strong for him. . . . Now the case is wholly altered. We have the same Ministers, the same principles, the same questions; but now the rule of Church law is, that everything may be done and dared for the Government, but that even a layman cannot be safely rebuked if he has the good fortune to render to the English Ministers the acceptable service of public prostitution.

.   .   .   .   .   .

At the time when I did my utmost to support Dr. Cullen against those who were his violent enemies and are now his violent friends, I did not know all the circumstances of the case. I knew Dr. Cullen as a priest standing high in general estimation; a strong opponent of Dr. Murray; a strong supporter of Dr. MacHale; a man so vehement against the very class of priests who now worship him and are consistent in supporting the Government, that he employed me to write down the priestly character of one of them. I was told that he was staunch in disconnecting the Church in Ireland from a Government alliance; and that he would exert himself to the utmost in organising the Catholic strength of Ireland so that it might be able to stand alone, and not lean upon hostile English Ministers for its support. This I was told, and this was Dr. Cullen's public repute, whether for good or evil, with the great body of Irish Catholics. But I did not then know, what I do now know, that while Dr. Cullen had earned for himself this character with Dr. MacHale, and had secured for himself in Dr. MacHale the warmest patron and supporter, he at the same time had secured the confidence of the Whig Ministers of that day; and that while Dr. MacHale was supporting him in Rome as a man who could be absolutely depended upon to make things safe for the Church against the Whig Ministers and any English politicians whatever—these same Whig Ministers were also supporting him in Rome, and were urging, directly and powerfully, his appointment to the

See of Armagh, as a man whom they knew to be safe for their own purposes. This fact, for a fact it is, was not known to me, nor was it generally known in Ireland; and if I were to publish it with the evidence on which it rests, it would tend a good deal to my justification, but not much to his Grace's honour.

.   .   .   .   .   .

What the grounds were in Rome of Dr. Cullen's appointment to the See of Armagh it is not for me to say. . . . But the grounds on which he was recommended by the English Ministers were, of course, exactly the opposite of those universally entertained in Ireland as to his sentiments; and it is no imputation on us to acknowledge, with the deepest regret, that when two opposite characters of himself were given to two opposite parties by Dr. Cullen, we should put full trust in the more honourable picture, while unhappily that presented to the enemies of the Church to secure their countenance was more consistent with the truth.

For some time Dr. Cullen maintained strenuously the course upon the faith of which he had been so recommended and welcomed by Bishop, priest, and layman.

Observe that this was long before Lord John Russell's " Durham Letter," or the Ecclesiastical Titles Bill. There was then no open aggression on the Church, any more than there is at the present moment. We had then exactly what we

have now, and what Dr. Cullen described with so
much unction in 1851—not a direct assault, but
"false friends," "smiles," "trifling favours," "the
pretence of being perfectly liberal," and insidious
designs against "the whole education of the rising
Catholic generation of the country." . . .

With the close of the year 1850 what Dr.
Cullen calls "the *more* dangerous" sort of persecution, "that of smiles" and "trifling favours,"
passed away for a short time, and was succeeded
by what his Grace calls the less dangerous sort
of persecution, that of "violence and force." The
exchange of a less dangerous for a more dangerous
persecution could not, of course, render Dr.
Cullen more hostile to the Government which inflicted both, nor more active against them, but it
brought him more before the public.

The first half of the year 1851 was occupied by
the session of Parliament in which the Ecclesiastical Titles Bill was proposed, debated, resisted,
and carried into law. So far as that law could
accomplish anything, it was passed, and there
was no present or immediate chance of repealing
it. But the example of twenty or thirty members
of Parliament severing all connection with our
"false friends" the Whigs, throwing aside all considerations of self-interest, and devoting their
days and nights to the service of the Church
against the Whigs and all other Governments
and enemies, inspired the country and Dr. Cullen
with new hope. Such a fortunate occurrence was

thought (by Dr. Cullen expressly) very much to outweigh the evils of the Ecclesiastical Titles Bill. His Grace publicly thanked God that we had bought such a blessing at so low a rate ; and it was resolved to try to perpetuate the blessing by establishing a Defence Association, which, under the guidance of Dr. Cullen, Dr. MacHale, Dr. Cantwell, and other Bishops, should give a wise and resolute direction to this new-born spirit of opposition and independence.

The session was ended. The Ecclesiastical Titles Bill was then law. No further persecution was then threatened or expected. The general possibility of new persecutions was of course recognised then as now ; but it was thought that the combination of members on an independent basis, irrespective of all Governments, was a new and powerful weapon providentially put into our hands at that moment ; and which it was our duty to employ, not for a session or two, but for a long course of years, during a series of protracted struggles to accomplish the redress of all our grievances. It was thought—Dr. Cullen thought— that perseverance in such a course, following up the example set by the Catholic members who opposed the Ecclesiastical Titles Bill, and adapting it to other grievances, was the true way of enabling us to obtain redress. This policy was not, as I have said, intended for a session or a year ; it was to be pursued through a long course of years ; and the specific things which Dr. Cullen proposed to himself for the Defence Association to accomplish are set forth in its rules, and in an address to the Catholics of the United Kingdom, which was signed by Dr. Cullen as chairman of the committee appointed to organise the Defence Association, and by Mr. Keogh as its secretary. They are, amongst other things :—

To repeal the Ecclesiastical Titles Act, and all other Acts restricting our religious liberties.

To get rid of the Church Establishment of the land.

To redress the religious grievances of Catholic soldiers and sailors, and of the inmates of workhouses, gaols, and other public institutions.

To procure the repeal of all laws that obstruct and endanger Catholic charities and endowments.

These were a part only of the task the Defence Association took upon itself. Not one of its objects has yet been accomplished; and what I wish to establish by this enumeration is, that, in forming the Association, Dr. Cullen contemplated work to be carried through Parliament that would necessarily occupy many years, and that in all probability would see many changes of Government.

A great part of the work of the Association was necessarily to be done through Parliament. What says the " Address to the Catholics of the United Kingdom," signed by Dr. Cullen, upon that subject ?

" They can never sufficiently impress upon the minds of the
people the great fact that all our hopes of redress, under Divine
Providence, are centred in the creation and sustainment of a
Parliamentary party ready to defend at all hazards with an
independent spirit our civil and religious liberties."

At the aggregate meeting over which Dr.
Cullen presided the same principle was laid down,
in words nearly identical, in a resolution signed
by Dr. Cullen and quoted by him in the body of
his address.   The words are these :—

" That as one of the great constitutional and practical means
of carrying out the objects of this meeting, we (Dr. Cullen and
others) pledge ourselves to make every effort to strengthen the
hands and increase the power of those faithful representatives
who in the last session of Parliament so energetically devoted
themselves to the formation of an Independent party in the
Legislature, having for its object the maintenance of civil and
religious liberty in the British Empire."

Now, first, what is an Independent party ? . . .
There is only one such party in the House of
Commons now ; there never has been but one
such party since that pledge was taken.   Mr.
Monsell was never a member of it ; Mr. Keogh
deserted it, and broke his oath to get a place.
Mr. Sadleir broke his oath and deserted it, for the
same motive.   Other members broke their pledges
with a like selfish object.   We remained true to it ;
we have not abandoned a tittle of its policy ; nor, on
the questions with which the Defence Association
affected to deal, have we gone one hair'sbreadth
beyond the plan of operations then laid down.

Yet, since these dishonest men broke from us to earn the wages of the Government, we have never received the smallest benefit from Dr. Cullen's pledge. He has made no effort to "strengthen our hands;" he has not striven to "increase our power;" he has done, I believe, everything in his power to weaken us and to strengthen the hands of those who have broken their promises for gold; and we are the party whom his Grace has laboured —sometimes insidiously and sometimes openly— to break down.

.   .   .   .   .   .

If it should be alleged on the part of Dr. Cullen that though he did not dissent in public from this theory of Independent Opposition—to support which indeed his Grace appealed to the people for subscriptions—yet that he did dissent from it in private, and so expressed himself amongst his friends, I could reply to such an excuse that I know it to be positively untrue, as far as conversations with me are concerned. About that time and later I had a great deal of talk with Dr. Cullen as to Mr. Keogh and several of his fellow-members of Parliament who have since deserted to the Ministers, and as to the course they had promised and sworn to pursue. I expressed strongly to his Grace my conviction that they did not mean to keep their promises, and that they would sell themselves and leave us in the lurch on the very first opportunity.

On none of these occasions, nor on any occasion,

did Dr. Cullen convey or endeavour to convey to me the impression that he dissented from the policy of Independent Opposition, and that he should be glad when it was abandoned. His Grace knew that I was becoming more and more deeply pledged to it, but never advised me against it—never intimated his dissent. On the contrary, he always spoke so as to convince me that he heartily approved the policy, though he believed many of the men who propounded it to be rogues. He gave me to understand that he was fully satisfied Mr. Keogh and his friends would leave us, and he assured me that he thought we should be stronger in their absence and after their desertion.

Everything happened as the Apostolic Delegate and myself had foreseen and anticipated. The moment Lord Aberdeen's Government was formed in the end of 1852, Mr. Keogh and Mr. Sadleir broke their oaths and their vows, as his Grace expected from the beginning, separated from the Independent party, and accepted the offices which, not merely in 1851, but again, only two short months before they accepted them, they had publicly promised to refuse. As we expected also, a considerable number of the party, connected with these leaders by family ties or previous arrangement, followed their example, and left us, as we had expected to be left, with a party cut in two.

.   .   .   .

Is it not strange that almost from the very

moment this desertion was accomplished, the hand of Dr. Cullen was heavy upon us and his discouragement of our consistency was distinctly marked ? For a time there was some effort to maintain appearances and to seem friendly. Always an open declaration in favour of the English Government was avoided ; but it became more and more clearly visible to which side Dr. Cullen leaned, and the very desertion which Dr. Cullen had helped me to predict, with regard to which his Grace had comforted me with the assurance that it would strengthen instead of weaken us, was used as a conclusive argument for following the example of the promise-breakers and for deserting us.

Section III.—*Dr. Cullen as a Peacemaker.*

I have been anxiously looking about for some —I will not say excuse—but for some explanation which could render intelligible the course taken by Dr. Cullen ; and in the course of my researches I have found it stated in one, I think, of the Government newspapers, that Dr. Cullen entered into the project of the Defence Association under the impression that the political efforts of its members would be not only "conducted with the strictest regard to truth, charity, and justice," but with the smoothest language and the utmost gentleness of phrase ; that in speaking of public crimes all vehemence of reprobation should be avoided; and that in speaking of men who betrayed their religion, not a phrase would be uttered to express the abhorrence which such conduct naturally excites. These expectations, they say, have been grievously disappointed. Hard words have been used; great abhorrence has been expressed; angry passions have been excited; a perfectly calm demeanour has not been preserved; and altogether Dr. Cullen has been so annoyed by the vehemence of the politics connected with this Independent policy, that he has judged it better and more becoming a minister of the sanctuary to withdraw from the strife, and to know no other course than that of a peacemaker and a reconciler of brethren. Let us see what this excuse is worth.

As to the political conduct pursued by the managers of the Defence Association, I am not concerned to vindicate it. I was carefully ex- cluded from the managing committee and from all share in its administration. A great many of the acts of its most prominent members I do not approve, but most strongly condemn, and I think that many of its founders did violate in the most shameless manner " truth, charity, and justice."

It was contrary to my notions of " truth," for instance, for twenty gentlemen to promise most solemnly that they would not support Lord Aber- deen's Government; that they would maintain for the Church's sake a course of Independent Opposition ; and for one of them to attest Almighty God to the truth of this promise by three solemn oaths ; and then on the very first opportunity, with hardly an interval between the promise and the act, to violate these promises and to break these oaths. Dr. Cullen, I admit, had great reason to be indignant at men who, in the name of God's Church, could be guilty of such scandalous turpitude.

Again, it was contrary to my notions of "justice" to ask money and subscriptions to support a policy of Independent Opposition, having the while the deliberate purpose never to carry out that policy, but to take the wages of the Government as soon as they were offered. This was a breach of "justice," indeed; and I admit Dr. Cullen might naturally feel displeased at seeing such an ignominious offence committed by those whom he himself commended to the people as the advocates of the Church.

It was contrary to my notions of "charity" to stand up before a number of poor electors on a hustings and induce them to expose themselves to ruin by voting against the will of their landlords, when the candidate on the faith of whose pledges this risk of ruin was incurred had not the smallest intention of keeping his engagement; and I am sure Dr. Cullen had the best possible reason to be angry with the perpetrators of this cruel fraud.

On the other hand, I have yet to learn that it is contrary to truth, justice, and charity, to call perjury perjury ; to stigmatise frauds as unjust ; to denounce those who victimise the poor as unhuman ; to try to relieve the Church from the odium of treating abandoned depravity as a venial offence ; or to inflict political chastisement upon political crime and to direct upon public offenders a just public abhorrence.

But the friends of Dr. Cullen seem to have reversed this order of things. Their notion seems to have really been that the offences I have enumerated were mere laughable peccadilloes ; that it made very little matter indeed whether men played false with what Dr. Cullen and Mr. Keogh jointly described as the basis on which " all our hopes of redress under Divine Providence " rested—though that redress meant and means salvation to the souls of thousands ; and that the only real offence, the great punishable crime, consists in giving its true name, and trying to secure its just reward, to this revolting perfidy. I can only pray that to the latest day of my existence I may hold an opposite opinion and act upon it ; and I can but regret that, since this perfidy was committed, Dr. Cullen, though of course he has not thought fit to approve it, has given no sign of his disapproval ; has so acted as to be in Ireland the greatest practical support of what others have done amiss ; and has steadily discountenanced those who were struggling for honesty and the service of the Church against fraud and selfish aggrandisement.

.   .   .   .   .   .

In performing this office—not a pleasant one to any man, but sometimes a duty—it is charged, and I neither admit nor deny the accusation, that in the vehemence of controversy occasional excess of language was noticeable.

Suppose the charge true; from how many warm political controversies, from how many theological controversies, is this same fault absent? It is a gloomy fact that not only political, but even theological disputants are touched with the infirmities of our nature, and that those who feel most deeply and honestly are sometimes the most tempted to excess in polemical warmth. But because this is so, is the cause of truth to be abandoned? Is error to be left in possession of the field? Are a few hot words, directed by a lay disputant towards men whose connection with the Catholic cause is a scandal and a disgrace, to be alleged as a reason for abandoning "the only means under Divine Providence" by which the redress of religious grievances can be attained and the perdition of thousands of souls prevented? . . . .

But if the charge of violence in political controversy be true, an explanation, painful indeed but accurate, may readily be given. If certain laymen were too warm in the dispute, it was perhaps because certain Bishops and priests showed themselves too cold. Too cold, did I say? To speak the whole truth, I ought to have said too hot upon the side of crime. It was hard to keep

the dead level of perfect moderation when one
saw the authority of the Church of God used to
prop up wickedness.   If all the Bishops in Ireland
had done their duty by the Decalogue on this
occasion, the word of a layman would not have
been needed ; but if Bishops will come forward as
the public patrons and encouragers of immorality,
we must not be surprised if disorders follow.
Having said this much on a painful subject, I conclude with a general denial that there was on our
side of the question any notable violation of
" justice, charity, or truth ; " and I challenge the
production of an instance in which a rogue was
charged with more than his deserts, or in which
any grievous or untrue imputation was made upon
an honest man.

I admit Dr. Cullen has always had on his lips
the words " peace " and " charity," but these
words have had very different meanings according
to the occasion.   In taking the chair at the great
aggregate meeting of 1851, his Grace did not fail
to impress upon the meeting the necessity of practising these virtues.   I quote his very words :—

" I call upon all to lay aside all bickerings and dissensions,
and to cultivate that charity which is the characteristic mark
of true Catholics."

.   .   .   .   .   .

Towards the end of the meeting one Mr.
Reynolds spoke on the same topic (of Independent
Opposition).   He said that "they had not twenty
true representatives of the people ; " and that " he

would not go to Parliament again unless he had fifty men with him," that is, unless—without dissension, of course—thirty Catholic members were turned out, and their places filled by better men. But Mr. Reynolds went on to speak of individuals. He vituperated Morgan John O'Connell (the nephew of the great O'Connell) as the " Kerry Whig hack," and threatened him with the loss of his seat. He denounced Serjeant Murphy, another Catholic member, whom he ridiculed for his " cockney" speech and his " nasal twang," and threatened him with the loss of his seat. He vituperated another Catholic member, Mr. Anstey, as " that political slave," and threatened him with the loss of his seat. He vituperated the two members for the county of Leitrim, whom he called " two Whig hack members," and he threatened them with the loss of their seats. He referred " to many counties which should be nameless," and told them " they would disgrace themselves" if they " again returned their present members."

This was the last speech of any length that was delivered on that day. It must therefore have been present in Dr. Cullen's mind when, at the close of the. proceedings, his Grace expressed " his unqualified and delighted admiration at the amenity of that day's proceedings." " Nothing," he said, " could be more decorous, or more decidedly characterised by courtesy and good feeling, than the deportment and conduct of all." " Not one word had been uttered which, when properly understood, could give the slightest offence." Thus we see that his Grace not merely presided during Mr. Reynolds' speech, but approved every word of it, and was particularly struck, it seems, with its decorum, courtesy, and good feeling.

We are, therefore, now in a position to understand exactly what Dr. Cullen meant in 1851 by charity, peace, and the absence of bickering and dissension. It meant to take part with twenty Catholic members, and to declare furious political war against twenty or thirty other Catholic members. It meant to do your utmost to drive those twenty or thirty other members from the House of Commons as unworthy to represent Catholic constituencies. It meant to hold up by name those Catholic members to the scorn and derision of the people, as " slaves " and " hacks," and a " disgrace to their constituents ; " and then to take credit for " courtesy, decorum, and good feeling," and to declare that "not one word had been uttered " to give those members or anybody else " the slightest offence."

But the words Peace and Charity have a very different meaning now.

　　　.　　　.　　　.　　　.　　　.　.　　　.

Union ! Charity ! I never spoke to Dr. Cullen on the subject since the summer of 1853 that his Grace did not strenuously advise me to *dis*union, and did not rebuke me for my too great charity to those whom he disliked.

Peace! By peace Dr. Cullen always means war with somebody. In 1851 his Grace's peace meant war against those members who supported the Government. In 1855 it means war against those who oppose the Government.

Peace and Charity! I believe, before God, there is no man now alive more active or more resolute in preaching and encouraging enmity and want of charity against those who continue to oppose the English Ministers than the Apostolic Delegate. The words used are Peace and Charity; the things encouraged are party spirit and service of the Government.

Section IV.—*Dr. Cullen as a Minister of Charity.*

It was my intention to have inserted here, for the information of the Holy See, a rather detailed exposition—by way of contrast—of the public men whom Dr. Cullen in his intercourse with me has done his best to favour, and of those against whom he has endeavoured to place me in a position of antagonism. But the delay that has taken place in the preparation of this Statement in consequence of my ill-health, and the continuance of that ill-health at the present moment, compel me to pass over this part of the subject more briefly than I should wish. What I shall say will consist mainly of proofs.

Dr. Cullen has always tried to excite in me

hostility against two persons—Mr. Gavan Duffy
and Mr. G. H. Moore.   He has always tried to
bespeak my favour for Mr. Keogh, of whose
moral turpitude enough perhaps has already been
said ; and for a certain powerful family of Sadleirs
and ——s, who are able to send five or six members to Parliament, and of whose character and
conduct I shall presently attempt to give some
notion.   I think the best clue to Dr. Cullen's
policy is to be found in inquiring who these persons severally are.

Dr. Cullen preaches charity, but I must say that
I never saw in his Grace any symptom of charity
towards Mr. Duffy.   His Grace complains of my
violence.   Those who were present at the conference I had with his Grace in the Irish College
in Rome were witnesses of the violence of his
passion against Mr. Duffy, and were *not* witnesses of his charity.   The pretence for denying
all charity for Mr. Duffy is that he is what is
called a " Young Irelander ; " that his principles
are those of Mazzini ; that he encourages the
Continental politics of the arch-enemy of the
Church of God ; and that his design is to play in
·Ireland the part which Mazzini has attempted to
play in Italy.   No opportunity is lost by Dr.
Cullen's friends and relations to make good this
statement, through the medium of those disreputable journals which, by an unhappy fatality, are in
Ireland the chief supporters of Dr. Cullen's new
policy ; though the calumny is so utterly without

foundation as to be, in Ireland, ludicrous rather than of any moment.

Twelve years ago there was a Young Ireland party, consisting for the most part of very young men with strong feelings of Irish patriotism and very unformed views. Some of these had unconsciously, some perhaps consciously, views hostile to the true interests of the Church. Others were zealous sons of the Church; and the whole party had no recognised object except the liberation of Ireland from English misrule. About that time (1844), I first made acquaintance with Mr. Duffy and several of his friends. I thought some of them were extremely estimable for frankness, candour, and good intentions; but it seemed to me that they were entirely misled on questions connected with the Church, and that some of them had been so far misled by the influences of the world as to have no very definite loyalty to the Church itself. I fancied, however, that this temporary aberration was *only* temporary; and I used every opportunity which their kindness for me afforded both to urge upon them other views and to make them acquainted with clergymen whose influence I thought would be useful to bring them back to the right path.

I think it was in 1846 that Mr. Duffy intimated to me a wish to make a sort of spiritual retreat under the guidance of the Very Rev. R. J. Whitty, now the Provost of the diocese of Westminster. He had, it seems, not been very regular in the performance of his religious duties, and had even loosely entertained some sceptical impressions, to which, however, he had never fully surrendered his mind.   For certain reasons this retreat took place in my house, and after about a week, I had the happiness of receiving the Holy Communion by his side, when, under Dr. Whitty, he had been reconciled to the Church.

Since that time Mr. Duffy has been a monthly communicant.   In 1849 his confessor, Dr. Moriarty, now the Coadjutor Bishop of Kerry, publicly swore in a court of justice that Mr. Duffy was a good Catholic and was a monthly communicant ; and the present venerable Bishop of Kilmore also testified from his own knowledge to the excellence of Mr. Duffy's character.   It is a singular fact that two of Mr. Duffy's closest political associates in those early years of his public life, when his Catholic character was least estimable, and who were as deeply engaged as Mr. Duffy in the counsels of the Young Ireland party when that party was least Catholic, have been actually selected or approved by Dr. Cullen as fit persons to instruct the Catholic youth of Ireland in the new University.   I refer to Mr. John O'Hagan, Professor of Political Economy, and to Mr. Florence MacCarthy, Professor of Poetry.

One of the leading questions which Mr. Duffy, as editor of the *Nation* newspaper, has had to discuss, has been this very question of the

Catholic University. ·His original view, and that of most of his friends, was in favour of the Queen's Colleges ; and he upheld that view with great ability and perseverance until in 1850 the Synod of Thurles pronounced a decree hostile to the Queen's Colleges. At this time Mr. Duffy had the greatest possible temptation to resist the decision of the Bishops. The support of a mixed system of education has become a point of honour with the party of which he was one of the chiefs. Many of the thoughtless among his followers looked to him to go all lengths in support of that point of honour; and while he was sure to encounter derision and obloquy for bowing his neck to the Church, there was not wanting to him, as the Holy See well knows, episcopal example to sanction and encourage a contumacious course.

What did Mr. Duffy do? He did not take advantage of the Episcopal encouragement openly held out to him. He did not even wait for the confirmation of the statute of Thurles by the Holy See. But the moment the decision of the Synod was made known, Mr. Duffy (on the 21st September 1850) published the most formal act of obedience in an article of which the following is an extract. After re-stating briefly the views he had previously entertained, he thus expresses himself on the subject of the obedience due to the Church :—

"These were our opinions throughout, and there are few

things we would not do to give them effect. But there are some things we cannot and shall not do ; and one is to encourage a schism among the Catholic laity in the face of a unanimous condemnation by the Prelates of the Church. The Pastoral of the Synod, published as the unanimous voice of the Bishops (and which we copy to-day), brings the question to this pass. We believe it leaves us no option, if we are not prepared to encounter the moral responsibility of encouraging disobedience to the decision of a National Synod. We value the education of the middle classes not an iota less than before. We believe the duty lies heavily upon the Irish Bishops to found without delay new colleges or negotiate with Government the possession of some of the existing ones. But our duty as a Catholic layman is not less plain—it is to submit to the decision of the Church in a matter distinctly within its province, and on which it has unequivocally pronounced. If the decision had been in favour of the Colleges, acquiescence would have been a pleasure, but a duty is not the less plain because it is unpalatable." [1]

If I am not very much mistaken, the Holy See would have been spared a great deal of trouble if the present Bishop of Ossory, and some of his Episcopal brethren, had shown as much docility in giving on this subject to the Successor of St. Peter an unquestioning obedience and a frank co-operation, as Mr. Duffy showed in giving obedience and co-operation to the decision of the Irish Bishops. Since that time, whatever obstacles Bishops may have put in the way of the Catholic University, Mr. Duffy at all events has never wavered in its support or in his loyalty to the Holy See. I venture to say that he has risked as much, and done as much, as any man

[1] *Nation,* September 21, 1850.

in Ireland, with perhaps one or two exceptions, to bring over to the Catholic University the support of a large section of public opinion in Ireland.

As to his being a disciple of Mazzini, it is a calumny of which any man should be ashamed. Since the attempted outbreak in Ireland in 1848, the Young Ireland party with reference to Continental politics has divided into two sections. Some of them, chiefly amongst those who took refuge in America, have indeed upheld and countenanced the principles of Mazzini and his allies. Mr. Duffy has been the head of that party which took the opposite course. For several years he has written in the *Nation* repeated and voluminous articles denouncing Mazzini and his designs. The originals of these now lie before me. They are known to every man in Ireland who interests himself about these matters; and they are particularly known to Dr. Cullen, because I have myself specially and emphatically brought them under his Grace's notice. Dr. Cullen knows full well that Mr. Duffy has broken publicly and personally with all his friends who have publicly identified themselves with Mazzini, and that he has been most influential through the *Nation* newspaper in preserving a large section of Irish public opinion sound on that important question. His Grace knows that Mr. Duffy has rendered this service to the Church at considerable risk and under considerable obloquy. He knows also the zealous and effective services which Mr. Duffy has rendered to the Catholic University. But because Mr. Duffy has shown himself forward on all occasions, not merely to defend the University against the indocile section of the Irish Bishops, but against the same section of the Irish Bishops now strengthened by the active support of Dr. Cullen; to defend the independence of the Church and the rights of the poor, assailed by the unhappy subservience of these Bishops to the English Government, Dr. Cullen has neither charity, nor candour, nor mercy for him; and though tolerant of such public perjurers as Mr. Keogh and Mr. John Sadleir, his Grace thinks (so he told me in the Irish College) that for a good Catholic and an honest man like Mr. Duffy, before he is admitted into public life again, there should be exacted (I use his Grace's very words) " a penance of fifty years upon bread and water."

From the many articles which have appeared in the *Nation* from Mr. Duffy's hand or with his signature in vehement opposition to Mazzini, I will merely extract one or two passages; and I do so only because during my stay in Rome I found that it was part of the tactics of Dr. Cullen's friends to lose no opportunity of calumniating Mr. Duffy by the most outrageous fabrications. Words were attributed to him which he never used, and the most outrageous forgeries were reiterated after repeated confutations. It is, of course, impossible to stop these slanders, because it is the natural fate of every man who upholds the independence of the Church and the rights of the poor to be slandered with peculiar malignity. But it is proper from time to time to put on record the truth, and it is also proper to warn those whom it concerns that one of the weapons with which Mr. Duffy and the rest of us are attacked is not merely slander, but forgery—the invention of passages pretended to have been written and published by us which never had an existence except in the mind of the inventor. The following is a true extract from a long letter, which, on the 25th of April 1854, Mr. Duffy addressed to Mr. Meagher, one of the Irish exiles in America, to remonstrate with him on the countenance he was giving to Mazzini. This letter occupied several columns in the *Nation* newspaper ; and in order that it might have a wider circulation, it was reprinted and disseminated in the form of a pamphlet. In both these shapes it now lies before me :—

"But Mazzini wants the rogue's virtue of fidelity to his accomplices. More recently, to gain the Continental Deists, he has thrown Exeter Hall overboard, and proposed to substitute for the Catholic Church, not English Protestantism, but a hideous salmagundi of 'notions,' collected by the agency of universal suffrage ! Let us not speak of the profanity of this shallow coxcomb laying his hand on the Holy of Holies, but consider the scope of his capacity, who thinks that our perverse human nature, which falls into continual insubordination and neglect of laws delivered by the voice of God on Sinai or on

Calvary, will bow down before the fortuitous progeny of the ballot-box. Here are his words :—' The Pope being gone, it would become a necessity for us, and for the whole of Italy, to do what I shall call—feel the pulse of humanity as to our religious question. As we should do in political, so we should do in religious matters—ascertain the general opinion by a general assembly. We should summon as far as the resolution goes the clergy ; not only the clergy, but . . . . laymen who have studied the religious question, and we should know from them the state of feeling and opinion as to religiosity. We should have the actual transformations effected in the Catholic belief by time. We should have a Council by the side of the Constitutional Assembly. We should have universal suffrage, and we should know, not what is the individual religious belief, but what is the collective belief of the majority.' This is Mazzini, painted by his own hand ; painted as I fancy you have never seen him before—the sworn enemy of the Church of God. I make no appeal to you on this evidence ; it is far beyond the province of rhetoric. If you do not feel, like an instinct, that this is a man to be renounced as you would renounce Satan, the father of lies, if he set up his standard in proper person, there is no more to be said. ' Italy must emancipate herself from the old Catholic belief.' Is there any Protestant living who, if we presumed to invite his help in Ireland with the aim of abolishing *his* religion, would not answer with a curse or a blow ? And we who have only one grand element in the history of our race, its loyalty to that ' old Catholic ' belief, who have only one consolation in the poverty of our country, that she has preserved a moral purity which no wise statesman would barter for the wealth of Carthage—we who have been bred at the feet of Catholic mothers, and from boyhood upwards have watched with flushed brows the eternal conspiracy to root the creed of Patrick out of this island—what shall be our answer ? I will not insult you, Thomas Meager, by misdoubting yours."

It is a curious fact that along with his support of Mazzini, which Mr. Duffy thus resolutely de-

nounced, Thomas Meagher had another project
which Mr. Duffy equally denounced, but which
shows Mr. Meagher to be a supporter of Dr.
Cullen's policy, as the best means of supporting
Mazzini in Ireland. It was Mr. Meagher's special
recommendation that the Irish Catholic priests
should be excluded from politics; and on this point,
at least, there is abundant sympathy between the
follower of Mazzini and the Apostolic Delegate.
What one urges in the interest of the English
Government, the other urges in the interest of all
the desperadoes, atheists, revolutionists, and cut-
throats of the Continent of Europe. Though the
objects which these two personages have in view
are very opposite, their policy is the same. "Exclude the priests from politics." The one would
do it, I suppose, by an appeal to the people; the
other by the strong hand of power. But in substance both would do the same thing. And it is
my firm belief that, to a certain extent, both would
attain their object. Dr. Cullen, by encouraging a
corrupt prostration before the English Government, would produce in many thousands the result at which he aims—a generation of tame slaves
to English authority; and so far his end would
be accomplished. Mr. Meagher, by separating
the priesthood from the people, would, amongst
another class, no doubt, produce a generation of
Mazzinists, enemies alike to the Government of
England and to the Church of God. The same
blow would produce these two opposite calamities.

The success of Dr. Cullen would be the inevitable forerunner or accompaniment of the success of Mr. Meagher and Mazzini. Mr. Duffy takes his stand against both these excesses. He rebukes those who, in whatever station, encourage political corruption and a venal subserviency to the English Government. He rebukes also those who encourage disloyalty to the Church of God, and taint a spirit of rational independence with the schemes of atheists and enemies of the Church of God. Both the classes whom he resists preach up, for the accomplishment of their own ends, "the exclusion of priests from Irish politics." Mr. Duffy resists both of them by resisting alike the end which each has in view and the means which they both have in common. Of course Dr. Cullen does not wish for the success of Mazzini or of his principles; but, as I shall answer for it at the throne of God, it is my firm belief that the best friend the principles of Mazzini have in Ireland is the Apostolic Delegate, and that one of the most effective enemies of those principles has been Mr. Duffy.

Of Mr. Moore, who is the other Catholic politician against whom Dr. Cullen has repeatedly warned me, and from whom, in his efforts after union, his Grace has striven to *dis*-unite me, I need say very little. Mr. Moore is the representative of the county of Mayo, and is a gentleman of high honour and strong Catholic feeling, in whom the Archbishop of Tuam has always had great confidence. I know of no ground which Dr. Cullen can have had for endeavouring to run down Mr. Moore except the dislike his Grace is supposed to entertain to everything and everybody connected with the Archbishop of Tuam. Mr. Moore has always been a great advocate of those principles of exclusively Catholic education which are known to have the approbation of the Apostolic See. He was always opposed to the Queen's Colleges; always in favour of a Cathol'c University; always opposed to the scheme of a mixed National education for the poor of Ireland. And it is within my own knowledge that these opinions of Mr. Moore have not been taken up by him to please Dr. MacHale, but are the fixed and ineradicable convictions of his own mind, or rather the dictates of his Catholic instinct.

But not to rely upon my own knowledge, merely, of Mr. Moore's character, let me quote a sentence from a letter that appeared in the *Tablet* newspaper of the 16th of June 1855, signed by his own parish priest, the Rev. James Brown of Ballintubber. The letter is dated 31st of May 1855, and the following is a paragraph in it :—

" In proof of this I can refer to my own beloved, distinguished parishioner, G. H. Moore, whose great piety is always a most practical sermon in this parish. Trusted by all for his political consistency, admired by all for his great talents and learning, justly looked up to as a parent by his numerous tenantry on his extensive estates in this county—the example of such a man kneeling down among the monthly communicants at the altar of his parish church has given a popular sanction to his principles, and the Catholic clergy and people are proud of him."

If I had followed Dr. Cullen's counsel, I should have broken off specially from these two men of great practical piety, unblemished honour, and integrity; I should have had no charity for them, and I should have reserved my charity for men who have not in their nature the faintest tinge of practical Catholicity; who have become infamous by their public perjuries, and whose connection with the Church is a scandal to religion and morality. For my part, I shall never blush at not having followed his Grace's counsel in this respect.

Of Mr. Keogh I have said enough, and also of Mr. John Sadleir. But it is necessary for me to say a few words, not about Mr. John Sadleir himself, but about the family and connection of which he is the political head, and with which Dr. Cullen, while proclaiming war upon Mr. Moore and Mr. Duffy, has always wished me to be at peace. I have given Mr. Moore's character as it is represented by his parish priest. With regard to the Sadleir and —— family, I will here set down, not my own words, but the words of three priests who belong to that part of the country in which these gentlemen live, and who know them well. It is not every priest who has the courage to put his name to such a certificate of character as I am about to transcribe; but I know that the hideous portraiture is in strict accordance with the feeling and the knowledge of numbers of priests in that diocese with whom I have spoken.

"DEAR SIR,—In reply to your letter, dated Rome, 12th May 1855, inquiring into the religious character of the ——s and Sadleirs, both in past times and at present, we have to say that the fathers of the present generation of ——s were most immoral men. . . . As to the present generation, Mr. Vincent —— and his four brothers have done more to root out the Catholic population of Ireland than any of the most bigoted Protestants or most violent enemies of the Church of God in this country. Wherever these men came into possession of land, they drove out the old Catholic inhabitants and turned their farms into sheep-walks or bullock pastures. Vincent —— holds about 900 acres without a human being now living on them, although these lands owned a population, not many years ago, of over sixty families.

"His brothers James and Rodolph exterminated over sixty-six families. His brother Thomas cleared about 800 acres, which he converted into sheep-walks and bullock pastures, and from which he expelled about twenty families; and his brother William cleared in like manner about 800 acres more, and expelled therefrom about thirty families. The five brothers cleared about 3000 acres and banished near 200 families from their lands. These poor creatures were tolerably comfortable, and could pay their rents if they were allowed. But they were cast on the roadside. Some few of them fled to America, but most of them perished in misery. Thus from 1000 to 1200 Catholic people were swept from the Irish Church by this one family.

"James ——, brother of Vincent ——, was murdered. Common report is divided regarding the cause of assassination. Some say he was shot by . . . . others say that he was murdered by some of the unfortunate people he had exterminated, or was about to exterminate. Another poor man was shot by one of the ——s in the act of dispossessing some families from their property, for which he stood trial, but escaped because 'the man was killed by the said —— in the exercise of his legal rights.'

"As to the Catholicity of Mr. Vincent ——'s brothers, we need only refer to the letter of the Rev. James Mullally, late pastor of New Inn, written in the year 1841, when he was curate of Kilfeacle, in order to induce Mrs. —— to subscribe for the building of the chapel of Kilfeacle, which the poor of the parish were endeavouring to erect, and which was situate within a quarter of a mile of the ——s' residence. We have only to add that not one farthing was subscribed by the —— family for the building of their parish chapel, while all the poor people emulously contributed the whole sum with which it was erected.

"In like manner, when the chapel of Moycarkey was in a falling state, William ——, brother of Vincent ——, was applied to for aid to repair it. But he refused to give a single penny, although he was after clearing 300 acres of good and honest Catholics in the parish, and left only two families out of twenty on his property in that neighbourhood.

"As to the Sadleirs, they have been remarkable for their money-making propensities and nothing more. They have never done anything for religion. They have but a small share of land, yet they have cleared nearly all of it of tenants. The late parish priest of Latten built a house and offices at a cost of nearly £1000 on ten acres of land which he held from Mr. Sadleir at the exorbitant rent of £50 per year. At the death of Father Hanley, the parish priest alluded to, Mr. Sadleir appropriated the whole of the buildings and land, and insisted that the new parish priest should pay £60 a year for the premises, give one year's rent over and above, besides £35 to the relatives of the late parish priest. Thus the parish was deprived of the fruits of the industry and outlay of the good parish priest, and his successor had to pay over again for the house and glebe land.

> "J. HICKEY, P.P. Doon, County Limerick and Tipperary.
> "WM. COONEY, C.C. Newport, County Tipperary.
> "J. O'DWYER, C.C. Doon, County Tipperary.

" *June 4th*, 1855."

SECTION V.—*Dr. Cullen as a Minister of
Truth and Justice.*

This section contains the account of the meeting
in Dublin referred to in Chapter viii. of the Third
Book. At that meeting John Reynolds was put
up by Dr. Cullen to inform the world that Lucas
had, in an article on the requisition issued by the
committee who called the meeting, stigmatised
the Bishops who had signed the requisition as
"knaves or fools."   This would have included
Dr. Cullen, who had himself been one of the
signatories. When Lucas essayed to repel the
charge, the Lord Mayor, who occupied the chair,
and who was a Whig Catholic of the most syco-
phantic type, and also a tool of Dr. Cullen's, refused him a hearing, as already mentioned. The
whole of the proceedings—but I have not thought
it necessary to reproduce them—are detailed in
this section. The persons concerned in the out-
rage are dead ; and I imagine the particulars
would not be of any general interest at the present day. The immediate effect was, as we have
seen, beneficial to Lucas rather than otherwise,
since nobody who knew him believed the charge.
Even staunch political opponents came to him
at the close of the meeting and expressed their
deep regret at the insults he had received, while
the " Statement " says :—

In England those priests and laymen for and

with whom I had been labouring to the best of
my ability for the redress of Catholic grievances
in which they were interested, were displeased
with what had taken place, not so much from personal kindness for me, but because they thought
it was not for the advantage of religion that I
should be run down with indignity at the very
moment I was devoting all my ability (such as it
was) to procure the redress of grievances. With
this view, and to strengthen my hand in · the
House of Commons and elsewhere against the
common enemy, a great number of clergymen, of
whom I am proud to name first Cardinal Wiseman, subscribed to a testimonial, which, along
with a most flattering address, was presented to
me as I passed through London on my way to
Rome in the month of November last.

.   .   .   .   .   .

When the testimonial to me was first spoken
of in England, Dr. Cullen was highly indignant.
He had laboured to discredit me by every means
in his power, and it certainly seemed hard, when
John Reynolds and his hired ruffians had just had
so brilliant a success against me in Dublin, that
so many dignitaries of the Church in England, so
many deans and canons, so many heads of colleges, so many members of religious orders, so
many priests, and so many respectable laymen,
and at their head the Cardinal Archbishop of
Westminster, should spontaneously come forward
to give me the unsought expression of their con-

fidence and esteem. Accordingly his Grace applied himself with characteristic activity to assail me in private, as a means of deterring my English friends from lending me any countenance or support. I was absolutely to be struck down; the foulest men and means were to be enlisted against me; and, if Dr. Cullen could have had his way, not a friend was to dare to raise his voice in my favour.

. . . . . .

Dr. Cullen wrote forthwith to one of the English Bishops a letter of remonstrance. His Grace expressed great surprise that the English Catholics should choose for a compliment to me a time when, as he was pleased to say, " I had so lately not only declined to co-operate with the great body of the Irish Bishops on the Convent Petition, but divided the supporters of that petition into the two classes of knaves or fools." His Grace then expressed great surprise that such a compliment should not have been paid me for my services in the *Tablet* to the cause of education (*i.e.*, when I was helping Dr. Cullen to attack Dr. Murray, and to combat half at least of the Irish Bishops), but should have been delayed to such a moment as that at which it was actually proposed. His Grace proceeded to speak of the testimonial as a most impolitic as well as ill-timed measure, inasmuch as it must injure the position of Catholics to identify themselves with so unpopular a person as my humble self.

. . . . . .

390 LIFE OF FREDERICK LUCAS.

At the conference I had with Dr. Cullen here in Rome, I referred in a friendly way to the letter which his Grace had written, charging me with having publicly called the Irish Bishops "knaves or fools." His Grace evidently was not prepared to make good such an accusation against me,—it was too evidently false ; nor had he the courage to do me justice. But he took refuge in the simpler process of an absolute denial. He had not written such a letter as I described. How Dr. Cullen was enabled to reconcile this denial with verbal truth I am not able to say. All I know is that his Grace *did* write the letter, and that the letter was sent to the Bishop of Beverley, Dr. Briggs, by the Bishop to whom it was written ; that it was read by the Rev. Mr. Oakeley of Islington, and that the documents of Dr. Briggs and Mr. Oakeley attesting both the letter and its contents will accompany this "Statement."

I am sorry to have been obliged to take up so much time and space with this miserable business. But it must be remembered that these are the acts not of a mere Bishop, but of an Apostolic Delegate, whose friends everywhere represent him as being all but another Pope. The opposition of such a person, however it manifests itself, is ordinarily taken as the expression of the highest ecclesiastical censure. To the opposition of the Apostolic Delegate, so long as he is understood to represent the Holy See, I certainly can never

be indifferent. If I occupy towards the Holy
See the position which it is obvious Dr. Cullen
compels me to occupy towards himself; if *his*
opposition is *its* opposition; if his desire to
weaken my hands, to discredit, disown, and degrade me, be the desire of Holy See; if these
acts are to be taken as the acts of the Holy See,
a much shorter and less troublesome method
might have been used. A word from the
Supreme Pontiff would accomplish what Dr.
Cullen is attempting to bring about by defama-
tion and calumny. If the Holy See thinks my
efforts injurious to that religion of which not I,
but it, is the appointed guardian, I will at once
cease to concern myself about these matters, and
leave the responsibility of them to others. Monsignore Barnabo has repeatedly informed me that
Dr. Cullen has done nothing in Ireland without
the express orders of the Supreme Pontiff. Is
this so? After the charges I have brought
against his Grace it is impossible this can be
true. When he said that, Monsignore Barnabo
did not know all that Dr. Cullen had done. No;
Dr. Cullen was *not* ordered by the Holy Father
to organise a machinery of slander for stabbing
the reputations of honest men. He was not
ordered to serve the Whig Government by de-
frauding every man who is too zealous a friend
of the Church to wear their degrading livery.
These and many other things he has done he
was not ordered to do; and, until I am otherwise

informed, I shall presume that they are quite at variance with the spirit and practice of the Holy See.

But there is another point of view in which this case required from me a minute exposition. In the first audience with which I was honoured by the Holy Father, amongst many condescending expressions and most flattering compliments in reference to my parliamentary course (of which his Holiness said nothing but praise), his Holiness added that he took a distinction betwen me as a member of Parliament and as the editor of a journal; that in the former character I had been a real apologist of the Catholic religion, and that for what I had done in that character he gave me in a marked manner his especial benediction. But that as an editor of a journal I too often withdrew myself from the domain of patience into that of impatience. His Holiness, in the spirit of that paternal kindness and condescension which he has twice manifested to me, and for which I feel more gratitude than I am able to express, evidently made a careful choice of the words least calculated to wound the very humblest of his children, and intended to convey a stronger meaning and reproof than the words necessarily implied. With all my heart and soul I thanked the Holy Father for his admonition, and promised with all sincerity to turn it to the best account I was able; and by the blessing of God, if I ever write in a newspaper again, that promise I shall not fail to keep.

But as I am sure the Holy Father cannot himself find time to read the *Tablet;* as the Secretary
of Propaganda has more than once assured me
that he does not know a word of the language in
which it is written ; and as I believe that of his
Eminence the Prefect of Propaganda, amongst
his many great qualities, the same thing may be
said ; I naturally ask myself by whom have representations been made to the Holy Father as to
the contents and the spirit of the *Tablet?* . . .

SECTION. VI.—*Dr. Cullen and Maynooth.*

I have omitted this Section as no longer of practical importance. It was designed to show that
the increased endowment conferred on the College
by Sir Robert Peel had tended to foster Gallican
doctrines and unsound politics. Certain professors—from sympathy with the State—were in
the habit, Lucas believed, of minimising the
authority of the Holy See ; and of dissuading
those future priests who attended their classes
from considering it a duty to take part in politics,
or to encourage the people to make sacrifices for
political ends. As the endowment no longer
exists, any evils to which it may have given rise
have also ceased. For, as Chaucer teaches—

> " When the cause removèd is
> The effect surceaseth too."

SECTION VII.—*Dr. Cullen, Tenant-Right, and Proselytism.*

What Dr. Cullen's opinions about Tenant-Right were in 1851 we have clearly ascertained in spite of his own denial. He thought it was a work of Christian charity in which priests were very properly engaged out of their own dioceses; he encouraged his spiritual subjects to contribute to the Tenant League; he gave money himself to the funds of that "political association;" and paid it expressly to clergymen of another diocese, whom he authorised to agitate for that sacred cause of charity in his own principal town.

As his Grace has changed upon almost every point, so he has changed upon this. What his present opinions are we know—partly by the discouragement which he inflicts upon every man whom he has an opportunity of afflicting, and who remains true to the principles for which his Grace gave his money in 1851—partly by his resolute denial of the proved facts with regard to his own conduct at that period; partly by the opinions his Grace expressed in the conference I had the honour of having with him in Rome.

At that conference his Grace expressed some singular opinions. His main purpose seemed to be to vindicate his own consistency by taking a distinction. He admitted that the Irish tenants were most shamefully treated by the English law

and the practice of the landlords. He admitted
that they required protection by a change in the
law. He said that the existing state of things
was most inhuman, and that for a priest to protest
against it was either a necessity, or at least a
proper act of charity.

So far his Grace admitted that it was a religious
question, and one in which, while they confined
themselves to general topics, priests might properly interfere. But then came the question of
a remedy. The best measure to remedy the evil,
the specific mode in which the law should be
altered, is a question of politics. People differ
very much about the value of any particular Bill
or law. The Bill brought forward by the Tenant
League is disapproved by many persons; and for
the priests to interfere in such a concrete matter
as the clauses of an Act of Parliament, about which
people may differ, is in the highest degree objectionable, and is indeed politics. A strange theory,
it must be admitted, for a great divine.

To feed the hungry and to clothe the naked is
a duty in general. But the question of whether
a particular garment is a proper article of human
clothing, or is a poisoned shirt—the question
whether a particular loaf or a particular piece of
meat is wholesome or injurious to the body—these
are questions of physical science with which religion has nothing to do. The business of religion
is with the abstract; *that* is in some sense certain,
but facts are very doubtful; and the concrete is

physics, or politics, or something very dangerous for a priest to meddle with. The duty of a priest is to say, "Be ye warmed and clothed" in general, and not to give them those things which are necessary for the body in particular.

If a priest rashly and without proper caution administers poison instead of food, and puts on the body, instead of raiment, something which will torture and kill, he is very culpable and very cruel. But if he takes all reasonable pains to arrive at a sound judgment, and yet poisons or kills, not merely is he free from guilt, and if then, with a dying man before him, he were to abstain from acting on that judgment, he would be more culpable, more cruel, and more fantastically inhuman.

But how stands the case of the Tenant Bill which the Tenant League advocates? For years it has been under consideration. Everybody interested in doing justice to the tenants has been consulted. Humane landlords, farmers, great and small, priests, Bishops, lawyers, legislators, friends of the Government, enemies of the Government, every man in Ireland who could be brought to interest himself in the question, has had his opinion taken. Various meetings of fifty, a hundred, two hundred, picked men of all classes brought from every part of Ireland have been held to deliberate on this Bill. The newspapers on every side have discussed it. Constituencies have been appealed to and have pronounced their

opinion.   The whole country had this Bill before
it at the last general election.   And after the election, one of the largest deliberative meetings ever
held in Ireland, attended by more than forty
members of Parliament, including the present
law-officers of the Crown in Ireland ; priests from
all parts of the country, including the Rev. James
Maher, his Grace's uncle; farmers from many
parts of Ireland ; humane landlords in considerable numbers, presided over by a landlord of
large possessions, and an extremely shrewd judge
and watchful guardian of his own interest—such
an assembly held in Dublin in October 1852 pronounced with a unanimity altogether unbroken
that the Tenant-Right Bill which we support is
reasonable and just, and that "no Bill which does
not fully embody its principles can be satisfactory
to the country."

That unanimity, as far as any public expression
of it is concerned, is at this moment practically
unbroken.   There have been all kinds of attempts
made to evade the engagements entered into at
that meeting, but no one has as yet been found
to recant his opinion that the Bill so approved,
sanctioned, and sent to Parliament was and is a
Bill suited to the occasion, and capable of saving
the tenant from great oppression.   There are
indeed a few persons of extreme views, who are
for dealing much more summarily with the rights
of the landlords, and taking more violent courses.
These have expressed themselves dissatisfied

with the Bill; have abused me and my friends for agreeing to so moderate a Bill, and declare that nothing less than a complete revolution will satisfy the justice of the case. Between these men on the one side and the unjust landlords on the other, we of the Tenant League have held a middle course. With which of the extremes his Grace sympathises he did not vouchsafe to inform me; but this I know, that having to provide for a starving and naked tenantry, we of the Tenant League have neglected no means of arriving at a prudent judgment, and we do offer them a law which *we* have a right to consider, and which *they* do consider, to stand in the place of wholesome food and proper raiment. Dr. Cullen's theory is that for a priest to exert himself to procure that particular Bill—that precise food and that precise raiment—for the starving and naked poor is politics. The abstract is religion; general, aimless, unmeaning talk is religion; but the loaf and the coat are politics.

Great God! how happy the poor tenants would be if the inhumanity practised towards them were of the same abstract description as the charity which alone in a priest Dr. Cullen tolerates. But unhappily for them, they suffer the concrete pangs of hunger; their nakedness exposes their aching bodies to the winter's cold; the law robs them, in fact, and not in theory; it is in the body, and not in the spirit, that they are driven roofless upon the world; when their little ones send up their cries of misery to God and to their parents, it is into ears and hearts of flesh that this terrible sound pierces. Abstract religion will not cure these evils, and though an Archbishop and an Apostolic Delegate tells me the contrary, I make no secret of my belief that his Grace's morality is unsound, and that an endeavour to secure a definite practical good for these tormented poor of Christ is not—whether you call it politics or any other name—displeasing to the Redeemer of mankind.

Nor let the Holy See for a moment imagine, because the time of a general and national famine has passed away, that the sufferings and wrongs of the Irish tenant have passed away with it. Long before the famine, this grievance of the law and of the fact existed, and was put on record in a thousand official publications. It was in the midst of the sittings of a Commission appointed by the late Sir Robert Peel to inquire into the relations of landlord and tenant that the famine first showed itself ; and with the ending of the famine this peculiar suffering and wrong have not ended.

I will make this clear by a fact which is even now in the course of occurrence, and which I take from Irish journals and the records of our courts of law in the March and April of the present year. A Scotch merchant, Mr. Pollock, has lately bought property to the value of £55,000 (or above a quarter of a million of scudi) in the West of Ire-

land, in the diocese of the Bishop of Clonfert. Before the purchase was completed it was rumoured
that Mr. Pollock, the purchaser, intended to
remove all the tenants from it, to the number of
700 families or 2700 souls.   The Bishop of Clonfert, thinking it his duty to try to prevent so great
a calamity, applied to many persons, and to me
amongst the rest, to see whether, amongst the rich
English Catholics who sometimes lay out money
in Irish estates, one could not be found to out-
bid or replace Mr. Pollock.   This attempt failed.
Mr. Pollock became the purchaser, and at once
set about removing all the tenants from his estate.
The offer made to them by Mr. Pollock was,
"that they might remain in possession till next
November, and enjoy their holdings rent-free from
the time of his purchase (24th February 1854)
up to that day" (24th November 1855).   These
are the words of a trial at law as reported in the
Irish newspapers.   These families and their fathers
before them have lived on these farms for generations.   Some of them occupy five or ten, others
several hundred acres.   They are all or almost all
good tenants, their rents duly paid or ready to be
paid ; and they state that they are willing "to
undertake the payment of any reasonable rent he
may think fit to demand, and to lodge one year's
rent or more in advance for his greater security."
The terms Mr. Pollock offers them are to excuse
them their rent for one year and eight months.
Some of them have made considerable improve-

ments in building and other ways, which in their judgment much more than outvalues the twenty months' rent. But out they are all to go, good and bad, rich and poor, honest and dishonest (if there be any dishonest), solvent and pauper ; the entire 2700 are all to be sent about their business— to live where they can—on the 1st November, and if they can't find homes, or employment, or the means of living elsewhere, they must either steal, or beg, or live by vice, or father, mother, and children must be separated and shut up in the workhouse ; or, as a last alternative, they can, of course, die.

No doubt it is very wicked for a priest to deal with a law which should remedy this evil in the concrete. His business is with the abstract view of the matter, and we can only lament that starvation and damnation are such terribly concrete incidents of human life. The tenants in the meanwhile look less to the abstract and more to the concrete, and having an extreme dislike to any of the alternatives above stated, it is alleged by Mr. Pollock's friends that these tenants persecute Mr. Pollock's agents ; have burnt down a house which he has erected ; have taken violent measures to render proof of his legal rights against the tenants impossible ; and, in short, that in that part of Dr. Derry's diocese there is a state of war. The case is brought into a court of justice; a necessary witness is not forthcoming ; Mr. Pollock is defeated for the present ; the people present at

the trial manifest their joy by the wildest excitement; and the war is held over for the present,
with the tolerable certainty of producing a fresh
crop of crimes.   Of course all this is politics.   It
is the business of the laity to attend to this.   The
duty of a priest is in the altar, the confessional,
and the pulpit.   He is to speak of these things
(out of the chapel) in the abstract.   He must be
very charitable—to Mr. Pollock.   But he .must
see his people scattered to the four winds of
heaven, and sin and crime and misery generated
in a peaceful, happy, and innocent community,
without making a single effort to prevent it by
so wicked a thing as urging on his representatives
in Parliament the advocacy of any particular
measures of redress.

But is this case the only one?   No; as the
war goes on in the Crimea, and as the price of
various articles of provision rises in value, it
becomes more profitable to the landlords to have
cattle on an Irish estate than human beings.
The landlords being mostly Protestants, have
gone great lengths to sacrifice their Catholic
tenants, even at a loss to themselves.   What will
they do, or rather what will they not do, when
they can enrich themselves by the same act of extermination which banishes the Catholics from the
soil ?   Accordingly, I find by the latest accounts
from Ireland, in private letters and in newspapers,
that this driving out of Catholic families is just
now receiving a new and vigorous extension.

"Last week," says a journal of April 21st that now lies before me, "the Sheriff (of the county of Longford) visited a small property within four miles of the town of Longford, recently purchased, and eight families, numbering thirty-seven individuals, became homeless. These were no pauper tenants. They had been, even in the worst times, punctual in meeting the landlord's demands. More than three generations of them had grown from infancy to old age on the property, and their permanent improvements in any fair market had fully doubled the value of the land originally confided to them. All these improvements the law has confiscated for the benefit of the landlord. They offered to pay two years' rent in advance, and to allow the landlord himself to fix the amount of the rent.

"In the next county, Leitrim, matters are still worse. Notices to quit have become the most ordinary legal process. The summer quarter-sessions and assizes of the next year will be rich in ejectments."—*Midland Counties Gazette.*

What becomes of the unhappy victims of the law who are thus driven from the soil? I have in part answered this question already, but I must be more particular in my statements. The truth is sufficiently known to every one in Ireland, but it is not fully known either there or here.

Those of the poor families who have sufficient means, escape either to America or Australia, and in America it may be that they lose their faith. If they cannot go so far, they go to Great Britain, and in the great towns of England and Scotland they learn new vices, new sins; and, from there not being sufficient chapels for worship or schools for the education of their children, or priests to hear their confessions, they omit, many of them, the fulfilment of their duties as Catholics, and the next generation become infidels.

Or they do not go so far as to England. They troop up from the west, or south, or north into Dublin, and hide themselves in the most dismal streets of that metropolis. What do they find there ? In every quarter and corner where the poor congregate, the devil has his workshops in the shape of proselytising schools, in which the very poorest children are tempted literally to sell their spiritual birthright for a mess of pottage. In so large a town the families that come up from other parts of the country are not known to the priests, and have no connections among the people. So the devil sits down at their elbows, and offers them a good breakfast or a good dinner, and the only condition is that for this daily meal they shall learn to become Protestants. Whatever proselytism there may be in Ireland, I am told by inhabitants of Dublin, has its home, centre, nursery, and origin—as far as Ireland is concerned —in Dublin. This is the source from which the infernal influence radiates to the farthest corners of the island. The Bishop of the diocese, of course, does not like to admit this, nor does any parish priest in which the pestilence is found. I am not blaming them, nor am I saying that they neglect any duty ; but from the information I have received I have no doubt whatever that the facts are as I state them.

Here follows a detailed list of schools, homes, and other proselytising establishments in Dublin, the particulars of which fully bear out the above description ; but as the circumstances of many of them can hardly have survived till the present time, I have not considered it necessary to reprint six or seven pages of such details.

SECTION VIII.—*Dr. Cullen and the Redress of Catholic Grievances.*

I have sat two sessions in Parliament, and during that time have applied myself diligently—much more I am sure than any other member—to the redress of Catholic grievances. My opinion may be unfounded, but, with the limited abilities God has given me, and the best use I have been able to make of them, it is my deliberate opinion that during those two critical years of Catholic history in Ireland and Great Britain—presenting greater means and chances for the redress of grievances than any period within my recollection—one of the principal obstacles in the way of obtaining redress has been the Apostolic Delegate. That Dr. Cullen has had any such motive or purpose I am far from saying. I speak merely of his acts and their results ; and I repeat my strong conviction that Dr. Cullen's influence has contributed much more than any other single cause to make fruitless the opportunity given us by God in which service might have been rendered to His Church.

If what I have said in former chapters and sections be even tolerably accurate, there can be no question that this assertion has in it nothing extravagant. If, indeed, what Dr. Cullen proclaimed to us in 1851 be true, namely, that "all our hopes of redress under Divine Providence" rest upon an Independent parliamentary party; and if since that time Dr. Cullen has used his influence and spared no exertion to break up the Independent parliamentary party, and to carry over the strength of the Irish Catholics to Lord Aberdeen and his Whig successors; it follows, as a logical consequence, that Dr. Cullen has been doing his best to defeat "all our hopes of redress under Divine Providence."

For, in point of fact, there has been, since 1851, no change in circumstances or in persons that was not at that very time clearly foreseen by Dr. Cullen. The only unexpected change of any moment has been in Dr. Cullen himself. Dr. Cullen knew the sort of men out of whom the Independent parliamentary party in 1851–52 was to be formed. . . . He knew that some of us would remain firm to our principles; but at that time he had no reason to suppose that we should present so respectable a figure in the House of Commons after we were deserted by some of the older and more experienced members. His feelings of dislike towards Mr. Moore, one of our colleagues who has remained true to us, were in 1851 exactly what they are now. Of Mr. Duffy he had not nearly so much reason to speak and think in 1851 as an obedient son of the Church, as he has now.

Of me he had heard for many years what he now says of me, that I was a violent man, intemperate of speech, and rough sometimes in my way of treating Bishops and priests who were opposed to me. Whatever truth or whatever falsehood there is in these charges against me, they were as familiar to Dr. Cullen in 1851 when he defended and encouraged me, as now when he joins the cry against me and tries to run me down. The political events that have happened since 1851 are exactly what were foreseen by Dr. Cullen, and were a matter of conversation between his Grace and myself. There is absolutely no difference in persons, principles, or circumstances between 1851 and 1855, except in two things. One is that the (Crimean) War has rendered the policy of 1851 infinitely more feasible and easy than it then appeared; and, secondly, that Dr. Cullen has abandoned his principles, encouraged public immorality, damped the ardour of the people, stimulated corruption, and gone over to the side of the enemy. . . .

Some of the details I have already given. The fact that upon me principally, though not at all to the exclusion of others, the task fell of endeavouring to remove the *religious* grievances of the Catholics of the United Kingdom and the Colonies, gives a peculiar significance to the words and letters of slander against me in which Dr. Cullen has habitually indulged. When it fell to my lot to rise in the House of Commons and

address them on a subject distasteful to the
majority of its members, it seriously impeded my
chances of success to have it whispered amongst
my enemies, Catholic and Protestant, in the
House, that Dr. Cullen highly disapproved my
conduct; that he censured me vehemently.   It
tended much to obstruct my success as a Catholic advocate to have it said that Dr. Cullen
denounced my behaviour in Parliament as "de-
plorable," for taking with great moderation in
1854 the line with regard to Maynooth which
his Holiness has not scrupled to take in 1855.
It was a direct obstacle on the part of Dr.
Cullen when it fell to me to defend Catholic principles of education against his friend Serjeant
Shee, for Serjeant Shee to be able to produce a
letter from his Grace assailing me; and to boast,
as he did boast, and boasted truly, that Dr.
Cullen favoured his general views and policy
rather than mine.   It was no little obstruction, in
a word, when I devoted night and day to the
investigation and exposition of Catholic grievances, to have it said in the lobby and on the
benches that in "my extreme Catholic views" I
had not even the confidence of the Bishops whose
work I pretended to be doing, and that they disapproved of my extravagant and erring zeal.   I
know, of course, comparatively little of the
whispers that passed and the letters that were
written; but I know enough to be quite sure that
this kind of opposition was incessant and effectual,

and the more effectual from the astute secrecy
with which it was shrouded.

In the conference I had with Dr. Cullen in
Rome, every part of which was marked by an
extraordinary spirit of hostility, Dr. Cullen kindly
hinted that he thought my absence from Parliament would be very serviceable to Catholic interests, and that concessions were not made to us
because I who demanded them am so unpopular.
This view of the case marks better than anything
I could allege the animus of Dr. Cullen towards
me. The demands we now make are the same
in substance as we have had to make for thirty or
fifty years. They have to be made of precisely
the same Ministers as those by whom they have
been repeatedly rejected for ten, fifteen, twenty,
or thirty years—long before I was in Parliament,
or was even a Catholic. They have been pressed
on the attention of successive Ministers of every
party by the great O'Connell; but though many
things were conceded to him, and many political
and social acts of justice done at his demand,
these religious grievances of the poor he was
quite unable to persuade either friend or enemy
to remove. Yet it is to my unpopularity, it
seems, that the continued refusal of the same
Ministers is now to be attributed. Thirteen or
fourteen years ago I remember O'Connell telling
me that he was in communication with Sidney
Herbert, the late Secretary at War under Lord
Aberdeen, pressing him to redress the grievances

of Catholic soldiers and sailors. Exactly the
same grievances remain now to be redressed.
Except in name, the grievances then complained
of, and which have reference to a time of peace,
have not been altered or removed. The same
Sidney Herbert who refused O'Connell has refused me; but it is to my unpopularity that this
latter refusal is to be attributed! To what then
must we attribute the former?

Dr. Cullen forgets that during the time of my
endeavours for the souls of the poor, Bishops of the
Church of God have been going about to frustrate
my efforts, partly in plain words, partly by their
acts, partly by their aspersions on my character;
that they have both practically and theoretically represented me as a person to whom little attention
need be paid, and have done their best to smite
me under the fifth rib, while I, in my simplicity,
have been fighting the battles of the Church.

The last two or three years have offered peculiar opportunities for procuring a redress of religious grievances. Never were opportunities so
great sacrificed so deliberately. The formation
of a Catholic party, the peculiar disruption of
English parties, the apparent unanimity of Irish
constituencies,—the hopes and the fears of various
classes of our enemies making them competitors
for our favours,—all these things (and the absence
of strong political excitement in any other direction, leaving the field vacant for mere party
struggles and intrigues), did really create an epoch

in our affairs which a statesman (if Dr. Cullen had possessed the mind and capacity of a statesman, or, if not aspiring so high in intellect, he had possessed the quality of masculine common sense united to directness and straightforwardness of purpose) would have made memorable for good in the history of the Church in Ireland.   As it is, he has made them memorable indeed, but it is memorable for evil; memorable for scandals infinite; memorable for a lowered state of public morality; memorable for high hopes disappointed, for encouragement given to the enemies of the Church, and for a rude repulse to those whose highest ambition was to be its devoted servants.

.   .   .   .   .   .

On the 3d March 1854 I made a statement in the House of Commons on "the religious wants of Roman Catholic soldiers and sailors."   In my speech I stated that "the question I was about to raise was not in any way connected with the military and naval service of the country *in a time of war*;" and I occupied nearly two hours in laying before the House a string of facts and figures to explain the nature and details of the injustice which Catholic soldiers and sailors endure *in time of peace.*

I draw attention to this distinction between war and peace, because an attempt has been made by Dr. Cullen and others to sound the praises of Lord Aberdeen's Government for their wonderful liberality in sending out Catholic chaplains to the

Crimea. To any one who knows England and the facts, it must appear ludicrous in the highest degree to give the Ministry any particular credit for what they have done in this respect. It was not previously the custom of England to send out even Protestant chaplains with their regiments upon service in the field; and what was done in the Crimea was not to modify an existing arrangement for the benefit of Catholics, but to commence for the first time the sending out of chaplains of any religion, Catholic or Protestant. One-third of the army was Catholic. Three-fourths of the force before Sebastopol was Catholic. If Lord Aberdeen had commenced sending Protestant chaplains for the Protestant soldiers, and had refused to send Catholic chaplains for the Catholic soldiers, he would not simply have been then in the position of refusing to remove a grievance, but he would have made himself the author of a new insult upon us and of a new grievance. I venture to say that no Government, however bigoted, would have dared so to treat Catholic soldiers encamped amongst a preponderate number of French Catholic soldiers, upon whom they absolutely depended for safety. As a matter of policy and for their own interest, if they were to commence sending out chaplains at all, it was literally impossible for them to avoid sending out Catholic chaplains. For doing this a certain verbal civility would have been due to them—if in doing what they could not avoid they had not exhibited great

shabbiness and meanness in their way of doing it,
and in their way of refusing everything which it
was possible for them to refuse.   And I must say
that it exhibited either great weakness of mind,
or a great resolution to serve and to praise the
English Ministers at all hazards, to found upon
what they have done in this respect a claim to
our gratitude and confidence.

As a reply to the grievances which I explained
to the House, both Sir James Graham and Mr.
Sidney Herbert stubbornly refused to comply
with my demands; treated the notion of a redress
of our grievances with the most arrogant contempt, and told me that they could on principle
hold out no hope whatever of complying with my
requirements.   I know Dr. Cullen's theory is that
personal dislike to me was the ground of this refusal, and that if some less hated Catholic had
made the demand it would have been differently
treated.   This would be a very plausible theory if
we did not know it to be untrue; if it were not the
notorious fact that the Ministers themselves at the
moment assigned the true reason for the refusal,
which was this—that they had been taught by
Catholic Bishops to consider my demands as
extravagant; and that they need be under no obligation to satisfy me while they had already succeeded in satisfying Catholic Bishops.   Not my
unpopularity, but the weakness of Catholic Bishops
in consenting to the maintenance of grievances, in
upholding the persecutor against the advocate of

the poor, and in standing between the Catholic
soldier and sailor and the redress of his grievances—this is the true cause of the contemptuous
answer that was given.   When I made my demand, the Princes of the Church were on the side
of the enemies of the faith against me ; and I had
to contend not merely against the Minister of the
Crown, but against the Ministers of the Sanctuary.
What overthrew me was not the word of the First
Lord of the Admiralty or of the Secretary at War,
but the crook of the Shepherd of the Flock interposing between me and these ravening wolves.
Those pleasant-spoken members of Parliament
who are always free from the charge of unpopularity with the enemies of our faith can never be
got to attempt to render the service which I attempted ; that is, to collect the facts and lay openly
before the world the extent and amount of the
oppressions practised upon our poor, and to make
a public claim of redress.   They gain and keep
the good word of our enemies by never giving
trouble and never pushing their demands for us
beyond the limits of the convenience of our oppressors.   And when at length some one is found
—with inferior ability, it is true, but with a little
more zeal and devotedness—to state the whole
case regardless of anything but the spiritual interests of the poor, his efforts are rendered fruitless, and he himself is driven back by the authority
and at the desire of the Bishops of the Church.

And who were these Bishops ?   Not all, I know ;

and this well known to the Holy See. The Cardinal Archbishop of Westminster has acted towards me a most friendly part, for which I am bound to feel grateful, in making known most fully his sentiments both in Rome and in London. The Archbishop of Tuam, with his accustomed promptitude and zeal for the public service, at once and in a published letter disclaimed any participation in the Episcopal content of which the Ministers had boasted ; and with his Grace's words were supposed to agree the sentiments of those Bishops whose views of public affairs are ordinarily not dissimilar to his.

But there is another Bishop who was much more imperatively called on to speak out on this occasion—a Bishop who (only nominally I hope), representing the Holy See, is understood in Ireland to represent the section of Bishops who habitually oppose Dr. MacHale, and are more favourable to the English Government. I mean, of course, Dr. Cullen. The question of grievances affecting Catholic soldiers and sailors is one that peculiarly concerns Dublin and its Archbishop. There is in Dublin a considerable body of troops usually stationed, and the Irish metropolis contains many military institutions the inmates of which require spiritual aid. Wherever the Catholic soldier and sailor are they are mostly Irishmen ; and therefore an Irish Bishop, a Bishop of Dublin, a Bishop whose position brings him habitually into communication with the Government, could not, either both in public opinion or in fact, but be considered a most important personage in the practical settlement of questions of this kind. When Sir James Graham spoke in the plural number, of being in "communication with the heads of the Roman Catholic Church;" when Mr. Sidney Herbert boasted of being able to satisfy "those with whom he was in communication," it is impossible to believe that he was not in communication directly or indirectly with some Irish Bishop on a subject so interesting to Ireland ; and it is impossible to suppose, if such communications were going on, that Dr. Cullen was not a party to them.

When, therefore, the Ministers for army and navy had boldly asserted the contentment of the Bishops with whom they were in communication, the eyes of every one were turned towards Dr. Cullen, to know what his Grace had to say upon the subject.

We had not to wait very long. On the 3d March my speech was delivered; on the 5th or 6th March it was reported in the Dublin papers. On the 8th March his Grace addressed to the editor of the *Univers* a letter the main topic of which was the attack upon our convents. In that letter he took occasion to refer to what had passed in the House of Commons, and he did so in the following terms :—

"Will you allow me now to call your attention to the discussion which took place a few days ago in the House of Commons on the religious condition of Catholics in the British army and navy? The various facts brought to light on that occasion, especially in Mr. Lucas's speech, must have astonished every one who looks to England as the seat of religious equality and perfect tolerance. Yet it is gratifying to perceive that, through the liberal spirit of the present Ministry, some little inroad is to be made on the practices sanctioned by the bigotry of past times. The appointment of even two chaplains to the troops now sailing to the East is of good augury, and we trust that this first measure, however insufficient, will be followed by others of the same tendency."

The first thing that strikes me on reading this paragraph is, that neither in words nor by implication does Dr. Cullen deny the accuracy of the Ministerial statements that the Bishops with whom they were in communication had been satisfied. If any Irish Bishop was supposed in Ireland to be implicated by this statement it was Dr. Cullen; yet Dr. Cullen, writing at the time on the subject, and about the Ministers, says not one word from which an inference can be drawn that the statement as regards himself is untrue.

. . . . . .

Two parties were in presence on that occasion. Myself, taking greater pains than had ever been taken before to ascertain the facts, and resisting every kind of pressure put upon me in the House of Commons not to bring the facts to light; and the Ministers, who, when at much inconvenience I stated our claims, met me with a refusal as contemptuous in manner as it was decisive in substance, and publicly quoted the Bishops with

whom they were in communication as their authority for not trying to satisfy me.

Of these two parties, to whom does the Bishop,
speaking about that event, give public praise?
Not to me, of course. I am out of the pale of his
Grace's charity or justice. He was just then engaged in an attempt so to arrange the aggregate
meeting . . . as most conveniently to uphold
the Ministers and renounce the principles of
1851, by aid of the Lord Mayor and Mr. John
Reynolds ; and it was only a few weeks later that
his Grace invented or circulated against me the
invention that I called the Bishops of Ireland
"fools or knaves." To me, therefore, no thanks
were due or were paid ; nor was any kind of
moral support given to me.   As far as Dr.
Cullen was concerned, the public and the House
of Commons were studiously left under the impression that the Ministers who could not satisfy
me could satisfy Dr. Cullen ; and I, unsupported
and unthanked by the Apostolic Delegate, and
contemptuously resisted by the Minister, was
left to feel that all the hostility of Dr. Cullen
was reserved for me and my political associates,
and all his gratitude, love, and tenderness for
those who stubbornly refused justice to the
Catholic poor.

.   .   .   .   .   .

The clue to all this is that about that very
moment Dr. Cullen was devising a public protest
against the attack upon our convents, in which he

assured the world that, except that attack, we Catholics have no other grievances which require us to come forward as a separate class of the community seeking for redress. . . .

But though the Minister of War and the First Lord of the Admiralty insolently refused the justice which I demanded of them, perhaps of their own free will or at Dr. Cullen's instance, they, or one of them, made us some concessions which justify the gratitude of the Apostolic Delegate. My belief is that, with the exception of chaplains in the Crimea—which no Government could have refused—and some facilities given to sailors for landing now and then at home and on foreign stations for worship, nothing has been conceded by the Government; and that, on the whole, in this department things have been made worse rather than better since Dr. Cullen's friend, Lord Aberdeen, became Prime Minister at the end of 1852.

Let me take as an illustration a method of practical arrangement which, small as it is, may seem of the greatest moment in connection with the redress of the grievances of all classes of our poor. Whether in prisons, or workhouses, or lunatic asylums, or schools, or industrial establishments, or in the army or in the navy, there is one leading principle through an observance of which justice may in great part be secured to the Catholic, and without the observance of which justice is neither possible nor practically conceivable. This principle is that every man on entering the army, the navy, the prison, the workhouse, the school, the industrial or other public establishment, shall on his admission be allowed freely to enter himself as of whatever religion he pleases ; and that having once done so, he shall be treated as a believer in that religion without being obliged to make any further claim, until he chooses deliberately to declare a change of religion, should such occur to him.

The importance of this principle will appear more obvious by considering the principle which is generally maintained against it.   When our enemies or "false friends" wish to arrange matters so that there shall be an appearance of justice, with the certainty of almost universal injustice, they adopt a different arrangement.   They lay it down that *prima facie* every man is a Protestant ; Protestantism is the legal religion ; and the presumption is that every man is of the legal religion until he says the contrary.   When, therefore, a man enters prison, workhouse, or ship, their rule is to make no registry of his religion, but to treat him in the ordinary way—that is, the Protestant way— until he declares himself a Catholic.   If, however, he should not like to be treated as a Protestant, and should have the courage, in the face of his superiors and against their will, to avow himself a Catholic, then of course he must to a certain extent be treated as such.   But without and until this formal demand —which it too often requires very heroic courage to make—he must be treated as a Protestant.

It is hardly too much to say that, in all public establishments and institutions, the difference between justice and injustice to the Catholic poor consists in the adoption of one or other of these two rules. Adopt the former, and almost by a necessary consequence you secure justice, or at least you make justice easily attainable. Adopt the latter, you render justice in the highest degree difficult, and you make exercise of the Catholic religion for the Catholic poor man a practical impossibility.

The reason for this is very obvious. Take a prisoner, for instance, at the door of his prison which he is about to enter for the first time, and let an official of whom he knows nothing ask him, as a matter of course, what is his religion ; in almost every case the prisoner will answer truly according to his creed. If he is a Catholic, he will say so ; and if the prison rule is that when once so registered as a Catholic he shall thenceforth be treated as a Catholic, the chances of injustice and of grievance are in great part removed, and all reasonable arrangements are facilitated. But let the prisoner enter the prison without inquiry, let him find when he enters that all the authorities are Protestants, that he receives better treatment in many small ways for appearing to be a Protestant, and, above all, that by so appearing he earns the favour of his superiors,—in the vast majority of instances a man subjected to these influences will neither have the courage nor the will to demand formally of the prison authorities that they shall treat him as a Catholic.

The very first element, therefore, of the redress of the grievances of Catholic prisoners is expressed in these few words, " Registration of religion before admission." And precisely the same principle, with the same reason, applies to all poor Catholics who enter any public institution or service in which they are exposed to the influence of malignant or bigoted superiors. Of the prisons I shall speak presently more in detail ; but let us see what has been done with reference to this principle in the navy of late years.

THE NAVY.—I shall not take upon me to praise the motive with which Lord Derby's Government acted with regard to the Catholic Church in 1852, but one act they did which, if they had been saints or angels, they could hardly have done better.   The Duke of Northumberland was First Lord of the Admiralty, and under him an order was issued that the religion of every sailor " borne," as I believe it is called, "on the ship's books," should be formally registered.   (I am stating just now what I stated last year in the House of Commons without contradiction, and what I have repeatedly said elsewhere in public without contradiction.) I will suppose that while the motive of Lord Derby's Government was the worst possible, that of Lord Aberdeen's Government was the best possible.   Taking this for granted, the fact is that Lord Aberdeen's Government—that is, Sir James

Graham—rescinded the order issued by the Duke of Northumberland and put an end to the only possible safeguard of the Catholic sailor, by destroying the previous registration of religion.

My attention was first called to this subject by the late Bishop of Plymouth, Dr. Errington, now Coadjutor-Bishop of Westminster, whose experience among sailors and ships in Plymouth and elsewhere has been very considerable. . . . His Lordship told me that the Duke of Northumberland's order was the most fortunate, and Sir James Graham's the most calamitous, that could be imagined.

Under the Duke of Northumberland's rule, if the Bishop, or if a priest, went on board a man-of-war on which there were known to be many Catholics, made friends with the captain or other officer in temporary command of the ship, and requested to have the Catholic sailors assembled for the purpose of addressing them on their religious duties, an order given to the Catholic sailors would at once, and as a matter of discipline, be obeyed by every sailor who was registered or entered on the ship's books as a Catholic. Every registered Catholic sailor would obey the summons as a matter of course, and come with his fellows to listen to the exhortations of the priest. Under Sir James Graham's rule no sailor is known as a Catholic, or is bound to answer to that designation. An order given by a friendly officer to the Catholic sailors to assemble would not be an order which any sailor would feel himself bound to obey. No sailor (being unregistered) is bound to acknowledge himself a Catholic; he may conceal his religion, as in the majority of instances he has every motive to conceal it; and, unless my recollection deceives me, Dr. Errington told me he had more than once been deterred under Sir James Graham's rule from attempting to have the men assembled, because he had been told, and it seemed true, that the Catholic sailors would not answer the summons, and that his attempt would be worse than useless. . . .

In accordance with these views, which were stated to me with much earnestness and in considerable detail by Dr. Errington, I urged upon the House of Commons, and especially upon Sir James Graham, the alteration of the rule and the re-adoption of the system of registration introduced by the Duke of Northumberland and abrogated by himself. Sir James Graham flatly refused to make the change. The only reason he gave was that the custom of the British navy was not to force upon the men any distinction of religion, and only to recognise these differences when formally claimed by the sailors themselves.

As I am informed, this disastrous arrangement, abolished by our open enemies, and re-established and resolutely maintained by our "false friends" in 1853, still exists in all its pernicious vigour. I make no imputation on Sir James Graham's motives for this baleful policy; and the less so because I am under the impression that it was under what I may call the "Cullen-Grant influence," or at least in full accordance with the wishes and consent of these Prelates, that the old arrangement was restored.   At all events, this step was taken, I suppose, either with their consent or against their consent.   If against their consent, how can Dr. Cullen praise the special liberality of the present Ministers?   If with their consent, then it is unfortunately too true that, in advocating the redress of grievances in the House of Commons, I was speaking against those Bishops with whom the "Government was in communication."   Not the Admiralty or the War Office, but Dublin and Southwark were the authors of the grievances of which I complained ; and then indeed is made clear to me how it could be truly said that the Ministers, though they despaired of satisfying me, had satisfied and were satisfying "others."

REGIMENTAL SCHOOLS.—Having thus in a truly liberal spirit rendered for the navy that redress of grievances impossible, which under their predecessors was not merely possible but in a very high degree probable, let us see what they have done in the army for the regimental schools. Here, at all events, we have not what Dr. Cullen calls "the bigotry of past times," but the very latest expression of the newest liberality of the best of Ministers.   These regulations were issued, after a careful examination of the subject, in order

to satisfy the demands of the Catholics. The subject to which they refer—the religious treatment
of soldiers' children—formed a very leading part
of our grievances as regards the army. They
were issued after consultation with "the heads of
the Catholic Church;" and they were rather a
striking portion of that very liberal arrangement
by which Mr. Sidney Herbert had satisfied
"others," though he could not satisfy me. Indeed,
he was so far from satisfying me by this arrangement, that it formed one of the special grievances
of which I complained. I read the regulations
aloud in the House of Commons with the date
and Sidney Herbert's name at the bottom of it,
and I stated there the objections to it, which I
will now repeat.

We have seen that in the navy the Catholic
sailors are not registered as such; and Sir James
Graham, relying on the traditions of the service,
refused to have them registered. But in the
army it is very different. The Catholic soldiers
are all registered as such; and the Minister of
War has the means of knowing the exact number
of Catholic soldiers in every regiment on any
given day. Such returns for the whole army
have been made by Mr. Sidney Herbert, and
have been printed by the House of Commons, at
my request; and Mr. Herbert has admitted to
me that he could give such return with perfect
accuracy for every regiment and company, if it
were judged advisable. Soldiers' marriages are

also duly recorded ; and the military authorities therefore know with perfect accuracy the religion of every adult soldier to whom the school regulations apply, and of the parents of every child.

As a matter of course, almost, regimental schools are mixed schools—that is, Catholic and Protestant are taught in them secular learning. There is also religious teaching in them ; and the rule in this case might be very simple, that where the religious teaching is Protestant (as I believe it always is), those soldiers who by the registry are known to be Catholics, and those children who by the registry are known to be the children of Catholic soldiers, should *ipso facto* be exempted from attendance at the religious teaching. Under such a rule as this there could be no interference with discipline or the regularity of attendance. The exemption permitted would apply only to a certain number of individuals known beforehand and recorded, nor could any others from idleness or worse motives take advantage of it. Of course endless objections may be made to any proposal which is disliked ; but I defy any one to urge to this proposal any practical objection which cannot be instantaneously refuted.

Such a regulation, besides being just and practicable, could not have caused any public outcry, like those just concessions which end or begin in giving us money. Here there was no money in question, no vote of the House of Commons, no publicity in the nature of the case ; merely an equitable exemption, which no one out of the regiment in which it had its operation would ever trouble himself about.

But small and simple as this piece of justice was, it was too great an effort for the liberal mind of Mr. Sidney Herbert to compass it. His regulations are exactly the opposite of what I have proposed. They provide that all soldiers, and therefore in effect all Catholic soldiers, even though registered or known to be otherwise, shall be presumed to be Protestants of the Established Church. *Prima facie* every registered Catholic adult and Catholic child is presumed to be in heart a Protestant. At a certain hour on each school-day, every registered Catholic adult and Catholic child is required to attend Protestant worship and Protestant religious instruction. This rule is the starting-point. It is not as in the navy, where the religion of the sailor is studiously unknown. Here it is known and recorded ; and, with this full knowledge, Sidney Herbert sets out with the presumption that the known Catholic adult will prefer both for himself and for his children Protestant worship and Protestant religious instruction.

But then comes an exemption. All adults are exempt if they "object." They must raise a formal objection ; and they must, in the words of the order, "object on religious grounds." By a further provision as to adults, their "objection" must be formally "signified to the commanding officer or to the schoolmaster, if the commanding officer should so direct." And as to children, the objection is only allowed "provided their parents signify their wish to this effect *in writing* to the schoolmaster or schoolmistress." By this new rule Catholic parents are taken to prefer having their children brought up Protestants until they have declared the contrary in writing.

Now, what has been the universal complaint about regimental schools before this order was issued ? It was that fanatical Protestant officers used the influence over the soldiers which military discipline gave them to force Catholic children and adults against their will into Protestant schools, and that the fear of displeasing their officers made the poor Catholic privates silent. The adult or the parent must object, and even must object in writing. But suppose his Protestant officer is a great fanatic, who, like many, makes it his pride to proselytise and spread heresy amongst Catholic soldiers and children. To present this formal "objection," "in writing," is perhaps the most distasteful thing to his officer personally which the Catholic soldier could do. If he ventures to object, he draws down upon himself the displeasure of his officer, which will not be the less effective because its origin is concealed. It is now, therefore, provided by law that all Catholic adults and children belonging to or connected with the army shall be brought up Protestants unless they or their parents have the

courage to brave the hostility of a fanatic and
unjust officer by making a formal objection and
"in writing."

I hope I need not argue this case further.   I
urged these objections in the House of Commons
as well as I was able, and Mr. Sidney Herbert
flatly refused to pay any attention to them.
He could not satisfy me, but he could satisfy
" others."

Who are those "others?"   It was Dr. Grant,
the Bishop of Southwark, who kindly put into
my hand the regulations against which I have
now been arguing.   When I pointed out to his
Lordship their objectionable character ; and when
I showed that the necessity imposed upon the
poor Catholic, whether soldier, sailor, or prisoner,
of making formal objections to procure exemption
from Protestant worship and teaching, was a
question of much wider interest than regimental
schools; and that the principle, for good or for
evil, applied to every Government institution and
service, his Lordship recognised the validity of
my argument; but added, " I think you will
find it very difficult to persuade Sidney Herbert
to give way to your objection, because Dr. Cullen
was a party (or consented) to these regulations
before they were issued."

It is simply impossible that in May 1853 Mr.
Sidney Herbert should have issued new regulations about the religion of Catholic soldiers without consulting Dr. Cullen.   He was most anxious

at that time to secure and keep, what he did secure and keep, the political support of this non-political Archbishop. He would have been foolish indeed to meddle in such a matter without Dr. Cullen's consent, because nothing obliged him to deal with that matter at all; and the fact that he issued those regulations, that he afterwards boasted of satisfying Catholic Bishops, and that Dr. Cullen afterwards publicly eulogised his liberality in regard to the religious treatment of Catholic soldiers, is a proof that on this point Dr. Cullen and Mr. Sidney Herbert understood one another. Besides, I am prepared to declare (on oath if necessary) that Dr. Grant spontaneously assured me that such was the fact, and that Dr. Cullen's consent would form the grand obstacle to a redress of that grievance. I need hardly qualify such a consent by any epithet.

GOVERNMENT PRISONS.—It is not a little singular that just at the moment when the "heads of the Church," with whom the Ministers were "in communication," felt themselves obliged to abandon the one fundamental principle for the redress of Catholic grievances in the army and in the navy, I succeeded in procuring the acceptance of that very principle by Lord Palmerston for the benefit of criminals in jails. I urged verbally the very reasons which I now urge in writing. Lord Palmerston, then Home Secretary (1853), admitted their force to me in private; and when I represented the case of the Catholic prisoners

publicly in the House of Commons, he publicly
admitted the justice of my claim and promised
that it should be conceded. This was towards
the end of the session of 1853. My claim was
exactly what I have set forth in the case of sailors
and regimental schools. The existing law with
regard to prisons allows the Catholic prisoners
the exercise of their religion if they have the
courage to claim it. They may refuse to attend
Protestant service; they may send for a priest
when they require his services; and in all respects,
if they have the courage and zeal enough to insist
on their rights, they have a right to be treated as
Catholics. Their case is exactly the same as that
of sailors and soldiers or their children in the regimental schools. The practical grievance is, that
being more or less at the mercy of their superiors,
who are often fanatics and unjust, they have neither
the courage nor the zeal to make that formal claim
which the law requires as a preliminary to the re-
cognition of their right. The main remedy in all
these cases is one and the same. It is to provide a simple means of recording at first the religion of the prisoner or sailor, and then to make it
a matter of course and rule for him to be treated
ever afterwards according to the record.

With regard to prisoners, I proved that there
are many hundreds of Catholics prisoners who
make a point of denying their religion, conform-
ing to Protestantism, and practising hypocrisy in
what it is pretended are places of reformation,

merely in order to please their keepers and to procure the indulgence on Sunday of going to a Protestant musical service by way of recreation. I insisted that the religion of every prisoner should be registered on his admission to prison ; that to the Catholic priest a list of the Catholic prisoners should be furnished ; and that he should have free access to them at all reasonable times, in the same way as the Protestant chaplain has to the Protestant prisoners.

I urged this as well as I was able in the House of Commons, and when I sat down Lord Palmerston rose, and after thanking me for the courteous and friendly spirit in which I had brought this subject under his notice, he said he thought he could give me an answer that would satisfy me, and that would express the unanimous feeling of the House.   That answer was to concede everything I demanded ; and he promised, moreover, that in the estimates or financial accounts of next year a grant should be proposed for Catholic chaplains, to be expressly attached to every prison which is under the immediate management of the Government.   In giving this promise he repeated his challenge to members of all opinions that he expressed the unanimous sentiment of the House, that this was just and ought to conceded.   I noticed on that occasion the presence of some of our worst enemies, some of the greatest bigots and fanatics in the House ; but not one of them rose to contradict Lord Palmerston, or to protest against the realisation of his promises. It was a promise given by the Minister, and given by him in the name of the House. It was a unanimous concession.

But why this unanimity? The reason is very simple. Our Independent Catholic party was then strong, and though many had deserted us, it was thought we were supported by the Bishops and clergy, and specially by the Apostolic Delegate. Whispers to the contrary had got about, but they were not generally credited. It was thought that we were politically strong; and as we asked nothing for ourselves, and could only be conciliated by concessions to the Church and to the country, the Ministers were willing to try to conciliate us by such concessions; while their opponents did not like to protest against acts of justice done at the demand of us who sat on the same benches as themselves, and whose votes might sometimes be useful to them on a party division. Both sides thought it their interest to be friends with us, and therefore the fanatics of both sides allowed their bigotry to go to sleep, and consented to a cessation of hostilities.

All through the session of 1853 this state of feeling prevailed, and the fact that such a promise of absolute concession was made by the Minister, in the name of the whole House, without one dissentient voice, is the strongest proof that could be given of the feeling that prevailed. But after the session was over, and in the course of the next year, this state of things began to alter. It began to be understood more clearly in England among political parties that our force was not so strong as it had been considered ; that corruption had spread deeper and more widely ; that a large number of the Bishops and considerable sections of the clergy were in favour of a party connection with the Whigs and with Lord Aberdeen ; that by reason of Dr. Cullen's favour the Whig side in Irish politics was likely in the long-run to preponderate ; and that our side, or that of the Independent party, deserted by his Grace, was likely in the long-run to be defeated.

This change of calculation showed itself in the most marked way in the altered tone of Lord Derby's friends in the House of Commons in the session of 1854. They no longer thought us as powerful as they believed us in 1853. There were in the House of Commons quite as many Catholic members as before, but more of them were on Lord John Russell's side ; and that side seemed likely to increase in strength, while ours seemed likely to become weaker and weaker. The Tory enemies of the Ministers, therefore, had less reason to fear our enmity, less reason to hope anything from our favour. We had become of much less importance in their eyes ; and thus in 1854 it was a better party calculation for them to brave our enmity by relying openly on the Protestant bigotry of the country than it had been in 1853, when we were thought to have more strength.

Upon this calculation the friends of Lord Derby acted in the most unmistakable manner. They made less concealment than ever of their un-Catholic feeling. Leading members of their party, who in 1853 had carefully stayed away from anti-Catholic debates and divisions, came down in 1854 to record their votes and deliver speeches against us.

On the prison question, however, Lord Palmerston kept his word with me. He caused to be inserted amongst the votes, as he had promised, a sum of money for Catholic chaplains. But this year there was no unanimity in the House of Commons. Lord Derby's friends judged that on this point, as on so many others, more was to be gained by cultivating Protestant bigotry than by treating us with forbearance. They saw the number of Catholic Bishops who made themselves partisans of the Ministers. They had heard of the altered politics of the great ecclesiastical dictator, Dr. Cullen; and as they considered that the bulk of the Catholics were going over definitely to Lord John Russell and Lord Aberdeen, they resolved to show us all the enmity in their power. Accordingly, when the vote for the prison chaplains was proposed, an amendment was moved, and after a debate the proposed grant was negatived.

This was towards the end of last session. Nobody had been particularly active in that affair but myself. I had extracted promises from Lord Palmerston which astonished Dr. Cullen's friends, who to me expressed their unfeigned surprise. I had succeeded in securing the apparently unanimous sanction of the House of Commons. Under my management the attempt was carried to the very verge of success. And it is my solemn belief that nothing contributed to my partial failure (for total failure there is not yet), so much as the altered temper of the House of Commons, produced by the changed politics of Dr. Cullen.

A CHAPLAIN FOR KILMAINHAM.—Dr. Cullen has now got the upper hand in our politics in the House of Commons. His side—that of favour to the Ministers—is taken by the majority of Catholic members. These Ministerial politics are understood to be in the ascendant. The Administration gets all the benefit they are ever likely to get upon Catholic support; and now, therefore, is the time to estimate the value of the policy which hands over the Church as an inheritance to our "false friends" the Whigs.

I have watched with some care since I have been in Rome the proceedings of the session of this year. Administrations have broken to pieces, have been re-made, have followed one another in quick succession, have rivalled one another in weakness, and not one has been formed to which the support of thirty Irish Catholic members was not a matter of very great importance. Up to this time, however, I have not seen in the newspapers, nor do my private letters inform me, that anything has been done by Dr. Cullen's Catholic partisans to turn this favourable conjuncture to account for the redress of Catholic grievances. On the contrary, what has caught my attention has been something very opposite ; and I am very much mistaken if it is not true that, just as our opportunities are improving and the strength of Dr. Cullen's Ministerial supporters is on the increase, our position in regard to the redress' of grievances becomes worse and worse. In 1853 our chance of redress seemed to be flourishing. In 1854 our opportunities seemed greater, but the chance diminished. In 1855 the opportunities have increased a hundredfold, but the prospect of accomplishing anything has almost entirely passed away. The development of Dr. Cullen's new Ministerial policy is the exact measure of the augmenting discomfiture of Catholic interests and rights.

The hospital of Kilmainham is a public institution in Dublin for the reception of old and disabled soldiers, like the *Invalides* of Paris, only on a smaller scale. Last year there were 139 inmates, of whom 100 were Catholics, 35 Protestants of the Established Church, and 4 Presbyterians. From the beginning a very abundant provision has been made for the religious wants of the 35 Protestants. They have in the building a handsome chapel, and a resident clergyman, who has a salary of about 1400 scudi (£250). The chapel clerk has a further salary of nearly 90 scudi

(£18, 5s.); and sums are constantly voted by Parliament for the repairs and furniture of the chapel. This is for the spiritual accommodation of 35 Protestants. For 100 Catholic soldiers, as usual, there was not a farthing.

In the session of 1853 I privately drew Mr. Sidney Herbert's attention to this injustice. He professed entire ignorance, thanked me for the information, and promised that next year a provision should be made for Catholic worship. This was actually done, and last year (1854) a vote was proposed and taken for £50 for "a Roman Catholic clergyman officiating to the inmates." I remember being assured at the time in private by some of Dr. Cullen's friends that this concession was made, not to me, but to Mr. Monsell, who had also busied himself about the affair. Be it so. I willingly surrender the praise to Mr. Monsell, and will suppose that it was through his influence the concession was made.

Unhappily the concession only lasted a year. This year I see by the newspapers that it is withdrawn, and that no allowance has been voted for a Catholic chaplain for Kilmainham. Everything else remains the same, but the Catholic chaplain has no allowance made for him.

Mr. Sidney Herbert was the Secretary at War who proposed the £50 grant for 1854. The same Mr. Sidney Herbert, as his last act before leaving office, withdrew the grant. As far as I know, the need of it for the poor infirm and maimed Catholic veterans is as great as ever.   It is in Dr. Cullen's own city.   Mr. Sidney Herbert is the man on whose modern "liberality" his Grace particularly relies.

Mr. Monsell is in higher favour than ever with his Whig employers.   The number of Catholic members who support the Ministers and do Dr. Cullen's latest will is greater than ever.   Throughout many parts of Ireland a reign of terror prevails in the interest of the Government, by which Episcopal authority tramples down every independent sentiment, and would render our side as utterly prostrate as Dr. Cullen desires, were it not that some Bishops, of whom the great Archbishop of Tuam—may God reward him !—is the chief, stand boldly forward to resist this degrading tyranny. Everything favours the views of those who support the Ministers ; and in this particular case it is a personal favour to Dr. Cullen which is in question, quite as much as justice to the poor broken-down invalids.   Yet with all this, the last act of Mr. Sidney Herbert was to insult Dr. Cullen by withdrawing the allowance for a chaplain from him ; and it is difficult to describe the contemptuous, insincere, and uncandid indifference with which, according to the newspapers, the withdrawal of this provision was defended, and all rational explanation refused.   I may observe that the protest against this withdrawal of the chaplaincy was not made from the Government side of the House.   Mr. Monsell *did* not, and indeed *could* not, raise his voice on the matter. No Ministerial Catholic seems to have interested himself about it, but it was left to a Protestant member of the Opposition representing a Catholic constituency to make this claim, to assert our rights, and to be mocked and laughed at by Dr. Cullen's friends for interposing in behalf of the salvation of some poor old battered Catholic souls.

Here ends the whole of what Lucas wrote in Rome. On his return to England he occupied some time in adding another chapter on Scotch Education, intended to show how the breaking up of the Independent Opposition party had been as detrimental to the interests of Catholics in Scotland as it had been to the interests of Catholics in England and Ireland. I do not give this chapter, because it furnishes only one more instance of the fatal effects of the policy already fully exposed in the preceding pages, and adds, I think, nothing to their force.

Book the Sixth.

RETURN AND DEATH.

CHAPTER I.

RETURN AND DEATH.

LUCAS had not completed the "Statement" when he returned to London towards the end of May. His first visit was to his father in the City. He looked so ill that his appearance made us start. Indeed, so altered was he, that when he presented himself at the door of the House of Commons, the doorkeepers did not know him. He at once became the guest of Richard Swift, M.P. for Sligo, a true-hearted, genuine friend, one of the few who continued faithful to their pledges. In Mr. Swift's house at Wandsworth he remained for two months; then he went for a short time to Weybridge, then on a long visit to his father at Brighton, and finally to Staines, where he died.

While at Wandsworth, alarming reports as to his health and also as to the failure of his success in Rome appeared in some of the journals. In reply to these he on the 12th of June addressed the following letter to his friends through the *Tablet :—*

"Though I am naturally unwilling to speak about myself, yet respect for my readers and constituents, and a sort of necessity arising out of letters received from friends in different parts of the country, oblige me to explain why it is that, having returned to England, I am able neither to attend in the House of Commons nor to write in the *Tablet* for a short time. I left Rome with my business uncompleted, because it is almost impossible to remain there with any regard to my health. A rapid journey home, and two late nights in the House of Commons before the recess, completed what the uncongenial climate of Rome had commenced; and I now find myself, I trust with no serious or permanent indisposition, but for the moment a great deal weakened, and absolutely requiring rest both of mind and body.

"When I left Rome, it was with the arrangement, and even on a sort of condition, that I was to return in a very short time for the completion of what I had in hand. Want of health has retarded, though it has not in the slightest degree changed, my intention in this respect. Just as much as if I was in Rome, I regard the completion of what has recently occupied so much of my time and attention as my first, and, in my present state of health, I may say my only business. Until that is completed, whatever exertion I can prudently make is being, and must be, devoted to that one object; and as soon as I have done everything which it is possible for me to do 'here, I intend, with the doctor's permission, to return to Rome in order to put this matter finally out of hand.

"I hope this explanation will be satisfactory to my friends. I feel myself daily recovering, but for the present I have found that any little excess of exertion or excitement tends very definitely to retard my recovery of health. I am sure, therefore, I shall be excused for taking rest which, after all, is a necessity, and does not depend upon my own will.

"The stories which I see in one or two of the venal journals about my having failed to obtain a hearing in Rome, and about the adverse interest being stronger than ever, are, when I look closely at them, simply the words of a very accomplished and practised falsifier. It so happens that, almost without making an effort of the most trifling description, I have had a hearing much more complete than is at all consistent with my personal convenience; and as to the result of the mission, up to the present moment nothing, of course, is concluded; but

I will only say that I feel no reason to regret, and never have regretted, either the time, the trouble, or the expense which this mission has occasioned. I am more than ever satisfied that to communicate directly with Rome was the wise and prudent course; and as for the occurrences that are to happen, according to the writer of the paragraph to which I have referred, they are as purely imaginary as the romances of Arthur or Charlemagne. F. I.."

I call particular attention both to the closing paragraph of the above letter and to the following (addressed to the Rev. Thomas O'Shea, late of Callan), written more than three months later, and at a time when he knew that his recovery was impossible :—

"STAINES, *September* 28*th.*

"MY DEAR FATHER TOM,—I don't know whether I am glad or sorry that your notion of my disorder is so mistaken. The truth is that it is pretty fairly spread over most of the organs of my body; that I am now suffering under enlarged heart, bronchitis, congested liver, inert kidneys, a stomach that refuses food, asthma that forbids sleep, and, to crown all, the dropsy. As Sidney Smith says in one of his letters—'I have seven or eight complaints, but in all other respects I am perfectly well.' In plain and sober seriousness, my dear Father Tom, I have given up all hope of life, have received the Last Sacraments, and though perhaps not immediately to die—for this is in God's hands—yet I have now no other business than to make the best preparation I can for the judgment-seat of the Almighty, and to request all the prayers of my friends to help me through this fearful passage, which I hope may be from death to life.

"Thank God, I have no wish to live. I ask for no prayers for restoration to health. I have never valued life very much, and now less than ever. Dear Father Tom, it would be a great pleasure to see you again before I die. We have fought many a battle together, at your imminent peril, and I never found in you less than the courage of a hero, perfect unselfishness, zeal untiring, and a devotion to the cause of God and the poor that it will be difficult to surpass. Now, when, perhaps, I am presently to stand face to face with my Creator and Redeemer, I esteem it an honour to have fought so often by your side ; and though I do not regret for a moment that my exertions have tended to shorten my life, I do most bitterly regret that your nobleness and heroism have brought on you so sad a persecution. However, my dear Father Tom, let me say to you, and to our friends of your diocese, not to be downcast or disheartened. As sure as God is in heaven, your cause is the cause of truth and honour; and when your last hour comes, you will feel what a consolation it gives a man never to have flinched in the worst of times—as I may say of you—or given way in the public service to selfish personal considerations.

" My dear Father Tom, I would give a little world to press your hand once more and to receive your blessing. Make my kindest adieus to all our friends, particularly to Fr. Keeffe, your good brother the Archdeacon, Fr. Aylward, our friends in Tipperary, and my most worthy and venerated friend, the Archdeacon of Rathkeale.

" Your business, as far as depends on my Statement, is not yet quite complete. I am sorry for it, but I have done my best; and I have left such instructions as I hope will turn to the best account what I have been able to do. If I die, you will hear through one of my friends how the matter stands. At present I can add no more than that I am, my dear Father, most affectionately yours,   F. LUCAS."

To his friends in Meath he conveyed a message in a letter written by his wife, and addressed to Fr. Tormey of Navan, in which that gentleman is desired to "assure his constituents, that if, as he expects, this illness shall terminate his career, he is indeed proud to terminate it in the service of men whom he respects, esteems, and loves so much, both for their private and public worth . . . He prays God to bless you all, clergy and laity, and to reward you for the honourable and high-minded fidelity with which you have sustained him in difficult times. . . . If he were to begin to give his kind love to everybody, it would be impossible to put them all in writing," &c.

About this time it became generally known that he was in a very dangerous state, and the greatest consternation was felt among Catholics, both here and in Ireland. One journal expressed the grief of the editor thus : "We have no words to express our intense sorrow at this distressing intelligence. FREDERICK LUCAS lies dangerously ill at Staines. A great champion of the Church is stricken in the height of his pious and generous career. . . . We are sure that in every Catholic church prayers will be offered up for his recovery or happy death, God's will be done! but this is a blow stern and awful indeed."

The Bishop of Southwark, for whom he had a very high regard, and several of the Meath priests, visited him at Staines, and his Eminence Cardinal Wiseman wrote him the following letter :—

"LEYTON, *October* 12, 1856.

"DEAR MR. LUCAS,—It was my sincere desire to call upon you, and inquire in person after your valuable health, but Dr. Whitty assures me, of what I feared, that my visit would be over-exciting at a time when quiet is indispensable. I must, therefore, content myself with conveying to you in writing my warmest sympathy and anxiety for your recovery, and assuring you of my fervent prayers to God for this mercy, if not for your own sake, for that of the Catholic interests and the general welfare.

"At the same time, I am sure that your own earnest wish is that God's will may be accomplished in you, and I pray Him earnestly to give you grace to be in all things conformable to it and prepared for it. In this spirit I wish you and yours every blessing, and am ever your affectionate servant in Christ,   N. Card. Wiseman."

The following account of his last illness and death is given by Father Whitty, S.J., who was at that time Cardinal Wiseman's Vicar General, and head priest of Moorfields :—

"Mr. Lucas arrived in London from Rome somewhat unexpectedly on 23d May 1855, in very bad health. No thought of death, however, crossed our minds, nor did he himself at the time, as far as I know, apprehend that he was about to die. A mental depression had come on him in Rome, partly from the anxieties of his mission to the Pope, partly from the Roman climate, and no doubt partly likewise from the secret progress of the heart-disease of which he afterwards died. He told me that almost from the commencement of the 'Statement' he never sat down to it without a feeling that he should never complete it. It was not an expectation of death so much as a vague presentiment of an overwhelming difficulty against which he felt bound to struggle. This depression of mind revealed itself in several letters home at the time. 'With all my heart I wish for a decision (of the Pope) against me.' In two letters he says he prayed earnestly to be delivered from the bondage of public life; not that he was unwilling to serve the Church still longer as a member of Parliament and a journalist; but he felt the hopelessness of doing good for Ireland *as things then were*, even if a decision should be in his favour.

"After one or two attempts to attend in his place in Parliament, he had to give up all business except a little work now and then on the 'Statement,' in the hope of completing it. He spent the summer months with Mr. Swift and other friends in and near London, and on a long visit to his father and sisters at Brighton. On September 6th he went down to the house of his brother-in-law, Mr. Skidmore Ashby of Staines, very sick and ill. Before going, Dr. Williams had told his friends plainly that, humanly speaking, there was no hope of prolonging his life. For such a sentence his own mind was fully prepared. Even whilst there appeared some hope, he used to say, I am willing to live if it be God's will, in suffering, humiliation, and poverty, but I would rather die.'

"In my first visit to Staines, on my telling him the dismay which the intelligence had created among those who believed that he had been destined by God to do useful work for Ireland and the Church, he could not see how his removal could materially interfere with that work, and in this impression he was perfectly sincere. I have never met any one in my life so unconscious of his ability as Lucas. The only power he seemed to himself to possess was the power, as he said, of putting an idea he had in his own mind into the heads of others. And in that first visit to him, looking forward to death, he said to me, 'There is only one thing I regret. If it were God's will, I should like to have had the opportunity of putting the temporal power of the Pope before the House of Commons. I have been to Rome, and I have looked into the subject. I am so convinced of the truth of my view, that I do think I could make even a British Parliament understand the true position of the Pope in Europe and in the world. But such is not God's will, and I am quite content.'

" He had always been most attentive to his religious duties; but on learning his danger, he set about preparing for death with that same earnest resolution with which it was his wont to undertake everything else. On my asking him one day how much time the doctor still gave him to live, he told me the hopes and the fears, and ended in a tone and look of great solemnity, 'So in any case I cannot expect to see the end of the year; before then I shall have appeared before my Maker.'

" The last time I ever saw him alive, on my asking how he felt, 'Thank God,' said he, 'I feel every day getting weaker and weaker.'

" On another occasion Mr. Swift expressed a hope he might still pull through. 'Yes,' he said,

'I've no doubt whatever I shall pull through, *and find myself on the other side !*'

"During life he had often said he hoped he should have good notice of death. Terrible as a death by the hands of the executioner might seem, there was one feature in it, he used to say, that would to him make up for all. 'It gives one leisure to prepare for death. If they gave me time to make a spiritual retreat, I should not object to going out of the world thus in a good cause.' In point of fact, God did give him this time, and he employed it well.

"Many and warm as his public controversies had been, he had no personal feeling against any one. But he felt that he had sometimes been hasty and incautious in writing; and in one instance, remembering that he had thus imprudently expressed himself about the late Duke of Norfolk, then Earl of Arundell and Surrey, he asked me to convey his deep regret and offer of a public apology. As might have been expected, the Earl wrote back a letter of most cordial sympathy and charity, which gave him great comfort. Nor was this charity confined to words. For after the death of Mr. Lucas, hearing that some persons were anxious to contribute to the education of his son, he sent me a handsome donation towards that object.

"Diseases of the heart, as is well known, often involve much distress and suffering. It was so in Mr. Lucas's case. He had at times most painful attacks of spasmodic breathing, and at the end of them he would often say, 'Thank God for that,' meaning the suffering.

"On Sunday, September 23d, he went to Beaumont Lodge, then a Jesuit Novitiate, and the nearest Catholic chapel to Staines. On that day dropsy first appeared. He had much difficulty in the evening in getting upstairs to his room, whence he came down no more. He felt a great desire to receive Holy Communion often, and he had this happiness, I believe, twelve times altogether during his six weeks in Staines. On September 25th he made a general confession to Father Tracey Clarke, the Master of Novices at Beaumont, and received the holy viaticum. Next day I came from London to administer extreme unction. He received the viaticum on several other occasions, and finally on the Feast of the Purity of our Blessed Lady, just the day before he died. The next day, October 22d, in the afternoon, he saw and conversed with his father for a considerable time. After he was gone he said, 'I hope I did not speak too much of myself, but I tried to give the conversation a Catholic turn.' A little later he had a violent attack of the painful breathing and became very faint. He was sitting up, having been unable to lie down for some time. As soon as the change in his countenance was perceived, the little indulgenced prayers were repeated to him,—'Jesus, Mary, and Joseph, I offer you my heart and my soul,' &c. He responded by a most emphatic 'Thank you,' bent forward, as was his wont in order to breathe more freely, then leaning back in his chair, expired without a sigh.

"It was a Christian death, cheerfully accepted from the hands of God, at the early age of forty-four, and well prepared for. His career, short as it was, is one for which English and Irish Catholics may well feel grateful to God. A convert to the Catholic faith, he from the first seemed to have imbibed the spirit of that faith in its fulness. No one, I think, could have known him intimately without seeing a certain resemblance between him and Sir Thomas More, the Chancellor and martyr, as we hope he will one day be declared by the Holy Roman See. In natural character of mind and heart both were Englishmen of the noblest type. Both had the same gentle yet resolute spirit, the same love of truth combined with considerateness for the convictions or prejudices of others, the same ready wit in reply and argument, and above all, the same irrepressible playfulness of spirit, even within sight of the solemn moment of death. Not that there was in either any want of reverence. On the contrary, the very characteristic of their piety, I should say, was a profound sense of God's rights. But they felt like God's children all the same, and as children they could feel no gloom in going into their Father's presence.

"Like Sir Thomas More, too, Lucas was, above

all things, a loyal child of the Holy See. It was
not indeed given to him, as to Sir Thomas, to die
for the divine rights of the Successor of St. Peter;
but he had the stuff in him of which, by God's
grace, martyrs are made. Since the sixteenth century England has been the great rebel in Europe
against the Holy See. Amid all the variations of
her sects and doctrines she has remained faithful
to this one dogma of No Pope and No Popery.
Even in these days of indifference to all creeds,
this hostility is as deep as ever. Personally
Catholics may be, and are, esteemed and liked,
and the Pope individually may be an object of
interest and veneration; but submission to his
spiritual rule seems to the English mind incom-
patible with the very existence of the British
Empire. It reminds one of the old Jewish sentiment—'The Romans will come and take away
our place and nation.' Yet in the midst of all this
hostility, God has never left this Catholic faith
without noble witnesses in England. From the
days of Cardinal Fisher and Sir Thomas More,
a long line of gifted Englishmen have by their
blood or their writings protested against the
sacrilege by which their country was separated
from the Church. This nineteenth century has
had its witnesses too. When, at its close, the list
of their names comes to be drawn up by the his-
torian, not the least among them will be that of
Frederick Lucas."

When his death became known, the expressions

of regret were, as we shall see in the concluding chapter, very general, not only among Catholics, but among Protestants too. It was said, and has since been repeated, that, disappointed at the failure of his mission to Rome, he had died of a broken heart. But that was not so. His was not composed of the stuff that breaks. The two letters given above show that he did not consider he had failed, since he had not yet completed his work; and the correctness of this view is confirmed by some circumstances related in the next chapter. The fact was, that his labours since the foundation of the *Tablet* had been enormous; he had crowded the work of a life into those fifteen years. Moreover, though his physical frame had the appearance of being robust, he had not a strong constitution. When quite a young man he was subject to violent headaches; and he never dared to retire for the night till some hours after a meal. As a remedy for this, he at one period for some months restricted himself to a vegetable diet. He died, as he said of O'Connell, broken—but not broken-hearted—with the storms of state.

His remains were removed from Staines to the Church of the Oratory at Brompton on the evening of Friday the 26th of October 1855, when the office for the dead was sung, and on the day following he was buried in Brompton Cemetery. As Canon Oakeley beautifully expressed it, "On his deathbed St. Ignatius watched with the tenderness of a father over one who seemed to bear the character, without sharing the privileges, of his noble sons.   When dead, St. Philip received him out of St. Ignatius's arms, and kept loving vigil over his remains." ·

CHAPTER II.

*ESTIMATES OF LUCAS'S CHARACTER—PRESENTATION
OF THE 'STATEMENT' TO PIUS IX.—RESULTS.*

On the day of his funeral Dr. MacHale had a
solemn requiem mass celebrated in Tuam for the
repose of his soul.   A week later seventy priests,
invited by Dr. Cantwell, assembled at Navan for
a similar function.   These were followed by others,
too numerous to mention, during the space of three
months.   And for the same length of time, articles,
letters, notices, recollections, continued to appear
in the journals of many nations, and of the most
opposite politics.   To this day his name is held
in benediction throughout a great part of Ireland.
Perhaps the most touching—certainly the fullest—
appreciation of Lucas is contained in a sketch by
a friend who had ample opportunities of observing
his character closely—Mr. Ornsby (M.A. Oxford),
for many years, and at the time of Lucas's death,
sub-editor of the *Tablet*.   The following copious
extracts contain some few remarks such as have
already appeared in the foregoing pages.   The
reader will not, I hope, find their confirmatory
testimony altogether superfluous :—

  " Frederick Lucas was of tall and commanding

stature, fresh Saxon complexion, fair hair, which
latterly had turned prematurely grey, and very
lofty and massive forehead.   His conversation
was richly furnished with reading and thought,
both being of the most vigorous and masculine
kind.   His favourite authors in literature—of religion I shall speak afterwards—were Tacitus and
Shakespeare ; but his range of study was very
wide, and his power of acquisition highly remarkable.   Whatever book he took up, even of a
trifling description, he seemed to have the talent
of eliciting from it some solid and valuable result.
The study, however, to which his inclination most
led him (though very likely it only appears to me
to have been so because he chiefly conversed with
me on that topic) was Latin literature.   The subject of the Roman empire, its polity and laws, and
the transmission of these under altered forms of
modern civilisation, was a subject which had for
his mind a special charm.   He used to say that
if he wrote a book, he should like to take for his
subject 'the Roman Province;' to describe the
method the Romans used in the formation of a
province, and the social changes it went through
at different epochs.   The materials for this, he
thought, were very abundant, and instanced in
particular the details we have of the Province of
Cilicia in Cicero's letters, and afterwards of the
province of Bithynia in the imperial age in those
of Pliny. . . .

   "As might be expected from what I have already

said of Mr. Lucas's mind, Cæsar's Commentaries
was a favourite work with him. I recollect his
saying that to him it was an *awful* book; the
actions of Cæsar gave him the idea almost of an
angel—not, as may be well imagined, for their
goodness, but for that unruffled tranquillity with
which he accomplished and described the most
terrible deeds. . . .

"When I observed to him how much better for
the world it would have been had Cæsar lived,
and not been cut off when he had just begun so
wonderful a career, 'I don't know,' he replied;
'there are some men who seem destined to be
the *beginners* of things, and others of inferior
powers, but better qualified to bring to completion what has been begun.'[1] . . .

"He used to admire the grand moral sentences
which here and there meet one in Virgil. One in
particular I recollect his quoting. It is a well-
known passage, but might be applied to illustrate
the plain and honourable character of Mr. Lucas
himself :—

> 'Aude hospes contemnere opes, et te quoque dignum
> Finge Deo.'

"He amused himself sometimes with Plautus,
and he remarked with great interest on that singular passage in the prologue to the 'Aulularia,'
where the Lars Familiaris speaks of the way in

---

[1] Nearly the same thought he had expressed in his article on the
accession of Pius IX., where he refers to the life of Gregory VII.

which he had repaid the devotion of the daughter of the house. It struck Lucas's imagination by the extreme vividness with which it represented the Pagan religion when actually energising among the ancients. Whatever he read in this way, he read, not like a mere literary student, but like a *statesman;* and his articles always bore traces of these studies as he pursued them. . . . He was not acquainted, or but slightly so, with the Greek language, a circumstance he regretted, and endeavoured to make up for by the study of the best translations, from which his extraordinary acuteness enabled him to derive almost the value of the originals. . . . I remember his mentioning to me how forcibly he was struck by the power and energy of the orations of Demosthenes. Inadequately as these characteristics are brought out in translations, the fact that he could be so struck with them under such disadvantages is not without its importance in forming an opinion of Lucas's mind. The Greek author he best knew was Plutarch, who was perhaps nearly as great a favourite with him as Tacitus. . . . On the exceedingly minute legislation of Solon recorded by Plutarch, Mr. Lucas observed that he could not well understand how the sanction to such laws was obtained, how they were made operative. Yet, whilst the temperament of his mind thus led him in a classical direction, and whilst deeply impressed with the practical utility of those studies, he never lost sight of the real character of Paganism.

I remember once expressing to him, probably in extravagant terms, my sense of the beauty of a description in Ovid of the procession of the Consuls to offer sacrifice in the Capitol at the opening of the year. His remark was that such admiration must be greatly qualified by the reflection that the procession, which was invested with all that pomp and grandeur described by the poet, was, in reality, marching with all due solemnity—to hell. On another occasion, on my quoting to him Lord Bacon's remark, that 'if ever man had a great, serene, well-regulated soul, it was Augustus Cæsar;' Mr. Lucas observed, with some indignation, that 'that remark thoroughly showed what Bacon himself was.' I have said that in English literature his favourite author was Shakespeare. I cannot, indeed, at present recall any remarks of interest on this head, except that he was greatly impressed, in a philosophical point of view, with the play of 'Troilus and Cressida,' on which he would descant largely. He thought that the object of the poet in that play was to depict the apparent emptiness of human life, by bringing it into the closest contact with those vast means which seem to be applied to, and to result in, such paltry ends—the huge Grecian armaments set in motion on account of Helen. . . .

"The poet whom he really admired and talked of with enthusiasm was Dante. . . . For the literature of the so-called Augustan age of Queen Anne he had no great liking. . . . Although Mr.

Lucas seldom conversed on metaphysical subjects, when he did so he showed a great fondness for the most abstract speculation. I remember, in particular, a most curious discussion, in which he imagined the possibility, antecedently, of the parts of space being transient, and those of time simultaneous. A good instance of his metaphysical subtlety may be found in an article in the *Tablet*, in which he argues most acutely against the objections of infidel geologists, by showing that creation is like a series, which, at whatever term it commences, must of necessity presuppose earlier terms, though in fact those terms never existed ; for example, if a horse were created, its teeth must indicate some age or other, and the construction of its organic system would imply previous sustenance, and the consequent existence of vegetation, &c., before its creation. . . . It is thus evident that Mr. Lucas possessed a mind of great fertility and cultivation. . . . In general, I may say that there could not be a more mistaken estimate of his character than to imagine him of a revolutionary temperament. His natural disposition was conservative, or, I should rather say, aristocratic. . . .

" What, however, his whole nature shrunk from was anything like a tendency to fawn upon people placed in a distinguished position—upon 'society' irrespective of real merit. He appreciated, though as an external fact (not as springing from right motives), that perfect polish and

evenness of manner which is attained by familiarity
with high life. 'It was something transcendental
—a solecism in good-breeding was their hell.'
He valued dignity of demeanour, which, however,
he said he could hardly recollect having recognised
in any one. But he detested what, for want of a
better word, may be summed up in the popular
term 'flunkeyism.' For this he had no patience
and no mercy; any manifestation of it, where
principle was endangered, caused him to feel a
distress which he could not control. The simplicity and extreme straightforwardness of his own
mind led him not to feel the inevitable offence he
gave by the expressions of indignation to which
he gave utterance when thus grieved. In his
mind the sense of justice and truth was so powerful, that no other consideration (in a public point
of view) could outweigh it, and to that he devoted
his life. I recollect early in 1852 a striking
conversation, in which he said with great energy,
and as if he were thinking aloud, 'When a man
can work and *will* work, his work will tell.' . . .

" He used to set a great value on the opinion of
others, even on those of persons quite behind the
scenes, but on whose good sense and good-will
towards him he could rely. He used to consider
that the judgment of one plain sensible man was
a test of what such people in general would
think. As an editor of a paper (paradoxical
as the assertion may seem to those who did
not follow with an unprejudiced eye his whole

conduct of his journal and compare it with that of others), rashness was by no means his characteristic, but rather the opposite tendency to caution. If you mark off what he said on the principles of duty, to which I have referred, and on which opinions may differ, all that remained was pervaded by a tone of dignity and a sense of responsibility, which I am much mistaken if you will commonly find among journalists in general. . . . In composition, and indeed in affairs generally, his principle was different from that of many great men, who keep their ideas and purposes a close secret, and think they are enfeebled by their being divulged. Lucas no sooner thought of an idea than he conversed about it with his friends, and they continually recognised in his articles the condensation of his table-talk. Latterly his articles were entirely dictated, and I cannot help adding that his amanuensis was his virtuous and noble-hearted wife. Most of his correspondence during his last illness, down to the letter in which he took farewell of one of his dearest friends, in words that even strangers could scarcely read to the end without tears, was dictated to her. I don't know that the same fortitude which earned the wife of Lord Russell her name in English history was greater or nobler than this. . . . His favourite theological author was St. Thomas, and I recollect his remarking what an admirable book might be made of the ethical wisdom which is so abundant in the writings of that great Doctor.

St. Augustine was another great favourite of his. Of lighter religious reading, he was perhaps fondest of St. Francis of Sales, particularly the *Esprit;* of St. Theresa, especially the *Foundations;* and of St. Alphonsus Liguori, whose *Visits to the Blessed Sacrament* was his usual devotional book. He said it seemed to contain everything. I need hardly say that the faith of this acute and capacious mind was child-like and undoubting as that of the humblest Catholic. . . . He was very devout to the Blessed Virgin. I recollect, when the *Tablet* was first removed to Ireland, and great difficulties were overcome in the course of its transference, he said, ' I believe it was the Blessed Virgin that did it, and nobody else!' He had a great devotion to the apparition of Our Blessed Lady at La Salette. In spite of many murmurs from those who did not understand him, he always retained the picture of the Blessed Virgin over the leading columns of his journal, and, I am sure, offered up all his labours to the greater glory of God by her holy and blessed hands. Before making his first speech in Parliament, he caused a novena to be offered up by his friends for his success. His house was the abode of domestic peace and happiness, and was beautiful to look upon, especially from the contrast it afforded to the troubled political existence it was his lot to encounter. What particularly struck me about it, independently of the image such a house gives one of that at Nazareth, was the noble simplicity with which he chose residences exactly in accordance with his means. He practised what he preached, and avoided all effort to make an appearance beyond what the circumstances in which the good providence of God placed him for the moment allowed of. A small house in the most unpretending quarter of the town contented him. If I had not perceived that he did this, not only from duty, but from a sincere love of holy poverty, when I visited his modest dwelling, I should have thought of Fabricius or Aristides. There was plain living and high thinking. No expensive carpets, no rich hangings, no liveried servants, but a cordial welcome to the house of a man whose greatness needed no such adventitious ornaments. It afforded, I am sure, a most useful lesson to society and to an age like the present."

Time and space would fail to repeat the great things said of him. But I will just quote a few from the pen of one qualified to speak of him better even than Mr. Ornsby, by reason of his longer friendship :—

"He had an intense feeling of the responsibilities of life. As a father, a husband, a journalist, and member of Parliament, he had a high ideal of duty—an ideal such as rarely, if ever, enters into the minds of ordinary men. He seldom spoke of himself, or of his own feelings on religion, or any subject. But it was this deep consciousness of the responsibility of life which made him shrink from advancement, and made him, though in secret, and in submission to God's will, often sigh for the grave." And again :— " Reverence for ecclesiastical authority was one of the leading features of his religious character." And again :—" I firmly believe he never took a side without feeling that he had the weight of ecclesiastical local authorities, speaking generally, of the United Kingdom in his favour, and never took a part against any ecclesiastical authority without great pain. Many blamed him for not remaining altogether silent on such questions. But this was not the view either of himself or of those to whom he looked up for advice and guidance."

In a sermon which Canon Oakeley prepared, but was unable to deliver at his requiem Mass, the intending preacher remarks :—" A word of encouragement from one of the Church's constituted authorities would light up his countenance with the sunshine of thankfulness ; a reproachful or a mistrustful word would cut him to the quick. I am told on the best authority, that when he once supposed (though most mistakenly) that he did not stand well with the Holy See, he was affected even to bitter tears." [1]

But I must draw to a close. It was not till some six months after Lucas's death that the

---

[1] This was in the time of Gregory XVI., and probably occurred in reference to a passage in one of the articles on " How to Set our House in Order," mentioned in the first vol.

"Statement" was presented to the Pope. Lucas regretted the incompleteness no less than the length
of the document. But his sense of what was due
to the Holy See and to truth in matters of such
grave moment, would not allow him to produce
a shorter or more speedy document. And in all
that he had written he declared that he was not
conscious of any personal feeling against any one.
His only wish, he said, was to fulfil to the best of
his power the duty imposed on him by the expression of the Holy Father's will.

There being no one left after Lucas's death to
prosecute the appeal, Dr. Cullen's friends in Rome
remained masters of the situation. In Ireland the
disastrous effect of withdrawing the clergy from
politics soon became apparent in the rise of the
Fenian Brotherhood. According to James Ste-
phens, late Fenian head-centre, the foundation
of this society would have been exceedingly difficult had the old order of things been allowed to
continue. In an article in the *Contemporary Re-
view* for May 1884, he attributes his success to
the fact that all hope of the redress of grievances
through the channel of the Legislature had become extinct, or nearly so.

As to Dr. Cullen, long before his death he discovered his mistake, and Sir Charles Gavan
Duffy tells us that he had actually asked him to
undertake the management of a journal on
Nationalist principles, for which Dr. Cullen
would furnish a considerable portion of the means.

He has lately been represented as adhering till towards the last to the opinion that Irish Nationalism was of a piece with the Continental Revolution. This scarcely seems compatible with the offer to Sir Charles Gavan Duffy.

THE END.

PRINTED BY BALLANTYNE, HANSON AND CO.
EDINBURGH AND LONDON